p. m. Freestone

SHADOW SCENT

SCHOLASTIC PRESS/NEW YORK

First published in the United Kingdom in 2018 by Scholastic UK Ltd., Euston House, 24 Eversholt Street, London NW1 1DB.

The publisher does not have any control over and does not assume any responsibility for author or third-party websites or their content.

Library of Congress Cataloging-in-Publication Data available

ISBN 978-1-338-33544-6

10 9 8 7 6 5 4 3 2 1   19 20 21 22 23

Printed in the U.S.A.   23

This edition first printing November 2019

Book design by Baily Crawford

*FOR ROSCOE, LAUREN, AND AMIE:
THERE'D ONLY BE THE FAINTEST WHIFF
OF THESE WORDS WITHOUT YOU*

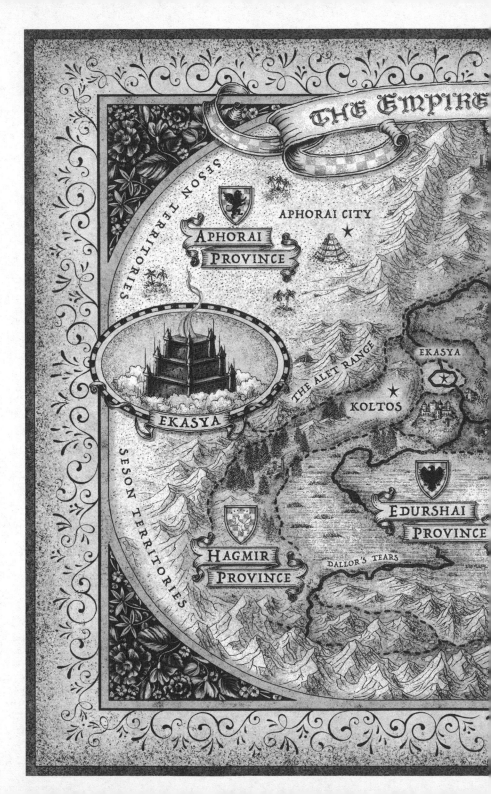

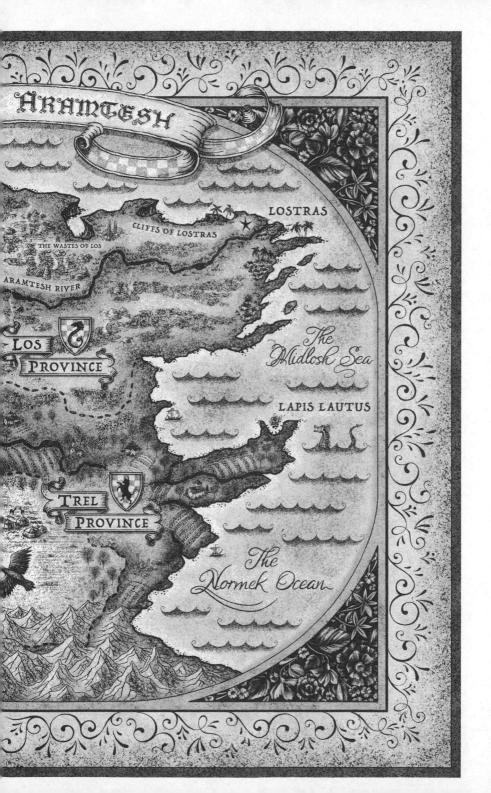

CHAPTER 1
RAKEL

Home has always smelled of cooking fires and desert roses that only release their perfume after sunset.

Home has always smelled of the first water for miles.

I lean out of my bedroom window and take a deep breath of night. When you fear you could soon lose something, you take every chance to savor it.

This is the place Father adopted after my mother died. An oasis on the road to nowhere, shaped like two cupped hands holding a pool of water safe from the greedy sand. Fish swim in the pool. Tortoises, too. Rock figs ring the shore, providing all the fresh fruit we can eat in season and enough to dry for the next turn. There are no leftovers. No luxury. But Father left the city and the Aphorain Province army when I was young to give me the chance of a carefree childhood. The simple, clear-aired life I loved.

Until the Rot.

Now home smells of Father dying.

With a sigh, I close the shutters and steal into the next room.

The bronze officer's sword still hangs on the wall. The symbol of the respect Father once commanded. But loved or scorned, once the Rot burrows under your skin, your moons are numbered. There are ways to extend the count, but that takes zigs. Gold zigs. Far more than I'll ever earn concocting village perfumes or salves to soothe sand-stinger bites. More even than what my best flower oils fetch on Aphorai City's black market.

With one skill to my name, I only have one option.

At least that's what I tell myself as I inch open the trunk at the foot of Father's bed. I tuck my prize—his signature seal—inside my robe.

"Rakel?"

My heart lurches. *Calm. He's out the front.*

I lower the trunk lid, ensuring the lock clicks back into place as if I'd never gone near it, and slip outside.

Everyone in the village has found sleep. Everyone except Father. He sits on a high stool against our mudbrick house, built using his own tweaks on military methods to withstand all but the greatest groundshakes. His experiments are the reason our home stands where others have crumbled.

Now his wooden crutch leans within arm's reach, his face lit by the last coals in the fire pit. Bergamot incense curls around him. The insects of dusk it repels have long scattered, but he likes the clean scent. Under normal circumstances, it'd be a waste. But I know I'd go mad if I had to live with the stench of my own flesh decaying.

"Couldn't sleep?" I keep my voice light despite the guilt, breathing as shallowly as possible.

Father draws me into a quick hug, careful to only let me touch his good side. "Ran out of willow bark."

"I thought we had a moon's worth."

He shrugs.

This is bad. Really bad. But it only strengthens my resolve and makes my plan easier to justify, easier to conceal.

"I'll pick up some supplies in Aphorai." At least that part's true.

He shakes his head. "It's fine. Don't worry yourself."

"In the sixth hell it's fine."

"Watch your tongue."

I stick my tongue out and go cross-eyed looking down at it.

Father chuckles. "I couldn't stop you from going if I tried, could I?"

"Not likely. Anyway, I already said I'd give Barden a ride. His leave is up." I shoulder my satchel and kiss Father's stubbled cheek. "Try to get some rest, will you?"

He nods.

"Promise?"

"Promise."

Footsteps scuff in the sand behind me. Right on time.

Barden's sword belt and kilt are so new they still smell of the thyme used to cover the pigeon piss of the tanner's vats. Behind that there's familiar sweat, drowned out by the amber oil the Aphorain palace guards are required to wear to ensure they don't offend any aristocratic noses. And I bet aristocratic eyes aren't at all troubled by the way the oil gleams off muscle. In the few short months since he was accepted into service, daily training has filled out Barden's chest, though it had already been broad enough to turn the head of half the people we grew up with in the village; as if he were Ashradinoran descended.

And doesn't he know it.

"Barden." Father greets my oldest friend. "Back to the service of our province's illustrious governor?" There's a faint note of bitterness in his voice as he struggles to stand—he'd served the Eraz of Aphorai before Barden was born.

Barden moves to offer Father his arm. "Can't drag my feet if I want to get ahead." He looks to me. "But nothing's better than time at home."

I avoid his eyes, straightening a satchel strap that wasn't twisted in the first place.

Once upright, Father leans heavily on his crutch, the remains of his left leg—now barely reaching past his knee—hanging useless. I squint in the moonslight. Are his bandages wrapped higher than they were yesterday?

He limps toward the door. "I'll see you tomorrow night, yes?"

I nod, not trusting my voice to conceal the lie.

3

When Father has retreated inside, I turn to Barden. "Ready?"

"As I'll ever be."

Barden follows me behind the house. A mare and gelding wait beyond a post-and-rail fence, heads lolling, each resting a hind leg on the tip of a hoof.

Lil is the biggest horse Father has bred, bigger even than her older brother beside her. Father gifted her to me on my twelfth birthday, and we've been together for the five turns since. I named her after the lilaria from our village storyteller's tales, because she's blacker than the shadow demons of ancient legend, twice as fast, and with a temper to match. Father said the name was bad luck. But by that stage I didn't give much care to Luck, or its cousin, Fortune—both had turned their backs to me. Lil was a demon, and we were going to suit each other just fine.

Now the demon wakes. Lil's ears flick back as she moves toward us.

Barden's steps slow. He eyes my horse. "She ever going to get used to me?"

"How many times have I told you it's not personal? She doesn't like anyone." It's at that moment that Lil chooses to swing her head over the rail and nuzzle my shoulder.

"Riiight."

Barden hands me his gear bag, packed to bursting.

"Stenches, Bar. What have you *got* in here?"

He shrugs that off. "You're still going through with this?"

I don't trust myself to speak as I fasten his bag and my satchel to Lil's saddle.

A huge hand stills one of my own. "It's not too late to settle for an incense-grinder post, you know. It wouldn't make the moons collide. You might even get used to it."

Here we go again. Barden thinks things are as they are for a reason. That everyone has their destined place. That it's written in the starwheel long before anyone is even old enough to know about the stinking starwheel. It's one of the few things we've never agreed on. I slip his grip and twine my fingers in Lil's mane, pressing my cheek to her neck, breathing warm horsiness as if hiding under a blanket.

"Powder rat wages are barely enough for one person." I look toward the house. "One *healthy* person. It's perfumer or bust. And it's *got* to be now. Father can't wait another turn."

Barden winces at the truth of it, then takes me by the shoulders. "There are other ways, Rakel. I'm climbing the ranks. Already sending half my wages to my sister. Soon I could support you, and your father." He steps closer and wraps his arms around me.

I take comfort from his familiar solidness, even though I can't leave it to him to solve my problems. By the time his ambitions bear fruit, it could be too late.

"And then," he murmurs into my hair, "you wouldn't need to take so many risks."

I tense. I love our village, but out here doing things differently means you've lost your way. The Eraz's perfumers, on the other hand, are rewarded for new creations. Richly rewarded. If I were one of them, I'd never have to worry about the price of the best supplies to slow the Rot and buy Father time. I might even discover new treatments. And I'd be able to make choices about the future on my own two feet, not kneeling in the dust for Barden's charity.

He straightens. "If you won't promise me that, promise me something else?"

Bravado won't fool him at this point, even if I did have the strength to muster it. I tilt my face up, but he's silhouetted against the moons and stars, expression hidden.

"Promise me you'll be careful," he says, voice husky. He lowers his chin and leans almost imperceptibly closer.

I duck away. "It's late, Bar. We should get going." I gather Lil's reins and set my foot in a stirrup.

With a sigh, Barden climbs up behind me. "Here." His voice is soft in my ear. "Lean back."

Despite this growing tension between us, he's still my best friend. My *only* friend. And he's always kept my secrets. I let myself relax against his chest. It's a night-and-day ride to the city. May as well get some shut-eye.

"Lil," I murmur, closing my eyes. "Keep Barden in his seat, would you?"

* * *

At times like this, I wish I had the nose of the next person.

Aphorai isn't yet in sight when a breeze threads through the dunes, carrying the perfume of the city's streets. One moment the desert is calm—there's just Barden, my horse, and the lingering tang of the camelthorn bush she crushed under her hooves some ways back. The next, I'm hit with a barrage of dried fruit, sour armpits, and everything ripe and rancid in between.

Barden gives my shoulder a reassuring squeeze.

I swallow down the urge to gag and give Lil a light tap of booted heels. I've got a meeting to keep.

The first building to appear above the dunes is the temple. The stepped pyramid hulks over Aphorai City like a crouched beast. One of the few structures to survive the centuries of groundshakes that heave and lurch underneath the province, believers say the temple was built by the gods themselves. Only way that theory has a whiff of truth is if your gods are indentured labor and a bottomless purse.

It's not until Lil whickers and tosses her head that I realize I've tensed from shoulder to thigh, my hand straying to the silver locket tucked inside my linen robe. I lean forward to stroke my horse's neck. "Sorry, girl."

From this distance, the priestesses really do seem like their namesake—tiny firebirds climbing the temple's main ramp in their crimson feathered skirts. As they reach the top, a column of blue smoke snakes from the great altar and into the sky. It's followed by another, white and rare as a summer cloud. Then a spiral of orange, one of dusty green.

Barden nudges me as the final plume rises. Imperial purple.

"What's that about?" I ask over my shoulder.

He huffs. "No idea. Only officers are privy to Empire matters."

"Oh? Thought the garrison sergeant was sweet on you."

"Not *that* sweet."

"You aren't his type after all?"

He pokes me in the ribs. "He expects I'll marry a nice girl."

"It's not like you're the eldest," I scoff. Barden's a lucky younger sibling—free of responsibility to continue the family line. "You can be with whoever you want."

"Can I?"

I sigh. Walked right into that one.

My mind flails for a way to steer the conversation elsewhere, when the ceremonial smoke reaches my nose, stirring up embers of long-held anger.

The temple controls believers' lives with rules and rituals. It starts from your first breath. The richly priced ingredients burned in candle and brazier proclaim to the sky the spokes of the starwheel between which you were born—so that the gods will hear your prayers until death.

But there were no sacred scents burned at my birth. No treasured incense I turn to for prayer.

Mint, leather, rosemary, sweat.

Those were my first scents.

Mint soap, seasoned leather armor, and rosemary beard oil made from the plants that still grow in fired clay urns at our door. Father's unmistakable uniform. All mixed with the work he'd done that day in the garrison's training yards. Those four scents drifted around me as he carried me on his shoulders through the markets when we visited

Aphorai City. Even so young, it was easy for me to single them out: my own personal fortress against an onslaught of tanning yards and camels, sandsquab stew and the cheap incense of a back-alley salon.

But that was before the tiny blister appeared on the arch of his foot. Before the scab that cracked open day after day to reveal a slightly larger wound. Before the pain became too much for him to bear his own weight, let alone mine.

A flock of swallows twirls and dips above us, their chatter interrupting my brooding as they prepare to roost in the archer's holes along Aphorai's walls. *The only city fortifications unbreached across the Empire during the Shadow Wars*, Father used to say. Guess the groundshakes helped our province prepare for another sort of violence.

Today, the walls defend against the sun—hot as a forge as it melts toward the horizon, gilding the desert in molten metal. When we reach the fifteenth gate, Barden slides from Lil's back. A group of ragged children instantly appear from the shade, crowding around us. Barden laughs good-naturedly and opens his gear bag, handing out rock figs. So *that's* why he had it overstuffed.

He gives my knee a squeeze without having to reach up. "See you at the trials, then?"

I nod.

"And, Rakel?" he calls over the children's excited voices.

"Yes?"

"Stars keep you."

I nod—Barden knows I've never said a prayer in my life—and ride on.

I leave Lil beside a fountain in a small square. She'd be less out of place if I'd taken her to one of the trade camps outside the walls, but that takes zigs. No matter. If this neighborhood is rich enough to keep a water feature in public, nobody will bother stealing a horse. Especially when most people think her more valuable in spit-roasted chunks than she's worth alive. And if they did lay a hand on her? They'd probably lose it.

Lil snorts in indignation at being tethered and abandoned.

"What?" I ask, giving her flank a rub. "You hate the night market."

She refuses to look at me.

I rummage in my pockets for a servant-yellow scarf, wrapping it over the dust and tangles in my hair. Nobody from inside these shaded walls dresses for the desert, so I roll the cuffs of my robe to the shoulder in city style. My locket serves as a mirror to check my face isn't smudged with dirt. Then I dab a smear of the locket's contents at my temples, behind my ears, along my wrists. Beeswax imbued with hyacinth and lily, with a hint of clove. It's sickeningly flowery, but it will help me blend in as much as short sleeves and drudge colors.

I give Lil one last scratch behind the ear, then shoulder my satchel— carefully, so as not to jostle its contents. With my starved purse tucked well inside, I set out.

My route takes me at first along broad, palm-lined avenues. Servants in saffron robes pay me no heed as they run late errands. A tiny cat watches me from atop a wall, the scent of ripe persimmons floating from the garden beyond. I stride purposefully, trying to stay alert without looking furtive, all too aware of the moons of work I'm carrying in a few precious jars.

Overhead, the sky bruises to dusk, the last eddies of temple smoke tattered and frayed.

Good riddance.

Closer to the markets, the streets narrow. Spices mingle along them like old friends, undertones of sewer seeping below. Breathing shallowly, I weave through the stalls, swerving chicken sellers and squeezing between tables mounded with dunes of sumac and constellations of star anise.

Then I'm back under open sky. Stalls line the plaza, the wares more decorative than useful, the air thick with dragon's blood incense. I take a deep gulp of the official scent of Aphorai—produced only by the Eraz's own perfumery. In this part of town, it smells more ambitious than aristocratic.

And behind it all, there's something terrible and familiar.

A man props himself against a nearby wall, a small wooden cart beside him. I squint in the fading light. Is he kneeling? No. His legs end above where his knees should be. Filthy, ulcer-damp bandages hang from the stumps, damp from the ulcers beneath. He hasn't got long.

Every passerby avoids his searching gaze. Servants study the flagstones. Merchants cover their noses with squares of perfumed silk and steer a wide path. When they're ten paces clear, the fabric flutters to the ground. Stall porters rush out to retrieve the scraps with long-handled tongs.

Superstitious fools. You can't catch the Rot just from breathing its stench: I'm living proof of that.

The man struggles to heave himself into the cart, but falters when a porter prods him with the tongs, prattling about calling the city guards.

My fists clench and unclench at my side. I stride over, pushing past the porter to crouch next to the man. "Take my arm."

He grimaces as we work together to settle him in his cart.

I rummage for the near-empty jar of willow in my satchel. It's the last of my personal store, but I'll be picking up supplies soon enough. "Here. It'll ease the pain. Best taken in kormak. But not too much," I warn, eyeing his bandages, "or it'll prevent clotting and you'll bleed."

"Thank you," he says, voice thick.

"Do you have somewhere to go? Can I help you get there?"

"I'll be fine." We both know that's a lie.

"Are you sure?"

He glances across the plaza. A commotion confirms the porter has found a patrol. "You should be on your way."

Now *that's* the truth. Last thing I need is to run afoul of a guard captain having an off night.

"Stars keep you, sister," he says firmly.

"And you."

Across the plaza, my destination is aglow with copper braziers. A row of young servants lines the threshold, their features smooth and fine, bodies lithe beneath kirtles of gauzy silk. Each bears a fan of woven palm fronds, wafting sweet red-tinged smoke into the street, beckoning buyers to come and indulge. The line of guards behind them says you need to be the right kind of buyer to be welcome.

I am *not* the right kind of buyer.

Good thing I've no interest in taking the front entrance.

At the rear of the building, a stone staircase leads down to the basement.

The guard on the door, dressed less garishly than those at the front, gives me a curt nod. I make my way along the corridor, almost tripping on the splayed limbs of a sleeping couple, the remnants of their elegant perfume overshadowed by the smell of empty purses and emptier heads. Dreamsmoke.

In the main chamber, a crowd of onlookers surrounds a waist-high marble table near the center of the room. Four men and a woman step up to the slab, and a servant brings them tiny glasses arranged around the edge of a silver tray, at the five points of the starwheel. The cups could have been filled from the end of a rainbow; the liquid in each gleams a different jewel in the flickering candlelight.

Ah, this game. Death in Paradise. The cups contain a cocktail of poppy milk and stiff spirit—each flavor sure to give the drinker a nightlong love of the entire world and everyone they meet. The risk? One glass may or may not be laced with night jasmine: virtually undetectable in the honeyed liquor, and lethal within heartbeats. A test of skill. Lacking skill, a test of nerve.

"Bottoms up!" The first player—a curl-headed youth wearing a robe dangerously close to imperial purple—raises his glass and empties it in a single swallow. His companions gasp, their expressions intent. But after a minute, he upends the glass onto the tray with a flourish and a grin. "I'll smell the gods' perfume another night."

Onlookers whoop and clap him on the back. I don't bother masking my derision as I cross to the bar. If they do look in my direction, their gazes will slide over me. Nobody sees the help.

The bartender and I have never played at friends, and there's no attempt at niceties when she eyes my satchel. "Leave that in the store. There's a half weight of zigs waiting for you. Next order due at half-moon."

"I want to speak to Zakkurus this time."

"No chance."

I pat my satchel. "Want me to take this over to Rokad's instead, then?" It's only part bluff. Rokad pays better, but he's also got a reputation for selling out his suppliers to the regulators.

She sighs and reaches behind the bar. Half a minute of telltale clinking later, five cups are arranged in front of me. "Choose."

"I'm not some puffed-up sniffling seeking a thrill on the dark side of town."

"And Zakkurus isn't a charitable benefactor willing to waste his time on whatever the cat dragged in. You want an audience. Choose."

Stink on a stick. I hadn't bargained on this. But what choice do I have? If it's not now, the apprenticeship trials will come and go for another turn. Call it the Affliction if you want to be official, but the Rot waits for no man. Or girl.

And with the gods and the stars and that lack of, well, *deference* my life has shown them, there's no other way. I need to know what perfume the Eraz's daughter, Lady Sireth, will favor in the next turn of the starwheel—the scent that anyone who is anyone or *wants* to be anyone will be clamoring to douse themselves in. The scent that will be the final test in the trials.

Willing my hand not to shake, I wave each cup under my nose, letting the bouquet envelope my senses. The third gives me pause. It's the only one with a hint of bitterness, no doubt meant to deter. It's also the only cup that lacks a cloying sweetness—the only one that's clean. I'd bet my life on it. I'm *about* to bet my life on it.

"Four?" I raise an eyebrow. "Stacking the odds in the house's favor, eh?"

The bartender shrugs.

Meeting her stare, I bring the bitter liquid to my lips. Then I tilt my head back, and drink.

For a breath or two, I feel fine.

Until the floor rushes up to greet me.

CHAPTER 2
ASH

Palace guards are trained to endure physical challenges. Imperial Family Shields face greater tests—learning to read the knife-edge niceties of court politics, while maintaining the illusion of being none the wiser. I may not be able to ignore the reek of Affliction permeating the imperial bedchamber, but by divine mother Esiku's mercy, my face will not reveal that fact.

The servants have done their best. The silk drapes are tied back to let a breeze slide through the windows. Braziers smolder, their embers agleam in the mirrorlike surface of the black granite walls. Cuttings of bay tree lay strewn across the mosaic floor, while sticks of incense emit tendrils of fragrant smoke. Yet none of it disguises the stench marking the boundary between the world of the living and the realm of the gods.

Anyone who entered the room would know it, as plainly as they would know their own nose: The Emperor of Aramtesh is dying.

Correction. Emperor Kaddash has been dying for ten turns of the starwheel. He's been dying longer than I've been shaving. But just like everything else he's botched during his reign, when it comes to leaving this life, he can't seem to do a half-decent job of it.

Kaddash lies propped on a mountain of pillows. Barely on the sunset side of fifty turns, he looks seventy or more. Skin stretched parchment-thin, eyes sunken beneath a once-proud brow. Then there's that undeniable fetor.

First Prince Nisai sits in a low, ornately carved chair by his father's sickbed, his slender form folded in on itself. As it is for almost every hour of almost every day, I'm at his side.

Well, not technically his side. That wouldn't be appropriate for the occasion. I'm keeping a respectful three-pace distance, clear view of the window and door, ample space between the twin swords strapped across my back and the wall, the polished stone cool beneath my palms.

Watching Nisai's expression hover between hope and grief sends a pang of feeling through me, like the dull ache of a scar before rain. With the well-worn ease that comes with turn upon turn of practice, I push the emotion down, shutting the lid tight.

"Father," Nisai pleads, gaze downcast.

How I wish he wouldn't. A First Prince should never, ever plead.

He takes a shuddering breath and lifts his eyes to meet the Emperor's. "Please, Father. Appoint a Scent Keeper. I've found references in the old texts—several references—suggesting their records go back longer than ours. They might know of something to improve your condition."

He looks to me on the last, as if seeking a supporting voice, though he knows full well I'm obliged to stay silent.

Kaddash scowls. "Have you lost your wits? They're charlatans. Witches. I'll drive them to the far reaches of the Empire. See how they fare in the Losian Wastes. Or in that Lautus cesspit! There will not be another Scent Keeper in Ekasya while I draw breath." Spittle collects at the corners of his mouth. "I would rather dine with Doskai." The last comes out as a hiss, the sibilant name of the Lost God uncannily loud in the otherwise quiet chamber.

I rub a palm over my stubbled scalp and glance around the room. It's a convincing enough illusion of family privacy. But even I can't guard against the walls having eyes and ears. Taking so long to appoint the imperial capital's next Scent Keeper after the last went to the sky was controversy enough. If the provinces caught wind of the true extent of Kaddash's shunning of the Accord . . . well.

Nisai sighs, resigned. "Try to stay calm. No good can come from upsetting yourself."

The Emperor's shoulders had risen like hackles during his tirade, but now they slump into his scented pillows. "Calm. Yes. First useful thing you've said all day. A little dreamsmoke would help. Recommended by the Guild in medicinal measures. Yes, yes. Summon the physician."

A young page appears, quiet as a dockmouse slipping into the river. He tugs a rope concealed behind the drapes. The bell chimes, thrumming through the stone of the palace so that I feel it as much as hear it.

The door opens, and the page whispers something to the guard outside.

I look to Nisai. A tiny furrow appears between his brows, the one that says he's skeptical but too diplomatic to voice it. The Guild of Physicians is gaining prominence, though for all their insistence on new "empirically proven" methods and practices, I've heard of few cases in which a patient has been healed without loss of something—sense, limb, or, at very least, a significant portion of their purse. And when it comes to the Afflicted? The Guild may extend lives, but only the gods can save them.

The physician arrives swiftly.

Always waiting in the wings.

The Guild's uniform of somber black seems a direct rebuke of the lustrous feathered dresses of the temple. Dark, rough-spun wool can't be comfortable on a morning like this: The breeze attempting to whisk the sick stench from the room is decidedly warm; the last of the turn's snow melted from Ekasya Mountain moons ago.

The page clears his throat. "Zostar Alak, Guild of Physicians."

Black Robes doesn't budge.

The page looks to Nisai, then back at the new arrival, his face flushing as he realizes the physician is expecting more. "By personal appointment to Emperor Kaddash the Fourth!"

Black Robes gives a satisfied nod. He bustles across the chamber in that way short men often do—as if they're trying to give the impression of meriting more space. I'm no master perfumer, but even I can smell the cloud of vinegar fumes trailing behind him.

I shift my weight, reinforced leather vest creaking underneath my palace silks.

The physician's eyes dart toward me.

I give him my blankest, most dull-witted look.

Suspicion pinches his brow, but he continues toward Kaddash, placing his bag on the bedside table with a clink of glass. He pinches a honey-hued cube into a tiny dish, igniting it with a taper lit from one of the braziers.

Nisai sits back in his chair, coughing as he waves the smoke from his face.

"Keep clear, my Prince," the physician instructs.

I pull one of my knives from the sheath at my wrist and run the tip under my nail, cleaning a nonexistent speck of dirt. Angled just so, the blade catches the morning sun, splaying light across the physician's face.

He glares at me.

I pretend not to notice.

Nisai gives me one of his "did you have to?" looks. Yes. Indeed, I did. Old Black Robes has been getting too big for his sandals these past moons. I've heard some of his quips about "true medicine." It's not hard to deduce where the Emperor's more blasphemous ideas are coming from.

After more fussing and clinking, Black Robes retrieves a vial of cloudy liquid. He taps several drops into a goblet, and a servant slips forward to fill it from a kettle of steaming water. The Emperor smiles and leans over the cup, greedily breathing its vapors.

Placated, Kaddash pats Nisai's hand. "There's a good boy. Why don't you run along now? Time for Papa to rest." His tone has shifted to the singsong of someone who thinks he can roll back the starwheel and speak to the small boy he neglected for so many turns.

"First Prince, if you would excuse us. The Emperor is ready for his Therapeutic Calmative Insufflation." Black Robes enunciates each term as if it warrants its own sentence.

"Therapeutic." Say that of anything and it transforms an idea that's all smoke and no scent into a socially acceptable treatment.

"Calmative." Oh, I don't doubt it. Nor do the highbrow merchants and aristocrats ensuring the dreamsmoke dens across the Empire do a roaring trade.

"Insufflation." Call it what you will, but it is what it is. Blowing smoke up the Emperor's arse. Literally.

I'm grateful when Nisai says his goodbyes and makes for the door. I follow without a backward glance.

We begin the walk to the First Prince's chambers in silence. Along the Hall of Emperors, I can't help but wonder what the men in the finely stitched tapestry portraits would have thought of Aramtesh's current ruler. Sawkos the Great is too intent on hunting feather-maned lions from his chariot to spare a care for the future. But I swear there's a frown of disapproval from Emoran the Lawmaker. And vague disappointment seems to emanate from Awulsheg II, framed by the colonnades of the imperial university as he puts quill to scroll.

As we pass the scholar and his successors, the rulers who presided over the Great Bloom of the fifth and fourth centuries pre-Accord,

Nisai runs his fingers along the polished cedar rods beneath each portrait. They keep the tapestries from curling, but they seem something more to the Prince. Talismans. Touchstones.

Nisai pauses underneath the final tapestry. Kaddash is seated on one of Ekasya Palace's many glossy black stone balconies overlooking the river plains far below, a lute before him, his fingers plucking at the strings. He's surrounded by beautiful young courtiers, some laughing with cups full, some drowsily reclining on cushions with dreamsmoke pipes. There's no title beneath the portrait, but it could easily have been *Kaddash, Life of the Party.*

"What makes a good Emperor?" Nisai asks.

I answer without hesitation: "That's for you to decide."

"Is it?"

He wipes an invisible speck of dust from his father's portrait and continues down the hall.

Issinon, Nisai's valet, waits outside the Prince's chambers. He dips into a deep bow, hand clasped around the purple silk sash denoting his office. Straightening, he proffers a tiny scroll. "First Prince."

Nisai shrugs off the weight of the morning and gives his valet a genuine smile. He waits until we're alone before unrolling the message.

I raise an eyebrow.

Nisai holds the parchment under my nose.

"Is that exactly what it smells like?"

He only grimaces and theatrically draws his finger across his throat.

We've been summonsed.

* * *
*
*

The scent of power presides over the Council chamber.

I remember the first time I smelled that combination of nectar and spice. It was long ago, at the base of Ekasya Mountain, between the walls of the imperial capital and the river. Down where the slums cling to the slopes like clusters of freshwater mussels. In that no-man's-land, where everyone is provinceless, nothing had ever smelled as sweet as when Nisai led me, a grubby street runt stinking to the sky of only Riker knows what, before his mother: a regal figure in robes of imperial purple, a diadem of amethyst and ruby glinting from her brow.

I stood there for what seemed like eternity, my throat dry, my child's heart mocking me—thumping so loud I thought she *must* have heard it, that with each beat it was betraying to her my guilt and shame and fear, as clear as temple drums declare the starwheel turned. But her perfume embraced me while her eyes held me captive, measuring but merciful, as if her son had brought a stray tabby home and asked to make it his pet.

Then she smiled at me with her wide, white-toothed smile, rose to her feet, and declared: "If my son wishes to take him to the palace, he will come to the palace."

And that was that.

Whether she saw my secrets, whether she knew the truth of what I'd done to save her son, I'll never know, and I'll never ask. Nisai and I agreed on that from the start. Too risky. What happened earlier that day must always be kept between the two of us. Only us.

Now Shari regards us from across the circular table dominating the room. Carved from smoky volcanic glass, mined deep beneath Ekasya Mountain, its polished surface is inlaid with gems in a stylized map of the starwheel on the night of the Founding Accord, the twin moons in gleaming mother-of-pearl.

The remaining four Councillors, Kaddash's other wives, are seated before the constellations of their respective provinces: the Losian cobra ready to strike, the aurochs bull of Trel, the golden eagle flying high over Edurshai, the line of stars tracing Hagmir's snowfox from nose to tail tip. I doubt that Shari's place at the winged lion of her heritage just *happens* to be opposite the door. The Council of Five may be egalitarian by law, but these days it hangs on the words of the Aphorain imperial wife.

Shari wastes no time getting down to business, her manner formal. After all, the Council has summonsed the heir of the Empire, not simply her son.

"Aphorai has announced the date of the Flower Moon." She states the obvious—the Ekasya temple sent a rainbow of smoke skyward yesterday—one link in a chain since Aphorai lit up hundreds of miles away. Signals are burning across all Aramtesh by now.

"The Aphorain Eraz extends his warmest invitation to the capital on this auspicious occasion. It is imperative we send imperial representation."

Galen, the imperial wife from Trel, inspects her manicured nails. "Auspicious?"

"Fortuitous. Lucky. Once in a generation," Shari snaps. She and Galen have long fulfilled their duty to provide the Emperor with imperial sons, so there's no sanction against their romantic interests finding each other. But Shari always seems to overcompensate in front of Nisai lest she be seen to officially show favoritism to a rival province. Then Aphorai, her home province, might sanction her. Even replace her on the Council.

"Oh! Indeed!" Galen nods, her braids—as gold as Trelian wheat fields—staying neatly arranged atop her head. Her eagerness makes me wish Shari wasn't so harsh on her in public.

Nisai clasps his hands in front of him. "Our great-uncle is magnanimous. And it heartens me that the Council will be honoring the imperial commitment to our province. I am at your disposal to assist with preparations for the delegation, cognizant of my father's needs. His journey will not be easy, but there are ways to ensure it is as comfortable as possible."

Shari taps a scroll against the tabletop. "The Council requests you assist in a different manner, First Prince."

"Of course, Councillor," Nisai addresses his mother formally.

Shari looks around the table, making eye contact with her four counterparts before returning her gaze to her son. "Let's be frank. It's time you took over some of your father's duties."

"Councillor, the Emperor is still very much alive." Nisai's loosely interlaced fingers lock together.

"We both know that Kaddash isn't going to leave the palace again until his body is borne to the heights of the temple."

Nobody has uttered it, but I'd wager my swords that everyone in this room has thought it—the longer Kaddash lingers, the worse off the Empire. But it was the Council who had named him to the throne as worthier than his brothers, just as they had named his father and his father's father and every Emperor going back to the edge of memory.

The Founding Accord has served its purpose for centuries, ensuring the most powerful position in the Empire is drawn from a different province each generation. Local dynasties can't overreach their bounds. Border disputes are tamped down before they ignite, lest the Emperor's office, and the imperial army that comes with it, fall to a slighted neighbor on the next turn.

It's assured relative stability across the Empire, allowing people with the wits and means to find ways to prosper. Though those with means without wits, or wits without means—well, that's another story. One I'd rather keep behind me.

Shari slices her hand through the silence. "Aramtesh waits for no man. Your father included." They're carefully chosen words, with truth and treason separated by a blade's edge.

"Indeed, Mother. But I'm still unsure what the Council needs from me."

"We're lifting the seclusion order."

I've always found Shari's decisiveness reassuring. Until now. Lifting the order? What is she *thinking*?

"Forgive me, Mother, but can you do that?"

Shari pushes the scroll she's been holding across the table. "By unanimous agreement, the Council of Five can overturn an imperial decree in situations where *not* doing so poses a risk to the principles of the Founding Accord. Much has changed since your confinement to the palace. I wish it weren't so, but your safety is no longer the most important thing at stake."

Nisai looks shocked. "You undermined Father?"

Two seats from Shari, Esmez leans forward. The Hagmiri imperial wife is the very picture of matronly motherliness, contrasting with Shari's statuesque poise. "We didn't need to exploit the legal loophole, sweetness." Esmez speaks in soft tones as if calming a spooked animal. "The Emperor signed the document. His physician forbids him from making the journey in his condition. So, don't worry yourself. At least not on your pa's account."

"Also," Shari adds, "your brother has been recalled. He should be with us within a half-moon. The Rangers will need no more than three days to resupply. Then you'll leave. Together."

Galen veritably beams with pride at Shari's mention of her son. As the only imperial child ineligible to inherit—given his mother and the Emperor hail from the same province—Prince Iddo could have done much worse than rise through the ranks to become Commander of the Imperial Rangers. Or maybe Galen's just excited to see her son— all the other wives must visit with theirs outside the capital since the seclusion order.

"It wouldn't be a good show of faith to send the Ekasyan palace guard," Shari explains. "Too partisan. But the Rangers are drawn from across Aramtesh to serve the whole Empire. You'll have your personal staff. And Ashradinoran, of course."

I cringe at the sound of my full name, even if Shari only uses it for the sake of the scribe sitting in the corner. These are official proceedings. And officially, I'm the Shield to the heir of Aramtesh. His closest guard. Sworn by ancient law and, like all Shields before me, marked for life with my charge's family sigil. The stylized winged lion tattooed over my body—fanged head to feathered arms and clawed heels—binds me to defend the Prince at all costs.

Unofficially, I'd willingly go to the sky if at any point there was a choice to be made between me and him. Even if I've returned the favor several times already, it was Nisai who first saved my life with his silence, and his friendship saves me anew with each passing day.

Now Nisai veritably bounces on the balls of his feet. I can't blame him for being excited. He's just been handed permission to leave Ekasya's palace complex for the first time in turns, since Kaddash first knocked on death's door and the Council did something that history has never witnessed: prematurely named the Emperor's successor, bringing on the seclusion order.

For a heartbeat, I think Aramtesh's next ruler is going to run around the table hugging each of the Council members in turn. Then he contains himself. "I thank the Council for its confidence in me."

I can only stand there, blinking, mouth opening and closing like a river cod caught in a net. In twelve days, the First Prince will be leaving the palace for the first time in as many turns of the starwheel.

That gives me eleven days to talk him out of it.

CHAPTER 3
RAKEL

Mint, leather, rosemary, sweat.

I cling to Father's shoulders as he carries me through the streets, taking us deeper and deeper into Aphorai City. Every soldier we pass nods to their commander, fist to chest, respect so sure it could be engraved on their features. They don't seem to pay any mind to the torrent of aroma and stench surging around us. To them, it's nothing but a gentle stream babbling in the background. But to me, the flood of odors turns Aphorai's broadest avenue into a mighty river—rushing at me, over me, a wall of water roaring down from the mountains at snowmelt.

If I don't scramble free, find some clear air, I'll be engulfed. The invisible hand of panic clamps around my throat. My breaths come short and sharp. Is this what it feels like to realize you're going to drown? I can't—

Control it, I tell myself, scrunching my eyes shut and pinching my nostrils together. Now, one at a time. Single them out. Found one? Hold tight. Count. Inhale . . . mint. Exhale . . . leather. That's it. Breathe. Just breathe.

I've regained a semblance of calm by the time we reach the walls of the temple complex. Father lifts me from his shoulders. When we face each other, I notice he stands only a head taller than me. Are we on a staircase? No, a level path. Strange.

"You'll have to walk on your own from here, little one."

"But I want to stay with you." Tears prick my eyes. "Please."

His only reply is to drape a necklace over my head—a silver chain and locket. My eyes widen at the locket's delicate engraving, tiny stars strewn across the metal as if it were cast from a piece of the night sky. I throw my arms around Father. "Thank you."

"Open it."

I do as he says. On one side, there's an empty balm container. I bring it to my nose. Nothing.

"When you're old enough, you can choose your own." He points to the other side, the lid, lined with a tiny portrait of a woman. "Your mother."

I can't remember her scent, so have no chance at recalling her image. But if she did look like the cameo, she was striking. Noble forehead, straight nose, high cheekbones. A set to her jaw that warned of a will implacable as stone beneath the smile.

"You grow to look more like her each day."

I take a closer look. I think he sees what he wants to see. Though there's no denying my eyes are set in the same slightly-wider-than-I'd-like way, and that my hair grows in flyaway strands that make it a battle keeping it off my face, let alone trying to tame it into sleek braids. Even now, frizz tickles at my nose. I swipe it away with a scowl.

Father laughs softly. "You have her temper, too."

At least *that* sounds like the truth.

"What did she wear?" I ask, holding out the locket, balm container facing up.

His weathered face takes on a wistful cast. "Desert rose."

Like countless times before, I close my eyes and try to remember. Desert rose. With a hint of cardamom for richness? Maybe a note of black pepper to make it her own? That could be it. Was it? I don't know. And if it was, why can I only smell lavender? Lavender filling my nose, my sinuses, my throat. Lavender meant to calm the injured. To soothe babies to sleep. But by the six hells, this lavender *burns*.

I surge awake, gasping for air. The girl leaning over me jerks back. She's dressed in yellow, but the fabric that slides across my arm is as smooth as water.

Silk? For a servant?

Satisfied that I've come to, the girl straightens and stoppers a small glazed pot.

Smelling salts.

Something itches at the corner of my fogged mind as I realize I'm lying on my back, cold marble under me. My eyes trace the fanciest reed-woven ceiling I've ever seen, a five-spoked candlewheel above me casting a single pool of light in the room. The only item of furniture I can see is a low stone bench piled with blue cushions—indigo, cobalt, azure, and then some.

With a few more breaths, the assault of ammonia on my nose gives way to the warm richness of Aphorai's prized incense. It's the pure kind, not that coarse powdered version they burn in the streets.

Dragon's blood.

It worked. I'm here.

I shove myself into a sitting position and press the heels of my palms to my temples, head clanging like someone clashed cymbals between my ears. By the time the ringing subsides, the servant girl has retreated into the shadows. It's doubtful I would have noticed the two guards hulking there were it not for the pungent waves of stale garlic and last night's beer they're sweating.

Whether it's the thought of them having worse headaches than I do, or the residual effects of the concoction I swallowed, I begin to laugh. It's more mad than merry, and the movement sends pain shooting down my neck. I bring my hand up with a wince. Guess I strained it when I passed out.

It's then that I recognize the prickling feeling of being watched. Sized up.

Fine. I've played the game so far. No point in pulling out now.

"Mandragora," I say to anyone listening beyond the flickering candlelight. But my voice is hoarse and barely carries. I clear my throat and try again. "It was mandragora you slipped me, wasn't it? Masked with bitter melon."

Nothing. Then, from the shadows, comes slow, deliberate applause.

"Bravo."

I snort.

"Truly. I don't know another nose in this city that could have deduced that."

The man who could only be Zakkurus emerges from the gloom. Tall and lithe, the dark silk of his robe blooms with tiny lilies in silver thread. His midnight hair is pulled back with a silver band, the fine features cast in pale hue of a life lived sheltered from the desert. With sinuous grace, he crosses the floor, lips curled in a smile. It's subtle, but I wonder if he stains them with pomegranate. Given the intricate swirls of rur ink outlining his eyes—cold and lapis blue in the candlelight—I wouldn't be surprised.

So the rumors are true. Aphorai's chief perfumer *is* as beautiful as he is reclusive. Younger than I thought, too. I'd never really believed someone could rise through the ranks that fast. But as he settles on the cushioned bench before me, my skepticism is shaken. He couldn't have seen a handful of turns more than me.

Zakkurus folds one long leg over the other and silently regards me. I resist flinching when he reaches forward and cups my chin. His skin is incredibly soft, and so is his scent. The fleeting freshness of violet water spills over me. It sends my imagination away from this strange dark room, away from this situation, so that I'm strolling through a garden in the cool of morning, new dawn dancing colors in the fountains, rare blooms in each terraced bed waiting to unfurl in the sun. I sigh and the scent dissipates, leaving only my longing and envy as its echo.

Zakkurus turns my head, inspecting me like a pack animal in the auction pens. "Did they hurt you, petal?" The perfumer's gaze flicks toward the hungover guards. "I told them you weren't to be harmed. But someone in my position must be ever so careful when receiving unofficial guests."

"I'm not exactly a—"

"Delicate flower?"

I shrug.

"No," Zakkurus says, lounging back on the cushions, gaze taking a languid wander from my dust-crusted boots to where my hair escapes its wrap. "You wouldn't have made it this far if you were." And with that, he pulls a bag into his lap and begins to examine its contents.

My satchel.

Somewhere in the back of my mind, I hear Barden's voice. *Be careful*. I shake my head, trying to clear the last of the wooliness.

"Well then, my *indelicate* flower, care to tell me how you stumbled across a small fortune of pure desert rose oil?"

I meet his eyes. *Don't flinch now, Rakel.* "I made it."

I'm damn proud of it, too. An entire season of scrabbling through canyons, harvesting by my own hand. It's the purest I've ever refined, far better than the cloudy dregs found in the market after the best stuff is shipped off to the imperial capital. The secret? Oil, not water. Unless you want to send it straight to the sky, there's no point distilling rose petals, boiling and steaming their essence from them. That's too aggressive. Violent, even. Things go much better if you coax the scent out. Gently. They have to *want* to give up their perfume. Press them between layers of solid fat over days, not hours, and that's what they do.

Not that I'm about to volunteer that information.

Zakkurus is still smiling, but his eyes have hardened to sapphires. "Come, now. Business associates must afford one another respect. Particularly those who have the . . . *vision* to bypass imperial regulations, no?"

Respect. Easy to demand, hard to give. I nod grudgingly.

"Lovely to know we're burning the same taper. Now, where did you get this?"

"I. Made. It. You haven't even checked for the maker's mark. Where's the respect in that?"

Blue eyes bore into me.

I hope they don't notice my pulse quicken in my throat.

He waves his hand as if swatting at a sandfly. "Leave us." Several pairs of feet shuffle away in the darkness.

I smirk in satisfaction when he unstoppers the lid, peering inside as if he were trying to read the stars in the bottom of a cup of kormak. Then he circles the jar under his nose. He frowns and makes another swirl, closing his eyes and inhaling deeply.

"By all means, take your time." There's nothing preventing me from standing. Except the fact that my legs have gone to sleep. I grit my teeth and force myself up, pacing through the prickling pain, not daring to leave the pool of light.

Zakkurus produces a sampling reed from inside his robe. With a steady hand, he dips it in the jar, then holds it above one of the candles. The flame devours it quick as a sniff, charred remains dropping into a copper dish. He rubs the ash between thumb and forefinger, staining them gray, and gives one final huff.

By the time he's finished his inspection, my blood has reacquainted itself with my toes.

"Satisfied? There's more where that came from. Question is, are you in the market?"

"Why are you *really* here, petal?"

I'd rehearsed this over and over for moons. Just not when my mouth was so dry, my tongue this thick. I can barely swallow down my nerves. "The apprenticeship trials are three days from now. I—"

"Even if your skills are what they appear, the trials favor the brats from the five families."

I was hoping for this: that he hadn't forgotten who he was, where he came from. I allow myself a small smile at his disdain.

"By Esiku's beard, you *do* think you have a chance." He throws back his head and laughs.

Heat flushes my cheeks. The only thing stopping me from turning on my heel and storming out the door is that I'm not sure where the door *is*.

I claw back my temper. "Have I ever botched an order? No. You make good money from me, Zakkurus. Hear me out, and you could make more. Much more."

He raises a perfectly groomed eyebrow. "Go on."

"Tell me the final fabrication test."

"You're asking me to help you cheat in my own selection trials? Has all that dreadfully hot out-of-town sun withered your wits?"

"I prefer 'leveling the field.' If I win, you can be as sure as scat stinks that you've selected the best of the best new apprentices, not just the ones that could afford a full kit. Imagine the reputation I could help you build. Catch the attention of the capital. Put Aphorai back on the map."

His eyes widen ever so slightly. I'm getting somewhere.

"And if you lose?"

I hold up a jar of desert rose oil. "It's not just this. I've already tested the method on white ginger blossom. Jasmine, too." I point to his robe. "Bet it'd even work on water lilies." I step past him, out of the light. My eyes take a moment to adjust to the gloom. A patterned carpet drapes down the wall—soft under my palm, worth more than a lifetime of toil for most people from my village. The bitter taste of unwanted sureness coats my tongue. There's no other way.

"If I lose, I'll give you ten turns exclusively. I'll supply you and you only. Still off the books. Tax collector none the wiser."

Zakkurus taps one long finger against his thigh, my bargain hanging between us like noxious smoke.

I clench my jaw.

Four taps.

Five.

He leans forward. "I'd want full indenture. Nothing less."

My stomach churns. Indenture. Typical that someone who no longer struggles can speak the word so easily.

"I know I'm the best." I manage to sound more confident than I feel, now that this unfamiliar room in only-stench-knows what part of the city, has become a cliff edge.

His eyes search the shadows. "You're not the only one to have stood there and said those words."

"And back then the risk was worth it, wasn't it?"

He doesn't flinch at my stab at the truth. "Let's say I do decide to help you. What is there to keep you from tragically suffering memory loss and wandering off to a distant oasis?"

With no small measure of guilt, I wonder if Father has discovered his seal gone. I wish I hadn't needed to take it, but if he had any idea what I'd planned he would have forbidden me from leaving the house.

"I have people I care about."

He sniffs. "I deal in scent, not sentiment."

I reach into my robe for Father's seal. "That's why I'll put it in clay."

We both stare at the object in my hand—the stone carved with a series of pictograms—a rose, a battle helmet, the zigzag of a mountain range—our family name and crest. For the thousandth time, I wonder if there's another way.

My thoughts are interrupted by a sharp clap of Zakkurus's hands. The servant girl reappears, nods at the perfumer's instructions, and scurries away.

Soon after, a table sits between us.

Most of the contract's language is beyond me, but the phrase "ten turns" is clear as freshly distilled water. I'm gambling on a decade of my freedom, and yet I'm strangely numb as I press the cylinder seal into the unfired tablet, rolling it until Father's full signature is indisputably indented at the bottom of the contract. Next to it, I press my thumb into the clay, the swirled lines confirming my identity.

It's done.

The servant whisks away the tablet. In its place sits a blue faience bottle.

"Go on," Zakkurus says. "It won't bite you."

I work the tiny stopper out, waiting for its contents to greet me.

There's simple enough topnotes. Star jasmine. Honey vine. Purrath blossom. So far, so good.

The base is . . . amyris? Interesting. I would've thought it too plain. Then again, it wouldn't overpower more delicate ingredients like a sandalwood base would. Spicy midnotes are overlaid through. Cinnamon? Yes. And something earthy grounding it. Carrot seed is my guess. Good. I've got enough of those in my stores.

But there's something else.

It's barely traceable. Yet it lends a distinctiveness. Lifts the perfume above the common. Something about its combination of tart crispness and lilting sweetness tickles at my memory.

I was very young. Father still served the Eraz, leading a campaign to put down border skirmishes in the foothills of the Alet Range. I'd stayed with Barden's family, night after night clutching my locket and wishing on anything—the stars, the gods—that he would return safe. They didn't listen. And I vowed I'd never ask them for help again.

31

Instead, I wished on the lost memory of my mother.

I'd grown a half hand taller by the time we were at the palace, where they'd put a new sash on him. The Eraz had his own daughter do the honors; Father knelt so she could reach. Lady Sireth and I were of an age, yet the scent she wore set us worlds apart. At first crisp and sweet like a pomegranate in early autumn. But then more, so much more. I no longer believed, but I understood how others could think anyone who smelled like that could only be descended from the heavens.

That's *it*. Next season, the Eraz and his family will remind everyone of the source of their power, beyond their imperially sanctioned rule in Aphorai. They'll anoint themselves with the perfume of a god.

"Dahkai," I breathe.

Zakkurus regards me, amusement dancing in his eyes. "Yes, yes, petal, the darkest bloom. Though calling it that seems—how should one put it—disrespectful. It's the prettiest, most darling little flower for those fleeting hours."

A darling flower that has started wars and ended dynasties since the edge of memory. A flower worth more than a lifetime of indentured labor. And a flower I now need if I'm going to help Father.

I choose my words carefully. "I can't get dahkai in the markets."

Rounding his lips into an O of mock horror, the perfumer produces the tiniest vial I've ever seen. No bigger than the tip of my little finger to the first knuckle, it's in the same signature blue as the perfume bottle. He gestures to the jars of desert rose, so plain and unassuming next to the showy faience. "I'll consider these, and your contract, a down payment."

"That's a moon of food and—" I stop shy of saying "medicine." And I bite down on the other things I want to say—that I thought we had an understanding, that we recognized each other. That Zakkurus remembered what it was to be desperate.

"I'll take a risk on you, petal. But I'm no charitable benefactor."

Charitable benefactor. The bartender's words chime a duet with Barden's "be careful."

I've traded everything for a vial of the most valuable substance in the Empire—so precious that every last drop is regulated. Try to sell it and I'm more likely to find myself in a dungeon than find zigs in my purse. But what else could I have done? What else *can* I do? If I leave the dahkai essence, I've lost the trials already. I scoop up the vial and snatch my now-empty satchel from the table.

The perfumer waves a manicured hand and the servant girl slips once again from the shadows, her face downturned as she hands me a cup. One sniff is all it takes this time. I never forget a scent. Mandragora masked with bitter melon.

Zakkurus smiles his snakelike smile. "Now be a good girl and take your medicine."

CHAPTER 4
ASH

I still don't understand why *you* have to be the one to go."

Nisai gives me his "I thought we'd already settled this" look before lunging into his next spear strike.

It's a predictable move, easily deflected. I circle him, my feet drawing lines in the sand, shadow stretching behind me as morning sun edges over the top of the arena. "Would it not be more appropriate to have Garlag represent you in this?"

What I really mean is, what's the point of paying exorbitant wages to a dandy of a chamberlain if you can't send him scrabbling around the Empire at your bidding?

"You heard the Council. It's time I took on more duties." Nisai feints toward my right. His eyes give him away, and my left arm is up well before the real strike. My gauntlet takes some of the impact, but it still jars along my bones.

Maybe his heart *is* in this after all.

He presses his attack. "It could be tomorrow, it could be turns away. I might wish it weren't so, but coronation day will come. When it does, I'll need to know my lands." Another strike, this one parried with a crack that reverberates around the empty spectator terraces.

My feet keep moving cautiously, my thoughts racing ahead. It's been turns since we last left the palace. Yet I can't help but think this expedition premature. Is he ready?

Am *I* ready?

"Wouldn't missives keep you up to date more efficiently than spending the best part of a moon on the road there?"

"Missives tell but one man's story." The butt of Nisai's spear, aimed to wind me, passes just by my left hip.

I eye him critically. "Keep your weight balanced."

"I *am* keeping balanced."

There's my opening. With a spin, I crouch behind his guard and sweep a kick that takes his feet from under him.

He lands on his back with an *oof*, though the river sand cushions his fall. If he were egotistical, his pride would bear the worst of his injuries. But Nisai? He just props himself up on his elbows and grins at me. "Is Aphorai rustic? Perhaps. Antiquated? Quite possibly." He taps his nose. "But honoring tradition means my uncle still finds himself presiding over the only dahkai plantation in the Empire. Half my father's court would turn on him if they lost access to the main ingredient in their most precious perfumes and prayers."

He stands, dusting sand from his plain-spun tunic. It's probably the only thing he enjoys about physical training—not having to wear the imperial purple silks he's expected to don the rest of the time. "Aren't you remotely curious? We'll probably only see two Flower Moons in our lifetimes. Three, if we're lucky enough to be long-lived."

I shrug. One flower is the same as the next.

"Imagine watching dahkai petals unfurl. And that first breath of perfume." His focus drifts to middle distance. "It'll be magical."

"Magic belongs with our shadows. Behind us." The proverb escapes my lips without a thought. After so many turns, it's become reflex. A necessity.

Nisai shoots me a narrow look. "It's important to the people that their ruler attend a Flower Moon. A good omen. Even my father attended one."

I grimace. Important, yes. Dangerous? Absolutely. The very thing I'm supposed to protect him against.

"Trip or no trip, no need to miss a session." I hand Nisai his spear. "Let's go."

He groans. "Couldn't I just slip away to the library?"

I reply with a flat stare.

"Fine, fine."

But he barely defends the simplest of attacks, even the ones we danced when we were children, bashing at each other with felt-cushioned poles and wooden swords, before Blademaster Boldor singled me out for Shield training. "Keep your guard up!" I snap. "That's thrice dead. Do you want to join the gods before you've even left the city?"

"Of course not. That's why I have you." There's that easy smile again.

"You should at least try to show *some* sign of strength. You're about to go halfway across the Empire. You don't want enemies thinking you're an easy target."

"There are other sources of strength than a blade. Hope. Empathy. Compassion. Love. Kindness." He counts off the words on one hand.

"Are you trying to make me bring up my breakfast?"

"Information. Knowledge. Intelligence. Cunning. Wisdom." He drops his spear so he can count them off on the other hand.

"Enough already."

Nisai grins. "To the library, then?"

I look to the sky. "Oh, Mother Esiku, grant me patience with this wayward urchin."

*　　*
*　*
*

The imperial library is divided in two—clay and parchment.

Clay tablets for trade contracts and laws proclaimed by Emperor or Council. Longer texts are committed to parchment—history and military tactics, celestial events, and even myth from beyond the edge of memory—nearly all destroyed in the Shadow Wars and the turns of chaos that followed—except for the records salvaged and reassembled in the capital by the scholar Emperors, kept under lock and key ever since.

We pass under the library's great portico, Nisai making a beeline for the scroll collection. If anyone ever inquires, he says it's to make sure he's informed when it comes time to rule. History is the best teacher.

But it's more. He's looking for an answer. Forbidden knowledge. To explain what happened that day when we were boys, what he thinks he saw. To explain who he thinks I am. *What* I am, beyond the legends and the bedtime stories parents use to scare their children into good behavior.

The manuscript room is wall-to-wall with shelves, ladders leaning against each bank. Light streams through the single window, illuminating the dance of dust motes. The rest of the room is lit by citrus-scented candles to aid concentration. The clean scent mingles with aging parchment and the cinnamon the curators use to ward off mold, or so I'm told.

Nisai takes a deep breath, eyes closed, like he's sampling the most exquisite perfume. "Hello, friends," he murmurs to the shelves. "I've missed you."

"We were only here yesterday."

"Are you saying it's not possible to miss someone for a day? I pity your shriveled heart."

I smirk. But I'm hoping Nisai's parchments aren't the only friends we meet today. And I'm hoping that the others will do better than I have, to dampen his enthusiasm for the proposed expedition.

Sure enough, a willowy young woman perches at the top of one of the shelf ladders, one hand trailing along the scroll cylinders. Nisai waves and Ami, one of the library's curators, smiles absently as we pass.

Farther ahead, a familiar, pale-faced figure jumps up from Nisai's favorite table. As we near, Esarik Mur bows to us both in turn, mine shallower than the one directed at Nisai, but still far more than is required from a noble to a bodyguard. "My Prince!" he exudes, Trelian accent trilling over the title. "If I may say, you're looking well."

"Liar." Nisai embraces his friend.

"No luck with the Scent Keeper issue, then?"

"Afraid not."

"Bias truly is a brute."

"Afraid so." Nisai cocks his head to the side. "You're early this morning."

"What do they say? The first drop of dew is the sweetest." Esarik grins, pushing chestnut-and-gold locks from his eyes. A haircut wouldn't go astray with that one.

"This newfound dedication wouldn't have anything to do with rumors from the university that a certain someone is in the running for valedictorian, would it? Soon to be snapped up by the Guild and fast-tracked to full physician?"

Esarik shrugs. "Rumors? All smoke and no scent, I'm sure."

"Speaking of rumors . . ."

"I heard! You're bound for the desert!"

Here we go. Watching these two converse is like trying to keep up with a game of bodko ball.

Esarik clasps his hands in utter glee. "I was going to ask if I could—"

"Pack your bags, my friend!" Nisai grins.

I suppress a groan. Not Esarik, too. I thought he'd have more sense.

"Most certainly! But first I was going to read over—"

"*Zolmal's Journeys*? Volume eight? When he attends the first Flower Moon after the Accord?"

Esarik rubs his chin. "I think you'll find it spills over into volume nine. They don't call him Master of Minutiae for nothing."

"Ugh. I prefer Tek the Losian. Eminently readable."

"Likewise. We could cover one each?"

Nisai pulls a gold coin from his robe. "Flip for the Zolmal? Emperor or Temple?"

"Heads."

"Pyramid it is."

Esarik groans and reaches for an ancient scroll.

The rest of the morning is spent reading. Well, the Prince and the scholar read, and I play fetch for them—locating the next text as they delve deeper into the past. I can't say I mind. The library is secure, familiar, with manned exits at opposite ends of the building. A bodyguard's ideal scenario.

And Esarik is good for Nisai. Truth be told, I've always been a little envious of their friendship. Not for coveting Nisai's attention, but for wondering what it is like to be at ease and on equal footing with someone you care about.

The most devastating outcome of being named First Prince was the seclusion order squashing his dream of attending Ekasya's university. So, the Council brought university to Nisai, commissioning the most talented young scholars and tutors from the five provinces to study at the palace. Most moved on when their official term ended. But the young Trelian aristocrat has never let a week go by without a study session with the Prince.

It also doesn't hurt that Esarik's been sweet on Ami since he first arrived in the capital. He tries to keep it secret; his father has ambitions for his eldest son to marry high and Ami's family doesn't make the cut. But as he watches her thread through the shelves toward us, one arm loaded with scrolls, the other balancing a tray of food, Esarik's face lights up like dawn.

"How are my favorite scholars on this fine day?" Ami sets down the tray and gives Esarik's shoulder a squeeze that Nisai and I politely pretend not to notice. "It's high sun, I thought you could use a bite to eat."

"It's kind of you to take a moment from your work to bring us refreshment," Esarik says with a stiff play at formality.

"The Head Curator has been watching me like a hawk today," she murmurs, leaning in to remove the cloth from the tray. It's Nisai's preferred library meal, a simple platter of bread and white Edurshai cheese, Trelian grapes, and steaming hot cups of kormak, the stimulant drink from the terraced foothills of Hagmir. "And I hadn't had the chance to ask you about the Dasmai lectures. Are you going? They've discovered a heretofore unknown translation of the Gen texts. Third century pre-Accord."

"Wouldn't miss it for the world." Esarik's eyes shine with enthusiasm.

"Save me a seat?"

"With pleasure." Then he seems to realize where he is and blushes.

"Great!" She inclines her head to Nisai. "First Prince, I'll take my leave. But do seek me out if you need any assistance." Then she's off as quickly as she appeared.

Esarik stares after her until she's left his line of sight. Then he rolls his shoulders, clears his throat, and gets up from the table. "Time for volume nine," he says, moving off in the same direction Ami took.

I swallow a smile.

Nisai absently chews his bread and returns to the scroll he's been poring over. He runs his fingertips over a passage, squinting as he translates from Old Aramteskan, then reaches for his journal. Bound in aurochs leather, it's full of notes and sketches of plants and animals familiar and fantastic—the sum of his research.

He's convinced it's bringing him closer to an answer.

But I am what I am, only the gods could make it otherwise. Knowing the why or how isn't going to change anything. I wish Nisai could accept that. Then he'd be free to follow scholarly inquisitiveness, not some turns-old sense of obligation.

I'm contemplating how to broach the subject of the Aphorai expedition when a page runs in, skidding to a halt on the library's polished black floor.

"Highness." The boy winces as his voice warbles and breaks. He clears his throat and tries again. "Highness, Commander Iddo has returned."

Now *that* gets the Prince's attention.

* *
* *
*

Back in our chambers, Nisai sits at his desk, unrolls a map, and weighs down the corners with an incense burner and a vase of lilac flowers—a gift from Ami. As with all imperial maps, the capital—the holy city of Ekasya—is marked at the very center of Aramtesh, perched on a single mountain in miles upon miles of alluvial plains, the river splitting to flow either side of the peak.

Iddo strides into the room unannounced, ducking so his forehead doesn't hit the lintel.

Nisai does his best to feign nonchalance, not lifting his eyes from the map. "Mind the carpet. It's an antique."

"What's the point of a carpet you're not allowed to walk on?" The Commander of the Imperial Rangers stops one footfall short of the rug, looking like he could have leapt from a mural depicting a mythical battle. There's exactly five turns—to the day—between Nisai and his half brother, but the elder Kaidon son towers over his sibling and is almost twice as broad.

Neither of them have grown beards—unusual for princes—though Iddo's jaw bristles with several days' growth, his usually pale complexion deeply tanned from the road.

Nisai rises from his chair with an obvious sniff. "Could you not have come via the bathhouse?" His eyes dart to the corner of the room. A page melts from the drapes along the wall to light another stick of incense.

The Commander pushes back his traveling cloak, the fine white linen designed for protection against the sun. The stains from the road are the particular green-yellow of sulfur. He must have been far north in Los Province if he needed to cross the Wastes to return to the capital. The Rangers travel *fast*.

"Your message said, 'as soon as you return.' Who am I to deny the First Prince?" Then he ignores the earlier request and crosses the carpet to envelop Nisai in a lion's hug. "How have you been, Little Brother? Are you well?" He turns to me. "Been keeping him out of trouble, Shield?"

Nisai steps back and smooths down his robes. "I'd like to think I could keep myself out of trouble in my family's own palace."

Iddo gives me a conspiratorial wink. "Oh, but the palace is the most dangerous den of all. All those daughters of little lordlings buzzing around the honey pot of a prince." He squeezes Nisai's cheek.

Nisai swats his older brother away, this game almost as old as he.

The Commander throws his cloak over the back of a dining chair and flops onto a divan, crossing his legs at the ankle, boots still on. "A little birdy told me you're looking to take a trip."

Nisai glances at me. "Ash doesn't approve."

"With good reason." Iddo stretches, one shoulder giving an audible pop as he clasps his hands behind his head. "The Empire is simmering with unrest. I thought it was just the usual rumors, but it's bubbling over in places, especially in the outer provinces. Daddy dearest's turns of military neglect means they all smell opportunity. Los has especially never been good at playing equal partners. Fine for me—I like being kept on my toes. But you? You're going to have your work cut out for you when the old man finally goes to the sky."

"All the more reason to start now." Nisai points to the map.

"With Aphorai? Really? Sure you don't want to dip a toe in the water first? The Trelian Riviera is particularly pleasant at this time of turn. Warm days, cool nights. Good wine. Even better food—produce goes from plant to platter in a single day. And the lowing of the aurochs herds at dusk is surprisingly relaxing."

I could cheer Iddo. Nisai might not listen to me on this, but there's a chance he'll heed his older brother.

"You two can gang up on me all you want, but Aphorai is my province. And there's a Flower Moon on the way. It's time for unification, not for letting cracks widen to chasms."

Great.

Iddo sighs. "Eh, fair point. And who are we to deny our illustrious mothers? What do you say, house cat?" A familiar jibe, directed at me but delivered with a smile more charming than cocky.

Perhaps in another life, I would have served the Commander. Another life in which he didn't think me a pampered servant. My loyalties lie with Nisai, and always will, but there's something appealing about traversing the land as the eyes and ears of the Emperor. Guarding against invasion, quelling insurrection. Camping beneath the stars. A life free of courtiers and tedious politics.

I give myself an inward shake. Without Nisai, I might not have *had* a life.

"It's my duty to go wherever the First Prince wishes," I say, a little too stiffly.

If Iddo noticed the impact of his words, he doesn't let on. "The question, then, is when do you want to leave, Little Brother?"

"As soon as possible. The Flower Moon rises on the final day of Hatalia. There'll be festivities prior, which I should attend."

"Good. My Rangers get restless if all they've got to do is eat and drink and oil their kit. They'll carp about it, but I didn't spend all that time sharpening them up so they can go soft hanging around here."

I search his face, trying to determine if there was a barb in those words.

"The morrow, then?" The Commander rises to his feet.

Nisai nods. "Thank you, Brother."

Iddo shrugs. "Just doing my job."

"Will you dine with us tonight?" The Prince looks so hopeful, like he's still the boy who would spend hours waiting atop the walls for the return of a particular Ranger patrol, bringing tales of intrigue and adventure.

"I'll find something at the barracks. My men will take more kindly to the news if it's delivered over meat and beer."

Nisai looks affronted. "They'll be equally well hosted in Aphorai."

"Any Ranger with recent experience of the outer provinces will find that a stretch."

"I expect my uncle will surprise them."

"As you say. Until dawn, then?"

"Until dawn."

Iddo claps Nisai on the shoulder, then snaps his heels together and thumps his fist over his heart. "Your Highness." With a nod in my direction, he strides from the room.

"Well then," Nisai says, returning to his map. "Are you pleased? We'll have more than a full escort; we'll have the *best* escort."

"I'd be pleased if this whole trip were set aside. But I'm relieved. Somewhat." I shake my head and turn away. There's not much I can do now, other than damage control.

I fill a cup of water from the alabaster drinking basin and retrieve a silver flask from the array of jars and bottles in Nisai's personal store. "Iddo will be taking care of most things, but there's one matter you'll have to attend to before we leave."

"Oh?"

I give him a meaningful look as I measure three drops of near-black liquid into the cup. They sink through the water like strikes of dark lightning.

"Oh. *That*. Of course. I'm sure Esarik will be able to get his hands on some, and then we can restock in Aphorai."

"Esarik? You promised nobody else—"

"He thinks I get migraines."

"Oh." I give the cup a swirl and knock back its contents in one gulp, gagging at the bitterness. All these turns, and I've never managed to get used to it.

Nisai eyes me warily. "Haven't you already taken today's dose?"

"Yes." It comes out curter than I intend. We both know how addictive Linod's Elixir can be.

His wariness softens to concern. "It's getting worse, isn't it?"

"I'll be fine." As Shield, my duty is to protect the Prince. He has enough concerns on his plate, he doesn't need mine heaped upon them.

This is my burden to bear.

Mine alone.

* * *
* *
*

I knew this day would come, I simply didn't imagine it would arrive this soon.

Dawn finds the sky above the imperial complex cloaked in cloud. Below, the docks and slums are obscured by chill river mist. I wish I could forget what it is to dwell in that fog, down where the higher reaches of Ekasya Mountain may as well be the realm of the gods.

Here, in the palace's outer courtyard, barked orders and the brays of pack animals echo around the black granite walls.

Even among all the activity, Esarik is lost in his own world. He toes one of the massive hexagonal flagstones with his boot. "Six sides," he muses. "Honoring six deities. The more I consider it, the more I'm convinced this construction *predates* the Shadow Wars."

"I wouldn't go shouting that from the rooftops if I were you." Official history says whatever was here before was razed by the heroes who stood with the first Emperor to banish the Lost God. Stars keep their souls.

Esarik cringes. "Did I truly speak that aloud?"

"As I'm yet to master the art of mind reading, I'd say . . . yes."

"I didn't mean any offense, I'm sorry if—"

I pat his shoulder reassuringly. "Sometimes I wonder why you didn't stick to history. You certainly seem to like it more than medicine."

"If only." He gives me a wry smile and rubs his thumb against the fingertips of the same hand. "Father pays my stipend. Father chooses what I study. Whether I like it or not."

With the last of the supplies loaded onto the donkeys, Iddo points Nisai to the imperial litter, piled high with cushions. Four burly servants—handpicked by Iddo—wait to take up the pole at each corner. "I have two legs of my own, thank you. I can walk." The First Prince's usually diplomatic tone is indignant. "Ash?"

I hold up my hands. "I'm not the one in charge here."

"Choose your battles, Little Brother. The future Emperor doesn't make his first public appearance strolling along beside an ass."

"I won't be walking with you, then?"

The Commander arches a brow. "How very regal of you."

Nisai sighs and steps onto the litter.

Behind us, the temple soars, the gloss-black pyramid a wonder of divine geometry. There may no longer be a Scent Keeper in Ekasya, but that doesn't mean the temple has ceased operations. And today it is as if all the priestesses' festivals have come at once.

Columns of colored vapor rise in succession from the temple's apex, concluding with the rich purple of the imperial family. The last burns the longest, a reminder to Ekasya's residents that they live in the greatest of the Empire's cities. Or perhaps it's trying to mask the growing rift between the throne and the conduit to the gods.

Whatever the intent, the smoke has stolen any chance of keeping the delegation's departure circumspect.

I curse under my breath.

"Spectacle," Nisai observes from his litter, "is half the reason we're out here."

The Commander gives the order to move out and the palace gates swing open with stately grace, burnished bronze wrapped around entire trunks of Hagmiri Mountain cedar. As if I'd been standing in their way, the enormity of the situation finally hits me.

We've not left the imperial complex for half our lives.

And now we're about to cross half the Empire.

We descend into the outer city, where the commerce district never sleeps. When he was restless, Nisai used to watch from atop the palace complex walls, fascinated at the bustle continuing into the night. Now even thicker crowds choke the streets. Iddo's men march in formation, spearheading the procession and clearing the way. The Commander walks easily, erect but with relaxed shoulders, as do his Rangers.

Except for one about my age.

It's not that she doesn't look the part—her battle braids give her an inch of height over me and she's almost as broad, while her deep brown skin is layered over a wiriness that attests to the endurance of a Ranger. She's as alert as any other in the squad, scanning ahead and behind at regular, almost regimented intervals. But unlike Iddo and the others, she hasn't mastered the art of appearing nonchalant about it.

Iddo traces my gaze to where the young Ranger pulls her cloak tighter around her. "Ah. Kip, she's new. Typical Losian: a few clouds and you'd think it was the dead of winter."

I don't blame her for being on edge. This is unknown territory for me, too, with the velvet curtains of the imperial litter pulled aside, the hides scaled with silver discs rolled away. It leaves Nisai exposed on all sides, and it feels like I need to be looking everywhere at once—down the avenue, up to the gardens overhanging the balconies of the grand manses, around every lane corner.

Nisai does nothing to tamp down the crowd, waving regally, tossing coins with his father's likeness stamped on one side, the temple on the other. He's using his personal currency supply. Kaddash recently had the imperial mint replace the stepped pyramid with the Kaidon phoenix.

"Relax," Iddo says beside me. "Here, he's loved. They're just fascinated to see the Hidden Prince. Save your energy."

He may be right, but I'm relieved when the river comes into view, wide and deep and the color of milky kormak. The ornate imperial barge with its purple tent is moored at the docks, surrounded by the plainer vessels for the staff and supplies.

Iddo had relayed the plan before we left the palace—we're to board the imperial barge, shuck the trappings of pomp and pageantry, then slip out the back onto one of the nondescript vessels. Iddo's shortest Ranger will stand in as Nisai's double. No insurgent archer or competing Prince's assassin will be able to tell the difference from the banks of the river.

We make it to the docks without incident. Inside the marquee, Nisai dons the same plain-spun robes he uses for training. His ever-present journal peeks out from one of the deep pockets. The day is warm, and the cloak I've been allocated is warmer, but I pull the hood up all the same. My tattoos make me too recognizable, even from afar.

Suitably disguised, we slip through the unpicked seam in the back of the marquee. Nisai seems almost gleeful as he jumps from deck to deck. Me, less so.

With everything in place, the Rangers cast us off and the current tugs us away from the docks. Soon, the west arm of the river joins with its eastern sibling, the water racing us along.

Nisai leans on the rail, watching as Ekasya Mountain, standing sentinel above the plains, retreats into the distance. He closes his eyes and takes a deep breath, face to the sky.

"Smell that?" he asks.

I sniff. "What?"

"Freedom."

CHAPTER 5
RAKEL

I *hate* crowds.

I'd expected a turnout. The trials aren't as raucous as the barley harvest used to be, or as momentous as New Turn's Eve, but they're still a key date in the festival calendar.

Just because I knew there would be throngs at the six-sided plaza, doesn't mean it's easy to cope with half of Aphorai pressing up against me—the woman whose robes stink of fennel and root vegetable stew, the boy who must have sneaked his father's aftershave this morning, marjoram and bitter-lime following him like a stray dog.

Barden takes my hand and shoulders his way through the swarm. He's not wearing his uniform, but his bulk is enough to encourage a path to clear. My satchel feels so much heavier knowing that it contains dahkai—and with it my future—even though the vial itself weighs next to nothing.

Around the plaza perimeter, street sellers do a roaring trade, slicing off half-moons of melon to order, each fall of the cleaver sending bursts of sweetness arcing through the air.

Farther on, spice-rubbed mutton roasts over hot coals.

I hope I'll be able to block out the savory smoke once the testing starts. I wouldn't have held anything down had I tried to eat this morning. My two doses of mandragora, courtesy of Zakkurus's people, have had my insides sloshing about like a water bearer's bucket ever since.

Or maybe the stomach churning has more to do with wondering whether Father has realized what I've done. He'd have expected me home by now.

Barden leads us past moneylenders who've turned bookkeepers for the day, their scribblers hollering out odds on competitors before we've even lined up for the entrance task. They know the families expected to front a candidate. And they know the candidates who are expected to win.

They wouldn't recognize my name.

When we reach the edge of the plaza closest to the palace, Barden guides me in front of him. My traitorous stomach clenches all the more at the sight of the testing stage, rising five tiered steps above the plaza.

Barden bends down to speak into my ear so that I can hear him over the drums. "I would wish you luck, but you don't need it." He grins and gives me a playful nudge.

If he only knew.

At the base of the stage, a line of hopefuls has formed. I clutch my satchel and move to join them, pausing for one last glance back at Barden. "Get right up their nostrils!" he shouts, signing with the rudest of two-fingered gestures.

I do my best to muster a smile.

I'm not the only one in the queue who is dressed in plain garb. Even so, we're the minority. Like me, the commoners who've stepped forward stand still and serious, not laughing and jostling.

Ahead, it looks like the testing will take place over several rounds. At least that's something I expected. We'll only be allowed onto the second platform once we pass the entrance test, where the barley is sorted from the chaff.

On the third level, workbenches have been set up in a line. Mortar and pestle, and an assortment of presses and measures are neatly arrayed on each. At one end sits something I've long coveted—a full imperial-standard distilling apparatus.

The fourth platform is for the judge and any observers. For Zakkurus, the Eraz's representative when it comes to our province's perfume regulation and trade. For Lady Sireth, the Eraz's daughter, though given she's more interested in trends than techniques, bets are she'll be fashionably late.

The summit belongs to nobody but the gods.

Speak of the demon, Zakkurus emerges from the portico, clad in signature blue—today's as light as summer sky. As his gaze sweeps the crowd, I wonder if I backed out now, could I return the dahkai? Find another way? If I worked day and night, if the seasons were kind and the foraging yielded plenty, I might be able to scrape enough together by selling to Zakkurus *and* his competitors. As long as none of them, or the tax collectors, found out.

But then the sick-sweet rot of Father's leg comes to mind—the bandages that need to be fastened higher with each passing moon.

Turning back is nothing but wishful thinking.

At the edge of the platform, Zakkurus spreads his arms wide. "Ours is a lineage from beyond the edge of memory," the perfumer begins, his voice controlled and yet carrying. "Older than the Shadow Wars, the Founding Accord. We, fellow Aphorains, are caretakers of tradition. Beloved by the gods. The Emperor may rule us, but in the ways of the highest sense, Aphorai rules the Empire!"

Most of the crowd erupts into a rousing cheer, though a staunch imperialist next to us mutters something about walking the line of treason.

Zakkurus raises his hands, begging for order with false modesty. "But to preserve Aphorai's legacy, to ensure we remain above all provinces, we must recruit the best. Who has the dedication, the talent, to continue our reputation for excellence?

"Alas, I am but a humble perfumer," he laments.

The crowd titters.

"This is not a judgment I alone can make."

The crowd shuffled aside for Barden. Now it cleaves in two as people rush to clear a path. A figure threads their way across the plaza, clad in a dark cloak despite the heat, full hood pulled up. I'd assume Lady Sireth, but she wouldn't be seen in something so plain, even for the mystery. And for all the times she's waved from the battlements at festivals or ventured into the streets to hand out silver zigs on holy days, I don't recall her being so tall.

The new arrival passes the line of would-be apprentices in a swirl of labdanum—sweet and smoky and dark as the underworld. A seed of suspicion sprouts in my mind.

The figure glides up the ramp, hem dragging behind. For the briefest moment, it snags on a rough-hewn edge, revealing a glimpse of what's underneath.

Feathers. Black feathers.

No. It can't be.

Today is about perfume, not prayer. A competition of craft, not a consecration.

But everything is falling into place. The smoke from the temple as I arrived in the city, today's testing stage in tiers like a replica temple,

Zakkurus's talk of gods and tradition. I should have realized. A Flower Moon is on the horizon.

And that means . . . it's her.

Scents abound, it's *her.*

Joining Aphorai's chief perfumer on the second-highest platform, the figure turns to face the crowd. Silence falls like a sword as she pushes back her hood. She shrugs out of the cloak and Zakkurus scrambles—*actually scrambles*—to catch it.

Ordinary firebirds wear crimson. But this woman's dress is the deepest black, feathers shimmering rainbow in the sun like oil on water.

Her movements are as fluid and flawless as molten bronze. High cheekbones, elegant neck, and full lips defy age. And if gray or white streaked her hair, nobody would be any the wiser—her scalp is shaven clean.

Since before anyone alive can remember, Sephine has served as Aphorai's Scent Keeper. Link between temple and palace. Mediator between the gods and the rulers of us mere mortals. The woman who has sanctioned half a dozen Aphorain Erazes. The woman who could revoke her blessing and turn the people against their lord, removing him as surely as a decree from the Emperor.

An air of calm assurance surrounds her as she surveys the crowd. But what she sees with her Scent-Keeper eyes—completely black where others would have pupil and iris—I haven't the smokiest idea.

Does she see me?

Does she see my unveiled hate?

There's as many myths and stories about Scent Keepers as there are feathers in their dresses. All I know is that they'd rather demonstrate what happens when someone goes against the temple than save a woman's life. Even if that woman was once one of their own. Even if she had a husband and a newborn daughter.

I clench my fists, resisting the urge to let one hand stray up to my mother's locket.

High on the judging platform, Zakkurus hands off Sephine's cloak. "Now then, shall we begin?"

A succession of the perfumer's assistants lift cones of intricately decorated parchment to their lips, puffing pale pink dust into the air. Well before any of the billowing cloud has drifted over me, I catch the scent.

Desert rose.

The crowd lets out a collective sigh, the poorer among them trying to grab handfuls of the stuff, as if they could gather it and trade it for something they really need. A wave of nausea washes over me—I'm breathing my own wares, the least of what I've gambled.

With a flourish of the perfumer's fan, two more servants step forward and set down a great bronze chest. Each of us in the line of hopefuls is handed a small slate and chalk-tipped stylus. We're to take one chance at sensing what's in the chest. To miss an ingredient, or to misidentify one, is to miss your chance until the next trials.

It's agony waiting this far back. In turn, each would-be competitor bends to the chest, makes a note, and presents it to the scribe stationed at the entrance to the next platform.

Some are waved through. Others are turned away. Some react with a shrug. Others have to be forcibly removed by the guards.

The youth before me wears a robe dyed in rich magenta—the almost purple of the minor branches of the five families. I wrinkle my nose and resist the urge to offer my condolences on his lack of access to a water well—he reeks so strongly of musky agarwood he must have bathed in it.

At his turn with the entry test, he only gives the quickest of sniffs.

"Be sure," Zakkurus warns from on high. "Even up here I can barely smell anything but you."

A snicker escapes my lips.

Rich boy casts his answer. The scribe doesn't even glance at his slate before ushering him through.

I can't believe it. I had always thought a son or daughter of the five families won because they could afford the training, afford the materials. Not because they were handed victory on a platter.

Fuming, I look at the guards. Most don't bat an eye. Though one of the women shifts her feet, jaw tight.

Then it's my turn.

I clench my fists harder, using the sting of my nails digging into my palms to center myself and focus on the chest. It's long been empty, but a careful inhale reveals the silk lining still carries the memory of what it stored.

Melissa—citrus fresh but less vicious than lemon itself.

Violets. Of course, given Zakkurus's soft spot for them.

Under that, an earthy balsam. Vetiver. A perfumer's best friend, fixing fleeting scents in place.

Prayer candles. These ones for the twin deities of the waterways, Zir and Tro.

So far, so simple.

At the base of the ramp, I hand the scribe my notes. He reads with a nod.

"Name?"

"Rakel."

"Rakel who?"

"Ana."

The guard leans forward to peer over the scribe's shoulder, hair falling over a jagged scar on her forehead. "You're Commander Ana's daughter?"

I nod warily.

She snaps her heels together and thumps her right fist to her chest. "I served under your father. How is retirement treating the old boy? Still training those bizarre beasts of his?"

I smile despite myself. "I expect he'll be working with horses until the day he dies."

"And may the starwheel turn many times before. He saved my life.

At the battle of Azutrai. Lozanak's my name. I was in the fourth. Would you give him my regards?"

I nod. "Of course."

"Appreciate it." She lowers her voice. "Good luck up there. The way your father used to talk, you'd run rings around those over-perfumed pups." She claps me on the back in farewell.

Above, Sephine stands still as a gate guardian, Zakkurus beside her. I want to believe Lozanak is right. But all I can think of is the noble kid being waved through, no questions asked.

Zakkurus had warned me, hadn't he? But he won mere turns ago, and he isn't from an aristocratic family.

It's been done. It *can* be done.

Nerves threaten to undo me, but I don't have a choice.

I step up onto the platform.

Less than half the candidates have been welcomed onto the first level of the testing stage. Seventeen of us.

This round will test etiquette and politics, history and scentlore.

It's my danger round.

Unlike most of the candidates, I've had to glean what I know from eavesdropping and watching from afar.

I try not to fidget as Zakkurus works his way down the line. "A merchant wishes to arrange a marriage," he purrs. "He would see his daughter wedded to the third son of a noble family. He invites the son's father to his house. What incense would you recommend, to receive his visitor?"

Small mercy I didn't get that question. Wouldn't have the smokiest idea.

By the time Zakkurus stands before me, half a dozen competitors have been culled, their answers bumbling or incorrect or just offending the perfumer's so-called refined sensibilities. He fixes me in a stare as uncaring as a drought. "Candidate?"

I play along. "Ana."

"Candidate Ana. Now then. An indentured servant has succumbed to the Affliction. Her condition is grave. What funeral incense would you advise her contract holder to burn?"

This isn't straightforward. Many people, especially those whose luxurious lives hardly ever come into contact with the Rot, are so terrified of it that they become irrational, exaggerating its progress, wanting only to be rid of it. The girl may still have options other than funeral incense.

"Her wounds?" I ask. "Where are they?"

"Excuse me, Candidate?"

I grit my teeth. "Where are her wounds? Limbs? Torso?"

"That has no bearing on this situation."

It's all I can do not to punch him right in that cat-got-the-cream smile.

"Frankincense," I tell him.

It has cleansing properties. Burned day and night, it may slow the progress of the Rot; some say it can even halt its progress if you apply it topically. If you can afford enough of it, of course. It's no dahkai, but it's worth more by weight than gold.

"You would advise a noble to waste such a rich ingredient on a servant?"

Every life is worth trying to save, I want to shout at Zakkurus. But I don't. Because I need to save one particular life, more than I need to save my pride, more than I need to call them out as richly robed monsters.

I take a deep breath and swallow my shame.

"Sandalwood and thyme," I concede. "The first sweetens the air, the second invokes Azered, calling on the goddess to speed the patient's journey to the sky, and in doing so protecting the higher-priority visitors."

At least that's what your heartless visitors will believe.

I sneak a glance above. The Scent Keeper regards me and Zakkurus in turn. She blinks once and returns her gaze to the middle distance.

The chief perfumer smiles. "You may advance, Candidate."

Shouts of approval fly from the crowd. From this distance, they can't see the way Zakkurus's blue eyes burn into me like the hottest part of a flame.

On the third platform, there's only one workbench left free. Right next to the rich kid I'd seen waved through. The boy's hands hang loose and easy at his sides, unblemished with the burns and scars of the trade. Nothing about him suggests those fingers would ever strip thorns from stems. Ugh. Not only will I have to compete with the others as well as my nerves, but I've got to do it in a miasma of sweat-sticky agarwood cologne.

The task is announced. We're to make our most innovative perfume with the ingredients provided. Using our own supplies will result in instant disqualification.

I inspect the array of jars and vials before me, discovering several are mislabeled. Tonka-bean crystals are never that pale. But there's labdanum here. Violet water, too. A plan begins to unfold in my mind. I set to work.

I'm almost done, when I catch wind of something I've only ever come across once before, at a metalworker's. It has the most gorgeous notes of plum and nutmeg before it comes in contact with anything other than the glass jars used to store it.

What in the sixth hell is Rich Kid playing at?

I glance at Zakkurus, who paces the line of workbenches. Has he even noticed? The smell must have reached him by now. Sure enough, he halts in front of my neighbor's bench. "Why have you ceased work, Candidate?"

"I've finished." The boy puffs out his chest. Either it's a fearless bluff, or he has no idea what he's done.

Zakkurus claps his hands, seemingly delighted. "Then let's sample the fruits of your labor, shall we?"

Rich Kid proffers the jar.

The perfumer holds his palm up—a magnanimous "you first" gesture.

The boy shrugs. And then it hits me. He really doesn't realize what he's made. I tense, torn between shouting a warning and staying silent.

Too late.

The boy dabs the concoction onto the triangle of bare chest at his robe's neckline.

"Oh, do be generous," urges Zakkurus. "There's that cologne to contend with, after all."

The boy rubs more liquid onto his skin.

"Wonderful. Now you just hold tight until the others have finished." The perfumer pats the boy on the arm and turns his back.

Instinct shoves my thoughts away. In a handful of strides, I'm at my competition's side. "Fool! Open your robe!"

He doesn't make a move. "Excuse me?"

The pretty silk ties lacing up his front would be worth more than my entire wardrobe, boots and all. I grab them in each hand and rip them apart.

"How dare y—" His words cut off in a hiss of pain. He looks down at his chest, the outrage of a moment ago replaced with alarm. The skin has reddened. Then it begins to bubble. A smell in the same family as roasting pig reaches my nose. Rich Kid stumbles back a step, trips on his own bench, and collapses to the floor.

I ignore his howls as I douse the area in sak ointment, rubbing it in even though blisters burst and weep under my fingers. He tries to push me from him, but he's weak with shock and it's little more than a flail.

When I'm sure I've neutralized the effects and contained the spread, I step back. "Didn't anyone ever tell you not to steam-distil zesker essence? It turns caustic when heated to high temperatures."

A pair of burly servants appear. They half carry, half drag the now-gibbering mess off the platform. To where, I have no idea.

I look for Sephine. The Scent Keeper has gone.

Slow claps ring out behind me. "Lovely performance, petal. On any other day I'm sure you'd be rewarded for such heroics. Today, alas, we cannot tolerate interference with another candidate's materials."

"What?" I gape at him.

Zakkurus waves over a pair of guards. Lozanak is one of them. Though she doesn't look pleased, she obeys the command.

"Makes the heart sing when an investment pans out. Truly."

"You . . . you *knew* what he was making!" I sputter.

Rage courses through me. I'll give them *interference*.

Zakkurus reaches out and pats my elbow, the same gesture he'd used on the boy before his flesh had started to burn. It makes my skin crawl.

Then he's replaced by the guards. They hustle me down each of the platforms and out into the crowd, one clearing a path while the other holds fast to my arm.

I find myself surrounded and yet utterly alone. My breaths come quicker, shallow, the city's stench suddenly too thick for my lungs. The sunlight starts to darken.

Then Barden is there.

I flinch. There will be questions. Oh so many questions. Barden knew I was selling. He knew I had a meeting with a source about the trials. But I hadn't yet worked out a way to tell him about Zakkurus's contract. I'd hoped I'd never have to.

Now holding it in feels like trying to carry sand in a basket.

"Bar—"

"Don't struggle," he murmurs in my ear. "You'll only make it worse."

He sounds so sure of himself. "I'll find you. I always find you."

And then he's lost in the crowd.

CHAPTER 6
ASH

On the barge, Iddo's men play Five Cups and arm wrestle for coin or extra ale. I've never dared drink more than a watered mug. I can't understand why anyone wouldn't want to be in control of their mind, their body. For me it would be downright dangerous.

Nisai spends most of the time on deck, scribbling in his journal, debating the finer points of Aphorain history with Esarik, or needling his friend to make a proper overture to Ami. I've never seen someone blush as furiously as the Trelian does whenever her name is spoken.

On the third day, the horizon changes. The straight line of the plains wavers into blue-green foothills. Later, distant peaks appear, their heads and shoulders cloaked in white.

I've just finished my morning devotions and refastened my prayer band to my arm, when Esarik points. "The Spine of Hagmir."

"The Alet Range," Nisai says. "Did you know their full name is recorded in the old documents as *Asmatuk Alet Tupeshto*? Old Imperial Aramteskan for 'the mountains that bite the sky.'"

Esarik frowns. "Wouldn't 'the mountains that devour the sky' be a more representative translation?"

"Poetic. I like it."

"Why, thank you."

At the disembarkation point, several Rangers wait with a herd of camels. Iddo can certainly plan a journey. Half the animals are saddled with cloth and leather between their two humps, the others will bear our packs. Nisai grimaces at the litter, but doesn't protest, and we strike out toward the tail end of the Alet hills.

The river plains give way to parched scrubland, patterned with a network of dried-out irrigation canals. Esarik glances around, then frowns at his map. "They still haven't updated it."

"Updated what?" I ask.

"This used to be the breadbasket of Aphorai. But the Great Groundshake of 614 changed the course of the river. Little prospect of barley sprouting within these borders anymore."

I shrug. At least it's still flat.

But soon enough, we begin to climb. And as we do, everything grows quiet.

Too quiet.

There's no birdsong. No skittering of small creatures in the spiny vegetation clustered around the rock formations. By the time the road passes through a steep cutting, all I can hear is creaking leather and the snuffle and plod of the camel train.

Until a pebble rattles down the gully.

Iddo's hand goes to his ax.

An arrow shuttles past.

I unsheathe my twin blades and move my camel between Nisai and the arrow's origin. Another bolt arcs down, piercing Kip's camel's flank. The shaggy beast kicks out and lunges against its headrope, red blooming around its wound.

"Get control of that thing," an older Ranger barks at Kip.

"Human shield," Iddo bellows. "Two deep!"

Almost as one, the Rangers fall into formation around the Prince and Esarik, so tight their camel's rumps jostle for space.

Within the circle, I'm the last defense.

"Down," I say. "Now."

The porters lower the litter and Esarik scrambles from his camel.

"Brigands?" the Trelian asks. It's little more than a whisper, his knuckles white around his mount's headrope.

I don't reply. Surrounded by Rangers and camels, I can't for the life of me get a view of the action.

Another arrow whizzes past and *thunk*s into one of the packs, crude fletching sticking out.

Azered's breath. This is a far cry from the training arena. My pulse quickens, blood thrumming in my ears. I fight to keep it in check. I've *got* to keep it in check.

I catch a glimpse of Iddo outside the circle, ax aloft. A pair of Rangers breaks out from the ring, the others quickly closing the gap behind them, blocking my view.

Shouts and the clang of blades reverberate around the rocky outcrops.

A shriek of pain rends the air.

Then it's over almost as quick as it began. The formation relaxes enough for me to glimpse the two Rangers returning, half a dozen ragged figures driven before them.

I shake my head. Boys, old men. Apart from the archer among them, they appear to be farmers armed with rusted scythes and hoes. What were they thinking attacking fully armed Rangers?

"Is that all of them?" Iddo demands.

"Aye, sir. Well, all of them bar one. But he's not going anywhere."

The Commander nods. "Scout a perimeter. If there's any more, flush them out."

Orders given, Iddo turns his camel toward the ambushers. He doesn't bother with the first, who has dissolved into a blubbering mess.

The second of the group stares straight ahead, his nostrils pinched white. When Iddo's camel draws level, the brigand spits at the Commander.

Iddo raises his ax.

My eyes go wide. Surely he's not going to—

"Stop!" Nisai presses his way outside the ring of Rangers, who hasten to turn their blades aside. "Look at them, will you? They're skin and bone. I doubt they're even aware who we are, other than the first group to ride by when they were desperate for their next meal."

Iddo's expression remains implacable. "Treason is treason. On the Emperor's person or his roads."

"I'm not the Emperor yet." Nisai spreads his hands. "I'm not saying they shouldn't atone for their actions. But it needn't be with their lives. If they were escorted back to the capital, they could serve in Ekasya's fields until they've worked off the debt of the camel, and anything else you take inventory of."

Iddo shakes his head. "The Rangers have a saying: Free one traitor and a hundred more will line up to betray you. There's no choice in this."

"We *always* have a choice. And I'd risk those hundred other traitors than live with one death on my conscience."

"Then it will be on me," Iddo says. He signals to the nearest Rangers, Kip among them. "Get this lot out of the Prince's sight."

I'd swear the youngest Ranger's jaw clenched at the order. But then she squares her shoulders and prods one of the farmers into a stumbling walk.

Iddo looks back down to Nisai. "I'm sorry it needs to be this way, but I'll always choose what's best for you, Little Brother. And I'll always choose what's best for the Empire. You're going to need to learn to do the same."

Nisai watches Iddo ride after his Rangers, wearing an expression I've never seen him regard his brother with.

Disappointment.

"We always have a choice," the First Prince repeats softly.

* * *
* *
*

"So *that's* what old Zolmal was on about in *Journeys*," Esarik marvels when we crest the final ridge. He flings his arms wide, earning a snort from his camel. "Behold! The Sand Sea."

I've never seen the ocean, but looking out across this vastness, I'll take the scholar's word for it. Forget the scrubland and rocky foothills we've already crossed, this is true desert. The kind that features in tales of audacious merchant caravans bringing essences from Aphorai—desert rose, black iris, and the rarest of rare: dahkai flower.

Down below, a hundred-strong unit of camel cavalry awaits us, decked out in full desert military regalia. They must have been waiting for a while. Pennants with the Eraz of Aphorai's sigil—the winged lion on a gold field—flap from every tent in their camp. It's a strange feeling seeing so many of the stylized version of my own tattoo in one place, like returning to a home I've never been.

I can only see Iddo's back, his once-white cape caked in dust and tented over his camel's rump, cloaking any clues as to what he thinks. But his heels are firmly down in the stirrups. At the ready. Waiting.

The curtains of the litter part. "Is there a problem?"

We hardly passed a soul after the skirmish, and Nisai has made a pretense of sleeping through the heat, though he would have been analyzing yesterday's events, going over and over them in his mind like picking at a scab until it bleeds.

"Seems we have a greeting party is all," I reply. "They fly your uncle's colors."

Nisai sighs. "I was hoping we could avoid this."

"Ah, politics," Esarik says, heaving an exhausted sigh of his own and dabbing his brow with the kerchief he's taken to wearing on the road.

When we reach the camp, the Aphorain leader makes his way straight to Iddo.

"Commander." The man doesn't nod or bow in greeting, though he's technically a rank lower in the imperial military hierarchy. Bold move. "I trust your trip hasn't been troublesome." His tone suggests he knows otherwise.

Iddo bristles. "Perfectly routine, *Province* Commander."

"Thank the stars." He looks the Rangers up and down. "Well then, no need to keep your men suffering in this heat any longer. Mine can take over from here." He juts his chin toward the unit of cavalry behind him, mounted on camels in every shade from sandstone to basalt. They appear as relaxed as the Rangers.

"This is an imperial mission," Iddo says.

"Are you saying my men are any less servants to the Empire?" the Province Commander's voice drops to a dangerous tone.

"I'm saying my men are trained for missions of state."

The Aphorain officer makes a show of inspecting the Rangers. He gives a sniff of derision. "Oh, your lot looks the part. But this is our land. We know the desert. And I know how perturbed the Eraz of Aphorai will be if you don't accept his kind offer of an escort."

Nisai leans from the litter, artfully assuming an expression of wide-eyed naivety. "My uncle? Is he with you?"

The Aphorain slides from his saddle and bends one knee in the sand. "Forgive me, my Prince."

"There is nothing to forgive. Province Commander, I thank you for your candor. Indeed, I would hear more of our province."

"It would be my pleasure. And, as it pleases you, your uncle has arranged entertainments for your journey into his estates in these sacred days before the Flower Moon. Tomorrow is the Feast of Riker, and we shall hunt in honor of the youthful god. A feathered lion. The greatest beast you have ever seen."

For the first time, Iddo looks interested in what the Aphorain has to say.

But Nisai affects a crestfallen demeanor. "Alas, the only way ballads will be composed in my honor is as a wielder of words."

"No need for false modesty. You're Aphorain. You'll come into your reign anointed by the gods like the great kings of old."

There's the slightest tightening around Nisai's eyes, a change I'm confident only I notice. "My thanks. Given the day fades, do you have any objections to remaining at camp for the night?"

"Of course not, my Prince."

"Then let us eat, and rest, and set out fresh tomorrow." He nods to Iddo and the Aphorain Commander as a pair, neatly sidestepping their contest of rank. "Thank you, gentlemen."

We're shown to a tent in the center of camp. Before our bags have been brought in, Esarik's already off again, peppering the Aphorain soldiers with questions.

Nisai sets about lighting incense. Myrrh and oakmoss—an offering to Kaismap, the god of his starwheel spoke. The god of foresight.

"What's brought on this pious streak?" I ask, taking a seat on the edge of my bedroll and setting out the essential oils I'll need to re-infuse the prayer braid tied to my arm—a different scented strand for each deity.

He shrugs. "It's no stench up my nose to burn a few sticks."

After the last couple of days, I'd agree. I hate to think what else this journey has in store if the gods desire some idle amusement.

"Anyway," he says, "I like the smell. It helps me think." He sinks onto a rug piled with cushions, crossing his legs, leaning elbows on knees and chin on hands. He's looking my way but not *at* me, his attention caught somewhere in the air between us.

"Those men in the mountains—they were in such a desperate state. I thought the capital had sent aid to this region. Wasn't that the impetus for my father's last trip? After the shake? The reports said the situation was assessed, help was given to rebuild. But did you see any sign of that aid? Little wonder the Province Commander was prickly."

"You're still gnawing on yesterday?"

Nisai rubs his temples, a pained expression creasing his brow. "I should have handled things differently."

"How so?"

"I sounded impetuous in front of my brother, in front of everyone, and yet when I was challenged, I faltered. I let those men die. The Empire had already failed them, and I let them pay the ultimate price."

He buries his face in his hands. "Ash, what if I'm no better at this than my father?"

I've always felt a conflicted affinity to Riker, the young deity who struggled against his darker side to be true to the goodness in his heart. But when we cross from the dunes into the tended land, we're informed marks the outskirts of the Eraz's estate, embarking on a hunt in the youthful god's honor, I feel anything but heartened.

As we walk toward our chariot, I try to dissuade Nisai from playing along with this nonsense. There's no reason to expose himself to such risk. "My Prince—"

"Scents, Ash. Don't you start calling me that."

"Sorry. I was going to say . . . you don't have to do this."

"You're wrong about that."

"I thought you said we always have a choice?"

"We do. But this is a test, and I intend to pass."

I drop my voice to a level that will reach only his ears. "Your father's not here."

He halts midstride and rounds on me but keeps his voice equally low, wary of the Aphorain soldiers. "It's more than that, don't you see? Look at the way the Province Commander challenged my brother; dissent comes easier this far from the capital. With every word, every action, they're deciding if I'm fit to be Emperor."

"Killing a lion does not prove you fit to rule."

"For them it does. Even at Ekasya, the Emperors of old would kill any beasts that threatened flocks or farms. In times of peace, it was their only way to show their willingness to fight for the people, to show that the gods favored them to lead. It may have gone out of style in the capital. But here? It's an honor."

"You're the First Prince. Tell them to keep their sport for their own lords. Your uncle will get over it."

"And what of the capital? The Council? They may not care if I can hunt lions, but I *will* be judged on whether I can hold this lumbering beast of an empire together. Aramtesh has its faults, but it's staved off war for centuries. If that's not something to work for, I don't know what is."

We climb into our chariot, an Aphorain at the reins, an oversized brute about an age with Nisai and me, wearing nothing but sandals, leather kilt, and a sash across his broad chest. Nisai nods, and the Aphorain slaps the reins against the rump of our chariot's camel.

We're off.

I never thought I'd see a lion, especially not the ancient feather-maned breed. Their ilk no longer ventures into the cultivated land around Ekasya. But I suppose Nisai's right—out here is a different story. There's only so much fertile ground, only so many places for man or beast to find a meal.

The chariot wheels along a spring-fed rivulet trickling through the Eraz's estate, a grove of rock figs lining its banks. It broadens into man-made irrigation channels enclosing a tapestry of crop fields, from the gray-green spikes of leeks to fronds of carrots and dill. The green is incongruous with the dunes still rippling the horizon. Part of me wonders whether the gods upheave this land with groundshakes because they never intended for people to dwell here.

Our driver points ahead. A flash of tawny fur disappears over a rise, and we pick up speed. Nisai nocks an arrow to his bow, his features taking on a grim, wild cast I've not seen before.

We track our quarry to where the estate borders a rocky canyon, dunes rising from the other side. The lion comes into full view, and my grip on the side of the chariot tightens.

It's enormous. Far bigger than the depictions in the Ekasyan palace tapestries.

Massive jaws and watchful eyes are crowned with a full mane of feathers—one moment near black, the next swirling with iridescent color. Beneath the mane, it's all power, from hulking shoulders down golden flanks to hind legs ending in black talons.

Cornered, the beast circles, feather-tipped tail lashing the air, measuring us. It lets out a roar that thunders through my chest. As it reverberates, I can't help but think of kinship, of like greeting like, as if he can sense what I am, as if he is telling me he sees me.

There must be some way out of this hunt.

"Nisai." My first attempt at gaining his attention is lost in the thud of hooves and the rattle of the traces. "Nisai!"

But the Prince has drawn his bow, training his aim.

The lion charges. It's mesmerizing in its magnificent ferocity, muscle and sinew bunching and stretching beneath velvet hide.

Despite all the hours we've spent training, I've failed to make a better-than-average swordsman of Nisai. But he's an archer to rival Etru the Hunter. He holds his bow steady, stance wide, sure-footed on the bucking floor of the chariot.

An arrow catches the beast in the shoulder.

The lion roars. Roars, and keeps charging for us.

Iddo barks orders from his chariot. "Circle around! Come at him from the flank! Give our Prince room!" The eldest imperial brother rides without helmet, chestnut hair ruffled by the breeze. He's *enjoying* this.

The men on the other chariot holler, but the lion is having none of it, its golden eyes fixed on us. Blood blooms from the wound in its shoulder. It's only when I taste metal that I realize I've bitten my lip.

Nisai nocks another arrow. He may be keeping his composure, but his face is pale, his jaw clenched.

The lion changes tactic and angles for the camels. The beasts shy away and careen to the side, swinging the chariot wide. We lurch after them, heading for rocky scree at the edge of the canyon. It's about to become a bumpy ride, but there's nothing I can do. If I stop them, we'll be within reach of the lion in a heartbeat. I have to trust Iddo to take care of it.

"Hold on!" our driver shouts.

Nisai refuses to drop his bow. He lets fly again, somehow managing to steady himself. The arrow thwacks into the lion's flank and the beast's rear leg gives out before it rights itself. Surely the only thing keeping it going is pain and rage.

We're into the scree now. The chariot shudders beneath us, lurching to the side as the wheels slam into something. Then the world is tipping sideways.

"Nisai!"

I'm thrown clear, rolling to soften the impact. Ahead, Nisai lands awkwardly, bow pinned beneath him. He lets out a groan.

Finding my feet, I snatch up my spear. I launch into a sprint, intent on closing the distance, to put myself between the lion and Nisai. I've got a start on it, but it's so much faster. It narrows my lead in a few leaps.

Blood pounds in my ears.

I'm not going to make it.

Turn upon turn of Shield drills show me the only choice. I can't reach Nisai, but I could still reach the lion. I angle my strides toward it. With mere yards to spare, I throw my weight into its path, skidding through the scree.

The lion rears on hind legs, fixing me in its golden stare.

I should bury my spear in its chest, but against all instinct and training, I hesitate.

It's a moment too long.

Huge paws thump onto my shoulders, my knees threatening to buckle. Pain sears down one side of my chest, snatching my breath and the spear from my hand.

I've got to reach my swords.

I try to twist away. Claws hook into my flesh. Every muscle goes rigid as a voice tells me from somewhere deep, somewhere primal, that this is a mortal embrace. One false move and my lung will be pierced.

The lion slumps farther to the side, its breath hot and rancid against my neck. My vision blurs. I clench my jaw and shove down rising terror.

Then something gives way and I'm crumpling to the ground beneath the lion's weight, both of us bellowing in agony as we fall.

On my back in the gravel, I barely register a silhouette above me, ax flashing in the sun. The figure draws itself up to full height, weapon raised. The blade comes down, and the lion's crushing weight stops struggling.

Iddo drops his ax and somehow rolls the beast off me.

Nisai's face swims into view beside his brother's. He's covered in blood. Panic seizes me until I realize it's the lion's. And mine.

He reaches out a hand. "Can you walk?"

I wave him away. "Just a scratch."

His eyes tell me he sees through the lie.

CHAPTER 7
RAKEL

W here are you taking me?" I demand.

Nobody answers.

I'd expected to be dragged off to spend the next ten turns wherever Zakkurus keeps his indentured servants. Instead, the stepped pyramid looms before us, sending me lurching from anger to confusion to dread.

My escort is the veteran soldier from the trials, another of the Eraz's guards, and a pair of firebirds who met us at the temple gates after keeping us sweating in the sun for only stench knows how long.

Enough time to think up a dozen plans to escape or get word to Father. Enough time to dismiss every one of them as futile.

Outside the temple estate, the streets are dusty. Inside, rows of cistus flowers and vetiver grass stretch between high walls, spring-fed canals keeping the crops lush. A paved boulevard lined with bay trees leads to the pyramid's entrance.

The priestesses usher us along. I find small comfort that it's Father's old comrade, Lozanak, marching in front of me, her fingers twitching for her sword hilt the way mine itch for my locket. I wonder what has the soldier spooked.

I've got reason enough: My mother used to walk this path.

And after I learned the circumstances of her death, I swore I never would do the same.

We pass through a stand of orange trees dotted with apiaries. Buzzing fills the air. Under different circumstances, I may have reveled in the heady scent of neroli as much as the bees. Today the floral notes are soapy enough to curdle my stomach.

The priestesses halt when all that stands between us and the temple is a terrace carpeted in green.

"That will be all," the older firebird tells the guards.

Lozanak gives my shoulder a squeeze, her expression an apology. "Stars keep you." She brings her fist to her chest and turns on a heel.

I watch her go. Her loyalty was to Father, not me. But now she's gone I feel truly alone.

The priestess gives an exasperated sigh and points to my feet. Both firebirds have already slipped out of their sandals.

I tug my boots off and defiantly take my time about clapping them together to dislodge the dust. Then I shove them into my already bulging satchel—at least they let me keep it—and set out across the lawn. Three steps in, I realize it's holy thyme. Our footsteps release its rich, herby aroma, preparing us to supposedly cross from the mortal realm into the house of the gods.

A massive sandstone portico extends from the temple's entrance, portal guardians carved into either side. True firebirds—creatures from the edge of memory. The details of their feathers have weathered over the centuries, but the expressions on their human faces remain fiercely beautiful, the claws in place of women's feet no less cruel. As we pass under their gaze and into the shade, a shiver snakes down my spine.

The main hall is cool and dim; the only light beyond the entrance comes from widely spaced sconces and the glow from the doorway. Both priestesses face ahead as we pass, but I crane my neck at each opening.

Right now, I need all the information I can get.

The first doorways reveal scribes hunched over tablets and scrolls, their scalps shaved like the other firebirds. Farther on, zig counters balance weights against substances more valuable than silver or gold: frankincense resin, orris-root crystals, and tiny vials that I can't smell from this distance.

The firebirds turn us up a staircase that climbs and climbs until my thighs burn. How many feet did it take to wear these stones so smooth? Did their owners have a better idea what they were walking into?

Then we're emerging into open air.

I shield my eyes against the glare. It's some sort of garden. Set back from the edge of the pyramid's upper level so that it is only a dark smudge from below. Rock figs grow in clay urns taller than Barden, leaves rustling in a breeze that never reaches the lower city. Here, the air smells fresh.

Blinking, I draw a long breath. I've never seen so far across the desert. Toward the west, I sight my village, a tiny oasis tucked between the dunes. There's the snaking line of the canyons carved by the shifting riverbed—places Barden and I used to explore before he enlisted. Beyond that, the horizon stretches into mountains I've only glimpsed on clear days.

Anyone standing here can take in my whole world with a single glance. It's dizzying, like I'm weightless. Like I'm nothing.

I turn back to the firebirds. But there's only the dark maw of the stairwell.

I'm alone.

Except for a figure wearing plain linen as she tends a garden bed near a pavilion of stone pillars and arches. As if she felt my gaze, the woman lifts her shaven head.

The shade takes on a deeper chill. I shouldn't be surprised by now, after all these turns, after today. But who knew the most powerful woman in Aphorai got her hands dirty?

Sephine returns to planting out tiny seedlings. "Do you know the road you traveled to this place?"

I doubt she means the streets between the plaza and the temple. From what I've heard of Scent Keepers, they're not the literal type.

"I'm sure you're just bursting to enlighten me."

"Sarcasm will not serve you here." She sets aside the seedlings, gently covering them in damp cloth to protect against the blaze of afternoon.

Fluid and graceful, she unfolds from her kneeling position to stand head and shoulders over me. Her eyes, completely black so I can't tell where her pupils end and irises begin, are unnerving.

If sarcasm won't serve me, maybe silence will.

I lift my chin and meet her impenetrable gaze.

After what seems an eternity, she retrieves a tablet from a stand, then sits at the edge of a contemplation pool and begins to run her fingers across the clay. Is she *reading* with her hands?

She makes an amused sound that could be a distant cousin of a laugh. "There are many different ways of seeing. Now. The indiscretions that paved your way. Interfering with an official selection trial for the Eraz's perfumery."

"Interfering? I *saved* that fool."

"Trafficking regulated substances."

74

"Camel scat. You think I'm that witless?"

"Bribing an imperial official. The chief perfumer, no less."

"Prove it," I retort.

She raises her hand. "I need not be truth's champion. The chief perfumer has spoken . . ."

That reekin' pile of—

". . . and the trafficking charges corroborated by the sworn testimony of a palace guard whose wisdom surpasses his age."

My chest seizes. There's only one other person who knows I've been selling on the black market.

Barden.

I struggle to breathe as questions ambush me. What does she have over him? His family? His sister Mirtan's pregnant; maybe Sephine threatened withholding the temple's blessing from the child?

Or maybe it's more direct? Does she think him an accomplice to my black market deals? Scenes flash through my mind—convicts working in construction gangs, the skin where their noses used to be red and puckered, the holes plugged and cauterized with molten metal in one excruciating moment. I wince, sucking a breath through my teeth.

But all those thoughts are like smoke on the wind compared to one.

Why?

Why has my best friend betrayed me?

The Scent Keeper reaches for another tablet, this one still on its supporting board, dry on the surface, but unfired. And there at the bottom, the all-too-familiar imprint of Father's signature seal next to the whorls of my own thumb.

"You breathe the smoke of the incense you light."

No. This isn't happening.

"I have purchased your contract."

I take one, two steps back, and stumble into a tree planter. My hands go to the fired-clay rim, thankful to find something solid. This woman decided my mother's life wasn't worth saving. Now she talks of mine as if I'm a camel in the market pens, auctioned to the highest bidder.

My fingers tighten their grip on the urn, the chill I felt earlier replaced by rising heat.

Sephine's gaze is unwavering. "Suffice to say, I own you."

"In the sixth hell you do!"

Her black eyes bore into me, unblinking. Then she tilts her face to the sky as if she's talking with her gods, not me. "I kept my distance for seventeen turns, Rakel. But your nose has led you astray. You are your mother's daughter."

"Don't you *dare* speak of her. My father will—"

"Your father." She sniffs. "I cannot divine why Yaita fell for him. What did he tell you of her? That it's *her* aptitude you've inherited? Did he tell you she could have been Aphorai's Scent Keeper after I go to the sky?" Her voice is quiet now, almost soft. "Did he tell you your locket was my gift?"

"That's a lie!" My hand goes to my most precious possession. I'm momentarily reassured by its familiar shape, of how my thumb can pick out each tiny star engraved in the silver. "My father gave me this."

"As I instructed. So you would remember Yaita. I made a promise to her when she knew she didn't have much longer with you: Watch over you, ensure you had what you needed to survive."

How can I believe the words of this woman? She could have made an exception to the temple's laws forbidding priestesses to have children. And yet she had still let my mother be cast out, Sephine could have saved her from the birth fever. If what they say about Scent Keepers is true—she could have healed my mother with her bare hands.

But she didn't.

And my mother paid the ultimate price for bringing me into the world.

"If you really cared so much," I say through clenched teeth, "why didn't you help before?" I glance to the edge of the platform. The temple may have stood for centuries, but it bears the scars of a hundred groundshakes, cracks and pockmarks webbing the brickwork, just waiting to become hand- and footholds. Maybe there's a way to navigate down the outer steps of the pyramid. Maybe.

Ten turns indentured to Zakkurus was a hideous thought.

This is worse.

"I did what I could without drawing attention. Where do you think your father's pension comes from?"

"He served the Eraz for twenty-five turns. A *full* cycle."

"Dishonorable discharge forfeits any pension."

"He retired a hero!" It comes out almost a shout. There can't be any truth to what she says. But then why do I feel like I've swallowed a stone?

"A man is not noble for facing a field of enemies if he cannot face his own downfall. He put his whole company at risk, hiding his condition for so long."

I bark a scornful laugh. "*You* don't get to say anything about being noble. You let my mother *die*. You *chose* not to save her. Was that in the name of 'not drawing attention,' too?"

"Complexity begs sacrifice, though it is difficult to grasp."

"Try me," I sneer.

"In good time."

I cross my arms. "Sun's high. Light breeze. Perfect day for stories."

She fixes me in her unnerving stare. "There is no drug to cure a stupid man. Or girl, for that matter. Prove to me you can think for yourself, and you will have your answers. Show me you can learn, and when the starwheel turns, I will teach you how to heal."

"I can already do that."

"Then why haven't you healed the father you're so eager to defend?"

"There's no cure for the Rot!"

"Death is not sated with simple bread, true. I have dedicated a

11

lifetime to deciphering that contagion. How many of your turns have you given to that cause?"

I twist away to stare out over the city. The breeze tugs at flyaway strands of my hair. I don't attempt to smooth them.

"Come," Sephine says, gliding toward the stairwell.

I don't move. "You're not keeping me here?"

"Impossible. You are not ordained."

"Then where are you taking me?"

"My quarters on the Eraz's estate. An imperial delegation is on its way, and there is much work to do with the Flower Moon nigh."

I swallow the bile rising in my throat and follow in the Scent Keeper's footsteps.

* *
 * *
  *

My new routine is mind-numbing.

Rise at dawn from my tiny pallet in my tiny cell. Sweep Sephine's rooms, beat the dust from the ancient reed-woven mats, refill the vases with fresh flowers. Empty the ash from the incense holders and install new sticks: spicy clove for when the first moon waxes, smoky labdanum for when it wanes, and some concoction called onycha reserved for when the second moon goes dark.

Scent Keepers move freely from palace to temple, honored and respected in both. They are the go-betweens. I've tried to predict when Sephine will appear at the Eraz's estate, but every time I think I've sniffed the pattern, she does the opposite. I try asking questions of the other servants I pass in the halls, the gardens, by the fountains, angling for an opening that could lead to someone, *anyone*, agreeing to take a message to Father. But they either shy away and flee, or stare straight through me.

So I clean.

Every. Single. Day.

The only thing keeping me going is that even if Sephine hasn't found a cure for the Rot, I'll possibly find something here I can at least use to help prolong Father's life.

This morning, her quarters are serviced, so I move on to her common supplies, kept in a series of rooms and a cellar farther along the wing.

I dust the drying bunches of thyme and lavender. Check the racks of orris root are free from mold and fungus. Then move on to cleaning the equipment Sephine leaves on the shelves outside her laboratory door. It's locked, as always.

I scrub blown-glass vessels left from last night. Judging from the scent, they were used for a steam distillation of frankincense. I wonder if there's some way I could smuggle some out for Father. Maybe if I lean something against the wall and climb in through the high window . . .

I almost jump out of my skin when a voice, *her* voice, rings out behind me.

"Tomorrow you shall lift and divide the saffron crocuses. East gardens, second tier. You know how, yes?"

I huff my hair from my face. "I'll do it. But at least tell me this: After all these turns, are you close to curing the Rot?"

She keeps her all-black eyes fixed toward a point above my head. "A Scent Keeper may call on the divine will to heal an individual but not the throngs of Afflicted."

"Can you talk straight for once?"

"Words are never simple."

I bite down on the inside of my cheek so hard the taste of copper fills my mouth. I'm still not sure whether she enjoys baiting me, or whether it's pure, cold indifference. Still, I refuse to react in case it gives her satisfaction.

"However," she continues. "I believe in Asmudtag, and Asmudtag wills balance in all things. Every shadow comes from light. Every ill must have a remedy."

"Asmudtag?"

For the first time, her mask slips, annoyance flickering across her features. "The primordial. Self-willed into existence. What has your father been teaching you all these turns?"

I rinse out the now-squeaky-clean flask and place it with exaggerated gentleness on the bench. "Oh, you know, useless things like how to ride and care for horses, survive in the desert, not cut myself on my knife."

"Your first knife, was it bestowed upon you during infancy?"

"Of course not," I scoff. "Who would give a blade to a baby?"

"Indeed."

And with that, she strides away in a swish of black-feathered skirts.

CHAPTER 8
ASH

Time is a mirage beneath the desert sun. Caught between glaring white sky and burning red pain, I silently pray to Kaismap for focus. Iddo rides behind me, his hawk-eyed gaze boring into my back. But I heal quick. Blood has stopped soaking through the bandage Nisai's valet wrapped around my torso. And if I don't? It's almost a comfort knowing Iddo will be the first to call me unfit for duty.

It's early afternoon when we crest a great dune to look down on the province's capital. Where Ekasya is a city of black stone glinting like the night sky, Aphorai is a city of mud. The only buildings faced in stone are the outer walls, the manse atop the hill that I assume is the Eraz's estate, and the adjacent temple. The latter is as large as its Ekasyan counterpart—the only impressive thing about this place.

"Stars above. What a sight." Esarik winces as he shifts in the saddle. Days on camelback have disagreed with him more than he's let on. "Isn't it stunning?"

Nisai draws the curtains of the litter. "It does have a certain raw beauty—holding back the sands, resisting century upon century of the earth's attempts to bring it to the ground."

"Technically most of it has been *rebuilt* for century upon century," Esarik points out.

"Still," Nisai says, his eyes taking on a thoughtful cast. "There's dignity in such resilience."

An aurochs-headed stubbornness, more like it. And behind those walls? Just a baser, rougher-hewn version of every other city. The only reason this place is still relevant to the Empire is as a producer of Aramtesh's most valued goods—oils, spices, and, at the pinnacle of them all, the dahkai flower.

I hold my tongue. Nisai seems truly enchanted. Who am I to take that away from him?

As we near, Esarik stiffens in his saddle. "Cinder and sulfur," he mutters.

I follow his gaze to the base of the walls. I'd heard talk among Iddo's men, but I've not seen so many Afflicted since I left the slums of my childhood. Dozens huddle in the shade. Each bears a bandage on an arm or leg or what's left of both. We pass them at a distance, but they're malodorous enough to be smelled from the heavens.

May Azered guide their souls.

We enter the city through its main eastern gate. Our camels kick up dust on the unpaved roads and I cough. Warmth trickles beneath my bandages, a stinging trail of blood and sweat down my side. Nisai looks at me askance. I straighten in the saddle, forcing my features to relax.

The inner arches of Aphorai's fortifications have been lime-washed bright white, then garishly decorated in painted murals. The artist had some skill to transform these surfaces, but the result is crude compared with the faience mosaics that bejewel Ekasya's monuments.

As we pass beneath, I catch the scent of fresh paint. The show is for us.

Then I smell something else. A haze of crimson incense billows through the streets—only Riker knows why the Aphorains insist on calling it dragon's blood. What do reptiles smell of other than the last thing they've slithered through? Or, if you're Kip, who relished snaring and grilling snakes over a campfire on the journey here—lunch?

But it's not that. Riding off to the side, Esarik and Nisai catch it, too, judging by the way their noses wrinkle.

Up ahead, on a paved island in the center of the dusty road, is a larger-than-life bronze statue. There's one in every provincial capital across Aramtesh, replaced each generation to capture the current Emperor's likeness. Flies gather in a black swarm around this version. Emperor Kaddash is barely recognizable—the sculpture has been smeared from crown to foot in excrement. The whole thing reeks to the sky.

Today, Aphorai's officials may have arranged for the city to appear its best. But someone has made it clear they have opinions of their own: The ruler of Aramtesh stinks. Whether it's commentary on heavier-by-the-turn taxation, the growing dissent among the outer provinces Iddo reported, or Kaddash's Affliction, I couldn't surmise.

Perhaps it's all three.

Iddo draws his camel next to Kip's. The younger Ranger stares tight-lipped at the putrid statue, a patrol of Aphorain city guards now desperately trying to swab it clean.

"Find out who is responsible," the Commander says from between clenched teeth.

"No," Nisai says.

"Little Brother, such a direct insult—"

"Please, let's move on."

After that, nobody says a word until we reach the five terraces of dull sandstone leading upward to the Eraz's manse. We dismount and lead our camels up the steps of the first terrace, where stewards take our mounts. I pause, gazing out over the thatched rooftops, listening to the distant sounds of the markets, the bleating of goats in the stockyards.

"There's no shame in feeling a stranger," Iddo murmurs beside me.

I regard him quizzically. His dark eyes are serious, without any trace of his usual mocking. There's an opening here, if I choose to take it. "I guess you're used to being this far from Ekasya."

"When you spend as much time on the road as I do, it's hard to know where home is." He clicks his tongue and leads his camel forward, handing the reins to a steward.

I'd not thought of it like that before, always envious of Iddo's freedom, his ability to roam unfiltered. I shake my head. Ekasya will always be there for him.

Dusting off his hands, Iddo eyes Nisai. "Are you sure this is the entrance you want to make? There's a well-appointed establishment not far from here, we could clean up, change into state attire."

He's got a point. We're all travel-stained. And what I wouldn't give for some rest in a quiet moment of prayer.

Nisai straightens his simple robe. "This isn't about grandeur. I come here humbly. A nephew visiting his uncle."

I wonder if he would have taken the same approach before we came across the statue.

The gates swing wide and we're greeted by a page. A single page. Inside the eastern wing, we follow the boy down near-empty halls. Iddo and the Rangers form up around us. Esarik dawdles at the rear.

The page trots up a staircase to a pair of huge wooden doors.

Nisai runs his hand over the tiny six-petal flowers carved into the cedar. "This pattern . . . These doors must be older than the Empire itself. Imagine what they've heard, what they've seen."

"They're doors." I glance behind us. If they're locked, we may as well be at the end of a blind alley.

"My Prince?" the page asks, uncertain.

Nisai gives him a smile. "Lead on."

We emerge into an inner courtyard, partially roofed by eaves of woven reeds. Pools line the perimeter, the water pale against age-worn white marble, myriad cracks repaired with veins of bronze—seems the Aphorains don't care to conceal the number of times the earth beneath them has revolted.

If only shade and fountains were enough to combat the heat that prickles my skin, the desert air amplifying the fiery wound in my side.

We've been preceded by a gaggle of Aphorain courtiers. When Esarik catches up to us, several of the ladies follow his every move like cats sizing up prey, batting dark eyes at his green ones. With nervous hands he smooths his robe, the embroidered Trelian aurochs always somewhat incongruous on his slender frame.

I glance sidelong through the smoke. "Just tell them you're betrothed."

He looks wistful. "If only I could." Then he gathers himself and turns to Nisai. "Did you take a moment to examine the—?"

"Did I ever!" Nisai replies, eyes wide. "First century pre-Accord?"

"Stars, no! Earlier. Much earlier. Third, I'd say."

"Amazing preservation."

"Truly."

I shake my head. "What are you two even talking about?"

As one, Nisai and Esarik point back the way we came.

Oh. Right. Doors.

Esarik tilts his head toward the courtiers. "Meaning no disrespect, but, you don't think I could—"

"Take your leave?" Nisai finishes. "I'm sure there is much you could learn for our benefit."

Esarik dips a grateful bow and retreats.

We cross the courtyard, Nisai smiling and nodding politely when greeted. Officially, it's all respectful hospitality. But someone here may share the same opinions as Aphorai's imperial statue decorator. My senses are on high alert.

We're ushered into the main hall. It couldn't be much bigger than the Emperor's personal reception chamber in Ekasya. Once the members of the Aphorain court move in to line the walls, a quick scan suggests they number no more than two score, yet the room feels crowded. Stifling.

A bald woman almost Iddo's height stands at the back of the room, clad in a skirt of iridescent black lion feathers. Her eyes—in their entirety—are darker still. Shivers run through me despite the heat.

Received by the Aphorain Scent Keeper.

Nisai's uncle nowhere in sight.

What message are these *provincials* trying to send?

Above us, wooden lattices screen off the upper galleries. The hairs lift from the back of my neck as silhouettes shift in the shadows behind. Servants awed by the spectacle? Or something more sinister?

Slighted. Surrounded. Surveilled.

Part of me wants to draw my swords then and there. But if half a life at court has taught me anything?

This isn't the kind of danger a blade can defeat.

CHAPTER 9
RAKEL

Crimson smoke has been rising across the Eraz's estate since dawn. The incense tints the air as if we're caught in one long sunset. Or a pool of bloodstained water.

But crocuses wait for no man, not even a prince. With Sephine's rooms cleaned and the dishes scrubbed from her nightly experiments, I head out into the red haze.

The path leads past the Eraz's main hall and up toward the garden terraces in a mirror of the external ramp on the temple's stepped pyramid—a reminder of the connection between rulers and gods. The plants held by the raised stonework beds increase in value until the top, where Aphorai's centuries-old dahkai plantation grows.

Up ahead, servants cluster around the entrance to the hall's antechamber, jostling for the chance to see the first imperial delegation in Aphorai since the early turns of Emperor Kaddash's reign. Back then, Father had been away on campaign, so I'd journeyed into the city with Barden's family to watch the arrivals in all their purple livery parade through the streets.

Speak of the stench and it appears.

I knew I'd run into Barden eventually. The Eraz's estate is big, but it's not infinite. So when he breaks away from his post, I'm relieved that I have a genuine excuse not to stop.

"Rakel," he calls.

I quicken my stride, pretending not to have heard. The last few days have shaken me to the core; I'm not ready to deal with this part of it yet.

"Rakel, wait! I need to talk to you!"

He needs to talk to *me*? The poor kitten, is he feeling oh so bad about ratting out his closest friend?

I keep walking, retrieving a vial of cedar oil from my satchel. The breeze is in my favor, but the last thing I want is to catch the merest whiff of Barden. I'm not sure I'd be able to keep my composure in the wake of such a familiar scent. One that used to be so comforting.

Barden jogs closer and I take a deep breath over the vial. It helps me distance myself from my rage, my hurt, from the fact that I don't know if I can ever again trust my only friend.

"Rakel! Just give me a moment. Please." He reaches for the sleeve of my robe, but I've already anticipated the move and swerve clear.

"Can't stop for chat."

"At least let me give you some news from home. How your father fares?"

I shake my head. Using Father as an opening? I didn't think he could go any lower, but there it is.

"I know where Lil is stabled. Want me to—"

How *dare* he.

"No time," I snap. "I'm on direct orders from the Scent Keeper. Good friend of yours, eh?"

"I know you're angry. But you were being so secretive."

"When?"

"When what?"

"*When* did she get to you?"

"Does it matter?" he asks, voice strained.

I glare at him.

"Fine. I was worried what you'd got yourself into. I sensed something was off that night. I followed you, saw you go into that place. When you didn't come out, I went in to find you. You'd vanished. I couldn't report it to the garrison sergeant—I didn't know what you were involved in—for all I knew they'd arrest you. I figured your mother had been Sephine's . . . I didn't know who else to go to. But then you turned up at the end of my shift, acting like nothing had happened. And you can't argue that things didn't turn out just fine. I mean, did you ever think we'd both end up here, working on the Eraz's own estate?"

"Why didn't you *tell* me?"

He shuffles his feet in that all-too-familiar gesture of discomfort. "She said not to."

"You should have told me." My voice is flat, dead of all emotion.

I avoid his eyes and keep walking, keep breathing the cedar oil, keep thinking of places far from here.

There's part of me that still longs to throw my arms around Barden, bury my face in his chest, tell him every word of what Sephine said of Father, my mother, my life . . .

A much bigger part never wants to see him again. The sooner, the better. That part decides on a detour, escaping into the cluster of servants, weaving between them and up the stairs to the viewing gallery without so much as a backward glance.

Inside, the only source of light is what filters through the carved wooden screens concealing us common onlookers from the nobles in the hall below. Incense perfumes the air with the dark caramel sweetness of opoponax. Interesting choice. Respectful, but not fawning.

It's eerily quiet for a crowded space. I push my way forward, ignoring the grumbles from the other servants.

The imperials are already here, led by the tallest person in the hall. Must be the Prince's brother—love or hate the Rangers, the infamous Commander cuts an imposing figure. The next figure looks more like what I've heard of the Prince. Average height, medium build, warm brown skin made all the more striking by his imperial purple robes. He's younger than I expected, not more than a turn or two older than me.

At the other end of the room, my two favorite people stand on the dais.

Sephine, naturally.

And Zakkurus, the snake.

The Scent Keeper lights two silver braziers beside the Eraz's throne. I press my face to the holes in the screen and give an experimental sniff.

My heart forgets to beat.

There wasn't supposed to be hardly any of it left. But there it is. Unmistakable.

I clench my fists, nails digging into my palms. Trust Sephine to have sat on a personal supply for longer than I've been alive. And trust the welcome mat for a Prince to be worth more to her than ten turns of my life.

Dahkai.

Once the scent has permeated the hall, the Eraz blusters in, hair and beard beaded and gleaming with oil. I've only ever seen him from afar but even a beggar in the street knows he styles his image as one of the rulers of old: strong and fair unless you invoke his rage, the human embodiment of the Aphorain sigil. I've seen enough lions in my time—they approach our village when the dry season stretches too long. The Eraz's huge belly detracts from the likeness, but hulking shoulders and a straight back tell of the warrior before the fat.

He settles onto his throne as a girl—my age and clad in barely there silks—takes up position at his shoulder. Lady Sireth.

The steward clears his throat. "The Eraz of Aphorai, Malmud of line Baidok, welcomes His Imperial Highness, Prince Nisai, Named Heir to the Empire of Aramtesh, caretaker of the Seson Territories and the Palm Isles . . ."

The courtiers directly below me begin to whisper to one another.

"Think he's attempting to set a new style?"

"What if he simply can't grow one?"

"Can't grow a beard? Can't kill a lion? Can't rule an Empire."

Finally, thankfully, the steward runs out of titles and breath.

The Prince kneels before the throne, wearing a slightly lopsided smile that's at once sweet and sharp. "Will you receive me, esteemed Eraz?"

A grin dawns on the Eraz's face. "Rise, Nephew. You are welcome."

He stands and pulls the First Prince into a crushing embrace.

"We've come for the Flower Moon, Uncle. I hope it's not an imposition."

"Bah! Boy, the firebirds have been burning the purple stuff for weeks. Shame on us if it's an imposition by now. Though we'd prepared for a full delegation. Your party is quite"—he surveys the Rangers, the Commander himself, finally letting his gaze rest on the figure trailing the Prince, a guard in black sleeveless silks trimmed in imperial purple—"small. These are troubled times in the border-lands."

At that, the guard steps closer. The Eraz may still think himself a lion, but the figure behind the First Prince moves like one—all muscle and sinew and predatory grace. Square jaw as unusually clean-shaven as the imperial brothers. Angled, high cheekbones. Prominent, straight nose.

Black ink trails down the tawny skin of his arms, bare except for a prayer band of braided leather—each strand scented for a different god. So he's a believer.

I shift, finding a better angle through the holes in the screen so I can piece together the tattoo design—from the lines of the fangs etched into his shaved scalp, to the stylized claws on the back of his hands.

I bite my lip. The Kaidon sons might be a source of gossip, but the tattooed warrior and his ilk are the stuff of campfire tales. I never thought I'd see one. But there he stands, flesh and blood and an impla-cable scowl. A life-sworn imperial bodyguard. A Shield.

As if he senses my presence, the Shield's eyes search the upper gal-lery. His gaze seems calm enough, but sweat beads the tattoos of his shaved scalp. I'd think him just a soft capital type struggling in the Aphorain heat if it wasn't for the slight tremor in his hands.

Fever.

The Commander steps forward and salutes the Eraz. "I would have expected more of your own guard, Malmud. It must be a particularly nervous time for the steward of the most precious commodity in the Empire."

Nisai taps his nose. "Ah, but until the Flower Moon, there's no need. Dahkai provides very little of value beyond its bloom. The leaves are unremarkable, the sap a severe skin irritant. Even if anyone wished to steal a specimen, it would die on transplanting—it hasn't been suc-cessfully cultivated anywhere else since the Shadow Wars."

Huh. Wouldn't have expected the future Emperor to know the plant from the perfume.

The First Prince raises his voice. "Please do correct me if I'm wrong, Scent Keeper."

Sephine nods. "You walk the path of wisdom."

Zakkurus dips an elegant bow. "Rest assured, the guards will be tripled for the Flower Moon. The harvest must be completed in a single night. Naturally, our esteemed Scent Keeper will receive the traditional allocation for the temple's use. Per the Emperor's wishes, the remainder is earmarked for perfume. Once my people have formulated the fragrance, the Aphorain cavalry will escort the shipment to the capital."

"But is it true you let the populace in? Literally anyone can visit the estate for the Flower Moon?"

From the dais, Sephine levels her black-eyed gaze at the Commander. "It is a sacred night. It is not our role to deny that to anyone."

"Including the likes of those who've committed treason by desecrating my father's likeness? Lady, you would insult us."

So, they know about the scat sculpture. It's an Aphorain rite of passage, throwing dung at an increasingly unpopular Emperor and getting away before the city guard catches wind of it.

"An Emperor has turned his back on the Scent Keepers. Temple and province find an insult most grave."

Silence falls over the room.

The servants beside me shift nervously, blocking my view of the dais.

Then the clash of steel rings out across the hall. Someone screams. More than one courtier rushes to the nearest door.

I rise on tiptoes, desperate to see what's happened.

The Eraz carries his daughter from the room, Sephine following close behind. Guess the Lady Sireth had another one of her fainting spells.

But there's another prone body on the floor.

It's the Prince's Shield. The silks at his side are damp, and the metallic tang that reaches my nose whispers of blood.

The other servants scatter from the hall.

My feet start moving of their own accord.

CHAPTER 10
ASH

Lucidity finds me lying on a pallet. Nisai hovers at the edge of the bed, brows pinched in worry but otherwise unharmed.

Thank Esiku. I can relax.

"Out of my way!"

There goes that idea.

It's a girl's voice, and I turn my head on the pillow to see Issinon, Nisai's valet, standing in her way. The intruder is short, her plain-spun robes reaching ankle and wrist, the white fabric favoring her golden-tanned complexion. Boots, rather than the sandals of the palace servants, peek out from the hem. The strap of a leather satchel crosses her chest, and a utilitarian knife is sheathed at her hip. All parts of an equation that my fevered mind can't solve.

Issinon bristles: "How *dare* you issue orders to me? I am the imperial—"

"I don't give a sniff who you are. That wound needs attending."

"Wound? How did you—"

"The Shield's favoring one arm, and anyone whose eyes weren't painted on would know he's feverish. You could wait for the Scent Keeper, but she's attending the Eraz's daughter. Who knows how long that could take. Lady Sireth's turns are . . ."

A groan escapes me.

"Let her in," Nisai orders.

"I think I'd prefer Esarik see to this," I murmur.

"He's gone on a specimen-collecting expedition. He won't be back until tomorrow."

Translation: He's fleeing the attentions of half the maids in Aphorai.

Issinon stands aside and the girl bends over me. She sniffs the bandages around my chest, nose twitching like a deer testing the wind for danger. But this girl's not prey. She's something else. The way her amber eyes meet mine is almost wolflike. There's something vaguely familiar about her that I can't quite pin down.

"Take off the bandages."

Issinon intervenes. "But surely the bleeding—"

"Is less of a risk than leaving a filthy wound to fester."

"The wound wasn't unclean. I checked it myself."

The ferocity in her eyes flares. "And did you clean and file the lion's claws before they sliced him open? You all shared a friendly conversation in the bathhouse this morning, is that it? Gossiping while your feather-maned friend had his cuticles scraped and oiled?" She keeps talking, holding the valet's attention hostage while she slips her blade underneath the bandages and starts cutting.

I wince as the cloth dislodges from my wounds.

The girl's eyes go flat. "I'll need boiling water, clean linen, and needle and thread. Now."

Issinon decides it's in his best interest to do what she asks.

I don't blame him.

When the supplies arrive, the girl mixes a handful of what looks like pink salt crystals into the basin. She dips a square of linen into the steaming water, untroubled by what must be scalding heat as she wrings it out. Then she upends a vial, a stream of orange droplets blooming onto the white cloth.

The girl offers me the hilt of her knife. "It's clean."

She doesn't have to tell me this next part is going to hurt. I open my mouth. With surprising gentleness, she positions the hilt between my teeth.

The hot cloth sears the open wounds along my ribs, and whatever she doused it with stings like nothing else. I bite down. Hard.

The cleaning seems to take hours. The stitches seem to take longer. It's a frantic battle to not lose consciousness. All too aware of what might be revealed if I'm incoherent, I force myself to focus on the here and now, hone in on anything but the pain.

The flutter of the girl's breath against my skin as she works.

The faint scent of her perfume—roses?

The silver locket that keeps working its way free from the neckline of her robe, only for her to tuck it back in as if on reflex.

Afterward, she rinses off her hands. "He needs to sleep."

"No." My voice sounds weak even to my own ears.

Nisai steps forward. "You're no use to me in that state. The quicker you recover, the quicker you'll be back in action."

The girl puts a cup to my lips. "Take your medicine," she says, some kind of bitter irony in her tone.

How could she know I need a dose? I look frantically around the room—who else heard her words? Then sweet liquid pours over my tongue and I'm forced to swallow it along with any denial.

Sweet? It's poppy milk, not the Linod's Elixir I'm relying more on with each passing day. Something akin to relief washes through me.

The girl ushers everyone from the room except Nisai and two Rangers acting as guards in my incapacity, then follows, closing the door softly behind her. Nisai settles on a stool by the bed. I'm reminded uncomfortably of morning visits to his father in Ekasya.

He watches me, intent. "Something happened with you out there, didn't it? Ash, if those claws had . . . Rakel says if they'd gone any deeper . . ."

"Rakel?"

"The person who just had no small hand in saving your life."

"You don't think she could tell anything, do you? Can she be trusted?"

Nisai bites his lower lip, then nods. "I believe so."

Before I can question why, drug sleep claims me.

CHAPTER 11
RAKEL

That night, I sleep fitfully.

Every time I close my eyes, I dream in fragments. Dark eyes brimming with pain and a distant, almost-hidden sadness. Tattooed skin that smells of sandalwood and musk. A muscled arm encircled with a prayer braid—the clash of sacred scents loud enough to wake me.

My blanket's on the floor again, and I'm tangled in the sheet.

Then I notice another scent. One that shouldn't be in the air.

Smoke. Not incense or cooking coals but something else entirely.

I fling the sheet aside and shrug a robe over my sleeping shift. My house sandals stay at the end of the bed. Whatever's amiss, I'll face it in my boots.

The halls are quiet at this late hour. I rush along, not seeing another soul on the way to the Scent Keeper's estate quarters. I thump on Sephine's door, but there's no answer. I try the latch. Locked.

Where is she? She should have finished with Lady Sireth hours ago. Maybe she returned to the temple without telling me. Wouldn't be the first time since I've been here that she's vanished without a word.

Or maybe she smelled the smoke before I did? If so, where did it lead her?

I take a deep breath. Thick, pungent. Something green is burning.

The gardens.

I burst outside and leap up the terraces, catching myself just before I fall facefirst onto a sandstone path. If there's one thing I vow to do if I ever make it out of this scents-be-damned estate, it's never to wear ridiculous sleeping shifts again.

It's clear before I'm half there which of the gardens is burning. The top level is completely lost in the smoke. I blink once, twice, rubbing at my eyes. But they tell me the same thing as my nose does. I can only stand and gape.

The Flower Moon is tomorrow night, and the very plants that were set to bloom for the first time in a generation are up there.

Guards sprint through the gardens. Their shouts betray confusion and an underlying current of fear. Either the palace defenses have been compromised during the night, or someone on the inside has set alight the fifth terrace, and set it well enough that it burns from all sides.

Who would wish Aphorai's most valuable resource destroyed?

And if they did, who would be the first to try and save it?

Sephine. She's up there. I know it. And she's the key to so many things I don't yet understand about myself, my family. Things she promised to tell me in good time, as if there ever was a good time. If the Scent Keeper dies, that knowledge dies with her.

A guard I don't recognize grabs my sleeve. "Get out of here! It's too dangerous!"

I shake free and plunge into the smoke.

CHAPTER 12
ASH

I wake in the guest chambers. The candles are lit, the tapers retaining half their length. Late evening, then.

It takes another breath to realize something's not right. That's not Aphorai's beloved dragon's blood on the air. Come to think of it, it isn't like any incense I've ever smelled before.

And if even I can smell smoke, the fire must be raging.

I attempt to rise. Pain lances my side, snatching my breath. The physical agony brings its mental cousin in its wake, sending scenes of the lion hunt flashing through my mind, stark images like lightning flares in the night.

I press one hand to the bandages at my ribs and use the other to push myself up the pillows.

"Nisai?"

He must be intent on his books again.

"Nisai?" I call a little louder.

There's no answer. Maybe he's meeting with his uncle? Or perhaps Esarik has returned from his expedition?

Gritting my teeth, I cast aside the blankets and swing my feet over the edge of the bed. A quick glance confirms the wound has been dressed recently—the linen free of the stains of healing—but I'm otherwise naked. My cheeks warm despite myself. Who saw to me while I slept? Was it *her*?

The chair where Nisai sat at my bedside is empty, other than the clothes draped over it. Someone has oiled my leathers, leaving behind a distinct note of cedar. It's not displeasing.

I struggle into my trousers. Between my wounds and my bandages, I soon realize my vest isn't an option. I throw it down and shuffle into the antechamber. Two Aphorain palace guards are stationed outside the door. The youngest does a double take at my ink-covered torso.

"Where is the Prince?"

The older guard shrugs, pointing vaguely up the corridor. "He left some time ago."

"Who's with him?" I demand. "Rangers?"

"Said he had some urgent diplomatic business to attend to. We left him to it."

The younger guard nods emphatically. "We wouldn't want to be questioning the First Prince, no, sir. We're loyal to the Empire, you see."

Simpletons.

"Step aside."

"Ah, Shield, sir, First Prince says you're to rest—"

"Out. Of. My. Way."

CHAPTER 13
RAKEL

The smoke gets thicker as I stumble through the gardens. It clogs my nose and throat and burns my eyes, setting them to streaming tears. Even when I force myself to keep them open, it's hard to discern hedge from wall, fountain from statue.

I keep my sleeve over my nose and mouth, trying to breathe shallowly so I don't take too much acrid air into my lungs.

Up close, I realize this isn't any ordinary fire. There's a signature at its base. Krilmair oil. Used when you need to burn something that won't catch or stay alight with any run-of-the-mill flammable. Only thing is, it leaves a telltale scent behind the char and burn.

This fire was no accident.

A figure appears, indistinct and wavering in the heat and soot. It's not until he's closed to a few paces that I recognize the Shield. Either he's stupid or fool stubborn. Strict bed rest, I'd ordered. Yet here he is.

And he's not wearing a shirt. At another time I might have found that amusing.

He breaks into a shuffling run when he sees me, one hand clutched to his side.

"What in the sixth hell do you think you're doing?"

"I was about to ask you the same thing." His deep, rumbling voice rolls question and accusation into one.

"I don't know. Sephine, she—"

"The Prince?" He hunches over a little, grunting in pain. He shouldn't be here, he should be back in his chambers.

"He's not with you?"

"I wouldn't be asking if he was."

I squint out over the smoking terraces. The ancient plants that haven't bloomed for a generation, that would have burst into bud and flowered when both moons went dark this time tomorrow. Now their last flowering is the pall of smoke unfurling skyward.

Guards circle the garden now, buckets in hand, their shouts growing more desperate. If Sephine's not trying to save the dahkai along with the guards, where is she? What could be more important to her? *Who* could be more important?

The Shield sizes me up, calculating, as if he can see my thoughts.

He charges toward the flames.

Rancid *reeking* rankness. He's lucky to be on his feet, given the amount of poppy milk I gave him last dose. There's every chance he'll keel over in there.

Then his death will be on my hands.

I'm not about to let that happen.

I follow him into the heart of the fire.

I tear a strip from the hem of my nightdress. Pressing my sleeve to my nose again, I grab the Shield's arm and motion for him to do the same. Then I turn my back on the source of Aphorai's liquid gold. It's too late for the dahkai.

There's no sign of the Scent Keeper.

Think, Ana. Think.

Since Sephine made me her servant, I've learned very little about the person behind the Scent Keeper's mask, if there even is one. But I've noticed her strolling the coiled paths of the labyrinth in the next sector. It's as good a place to start as any.

I risk taking my sleeve away for a breath, except I can't smell anything but smoke and char.

I'll have to get closer.

The coniferous hedges have caught alight now. *Their sap is a natural explosive*, I think. As if on cue, a nearby trunk bursts apart with a *crack*. I drop into a crouch as splinters and coals spray in every direction.

Something stings my cheek. My fingertips come away wet.

I gesture to the Shield to keep low as we head toward the next garden over. It's choked with smoke, but the manicured lawns and swirling paths of the labyrinth are unscathed. For now. Something's out there, though: an indistinct shape on the grass. I move closer, careful to avoid the glowing embers amid the ash fall.

There. The outline of an arm against the lawn. Black feathers gleam for a fleeting moment in the firelight. I rush forward, dropping to my knees beside the Scent Keeper's prone form.

"Sephine!"

There's an answering groan. I take her by the shoulder and manage to get her onto her side. "What happened?"

She tries to speak, but it's interrupted by a cough. "It was too strong," she says, voice hoarse between ragged breaths. "Too quick. Too much . . ."

Then the Shield is there. "What was?" He's clutching at his bandages from that ridiculous lion hunt. "A beast?"

I shake my head. Even in the smoke-filled night, I'd see blood. And if I couldn't see it, I'd smell it.

"You must save the . . ." Her words are lost under the shouts in the next garden over.

"The dahkai? The guards will take care of it." There's no point in telling her it's a lost cause.

She coughs again, this time spitting blood. Dark blood. Internal bleeding, from somewhere deep. And there's a faint whiff of . . . Rot? Or just something rotten? Whatever it is, she needs care, and quick.

There would be some sort of justice in leaving her here, leaving her to die from circumstance, just like she left my mother.

But I'm *nothing* like Sephine.

"We've got to get you out of here." I crouch down farther and lift her arm, trying to prop it across my shoulders.

"No. The stars have seen my fate." She lifts a trembling hand, though whether it's to point at the stars or to grab at my night shift or something else, I can't tell. "Save the Prince."

The Shield leans closer, wincing. "Where *is* he?"

More dark liquid seeps from the corner of her mouth. On reflex, I dab at it with my sleeve. She turns her head away. Following her gaze, I can barely make out a prone form in the smoke, the deep purple robes serving as camouflage in the darkness.

The Shield curses and lurches to investigate.

Sephine rolls onto her back, reaches up, and grabs my locket with surprising strength, yanking my face close to hers. "I could only slow its progress. Heed the starwheel. When the lion wears the lost crown, he'll not live through the night. Follow the way of the stars. Find the order . . . Asmudtag . . . in . . ." The hand gripping my locket goes limp and falls.

"The darkness will bloom again," she murmurs, closing her eyes.

Her chest falls with a sigh and her fingers open. A tiny vial rolls from her palm and onto the manicured lawn. It's made of some sort of glass, its sides faceted like a cut jewel.

I feel Sephine's wrist for a pulse.

Nothing.

Check for breath.

Nothing.

No. This can't be. Scent Keepers don't die.

But Sephine is gone.

And her secrets have gone with her.

CHAPTER 14
ASH

Nisai lies unmoving on his back in the grass. I drop to my knees beside him.

On the name of every god, please, please let him be all right.

"Nisai?" I shake his shoulder.

No response.

"Nisai!"

There's nothing to show he's hurt. If anything, he appears asleep. Peaceful, even. Has he breathed too much smoke? What was the Scent Keeper saying about something being too fast?

"What were you doing out here alone?" I admonish his still form.

But he wasn't alone, was he? I peer through the smoke to where the girl rocks back on her haunches. I'm not sure if she's murmuring to herself, or to the Scent Keeper. "The darkness will bloom again," she mutters. "The darkness will bloom."

What in Kaismap's far-seeing name does that mean?

Too many questions. And the answers will have to wait. Right now, all I care about is Nisai.

I crouch down and lift him into my arms. He's slight, but straining my muscles reopens several of my wounds. Warmth trickles beneath my bandages.

Something drops to the ground and I almost trip. Nisai's journal. He'll be devastated if he loses that book.

But if I put him down to retrieve it, I'm not sure I'll be able to get back up.

And it's then, staring down at the journal, that I realize. He wasn't excited about coming to Aphorai for the Flower Moon. It wasn't just mobilizing to appease the superstitions of his future subjects, or shore up a supply of the most precious commodity in the Empire.

He wanted to come here for *me*. His book: He thought he was getting close to a better treatment, a cure, for my condition, rather than the daily dose of Linod's Elixir that barely keeps it in check.

He wanted to speak to a Scent Keeper. The oldest Scent Keeper across all Aramtesh. A woman whose scentlore transcends secular perfumery, who can use vapors to heal wounds, to force the truth from an unwilling mouth, to commune with the divine.

Nisai came to Sephine for help.

And look where that left him.

"I'm sorry," I murmur. "I really am. But you're more important than a book."

The way back to the palace feels so much longer than the way there.

One step, then the next, I chant inwardly, beneath the shrieking pain along my ribs. *One step, then the next.*

Kip is the first Ranger I recognize in the knot of servants and courtiers gathered in the relative safety of the palace's first terrace. She's still wearing boots and a travel cloak, as if she's ready to hit the road at a moment's notice. Esarik stands by her, wringing his hands, his expression a mix of horror and worry at the smoke and chaos.

Kip's ever-watchful eyes spy me and she breaks away from the group, rushing up the terraces in a few agile leaps. The Losian Ranger takes one glance at me staggering beneath Nisai's weight and lifts him into her arms as effortlessly as carrying a sleeping child.

She turns toward the palace, her usually stern expression unfaltering. "You're bleeding. Get inside. If you faint, I won't be able to carry both of you."

We cross over the courtyard where the courtiers gathered on the night of our arrival in this godsforsaken place and pass through the same doors Nisai had so admired.

Esarik follows at our heels. "Ash! Stars above, you look a fright. What happened?"

I can already tell that question is going to be asked of me a lot in the coming hours and days. I'll need an answer. But how I describe the events since I left my chambers will have heavy bearing on what could be a political disaster. If the capital thinks the Aphorains responsible for an attempt on the First Prince's life, the cracks between provinces and Ekasya will fracture deeper than in a groundshake. If the Emperor holds the Scent Keepers responsible, it could undermine the Empire's very foundations.

That everyone will assume I'm in shock is a blessing. Because right now, politics can take its pick of the five hells.

Esarik shakes himself. "What am I thinking? Here, let me help you." He bends his slim frame and gets a supporting arm around me. "Now. Details. I need details. Did you see who struck down the Prince?"

"No. He was out when I found him."

"Any bleeding?"

"Not that I could see. It was dark in there though. And the smoke . . ."

"Smoke inhalation. Yes. Likely."

"If it is just smoke, you can fix it, right?"

He swallows.

"Esarik?"

CHAPTER 15
RAKEL

I snatch up the vial Sephine dropped and give it a tentative sniff. Instantly, I wish I hadn't. Noxious fumes sting my nose and eyes more than the smoke billowing around us.

I rock back on to my heels. What *is* this stuff?

Surely it's not . . . poison?

If it's an inhalant, it's probably too late. Still, I turn away and hold a finger to my nose, blowing from either nostril in case there's any chance of getting it out.

But why would the Scent Keeper poison the Prince? More to the point, why would she poison herself? I've heard of people killing themselves after committing terrible crimes, but Sephine? History shows she's made of sterner stuff.

No time to ponder. If the barked orders of the palace guard officers are anything to go by, they'll be here in a whiff.

I think about slipping the vial into my satchel. But something tells me this isn't going to end well, not least of all the way the Shield staggered off with the unconscious Prince in his arms, so I'm sure as stink not letting them find me with this. I place the vial on the cloth I'd been using against the smoke and tie it tight against my upper thigh, then pull my shift back into place.

Just in time, too. One moment I'm alone in the garden, crouched over the Scent Keeper's lifeless body, the next I'm being surrounded by a group of guards.

"On your feet, girl." The stone-jawed officer's tone warns against argument.

Something tells me it's not the time to put that to the test. I clamber upright and reach for my satchel.

"I'll be taking that."

Oh, that's *too* far. "In the sixth hell you will. On what grounds?"

"Evidence." He retrieves the satchel, then straightens, sizing me up like I'm simple, but possibly dangerous. Like he can't decide if I'm a pet or a rabid stray. "Now walk."

I do as I'm told.

The guards march me down the stairs toward the palace. Fires still glow in the hedges and dahkai plantation, though they seem to be under control. Buckets of water are being passed along a line of servants and soldiers alike, dousing the flames with greater efficiency than the earlier chaos.

Half the Aphorain court seems to have assembled outside the palace. The Rangers who arrived with the imperial delegation are there, too, as is the Commander and the Prince's prickly little valet.

There's too much commotion to pick up any single conversation, but the words being uttered over and over by the gathering crowd send a chill through me.

Prince.

Assassin.

Treason.

A familiar face emerges from the throng of guards. Barden's jaw is tight, his usually smiling mouth set in a grim line. "Seems you're making a habit of getting arrested lately."

"You think *I* had something to do with this?" Is that an officer's sash? How much butt sniffing did he do for such a swift promotion?

He shakes his head. "How am I supposed to know these days?"

I've always thought spitting a filthy habit, so even I'm shocked when the glob of saliva splatters across Barden's face.

He draws close enough that I can see his cheek shine in the torch-light, see the warring anger and hurt in his eyes, smell the amber, the sweet orange oil, the tanner's thyme that still permeates the leather of his uniform. He fondles the cuff of my shift. Stench of stenches, what is he going to do?

He takes my wrist and raises it, using my sleeve to wipe his face. I struggle to break free, my fingers curled into a fist that wants nothing more than to punch the same cheek.

Then the Commander's towering presence is there, a sandstorm of fury in his eyes. "Get her out of here," he orders his Rangers. "I'll question her later."

One of his men takes Barden's place with a nod. "We can manage from here."

Barden steps back like the good little guard boy he is. The Ranger begins to manhandle me away, pinning my arms behind me like a trussed sandgrouse ready for the ovens.

I take a last glance over my shoulder before we begin the descent into the catacombs below the Eraz's manse. Barden is conferring with several of the imperial Rangers. He doesn't spare a look after me.

He's made his choice, distancing himself from the first whiff of suspicion.

So much for loyalty.

CHAPTER 16
ASH

We hurry after Kip through the halls.

Well, everyone else hurries. I manage to keep pace with a limping shamble.

The useless pair of Aphorain palace guards are still stationed either side of our chamber entrance, terror creeping across their faces at the sight of the unconscious Prince.

"Open that salt-sown door already," Kip demands, accent twanging even more Losian than usual. The guards scurry to respond.

Inside, Esarik rolls up the nearest rug and wedges it in the gap between the floor and the now-closed door. There's a grating screech as he drags one of the divans across the marble to the center of the room. "Set him down on his side. We want to give him the best chance of clearing his lungs."

Kip wordlessly follows his request.

"And someone cover that window."

A servant girl rushes to draw the heavy drapes. Something about her brushes against my memory.

I want to stay hovering, but now that we've made it here, the last stores of my strength drain away. I'm grateful when Kip pulls a chair over and motions for me to sit—close by Nisai, but not in Esarik's way.

The soon-to-be physician sets to work, peering in Nisai's mouth, smelling his breath, taking his pulse. Rolling the Prince onto his back, he prods his fingers experimentally into his abdomen. I clench and unclench my fists, controlling my urge to needle him with questions.

Esarik pushes his hair out of his eyes to reveal a creased brow. "I'm not entirely convinced this is smoke inhalation. He doesn't have a burn on him. There's no sign of soot in his airways. Not that I can see. I wish I'd gone in there with you. If I'd seen what happened, I might have been able to . . ." Esarik trails off, a pained expression on his face.

"What happened? It wasn't the fire?" I find myself mirroring the Trelian's gesture, running a hand over my recently shaved scalp.

"It could be in his lungs and I'm just not able to tell. Though usually there would be other signs if it was severe enough to keep him out cold like this."

"The Scent Keeper said there wasn't much time. She said something was 'too much' or 'too strong.' Does that mean anything to you?"

"Smoke-strewn skies, Ash: You think the *Scent Keeper* did this?"

"I've no idea what to think. But could this be poison?"

Esarik crosses his arms and props a thumb beneath his chin. "It's possible. Though most poisons that would put him in this state would have killed him already. To illustrate: Hagmiri formulas are derived from fruit seeds—readily available in the province's mountain orchards. Breathe in enough of the powdered form and a coma will result, but the heart will quickly shut down as well, the individual likely to experience seizures in the short interim. They call it Stonemason's Joy because it keeps the tomb carvers in business."

"Surely the Hagmiri aren't the only ones in the Empire who make poisons?"

Esarik begins to pace. "Of course not. The Trelians tend to use mineral by-products from precious-metal mines. But those are highly unlikely to deliver a life-threatening dose without sweating, jaundice, vomiting."

He taps one finger against his temple as if trying to dislodge the answer. "On the other hand, if it were Losian, I would hypothesize a derivation of a particularly potent snake venom. The name eludes me. Oh, but this is so difficult without my books!"

Kip has been leaning against the opposite wall, watching Esarik pace. Now she scowls. "Ralshig's Lament," she provides. "Makes you cry blood tears."

"The very one! My thanks."

Kip shrugs. "Makes you piss blood, too."

"Indeed! Enough venom can thin the blood so rapidly it starts to seep from the pores, and out of every—"

"I get the picture," I say, holding up my hand with a cringe.

"Sorry. I forget this sort of thing can be disturbing to a layperson." The scholar keeps pacing, muttering to himself, counting off thoughts on his fingers. "Oh!" He stops abruptly, paling more than I thought even Esarik could.

"What? What is it?"

His eyes lose focus. Then he straightens, shifts a chair, and steps up onto it, reaching for one of the candles from the lightwheel. His prize in hand, he returns to Nisai, gently peeling back each eyelid as he shines the flame close.

"Esarik!"

If I wasn't seeing it for myself, I wouldn't believe it possible the Trelian could blanche further.

"Stars, Ash. I've never so dearly wished *not* to have made a diagnosis." He gropes for the divan behind him and sits heavily.

With no small effort, I heave myself to my feet and cross to where Nisai lies. My hand betrays me, trembling slightly as I thumb back Nisai's eyelid. In the low light, it looks as if the normally crimson capillaries in the whites have turned into a fine web of black.

I squint and lean closer. Somehow, faintly wavering dark lines have appeared beneath the skin surrounding Nisai's eyes, between them, across the bridge of his nose. Scrunching my own eyes shut, I send a silent prayer to Kaismap for clear vision. But when I look again, the

shadowy threads are still there, radiating out like tiny streams meandering across a map.

Gnawing apprehension sinks into the deep bite of fear.

"She was right," Esarik marvels.

"The Scent Keeper?"

He looks up at me, confusion momentarily flickering across his features. "The Scent Keeper? Stars, no. I meant Ami. There are mentions
in surviving pre-Accord texts of a poison used by the small kings,
astronomically expensive because it was so hard to trace. Ami and I
debated whether it was merely myth. She argued that most myths are
borne of a smaller truth. And in my aurochs-headed stubbornness I
had refused to give her theory credence."

I sink back into my chair. "You think we're dealing with an expensive, ancient, possibly mythical poison?"

He pinches his nose between thumb and forefinger. "The evidence
suggests that's possible."

"Then we should focus on finding an expensive, ancient antidote."

"That, I'm afraid, will be *im*possible."

"Because?"

He takes a shuddering breath. "There never *was* an antidote.
Not in any of the texts I've seen. Though we only have fragments to
go on."

I look to Esarik, then to Kip standing stone-faced against the wall,
then to Nisai's unmoving form.

None of us utters a word until the sounds of a commotion echo
from outside the chambers, Iddo's voice carrying over the others. He
strides into the room, Issinon trailing him. The elder Prince crosses to
where Nisai lies, taking in the sight of his younger brother with a look
of sheer incredulity.

"Clear the room," he grates.

Light on her feet, the servant girl flits out the door.

Iddo clenches his hands into fists, corded tendons standing out
along his forearms. "I take an hour—*one* hour—to try to smooth

things out with the Aphorain Commander and everything descends into chaos."

Then he's back in control, pinning me in his hawk's gaze.

"How did this happen?"

Even if he didn't love his brother—and it's always been clear he does—Iddo has nothing to gain from Nisai's downfall. His Trelian heritage means he's the only imperial son who cannot inherit the throne. But he does have something to lose—what kind of Commander of the Imperial Rangers lets the heir be harmed on his watch?

What kind of *Shield* lets this happen on his watch?

I shake my head. "We're just trying to piece that together. Esarik may have a theory."

"Try me."

The scholar jumps to his feet. "We were considering the possibility of poison. But it's merely *one* possibility. I'm afraid I'm out of my depth, Commander. I'm a student, not a full-fledged physician." He wrings his hands. "With respect, it's no coincidence that after your father declined to appoint a new Scent Keeper in the capital, the Aphorain Eraz has declined to make any local appointments from the Guild of Physicians. We need to get the Prince back to Ekasya, where he can receive proper care from the Empire's best medical minds."

"Not yet."

Esarik takes a step back. "Forgive me, Commander, but when a patient is in an unconscious state, time is of the—"

"Understood. But not yet. First rule of survival in enemy territory—secure the surrounds before seeing to the wounded."

Enemy territory? Last time I checked, Aphorai was still a province on the imperial map. Then again, last time I checked, Nisai was in perfect health. And there's only one person in this room who rose through the ranks to become the youngest Commander of the Imperial Rangers.

House cat, I think bitterly. *I'm just a house cat.*

112

"Esarik," Iddo orders. "Begin a list of the best healers, religious or secular, Aphorai can offer—then do your own due diligence on their worth."

"There's an option close by," I suggest. "The girl who stitched me up knew exactly what she was doing. She was one of the first to the gardens with me. Maybe she saw something I missed."

"She was *with* you?"

"We arrived around the same time."

"Convenient." Iddo's eyes go flat, and I can't tell if he was speaking about the girl or me or both. He turns to Issinon. "Reconvene my meeting. If we're going to have a chance of identifying a culprit, we need to lock down the palace immediately. The Aphorains aren't going to like me pulling imperial rank. But I didn't come here to be polite."

He gives Nisai's shoulder a gentle squeeze.

"I came to protect my brother."

CHAPTER 17
RAKEL

They say the Eraz's dungeons, carved into the bedrock several levels under the palace, are darker than the Days of Doskai.

They're right.

It's so black I can't see my hand in front of my face. Then again, I'm not even sure if I *want* to see, given my nose only finds rats, unwashed bodies, and slop buckets of human excrement.

The rats are bigger than I'm comfortable with, judging from the skitters. And if the only guard standing watch over this floor has family? Poor them—he could snore a house down surer than a groundshake.

I block it all out by focusing yet again on Sephine's last words.

When the lion wears the lost crown, he won't live through the night.

Nisai's Aphorain roots mean he'll be the first Emperor for generations to fly banners with the winged lion facing the imperial phoenix. Was the Scent Keeper saying he'd only survive to rule Aramtesh for a day? Surely they wouldn't crown an unconscious Prince?

As for the other things . . .

The darkness will bloom again.

I was dragged down here before the fire was brought under control, but I'd bet my nose the whole dahkai crop had caught. There's no way those plants will be blooming when the moons go dark, nor at the next Flower Moon. They're gone.

The way of the stars.

Scent Keeper philosophy? Caravan navigation methods? Starwheel superstitions? I kick my heel against the cell wall and start pacing.

Asmudtag.

For someone who only first stepped onto temple grounds days earlier, mention of a near-forgotten deity is a sniff too mystical to interpret.

All I've got is those few words and a stampede of thoughts that reach the same dead end again and again. Yet the imperial heavies who've been taking turns questioning me think I know more than I'm letting on. Why haven't any Aphorains been among them? Father would detest the capital pulling rank if he were still one of the Eraz's officers.

Father.

Has word reached him of my fate? Would Barden have slunk home and told him, rubbing salt in a Rot-forsaken wound? And what would Father do then? Call in favors from an old army comrade? How many of those are left, and what would they be worth in the face of imperial command?

Air brushes past me, stirring me from my thoughts. A hint of sweet freshness, its visit cruelly fleeting. Someone opened the door to the outside world and shut it just as quick.

Sure enough, footsteps start down the corridor. My heart drums in my ears, instinct screaming for me to scramble to the rear of the cell and press my back against the wall. But how's that going to help? I've got no chance if the imperials decide on more direct interrogation methods.

The footsteps near. Just an average scuff. Probably a servant. In the darkness, I've lost track of all time. I've no idea how often they bring the barley gruel they call food in this place, or the last time they topped up the water bucket, its contents questionable enough for me to hold my nose every time I force myself to take a drink.

The footsteps slow and stop. So does the snoring. A man's voice—the guard. Then an *ooof* and a muffled thud. After that, nothing.

I strain to hear, canting my head to the side, ready to gauge the angles of the next sound. The darkness only answers with silence.

Candlelight flickers. A figure.

I edge backward. How could anyone move without a sound?

The figure steps closer. A girl in saffron robes and servant slippers. Black, chin-length hair framing a pale face barely older than mine. Huge eyes that could be any color under the sun—it's too dark to tell.

It's not too dark to tell that she's beautiful.

She pushes a tray through the slot under the bars. Gingerly, I lift the cloth. The homey waft of still-warm barley bread. A fat leg of roasted sandsquab. Honey-glazed Hagmiri apricots. A cup of what could only be Trelian red wine, transported barrel by barrel on camelback from the riverlands.

A meal fit for the Eraz. Delivered to a girl in a dungeon.

If they think I'm going to beg, they can think again.

"So," I drawl, hoping my voice is steady enough to mask my fear.

"We've skipped the trial and gone straight to the last meal? Care to tell me what it's laced with?" I bring the cup of wine to my nose, but all I get is a bouquet of dark berries and a hint of anise.

The girl raises a manicured eyebrow. "Satisfied?" She speaks with a calm assurance I wouldn't expect from a servant. Guess anyone can afford to be confident on the other side of these bars.

"What happened to the guard?"

"He's sleeping."

"He snores when he sleeps."

She smirks. "He's sleeping *very* soundly."

"Did you . . . ?"

"He'll be fine in a couple of hours. Won't even have a headache. Or any recollection that a servant girl brought him a nice cup of ale halfway through his shift."

"Then you *are* here to . . ." My voice finally betrays me, catching in my throat at the thought of dying here, now, in a dungeon.

"If that were my intention, it'd already be over with you none the wiser." She looks pointedly at the food. "Do you treat everyone who shows you kindness with such disdain?"

I try another angle. "Who sent you?"

"Someone who thinks you're worth saving."

Barden? Has the guilt finally got to him?

"It's not your pretty guard, if that's what you're thinking."

So, she's been around the palace long enough to note its comings and goings. Or she's someone with sources.

She waves her hand. "All of that's irrelevant, and I'd hate it if our dozing friend was discovered before we'd finished our conversation. I'll talk, you eat. Who knows where your next meal will come from."

I glare at her.

She stares back, unblinking.

My traitor stomach gurgles. Hunger wins the battle against suspicion, and I fall on the food.

"Delightful choice." She draws nearer to the bars. "Now. You'll be found guilty no matter what. They need a scapegoat. You're the newest servant on the estate, the Eraz can plausibly deny any of his staff was involved or had knowledge of anything you had planned. Sephine could have vouched for you, but she's gone to the sky."

The girl turns away. What was that in her expression? Grief?

Then she's all business again. "Whether you like it or not, they'll get a confession from you. There's been no major physical harm yet. But there will be. You've seen the chain gangs working the irrigation ditches?"

Noseless ones.

I swallow the mouthful of apricot I'd been chewing. It sticks painfully in my throat. Whatever this girl's motives, there's truth in her words. If there's anything I've learned from recent events, it's that those with money or power are the ones in control. No matter if I've done anything wrong or not, they'll decide my fate. Just as whoever employs my unexpected visitor is doing right now.

What's in it for them, I haven't the smokiest.

The girl sets the candle on the ground and pulls two metal pins from her robe. She jams one into the lock on the cell door and works the other like a tiny lever, clucking her tongue.

"They really should keep these things oiled. Where were we? Ah, yes. Someone high up wants the Prince healed before too many hotheads start us down the road toward civil war. That someone also recognizes that self-preservation is one of the best motivators, hence deciding it's worth adding you to the field. You've built a reputation in certain quarters for—how shall I say it?—unorthodox creativity. Tenacity, too. You'll need both if you're going to figure out how to save our next ruler."

The lock clicks audibly. She gives me a sly wink as the cell door swings open. "Guess I've still got it."

Who *is* this girl?

"Now. The nice thing about rich people not wanting to sniff their own stink is that the drainage systems go well beyond the walls. That's your way out. I've taken care of the grate."

I cringe. The dungeons are bad enough. But the *sewers*?

"Far from glamorous, but that's how it is. I've taken the liberty of having your horse relocated. I trust you'll take that as a sign of good faith. She's penned in the outer corral of the trader camp north of the walls. Two silver zigs say the stock boy won't be reporting any unusual noises tonight."

I choke back tears of relief. Guess if I'm going to be played by someone, I'd rather it to be the sort who takes care of my horse.

My lock-picking visitor leans a shoulder against the doorway, arms folded. "Circle wide of the city, then strike south, for Belgith's Canyon. You know the place?"

I nod.

"Lovely. Whatever you do, don't even think about taking a side trip to that village of yours. And here, you'll need this."

I'd noticed she was carrying a bag but couldn't make out the details given the cloak draped over it. Now she hands it to me and my hands instantly recognize its familiar shape, the strap fitted to my shoulder from turns of wear.

The weight suggests it's full, but I open the flap to check. Sure enough, the various vials and pouches of my stores are there, and some have even been replenished: yeb balm for starting fires, liquid torpi to aid a sleep so deep no pain is felt, even some Linod's Elixir. I haven't needed the latter since I was young, but I always feel better carrying a small amount for emergencies. I slip my hand into the concealed pocket, fingertips finding the tiny vial of dahkai essence.

The girl raises an eyebrow. "All in order, I trust? Now, this'll also come in handy." She hands me a pouch with the telltale jangle of silver zigs. "Oh, and I almost forgot . . ."

She produces a book from her robe. It's not much bigger than my splayed hand, but thick with pages and bound in what appears to be aurochs leather.

I've never seen a book up close—I don't exactly have reason to frequent the scroll merchant in Aphorai's market. It falls open at a random page, and I squint in the low light. Charcoal sketches. Scrawled notes from which I can only pick out every third or fourth word. Other scripts I've never even seen before.

"It was the Prince's," she explains. "May come in useful or shed light once you get to the Library of the Lost. If anywhere is going to have answers to the Prince's calamity, it'll be there."

A legendary library hidden somewhere in the depths of the Aphorain desert? I'd almost started believing this girl was serious. Dared hope there might be a way out of all this.

"And how am I meant to find it?"

"The map around your neck."

Stunned, I reach for my locket, my thumb tracing the constellations. *Follow the way of the stars*, Sephine had said.

She leans forward, peering at me searchingly. "Scents be damned. She told you nothing of the Order, did she?"

"Who? And in what order?"

"Sephine. The Order of Asmudtag."

Asmudtag. That's two out of three. What is going *on* here?

She rolls her eyes skyward, though a ton of rock stands between us and whichever god she's invoking. "What *did* she tell you? Don't bother denying it, I know she spoke to you before she passed."

"How could you—"

"Irrelevant," she snaps, all trace of her arch playfulness evaporated. "Tell me what she said. Word for word."

I consider resisting, but she's given me food and the promise of escape. "It was babble. Her usual riddles. Something about the darkness blooming again. And something about the Prince's coronation: 'When the lion wears the lost crown, he won't live through the night.'"

The girl hisses a string of curses that would make a soldier blush. "Not the Prince's coronation. *Tozran's.* She was speaking of the old calendar. Ours uses Kaismap's moon but pre-Accord calendars follow the fifteen-day cycles of Shokan, the moon of the Lost God. Feast days, auspicious dates, times of ill omen, were decided by its movement against the stars. When Shokan waxes full and crests the eighth segment, the moon 'crowns' Tozran—the lion constellation.

"Sephine must have had reason to think the Prince will succumb on that night. I don't spend my days hunched over starwheel charts but that's"—she purses her lips, staring into the shadows as she counts on her fingers—"sometime in Adirun."

Adirun. Three moons away. Fifty days, give or take.

Enough time to cure a prince, clear my name, and potentially stop my province feeling the imperial boot on its neck?

It'll have to be.

The girl checks the darkness over her shoulder. "I don't plan to be here when that guard comes around. Let's be blunt: You want two things—salves and tinctures for your father, and to understand who your mother was. The Order can provide both."

"My father needs treatment daily, not at the tail end of some smoke-brained quest."

"Arrangements have been made. He'll be well supplied, and someone will watch over him. So, are we burning the same taper? Take the sewer tunnel. Get your horse. Find the Library and a cure for the Prince before the lion is crowned."

Footsteps echo far above us.

My visitor retrieves her candle. "We need to move."

What choice do I have?

Stay and risk almost-certain punishment for a crime I didn't commit?

Escape and flee home for the hours or days I might get before I'm apprehended, implicating Father for harboring a fugitive? He wouldn't last long down here.

Or trust the words of a stranger who has gone to a lot of trouble to offer me a chance at a way out of all this.

I grab a last chunk of bread. With no better option before me, I follow the girl deeper into the tunnels.

"I'll be leaving you here," she announces when I've lost count of the turns we've taken and the floor has begun to slope downward.

"At least tell me your name before you go?"

There goes that arched eyebrow again. "You don't know many spies, do you?"

I answer with a glare.

A row of white teeth flashes in the candlelight. "Good thing you're so cute when you're pretending not to be out of your depth." She reaches out and lays her hand on my arm, her touch raising my skin to gooseflesh. "You can call me Luz."

She steps back. "Stars keep you, Ana. You just might be reckless enough to pull this off. If you don't end up dead first."

The barest hint of violets follows in her wake before it's swallowed up by dungeon reek. It's delicate, but it clangs in my memory. I never forget a scent.

Zakkurus.

She's one of *his*? What's he got to do with all this?

More to the point, what's he going to get out of it?

CHAPTER 18
ASH

Iddo's first order of business after declaring martial law was to station several of his Rangers in and outside Nisai's chambers with strict orders not to admit anyone who hadn't been pre-approved by the Commander himself, *especially* any Aphorain. The First Prince's safety, he said, is his paramount concern, a concern he'd "obviously have to take personal responsibility for" if he wanted it done right.

The second order was to appoint an interim Shield for Nisai from among his Rangers, considering my incapacity.

He appointed Kip.

A good choice, in my view.

She didn't object, but the disappointment in her eyes was obvious. Being one of the newest Rangers and having a reassignment to a comatose Prince? I expect the Commander's decision hinged on Kip's loyalty and her prodigious mastery of the deadly art of lo-daiyish, the unarmed combat style of her home province. But the way the other Rangers immediately began to let their gazes slide over the Losian— as if "out of the field" means "part of the furniture"—made me feel guilty and sympathetic in equal doses.

Iddo's third order landed me here.

Told to focus on my recovery, I've been reassigned to a chamber that appears remarkably similar to a servant's cell—four unadorned stone walls, bare ceiling, narrow bed, a candle in a simple holder providing the only light source.

The passing hours bleed into one another. Issinon brings food, fresh candles, and a reminder I'm to rest—my priority is to mend. Esarik pokes his head in the door as often as he can, giving me updates that aren't updates on Nisai's condition.

The Prince's heart beats.

Breath rises and falls in his chest.

His eyes stay closed.

The darkness remains.

The scholar grimaces when he speaks of the ratcheting tension as the Commander hunts for the culprit behind the fires and Nisai's condition. I want answers, too. But I've begun to wonder whether more energy is being spent on identifying and punishing the would-be assassin than on finding what ails Nisai, and, more importantly, what will cure it. Because who knows how long he will last in this state, how long it will be before he recovers or succumbs.

Sometime in the night, I wake to raised voices echoing down the hall.

I'm thankful that my wounds have crusted over well enough to allow me to pull on my armor. I exit my cell and hurry along the corridor, following the sound to Nisai's chambers.

The Rangers stationed on the outer door nod me through in unison. Their comrades on the inner door greet me in the same manner.

Inside, Kip meets my eyes across the room. There's sympathy in her gaze, but then the moment passes and she's stoic again, on guard at the Prince's bedside.

Nisai remains on his back. Someone has changed his clothes into his state robes—deep imperial purple with thread-of-gold phoenixes stitched into the silk. The sight makes me slightly uneasy—it's not what Nisai would have chosen. Not that you'd be able to tell: The Prince's expression is serene, eyes closed, hands clasped over his stomach.

Iddo, however, appears anything but serene. His shirt is uncharacteristically unbuttoned, his face shadowed where by now he normally would have shaved. He paces in front of one of his senior officers—by the look of the man's insignia and silver-sown hair—who stands next to an Aphorain guard. It's the same hulking brute who steered the chariot at the lion hunt. What's he doing here?

"An innocent doesn't run," Iddo fumes. "Find her."

An innocent? On the run?

The Ranger nods, his hands clasped behind his back. "Aye, sir. But we're stretched. We never thought we'd be holding a palace complex, and now the city is growing restless. Could we let some of the Aphorain guards resume patrols outside the walls? Handpicked, of course. Only those we judge to be loyal to the Empire. Like this lad already proved himself at the scene."

The Aphorain guard lifts his chin and puffs his chest. Smug bastard.

"Very well, Squad Captain," Iddo says. "But I want our men—not theirs—to see to the matter of the fugitive."

"There's the team helping the scholar vet the healers. There's only three of them, though."

"Enough to track one girl. And Issinon can assist Esarik to delve into healer credentials. It's not like my brother is in need of a valet at this point."

Divert resources from finding the expert Nisai needs? I want to protest—we need answers and we needed them yesterday—but I grit my teeth. No good can come of openly challenging the Commander. His frustration has built until he almost quivers with it, an over-wound bowstring ready to snap at the lightest draw.

I can't imagine the stress of having to take charge over a situation like this. And I can't imagine the grilling he'll receive with each messenger bird from Ekasya bearing the Council of Five's seal.

But surely there's another way.

I clear my throat. "You've found a suspect?"

The Squad Captain grunts assent. "The girl who was with you when you found the Prince. The Scent Keeper's servant."

"You think she did this?"

"We're shy of a confession, but we'll have one soon enough." He claps me on the shoulder. "Don't worry, we'll track her down. Then she'll talk. I'll make sure of it."

"What if she's innocent?"

Iddo sets his jaw. "Then it will still signal to the Aphorains that no leniency will be shown when my brother's safety is under threat."

The last makes the hairs on the back of my neck lift. I'd told Iddo the girl might have some insight into what ails Nisai, but this doesn't sound like reconnaissance. This sounds like vengeance. And for what? For being in the wrong place at the wrong time? For knowing more than she's letting on?

Whatever the girl's involvement in all this, I don't see her as an ancient-poison-wielding assassin. And Nisai trusted her, he said so, after she'd tended my wounds from the lion hunt. If he were the one giving orders, he'd want to find out what she knows; he wouldn't want her thrown behind bars, tracked like an animal and then tortured to confess to something she may not have done.

For the time being, Kip is in far better condition to stand guard over Nisai.

Esarik is screening potential healers.

Iddo needs all the men he can get.

"I'll go," I venture.

Iddo raises an eyebrow. "Go where?"

"To find the girl."

The Squad Captain guffaws. "I've never seen you bested in the training yard, boy. Ol' Blademaster Boldor—may Azered guide his soul—knew how to foster talent. But you were still squeaking like a girl when you came to the palace. What do you know about tracking out in the big wide world?"

"I, ah—"

He folds his arms. "Exactly."

I look to Iddo, imploring.

"The Squad Captain is right, house cat. Focus on your recovery. If my brother wakes, he'll want you."

The Ranger sniggers lewdly at the last.

Anger tightens my throat. *Mother Esiku, give me patience.* "But I—"

Iddo's eyes spark dangerously. "That's an order, Shield."

"Acknowledged, Commander," I say through clenched teeth.

Back in my cell, I slump against the wall, hissing a pained breath when the jolt smarts the wound in my side.

I've never defied an order. I never thought I'd need to. But my responsibility above all else is to serve Nisai. Until my last breath, I need to do everything within my power to cure him. If the Aphorain

125

girl knows something that could help, I *must* find out. And if I don't move now, I'll risk word spreading among the Rangers that I'm on orders to stay.

I start shoving my belongings into my travel pack.

A soft knock makes every muscle tense. I shove my pack behind the pallet and crack open the door.

It's the Aphorain guard. The so-called loyal one. He shifts from foot to sandaled foot, eyes darting up and down the hall. "Apologies, ah, Shield, sir. But I couldn't help but overhear."

"Spit it out, man."

"Do you think she did it?"

"Excuse me?"

"The girl who escaped. Do you think she hurt the Prince?" He seems so earnest, like his world turns on my answer.

"I believe she understands more than she's revealing," I say carefully. "But I don't believe she's a murderer."

He sags in apparent relief.

Footsteps come into earshot. I grab the guard's sash and drag him back into my room. "What aren't you telling me?"

He holds up his hands. "Nothing about the Prince. I swear. On my sister's life. But I do know about Rakel."

I've observed courtiers and merchants, ambassadors and bards, over my turns in the Ekasya palace. Something tells me this guard isn't a master of guile. I relax my grip.

He eyes my pack. "I might run, too." The implication is clear—a Shield is blood-sworn to his charge. If they fail in their duty, their life is forfeit.

"I'm not doing this for myself," I growl. "Now, the girl."

The guard studies me, cocking his head to either side as if he'll see something different from another angle. "I can't believe I'm here again," he mutters.

"Here?"

"You swear you won't hurt her?"

I glare at him. He doesn't shrink from my gaze. Seems when it comes to this girl, his bravery matches his brawn.

"If she means no harm to the Prince, she'll not be harmed by me." It's as far as I'm prepared to go.

It seems to be enough, because he leans forward, his voice dropping almost to a whisper. "I'll help you get out of here. You heard in there—your lot has approved us to resume patrols of the city. We'll smuggle you out at the next shift change. From there, find the horse."

"Excuse me?"

"You'll want to track a horse, not a camel. She's had a pet horse since she was a kid. She won't leave the city without it. Find the horse, find the girl."

"And you know this because?"

His expression turns soft, almost wistful. "I grew up with her."

CHAPTER 19
RAKEL

It feels like I've been picking my way through sewer reek forever—one hand on the wall, nose pressed into the other shoulder—when I make out the barest hint of light up ahead. I follow it, my breath loud in my ears, to the grate that Luz told me about. I give it an experimental push. It swings open with surprising ease.

Outside the city walls, it's night, though it may as well be day compared with the unnatural darkness of the dungeons. I suck in a breath. Sweet freedom . . . with a chaser of sewer. But after stumbling along those tunnels for stench knows how long, I'm not complaining.

If the smell of sodden char wasn't still drifting down from the palace terraces, I could almost imagine nothing was amiss in the city. But that, paired with the silhouettes of the Rangers that now patrol the walls, snuffs out any wishful thinking. And there's something distinctly unnerving about the sight of the larger moon, Shokan, covering the smaller and taking on a color I didn't expect.

Flower Moon?

Blood Moon more like it.

I do my best to combine casual with quiet as I make my way to the northern trader camp. The back of my neck prickles with every step— if Luz spoke the truth, the dungeon guard will wake up in a puddle of ale any time now.

One thing's true: They've corralled Lil in the stock pens, along with the sheep and goats that will become roasts and stews for travelers. My horse gives a soft whicker as I approach.

"Shhhh," I murmur.

But it's too late. A figure stumbles out of the small tent overlooking the pens.

I stop dead in my tracks. Seems Luz's plan was Rot-brained after all.

The stock boy approaches, something bundled in his arms. "What's your name?" he whispers hoarsely.

"What?"

"I need a name. If I don't tell her the right one, I don't get my second zig."

"Oh." Makes sense. "Rakel."

He holds out his arms. Lil's desert cloth, saddle, and the rest of her tack.

"Thanks."

With a sleepy nod, he heads back to his tent.

I saddle Lil as quickly as possible and lead her from the pens, keeping in her shadow when we pass any perimeter torches. Then we're clear of the caravan camp and heading across the scree for the desert.

I hold my locket up before me, turning it this way and that, squinting in the moonlight. I've always marveled at the skill of the artisan who engraved the silver with such accuracy that I could pick out several constellations of the starwheel even in childhood.

But there was one star near the locket's bottom edge that always stood out, larger than anything I'd seen near the southern horizon over Aphorai. I'd always thought it was a silversmith's error. A slip of the hand covered to look like a bright star.

If it's really a map, I have no idea how I'm going to read it. But first things first—put some sand between me and the city. *South,* Luz said. Her word has held water so far, so south it is.

Before I mount up, I take one last glance over my shoulder at the silhouette of Aphorai's walls. "Good reekin' riddance," I curse under my breath.

"Not. Quite. Yet." The voice is deep as midnight shadow.

I twist around, only for my eyes to find blackness.

Then my nose picks up the barest hints of sandalwood and cedar.

I spin back the other way.

A dark outline stands against the stars and eerie crimson moon, the scent of cedar stronger now I'm facing him. The Shield. Not for the first time, I wonder why I took the trouble to oil that armor. It's not like it was my role. I just had to do *something* with my hands while I watched over him that first night.

But that was before the fire.

Now all bets are off.

If I'm going to die here, it will be on my own terms. I draw my knife, though it's hardly more than a toothpick compared with the two swords strapped to the Shield's back.

But he doesn't reach for either of them. Instead, he tilts his head to the side. It's an unexpectedly boylike gesture.

What in the sixth hell is he playing at?

"Shouldn't you be with the Prince?" I ask, hoping on my father's life that the Empire's heir is also still in the land of the living.

He gently pats his side. "I'm healing, but I'm of limited use to him in my, ah, traditional role. Doesn't mean I won't do what I must to serve him. And you, it seems, might be able to help. I've no interest in causing you harm. If you know anything about what happened, now's the time to speak."

Another interrogation? No, thanks. "I was just a servant. I wasn't privy to—"

"Rangers are coming for you. It's only by Azered's mercy I found you first. So you can be honest with me, or I can leave you to them. Your choice."

I study him as I take that in. It's too dark to read his features, but he's carrying a travel pack, stuffed full. He expects to be gone some time. Maybe he *isn't* looking to drag me back to Aphorai as soon as he gets what he wants.

But what I know, where I'm going—why would an imperial body-guard believe me? Then Luz's voice echoes in my mind: *It was the Prince's.*

I rummage in my satchel, feeling for the book. It's not like I'm going to be able to decipher it on my own, so I doubt there's much point in withholding it from him. I heft its weight, then pass it over. "Do you recognize this?"

The Shield takes the book—so much smaller cradled in his square hands. "Where did you get this?" he demands.

"Some girl acting as a servant. But she knew too much for any servant I'd known. She said the book was the Prince's, then sent me to look for something to help him."

"I thought it was destroyed in the fire." He lets out a sigh and tucks the book into his pack. Then he straightens his shoulders, as if he's decided something. "You shouldn't go to your village. That'll be the first place they'll hunt for you."

I glare at him. "Just because I'm common doesn't mean I'm stupid."

"I didn't say that," he says, holding up his hands.

"So how did *you* find me?"

"One of the palace guards. Said you grew up together."

I grit my teeth. Barden.

"Lovers' quarrel?"

I turn away and climb into Lil's saddle, half expecting to be yanked back to the sand.

But the Shield doesn't move to stop me.

"Look," I say, my fingers twining in mane. "The only thing I know for sure is that I'm being played. Not like that's anything new these days. But I've got a lead on something that might help your Prince. It's flimsy, but it's a lead."

His face is only dimly lit by the stars and the bloodred smolder of the Flower Moon. Even so, there's something intimidating about his gaze, as if he's the one with the high ground glowering down at me.

"I'm going to find the Library of the Lost."

He snorts. "That's a myth."

"Like I said—flimsy. As flyaway as temple smoke. But the person who gave me that book also told me the only place to find answers for your Prince is the Library. I'm desperate enough to gamble. Are you?"

He kicks a boot in the sand and stares down at it for a long moment.

"There's something else, too. Something Sephine said before she died. Seems your Prince won't last to become Emperor."

His head snaps up. "What did she say?"

"'When the lion wears the lost crown, he'll not live through the night.'"

He mutters under his breath and begins to pace, more predator's prowl than nervous fidgeting.

"Why couldn't you just have a camel like everyone else?" he growls.

"What sort of question is that?"

"Do they not teach you history out here? Never heard of the demise of Emperor Mulreth?"

The Mulreth Saga? Please. It's one of Father's favorite tales from beyond the Empire. Though I'm betting it was told very differently to whatever version the Shield's heard. "Yeah, yeah, I know, the horses got one whiff of camel musk and the cavalry were routed. And fair enough. Camels stink." I wrinkle my nose. Right now, so do I.

"I don't care what it smells of. I do care what tracks it leaves behind. One horse in a thousand camels . . ."

"With this breeze, the desert will swallow her tracks soon enough. Lil and I have been together for turns. I know her weaknesses, her strengths. I trust her. Which is more than I can say for you."

He grimaces. Serves him right. I shouldn't be the only one who has to earn respect around here. "If you're coming with me, you've got a choice. On horseback, on foot with that love tap from your lion friend only held together by stitches . . . or go steal a camel. Good luck to you if you do, because Lil and I will be long gone."

He checks his pack, pulling the straps taut so it sits snug against his back. Without a word, he starts jogging south, the direction I'd been heading before he crept up on me.

Stubborn fool. I give him a mile, two at most, before his wound flares and he's sapped of energy.

I reach down and give Lil's neck a pat. "He's made his decision, girl. Let's go."

We don't speak as we leave Aphorai behind, too intent on whether we'll be noticed, whether an alarm will be raised. The Shield's pace matches Lil's—their footfalls drumming a muffled beat in the sand. How he keeps going with a wound like that is bordering on unnatural. The thought sends an extra ripple of unease through me.

When we reach the larger dunes, we slow to a walk for a spell. I look back toward the city. It's nothing more than an orange-gold smudge where the night sky meets the waves of the desert. Except . . . I squint. Are those lights moving?

I point. "What's going on back there?"

"Azered's breath," the Shield mutters. He scans the horizon in the opposite direction. "Where do these dunes end? How far until the landscape changes?"

"Days. Weeks, in some directions. But there's a gorge to the south. A bunch of seasonal streams run off it, like the fronds of a palm leaf."

"How long?"

"Depends how fast. A few hours?"

"Shuffle forward," he growls.

The next thing I know he's vaulted up onto Lil behind me. So much for old Mulreth.

"Go," he says, voice gravelly in my ear. "Head for the gorge, and if you want to live, don't stop. For anything."

We ride.

Lil surges under us, her powerful muscles bunching and stretching as she climbs dunes and gallops headlong down the other side. The Shield bounces around behind me. I'm afraid without the benefit of stirrups he's going to lose his seat, or worse still, make me lose mine.

"Wrap your arms around me," I tell him over my shoulder.

"I hardly think that's—"

"Just do it! You're slowing us down!"

His arms circle around my waist. Only minutes ago, I thought those same hands might choke or stab the life from me. They may still.

"Now, grip with your thighs, not your entire leg. Get your feet out of her ribs."

The weight behind me shifts again, his broad chest pressing against my back. Better balanced, Lil finds a renewed burst of speed. I crouch forward up the next dune, urging her on, and lean back again as she plunges down the other side.

The Shield moves with me.

He's a fast learner. At least there's that.

Cool night air brushes my cheeks, the headwind holding no clues as to whether our pursuers are gaining. But Lil soon begins to radiate with the heat of her exertion, and the grassy smell of horse sweat fills my nostrils. All I can hear is her labored breathing, her hooves churning the sand, my heart thundering in my ears.

I risk a glance behind. Lights trail out from Aphorai like gems threading a necklace. They're not gaining ground on us yet—their camels aren't as fast. But they can endure longer than Lil can, especially when she's carrying two people.

"How long can she keep this up?" the Shield asks, as if he's heard my thoughts.

"Not much longer. We're going to have to let her rest soon."

"We have to get to that gorge first."

"Come on, girl," I say, willing her strength. "You can do it. Not far now."

But the gorge doesn't appear, and Lil's head starts to lower, her sides heaving against my legs.

I check over my shoulder again, but we're in the valley of a massive dune and I can't see anything but dark sand and sky. "You can ride a horse to death, you know," I tell the Shield.

"She's not stopping."

"She won't. She's trained too well. She'll keep going until it's too late. We *have* to rest her."

"It'll be too late for all of us if we don't make it to that gorge."

I'm on the verge of calling a halt when the terrain begins to flatten. Lil's hooves strike something hard.

Sandstone.

The gorge.

There are too many dunes between us and our pursuers to spot their torches through the night. Unless, of course, they've put them out, so we can't tell where they are. There's a cheerful thought.

"Any sign of them?" I ask.

He scans the horizon. "No. But if they're Rangers, that's meaningless. Ride along the rock. They'll at least have to choose which direction we've gone when the obvious tracks run out. Hurry."

I peer down into the gorge as we skirt the rim. It's dark, with even darker shadows where the cliffs overhang the canyon floor. "If we're going down there, we need to dismount."

The Shield slides from Lil's back. He gingerly stretches his arms, hissing a breath through his teeth as one hand goes to the bandages around his chest. I'm going to have to look at those. And soon. The last thing we need is a reopened wound going bad.

I free my feet from the stirrups and drop down behind him. We move under an overhang at the lip of the canyon.

Lil snorts, spraying foam that had accumulated around her bit. I shove my waterskin into the Shield's hands and then cup my own, gesturing at him. "She needs water."

The Shield does as I ask.

It's not much but it'll have to do. I flip her reins over her head and tie them together so they don't snag on anything.

"You don't need to lead her?"

"She's better at finding her own path."

We head out from the overhang. The Shield finds a less steep section eroded out of the rock and starts down.

I've explored parts of the canyon, but I've never tried to descend at this gorge, and never at night. Barden and I used to come here when we were old enough to be let out of sight. More to the point—when my father deemed Barden old enough to accompany me in case we ran into trouble. Funny how everyone seemed fine with that, with us taking overnight trips, as if they'd already decided our future was fused together.

I glance back. No torches have appeared, and Lil has begun to pick her way down the slope, a silhouette as dark as starless sky. Good girl.

My foot comes down on a loose rock. It rolls out from under my weight. My ankle twists. The other foot begins to slide on loose scree. The gorge is a toothless grin, gleeful at the prospect of swallowing me whole. I teeter on the edge, arms flailing.

A strong hand grips my shoulder.

"What are you playing at?" the Shield fumes.

"What are *you* doing creeping up on people in the dark again?"

"If you need help, tell me. You can't expect me to predict what you're capable of and what you're not."

"That could have happened to anyone," I retort. "And I'm fine, aren't I?"

He grunts. "Mission first, pride second."

I flip two curled fingers at his back. Excuse me if almost plunging to my death got up *his* nose.

At the bottom of the gorge, silence reigns. Lil dips her head to drink from the pool and doesn't let up until I take her reins. "Go easy. We can stop again soon," I promise, rubbing her still-damp neck.

She snorts but lets me lead her through the water. The going is slow as we feel out each footstep on the slick pebbles, sometimes skirting around boulders, sometimes clambering over them—every time with my heart in my throat, worried about Lil's legs.

Part of me wants to leave the water and run again, run and never stop. But covering our tracks will buy us more time than a half-hearted sprint from an exhausted mare.

Because if it doesn't, we're all out of options.

CHAPTER 20
ASH

The girl threads her way deeper into the canyon, nimbly traversing the rocks.

I trail her, every sense on high alert for the first hint of our pursuers. By the time I'm satisfied we've evaded Iddo's men, dawn has begun to fade the only slice of starry sky we can see. We're safe for now. Though one thing is certain—they'll keep coming.

A Ranger never yields the hunt.

I draw even with the girl and gingerly stretch. My side aches, but the fire in the wounds has cooled. "Which way?"

She tilts her face to the sky, then squints down at her locket. It's engraved with what appears to be constellations. I surmise she's trying to get a reference point between it and the sky. But dawn edges closer, and the stars are blinking shut one after the other.

She gives a frustrated huff. "Map's decided to take a nap. May as well make yourself comfortable, Shield." She catches my eye. "Is that what I should even be calling you? 'Shield'?"

A derisive laugh escapes my lips. "I expect my days as Shield are numbered. It's probably already a lie to call me that."

She stares at me, tapping her foot.

I sigh. "Ash. Call me Ash."

"Ash? What kind of name is that?"

"Er, mine?"

"Is that your real name?"

"I just said as much, didn't I?"

"Ash." Her Aphorain accent draws it out like the sound people make when they're shushing a child.

"And you, Scent Keeper's Apprentice?"

"I *wasn't* her apprentice."

"Good. That would have been a mouthful. Nisai said your name was . . . Karel? Rikal?"

"Rakel."

I arch an eyebrow. "What kind of name is that?"

She lets it drop.

The girl hunkers down next to her satchel and points to a water-smoothed boulder. "Sit."

"Excuse me?"

"We're not going anywhere until nightfall. Your wounds need checking. No doubt some split last night."

"They're fine."

"*Sit.*"

I decide it's not worth arguing about and hunker down on the rock. She kneels at my wounded side and produces the same knife she used when she first stitched me up.

"What do you think you're—"

Too late. The scrap of silk that was my palace vest gapes open from sleeve to hem and slips from my shoulder. She wastes no time moving on to the ties of my armor, loosening the laces that run up my side with surprising deftness. My vest comes free and I suppress a shiver as the cool air of desert dawn washes over my torso.

The girl hisses a breath through her teeth.

"Bad?" I ask.

"The opposite," she says, her expression a mix of awe and suspicion. "It's . . . beginning to heal."

My mind scrabbles for something to deflect her curiosity. I attempt a smile. "Only thanks to you patching me up so well."

She frowns, seemingly unconvinced.

I gesture to my shucked vest. "You, ah, seem to know your way around armor."

She blushes, suddenly appearing self-conscious, and keeps her eyes on her work. "Military family."

Judging by her curt tone, I won't be getting any further details. She begins cleaning and rebandaging the wound, and I send a relieved prayer to merciful Azered in thanks for the silence that ensues.

Later, I find myself pacing the length of the canyon. At any other time, this place would feel miraculous. Pools cascade as clear and blue as polished aquamarine. Rock figs cling to the canyon walls with ancient, gnarled roots, their canopies fringing the water in shade.

If only I wasn't too on edge to appreciate it.

The slow passing of the day chafes me rawer than a new pair of boots. I climb to the rim to regularly check for signs of Ranger scouting parties.

If the Rangers catch up to us, only Kaismap knows what they'll do to the girl. And for my part? We're in unprecedented territory. Though I'd wager they'll come up with something more creative than incarceration. Something that makes the five hells look heavenly.

But what other option did I have? I serve Nisai, first and foremost, not the Empire. His life comes before politics, and my life is forfeit if his comes to an end. I was damned if I did, damned if I didn't.

The sun approaches its zenith painstakingly slowly, glaring into the canyon as if the gods are on the side of the Rangers. I retreat to the shade of an overhanging rock, where Rakel hunkers in the dust. She's using a stick to draw lines on the ground, then smooths them over with a hand and starts again. Her locket lies beside her.

"Follow the way of the stars," she mutters between a series of curses that wouldn't be out of place in a barracks.

"What was that?"

"The engravings on my locket were supposed to be a map." She points to the largest star etched in the silver, then at its counterpart in the dust. "I figured this one was a marker for where we need to go."

"Surely you weren't trying to follow a single star. You realize they traverse the sky each—"

"I don't have Rot for brains, all right? I get that they move. But this one isn't a real star. There's no match for it in the night sky between the snowfox and the winged lion constellations. Not even close."

I frown. She's right. I can't recall noticing anything bright between Kal and Tozran.

"And I think these are also odd ones out." The tip of her tongue peeps from the corner of her mouth as she marks another five points in the dust. "But I'd have to check at night."

"Don't tell me you've dragged me into the desert to search for a place that may not even exist, with a map that may not even be a map, and you've no idea how to read it?"

"I didn't *drag* you. And if you could turn the mind behind that sharp tongue to helping me figure—"

I hold up a hand. "Just . . . I need a moment."

She falls silent.

On one of my earlier surveys of the canyon rim, I'd collected some melons not much bigger than my fist. I've no appetite after this latest revelation, but I need to think about something else while I calm down. I cross to where I've stacked the fruit, take out my knife, and slice into the thick gray-green skin.

"I wouldn't eat that if I were you." Rakel's voice is more singsong amusement than warning. She's now perched on a nearby boulder, riffling through the pack I'd hastily thrown together last night.

I pause, knife still sticking in the fruit. "It's a melon. It's not going to bite me."

"Sure. Akrol melons are melons. But they *will* bite you. In the arse."

I give it a sniff. "Is it poisonous?"

"Nope."

"Then I'm eating it."

"Fine. But if you manage to get past the bitterness, don't complain to me when your guts turn to water."

I glance sidelong at the black mare. "Do horses eat them?"

"Nope. Too much sense for that."

She resumes her search in the pack, then holds up Nisai's journal. "You never said what this was."

"I'd prefer you didn't touch that," I say, flinging the melon across the gorge in disgust.

"What is it?"

"It's personal," I snap.

She raises her hands. "Hold your nose. I'm not trying to pry."

"Hard to believe when you're pawing through someone else's belongings."

"I just wanted to know how it could help us."

"I'd reckon nothing could help us at this point."

She shakes her head as she replaces the journal in the pack. "You've got to get over this failed-before-we've-even-started thing."

"Pardon?"

"You're acting like you think this is impossible."

"Isn't it?"

"Maybe. But if we don't try, we won't find out. So can we focus on the 'doing' bit and not the 'failing' bit for now?"

"You obviously don't comprehend what's at risk here. What's against us. I came after you because I thought you knew something, something useful that could help Nisai, and all it turned out to be was a nursery tale. This venture was doomed before it started. I should never have left."

She stands and balls her fists at her hips. "You've never failed at anything before, have you?"

"Excuse me?"

"You've never screwed anything up. You've always been on top of things. In control. Everything has gone your way. You've lived in a palace all your life. It's all been . . . roses."

If she only knew.

"I bet you didn't have to even try when they gave you arms training. You just strolled out there on the arena and your opponents didn't stand a chance, am I right?"

Taken aback, I answer honestly. "Close combat is the one thing that comes naturally to me."

She lets out a short laugh, full of contempt, but I can't tell if the derision is of me, or her, or something else entirely. "So you've never failed anything. But now you're facing it, you're terrified. Most of us didn't grow up in the imperial capital, living prettily perfumed lives. Some of us have to live every day with The Fear." She makes it sound like each word deserves its own sentence.

"The Fear?" I venture.

"The Fear that there may never be anything else. That we're nothing and will always be nothing. That no matter how hard we work, how dedicated we are, we'll never escape our lot. Does that stop me hoping? Taking the long odds? No."

She snatches up her own pack. "And you know what, Shield?"

"What?" I ask, tone subdued.

"It would make it a hell of a lot easier if you tried something other than sitting there sniffing your own stink." With that, she turns on her heel.

"Where are you going?"

"To *wash* if you must know. I can't think like this, caked in dust and sweat and the rat stink of that cell." Her shoulders slump. "And I can still smell smoke in my hair, in *this*." She plucks at the nightdress she's been wearing since we left.

"I understand, but—"

"I'll go just around the next bend."

I shake my head. "No. We should stay within sight of each other."

"I have no interest in putting on a show for you."

"Believe me, I have no interest in watching."

She glares at me, fire sparking in her eyes. Then she stomps off toward the bend in the canyon wall.

I watch her go, bewildered in the wake of her conviction.

Somewhere between our makeshift camp and her destination, she stops at the edge of the pool. It's short of leaving sight. Only barely, but still.

She sits on a boulder and I prepare to turn away so that I won't notice her unweaving her hair from its travel-stained wrap. And I certainly don't pay any attention when she sets aside her cloak, revealing arms banded by the sun like the sandstone of the canyon walls. And there's no way I'm going to watch as she slips from her tattered, ash-smudged nightdress . . .

There's a loud snort and pointed stomp behind me. I swing around to find a black muzzle inches from my face, teeth bared.

"What?" I ask, holding up my hands.

Rakel's horse slowly, deliberately, turns her back on me.

✻ ✻
✻ ✻
✻

I spend the morning with whetstone and oil in hand, working out the nicks and hairline notches in every blade I possess. I move on to inspecting my armor, but the servant who oiled it while I was drugged after the hunt did it so well it doesn't need any work.

In between, I scout. I'm checking the canyon rim for the third time, wondering how long a bath can take a person, when Rakel finally returns, wearing her hair in a braid and a damp smock shirt over loose leather trousers.

"Better?" I ask.

"Much better." She smiles. Actually smiles, one of her teeth snagging ever so slightly on her bottom lip. I'm surprised to find it disarming.

Despite myself, I smile back. "Only Kaismap knows how you fit so many things in that pack of yours."

"What do you mean?"

"Your new attire."

"This old thing? It's just my nightdress washed and hemmed." Her smile turns mischievous. "I used part of the offcuts on the belt, otherwise there was no way these were staying up."

I peer closely at the trousers. "Hang on. Are those my—"

"It was very generous of you to loan them. Thank you. Now if you'll excuse me, I'm going to check on my horse."

We rest in shifts through the afternoon, though I can only manage a fitful doze. At sunset, we share a meal of dried figs, the last of the coarse barley bread, and a slice of oversalted Aphorain cheese. The stars seem slower to appear than normal—watching the dusk sky when your next move depends on it is like waiting for an oil burner to steam.

Eventually, Rakel points. "There, see? Between the fox and the lion. Nothing."

The two constellations are in different parts of the sky from where they usually hang over Ekasya at this point in the starwheel's turn. But it's always easy to spot Kal—the milky patch of the gods' realm where the scholars say there are more stars than the eye can see. It's edged in seven brighter points, curving from the snowfox's curious nose, along its back to the sweep of its tail.

I move behind Rakel and follow the guiding line of her arm. The sparkle of the stars at the tips of Tozran the lion's feathered wings come into view. Between them is a distinct patch of dark sky.

She squints back at her necklace. "Some map. What are these stars meant to be? A constellation that appears at a different time of night? Or in the day? Or something else all together? Direction marker? A message? And where is this stinkin' lost library in all of it?"

My mind casts back to her sketch in the dust, the line she drew like a letter *w* to connect them. Something tickles at my thoughts like an unreachable itch.

The way of the stars.

"It's the canyon!"

"What?"

I reach for her locket. "May I?"

She hesitates a moment, then hands it to me.

"When I was keeping a lookout today, up on the rim, I got the lay of the land. There's a branch of the canyon that curves in exactly the same way as a line drawn between those five extraneous stars."

"Are you sure? Which way?"

"Farther south. We should be able to backtrack until the branches diverge, then follow the other until we reach this marker. If I'm right, two days at most. I can hardly believe the Library would be so close."

Rakel shrugs. "As good a place as any. There's no caravan trail, you can't grow crops. The only place you'd be getting closer to is the borderlands, and heading there without a death wish is kind of like sitting on a sand-stinger nest to avoid being bitten. Why would anyone strike out into the desert in the direction of nothing?"

Curiosity, comes Nisai's voice in my mind.

"Desperation, more like it," I mutter.

"Sorry?"

"Exploration. That's why someone might come out here. To learn something."

She nods, expression thoughtful. "I suppose I could understand that."

We gather our things and set out.

Other than a few short breaks, we walk all night. When the sun invades the gorge the next day, we rest beneath an outcrop, tense and barely saying a word. At times, the canyon floor is sand, the walls wide, so that Rakel can ride and I can keep pace beside her horse. When the canyon narrows so that there's only the barest sliver of sky overhead, I take the lead and we walk in single file. Not long before the next dawn, when the sky illuminates to a gradually paling blue, I call a halt.

Beside me, Rakel pulls her horse up and slides to the ground, tying off the reins. "Don't wander far," she tells the mare, who immediately lowers her head, closes her eyes, and bends one foreleg to rest it on the tip of a hoof. Useful skill, being able to sleep on command.

Rakel shoulders her satchel and peers ahead. I follow her gaze. Around the bend in the canyon, the cliffs are in shadow. It's a dead end.

But there's something precise about one line in the rock, something that seems intentional rather than the result of natural erosion. Or it could just be my imagination.

"Stay there," I tell Rakel quietly. "I'll scout ahead."

Keeping my back pressed against the canyon wall, I edge closer. If there does happen to be anything here, I need to assess how well it's defended. I unsheathe a knife, angling the blade to mirror around the bend.

It's deserted. Silent.

So far, so good. I creep closer.

At the dead-end cliff face, I discover my hunch is right. There's a pathway, barely as wide as my shoulders, that veers sharply to the right so that it's completely disguised from anywhere else in the canyon. I hesitate. The gap becomes a tunnel a few paces in, and the remains of several rockfalls are piled up around it. Who knows how stable the rest is. But it can't stretch on for too long—there's light beckoning beyond the gloom.

I take a deep breath, set my jaw, and venture onward.

Thirty, forty, fifty paces with my chin ducked to my chest and I'm emerging, blinking, into a circular ravine, the floor littered with rocks and long-dead vegetation the wind and seasons have deposited down here.

Another dead end.

"Well, dunk me in a tanner's vat and call me Pong," Rakel breathes next to me.

I turn on her. "I thought I told you to stay back there?"

"You did. And?"

I scowl.

"Look." She points. "Under that branch of flood wood. Is that a flagstone?"

"Who would pave a dead-end ravine?"

Hands on hips, Rakel stares up at the facade. "I don't have the faintest whiff. What I'm more interested in is who lives there now."

"Shall we go find out?"

I needn't have bothered asking. The words have barely left my mouth and she's already leaping ahead. I shake my head and start after her.

Then I notice them. I'd first thought they were rocks that had tumbled from the cliffs over the turns. But rocks don't bleach white like that. And they certainly don't have two dark holes where eyes used to be.

"Rakel!" I bark. "Stop!"

She turns around, annoyance pinching her features, her feet still moving backward. "Come on! I can see an opening from here. This has to be it!"

"Seriously, Rakel. Don't move."

Her posture goes rigid. But she's off balance. She teeters for a heart-beat, then stumbles back onto the flagstone behind her.

It sinks beneath her weight with a sharp, mechanical click.

CHAPTER 21
RAKEL

S tay still and look around you." Ash's words are low and quiet, his gentle tone reminding me of my own, back when I was first training Lil.

It stops me quicker than any haughty command.

Without shifting my weight, I cast about me. There. The telltale lines of a rib cage. And there? Is that the curve of a skull? A *human* skull? And why are they only in a few places? As if they'd collected in front of that opening in the rock only a few more paces from where I'm standing—

Oh.

Oh, oh, *oh.*

I could slap myself across the nose. Sideways.

If this truly is the Library of the Lost, it's of course going to have defenses. A place that lasted through centuries of spilled blood between the small kingdoms of old, a place that survived the Shadow Wars, doesn't persevere by letting you stroll up and wander straight in. Particularly the kind of place that legend says preserves every written work since written work began. Even texts the Empire has since outlawed. *Especially* texts the Empire has outlawed.

"Ash?" I call, voice hesitant.

The scrape of rock against rock grates in my ears. Then there's a grunt and a muttered curse.

"Ash!"

"Just hold on." His voice comes from off to the side. "I've got a plan."

He appears before me again, rolling a boulder along the exact same path I'd taken. "I'm going to wager that mechanism isn't hooked up to a welcome mat. And, given that we don't know what it *is* connected to, I'd greatly prefer we replace you with this." He eyes the rock critically. "Appears about the right size."

"*About* the right size? That's how confident you are?"

"I've been measuring opponents on the training field for over half my life. You're going to have to trust my judgment. Now, if this setup is what I'm thinking it is, we'll need to time it exactly. When I say, and not before—jump onto the flagstone I'm standing on. Don't go too early. Equally, this isn't a time to start hesitating."

"Got it."

"On three, then?"

I nod, dropping my hands to my sides, balancing my weight across both feet.

"One . . ."

If I managed to get myself here in one leap, surely I can get myself back again. But fear has made the pavers seem bigger than excitement did.

"Two . . ."

I wish I could shuffle closer to the edge of the sunken stone, but I don't dare.

"Three!" With a final grunt of effort, Ash tips the boulder onto the lowered flagstone.

I jump.

Both my boots land on the next stone.

Nothing happens.

Ash reaches out to steady me, and I grab for his arm. "Thank you."

"Don't thank me, thank my 'pretty' life in the palace. I'd never have learned about architectural defenses otherwise."

I resist the urge to roll my eyes at him.

With a new sense of caution, we pick our way toward the gap in the cliff face, testing each stone with the press of a foot before moving our full weight. When we're close, I catch sight of a line of spears arrayed in carved holes in the rock, as if ready to launch. Their tips are made of something resembling blue-black glass, the points cruelly barbed.

I look back down the path we've picked out. Sure enough, Ash's boulder is directly in line with the spearheads. I swallow. Human pincushion—not a way I'd like to go.

Ash only has eyes for the spears.

"What is it?" I ask.

"This glossy stone," he says. "I've only ever seen it in one other place. In the Council chambers in the Ekasya palace."

"You think that means something?"

"I don't know."

I peer inside the opening in the rock. It's dark. Really dark.

Careful not to step beyond the path we've already taken, I scoop up a bleached thigh bone. "Sorry," I apologize to the skeleton as sinewy bits stretch and snap, sending other bones to the ground with an unnerving rattle.

I retrieve the remnants of my old nightgown from my satchel and tie a few of them around one end of the bone, then smear them with a little yeb balm. It's not as flammable as krilmair, but even if I had any of that stuff, I wouldn't want to be carrying a flaming glob of it into a creepy tunnel full of stench knows what. And yeb balm smells sweeter.

Ash crouches beside me, gathering a handful of pebbles. He tosses one through the tunnel entrance. It clatters once, twice, three times across the rock floor. Then nothing.

I hand him the torch and glance back up the canyon to where Lil rests. I don't like leaving her, but I'd rather do that than risk her getting hurt—or worse—in here.

Inside, the tunnel has been lined with huge blocks of unadorned stone. It twists and turns in sinuous curves that remind me of the garden labyrinth Sephine used to walk. If she were here now, she'd have to crouch low—Ash stoops to not hit his head.

He runs a palm along the wall, the torchlight flickering over the stylized claws inked on the back of his hand. "Only Kaismap knows what the architect of this place had going through their mind."

The path spirals gently but steadily downward. I lose count of how many times we throw and retrieve the pebbles.

We emerge into a huge chamber, easily as big as an entire wing of the Aphorain palace. Pillars flare up from the floor, crossing over one another before joining the stone high up the walls. Sconces attached to the pillars are lit with some sort of alchemical fire that lends the vast space a greenish hue and smells completely alien. It's unnerving.

On the far side of the vaulted chamber is the largest statue I've ever seen, a massive figure sitting on a simple throne, carved from the rock wall behind. It's so big I need to crane my neck to take it all in. One hand rests palm-up on a leg, the other lies facedown. There's nothing to indicate gender, the huge chest slender but flat, no beard, head carved smooth as a freshly shaved scalp. No crown or jewelry. None of the trappings of any of the gods.

My breath catches when I look farther up. The ceiling is higher than any I've ever seen. It's made of the same blue-black glass-like substance as the spears at the entrance. But this is one single, magnificent piece, dotted with silver in what seems like an irregular pattern until I recognize the points of the horns in the aurochs constellation.

It's the starwheel in the night sky.

A woman's triumphant voice echoes across the chamber. "Here they are. I knew it! Pay up!"

"Shhh!" someone else hisses.

Ash shoulders past me and draws his swords, the blades shining in the strange light.

Two figures appear. They move toward us on silent feet, the toes of soft leather slippers peeking from the hem of their plain linen robes. They both wear their gray hair in a single plait down to the waist. As they near, their faces reveal the deep lines of age, and the scent of orange and cinnamon wafts from the simple pomanders hanging around their necks—the only adornment they're wearing.

"Sheer luck," the woman's companion says. He points at me. "There isn't a semblance of self-control in this one. Hardly a worthy wager."

The woman leans to the side to catch my eye, completely unconcerned with the sight of an armed Shield before her. "Don't mind Akred. These days he's outnumbered and that makes him grumpy."

The man scowls. "In case protocol has escaped your memory, all visitors must be escorted to the Archivist *immediately* upon arrival."

His companion sighs. "Stickler." She sweeps an arm back in the direction they arrived. "If you'd be so kind as to follow us. And you can put those away, young man."

I glance to Ash as we fall into step behind our escort. He's wide-eyed. Seems even someone who lives in the imperial palace can be awestruck.

"Are you sure we're in the right place?" I murmur.

He nods. "I've spent enough time in libraries to know when I'm in one. Nisai and Esarik are going to be beside themselves when they hear they've missed this."

Guess the legendary Library is *kind of* impressive.

Doors line the walls of the chamber. There must be dozens. Maybe more. Identically attired figures, almost all of them women, hurry soundlessly between them. Some bear armloads of tablets and cylinders. Others carry clusters of pale yellow candles—their wicks left long and braided together as handles—or trays of small pots and reed styluses. Everyone appears to have seen more turns than Old Maz, who could remember when my village was nothing but an oasis and a couple of huts.

Somewhere in the distance, there's a muffled echo of thuds. The sound comes in rhythmic bursts, like hammering, the impact vibrating the stone under my feet. I look up to the impossibly high ceiling, trying not to think of the sheer weight of the cliffs above us.

The friendlier of our escorts smiles. "Safeguarding the written word—law or literature—takes space. Don't fret, we've been expanding the Library for centuries. The Delvers may be our youngest members, but they know their craft."

Her companion huffs. "If only they could figure out how to do it quietly. Terrible imposition on serious study."

By the time we reach the far side of the vaulted hall, we've gathered a following, so that a small crowd gathers before a platform at the feet of the huge statue. There sits an elderly woman at a desk of blue-black glass, piled high with scrolls. She wears the same robes and is as wan as everyone else in here, as if they haven't seen the sun for half their lives.

"Archivist, we have visitors," our grumpy guide announces.

The woman at the desk doesn't look up. Her stylus scratches across a parchment before her, moving faster than the scribbles of an Aphorain auctioneer. "Thank you, that will be all."

Our escorts nod in unison.

"She is all," the friendly woman says.

"He is all," the testy man says.

Curious.

Ash steps forward. "Archivist, is it? We're grateful for this audience. I serve as Shield to First Prince Nis—"

She peers down her long nose at him. "I'm old, my boy. Not ignorant. Your ink has already announced you."

Her voice is high, and she speaks in rapid bursts like a chattering bird. "However, I'm afraid we haven't been a *public* library for nigh on a millennium. Third century pre-Accord. Though I suppose we didn't truly close our doors until the end of the Great Bloom. After those lofty heights of debate and inquiry, everyone was looking for a shortcut, not willing to put in the work to hone true expertise. I

152

remember one young man walked in our door not long after I was elevated to my current position—before we took those measures you encountered—marched right up to the catalogs and *dared* to lay his *gloveless* hands on—"

The male Chronicler who first met us clears his throat.

"What's that, Akred? You have something to contribute? I'm struggling to deduce how fifth-century Losian architecture could enhance our guests' understanding of the situation. Do enlighten me if you've been developing another specialism relevant to the conversation at hand?"

He looks at his slippers.

"As I thought! Young people today," she grumbles. "Seen eighty or ninety turns and they think they're knowledgeable. Well then, where were we? Oh yes. If your young Prince is missing something in the imperial collection, I suggest he dispatch you elsewhere. We reside here in the business of preservation, not loans."

And with that, she goes back to her parchment.

The dozen or so Chroniclers that had gathered around us begin to murmur, a pair of them wandering off.

I step closer to the platform and lift my necklace over my head. If we've got anything that will interest this woman, surely a map to her precious Library will spark her curiosity. Stretching on tiptoes, I reach up and drop it on the desk.

Her stylus stills. She sets it aside and picks up my locket, turning it over in her palm. "How do you know Sephine? Is she here?"

Relief washes through me, if only for a small part of myself to drown in it. It's true, then. My locket *was* the Scent Keeper's gift. Had she forced Father to have me wear it? And why didn't he tell me?

I clear my throat "I was her . . . I was Sephine's . . ." I can't bring myself to say "servant."

"Was?" she asks, suddenly intent on the point at hand.

I guess there's no point in waving a stick of incense around if you're not going to light it. "Sephine's dead."

153

The Archivist recoils as if I'd slapped her. "When exactly did her death occur?"

I lost track of time when I was locked up, but it's not like I want to blurt that out. This woman already seems like a hard sell, no need to add accused criminal into the bargain. "The night before the Flower Moon."

Her expression goes flat. "Then there's nothing to be done. One of my Chroniclers will escort you out. They'll provide sultis for you to ingest along the way."

Chew sultis leaf? In the sixth hell I will. My memory's staying right where it is. "You don't care about finding out how a Scent Keeper was poisoned?"

"I have more pressing concerns."

Ash stiffens. "More pressing concerns than preventing the Empire from erupting into civil war?"

"I doubt the veracity of that hypothesis. The Founding Accord has endured longer than any other political arrangement in history. Even if one includes the longer periods of peace between the small kings, nothing comes close. While the current Emperor doesn't care for Scent Keepers, his influence is nothing more than a grain of sand in the desert—necessary, but inconsequential, to the whole. The diplomatic ripples of Sephine's death will soon be nothing more than marginalia on a scroll."

"Perhaps," Ash says. "But there was another victim. First Prince Nisai."

The Archivist's white eyebrows arch so high they almost disappear into her hairline. "The Prince is dead?"

"He's unconscious, but alive." I grimace. "At least he was when we left."

Ash shoots me a dark look. "We've reason to believe there might be information on what ails him, and how to counteract it, here in your Library."

"Sephine thought so," I add. "She sent me here with her last words."

I still can't understand half of what I'm caught up in, or what kind of pawn I was in the elaborate plan the Scent Keeper had been distilling. But all I can think of is the way she spoke with her last breaths, her lips stained with black blood.

The Archivist folds her hands primly, pallid skin stretched over blue veins. "We serve Asmudtag—"

Ash glowers. "You turn away from the true gods in favor of an ancient idol?"

"We prefer 'primordial deity.' Asmudtag is a being of balance. Asmudtag is all. Any gender or other trait we assign is our own human foible," the Archivist says sniffily.

There's now two dozen or more Chroniclers gathered and hanging on her every word, and each time another wanders into the main chamber from one of the wheel-spoke halls they're drawn to the Archivist's platform, bringing with them a cloud of cinnamon and orange, dust and ink. They seem harmless, yet I can't help but tighten my hand around my satchel strap.

We're surrounded.

The Archivist gestures expansively. "It's true we revere the same deity. However, the Scent Keepers meddle in the political affairs of the Empire, while we Chroniclers decided centuries ago to keep the Library outside such pettiness. Whatever games the temple and the palace are playing in Aphorai, it isn't our concern. Perhaps it's time the capital let that territory secede from the Empire. Who can say?"

Ash steps up to my shoulder. "The Emperor. And the Commander of the Imperial Rangers. Prince Iddo is hunting for the perpetrator, and he'll have the Rangers scour every inch of Aramtesh until he apprehends the culprit. Your Library won't be lost for long."

"Pah!" a Chronicler shouts. "The entrance is concealed."

"To a caravan trader, perhaps. To the Empire's best trackers?" Ash smiles slowly. It's all teeth, and I'm suddenly, uncomfortably, reminded he's a trained killer.

The Archivist regards us over indignant murmurs and the shuffling of slippered feet. "Tell me what you've observed."

I recount the night before the Flower Moon, from when I first smelled smoke to being thrown in the dungeons. Ash fills in the gaps. Somewhere in the middle of our story, the Archivist pulls her long white braid over one shoulder, stroking it like it's a bizarre pet.

When we're done, she turns her stylus over and over in her fingers.

"Where I and my predecessors dedicated themselves to the preservation of knowledge, the Scent Keepers developed alchemical traditions, using scentlore to unlock intrinsic abilities within themselves. Sephine was the most senior and skilled in the Empire. If she couldn't save that young man, nobody could. I appreciate your dedication to your Prince. I do. As far as rulers go, what we've read of him speaks of great potential. But I cannot help you."

On her last words, she weaves her stylus into her braid. What is *with* this woman constantly playing with her hair?

"You mean you *won't* help us," Ash grates from between clenched teeth.

"If it gives you comfort to frame it as such, so be it. Now, if you'll excuse me, I—"

Akred steps forward, producing several scrolls from the voluminous sleeve of his robe. "Archivist, this is all very entertaining, but I'm still waiting for your approval of the minutes from the most recent meeting of the Committee for Pre-Imperial Parchment-Eating Fungus Management meeting. We also await your signature on the latest resolution from the Arbitration Board for the Safe Return of 'Borrowed' Styluses."

"—have work to do," the Archivist sighs. "My assistant will show you out."

CHAPTER 22
ASH

Our escort—the Chronicler who first greeted us—nods toward the distant side of the vaulted cavern. "Follow me."

We cross the floor in silence, until the thud of the Delvers' distant excavating resumes. There's something not right here. If the Archivist is so keen to keep her operation a secret, why allow two intruders to be escorted out by one unarmed elderly woman?

We're led through one of the myriad doors lining the main chamber, Rakel the only one of us who doesn't have to stoop to avoid smacking their forehead on the lintel.

Out of sight and earshot of the others, the Chronicler's demeanor changes, affable openness replaced with hushed tones. "It was half a century ago, but my second specialism was poisons; I should still be able to navigate the collections. We must hurry—Akred will pontificate at the Archivist until he turns blue, but even that windbag will eventually deflate."

"What's the point?" Rakel snaps. "We'll forget everything when you dose us up with sultis on the way out."

"I'll not be doing that."

"Oh." Rakel almost manages to appear contrite. Almost. "But your boss made it plain as stink she wouldn't help."

The Chronicler folds her arms, pushing each hand into the opposite cuff of her robe.

"Her mouth said that, yes. Her signals said the opposite, and it's my role to follow those."

"Heh," Rakel says, now looking impressed. "So *that's* what all the fidgeting was about."

The older woman sighs. "The Archivist does what is needed to keep our people united. Some, like Akred, believe we should sever all contact with the outside world. His fear is not without foundation—there has been more than one Emperor in the last cycle who would have gladly had inconvenient documents destroyed." She spreads her hands. "But what is knowledge worth if it is not shared?"

Hope flares. If I've learned anything at court, it's that the actions of leaders don't always match their words. That sometimes they must say one thing when they mean another to keep things together.

"If your Prince really is the future ruler the initial reports show, perhaps we needn't continue to dwell here in secret. He could safeguard the Library and we could coexist with the new ways." She sighs. "Or perhaps that's a dream the Archivist and I should have long woken from."

I press my palms together respectfully. "We truly would appreciate any assistance. As would Prince Nisai, I'm certain."

"If you could show me a sample of the poison, it would make the search swifter."

Rakel rummages in her satchel and holds out a vial of green-black liquid.

I've never seen poison, but this matches what I'd imagined, thick and viscous against the faceted glass of its container, a strange symbol carved into the stopper.

Every muscle in my body stills.

She had this all along? And didn't say anything? Why would she hide it?

Doubt creeps through me, fear breathing down its neck. I made the wrong decision, didn't I? The single time I act beyond the bounds of my role, this is what happens. I should have done my duty. Should have apprehended her and returned to Aphorai when I had the chance.

Should act now, if there's any chance of salvaging the situation.

I'm about to grab Rakel by the arm, when she hands the vial to the Chronicler. "Sephine dropped it in her last moments."

The older woman holds the vessel out at arm's length.

"It's sealed. I made sure of it."

"Some would say this is poison, in its own way," the Chronicler says. "It's the elixir of the Scent Keepers. The key to their ability to channel the will of Asmudtag—healing those that would be lost to any other intervention by taking the ailment into themselves. You can see it in their eyes—the more a Scent Keeper has healed, the more of her own light she's sacrificed."

"Could they use it to make someone sick?" Rakel crosses her arms, tone skeptical.

I shift my weight from the balls of my feet, poised and ready to move, back to my heels. Unless she is a better actor than the palace theater players, it seems Rakel knew barely anything about the vial.

"I've not seen any documented cases. The only accounts of related deaths describe an apprentice failing to survive the first absorption. Sadly, most fail. Even those who survive tend to have their minds . . . addled. I'm not the first and won't be the last to imagine what the Empire would have been if that weren't the case . . ." She sounds nostalgic, almost whimsical, as her eyes take on a faraway look.

"This isn't what poisoned your Prince, it's what Sephine used to halt the effects of the poison, taking more of it into herself than she was capable of absorbing." She hands the vial back to Rakel. "But without a sample of the toxin, it makes it difficult to deduce what class of poison was used, let alone the exact formula. Proceeding without all the information would be . . . How do they express it in contemporary parlance? It's to throw dice with the Lost God."

The blasphemy grates, but I keep my feelings hidden. "How so?"

"One poison's antidote is another's accelerator. Ignorance could be deadly."

I run my fingers over my stubbled scalp and exhale loudly. So much risked, so much forfeited, and we're back where we started. A theory about what the problem could be, and no convincing ideas of how to solve it.

I force my voice to evenness. "A friend had a theory that the poison's origin could be ancient. There was a particular symptom: lines of, well, darkness, spreading in and around the Prince's eyes. Like . . ."

"Sephine?"

"No, not like a Scent Keeper, more as if . . ."

The Chronicler's brows pinch together. "Was there a fever?"

"Not discernably."

"Strange," she muses. Then her eyes light up. "It could be nothing, but . . ." She trails off and strides away toward one of the carved stone halls.

Rakel frowns, and I motion for us to follow the Chronicler. The older woman's cerebral vagueness makes me think of Esarik. I wonder what he's made of my disappearance. I hope he would understand. I hope *Nisai* would understand.

Deep in the bedrock, the Chronicler turns into a side corridor that opens out into another chamber. It's narrower and plainly designed compared to the main hall but stretches back until it disappears in shadow. We pass shelf after carved-sandstone shelf, the first ones stacked high with new-looking scroll cylinders inlaid with familiar mother-of-pearl phoenixes against Ekasya obsidian.

"Keeping a closer eye on current politics than your Archivist would have us think?"

"We collect from every era," the Chronicler replies mildly.

We pass a small desk at which the first young Chronicler I've noticed hunches over a tattered manuscript, piecing it together with fine pincers. "That's coming along nicely," our guide notes, giving the younger woman a nod of approval.

Farther still, we arrive at a rack of tablets. The Chronicler counts silently down them, her lips and fingers moving. "Ah yes," she says, satisfied. "Here. Second century pre-Accord."

Rakel's eyes widen. "People wrote back then?"

I suppress a smile. For someone so streetwise, she can be unexpectedly naive.

"The written word is far more ancient than imperial doctrine would have you believe," the Chronicler explains as she pulls on one of the racks. It glides smoothly into the aisle on a track embedded in the floor. I make a mental note to share the idea with Ami if I ever see the Ekasya library again.

"Let's see," our guide begins, *"Emoran's Law Code. The Epic of Saryad. Enib's Descent into the Underworld.* Yes, here it is."

She blows dust from a cylinder, revealing dull yellow beneath.

Rakel gives a slow, disbelieving headshake.

It's made of solid gold. Engraved lettering runs down its length, the script so sweeping and elaborate it could only be Old Imperial. *The Dance of Death.*

Reverently, the Chronicler removes the parchment from the cylinder and unrolls it inch by careful inch. "I first came across this when I was cataloging as an acolyte. Your friend is correct—the poison itself is pre-Imperial, from the time of the small kings. Blackvein, they called it. I'm sure I don't have to explain the etymology. This particular account suffers from the paranoia of the time, and a Scent Keeper's predilection for the archaic and aphoristic, but what it distills down to—so to speak—is the formula."

I frown.

"A recipe," Rakel whispers.

"Obviously. But what use is knowing the ingredients of the poison when we've already identified it as the one threatening Nisai?"

"Ah," the Chronicler says, tapping her temple. "In this case, the poison and its antidote have the same ingredients." She clears her throat and begins to read:

When Riker's heart faced the eternal plight
The sky was devoured and the Twins' lives sown
When Azered's bones danced in the breath of blight
Esiku's first children were turned to stone
When the darkness bloomed across Kaismap's night—

The young Chronicler we passed earlier hurries between the shelves toward us, out of breath. "You're here, thanks be to Asmudtag. Chronicler, you're needed. Please, there's trouble."

The older woman nods. "Wait here."

As soon as she has disappeared around the shelves, Rakel rolls up the parchment.

"That's an important historical document." I gape at her as she scrunches the priceless artifact into her satchel.

"And we'll be an ink blot on an important historical document if we don't cure your Prince."

"You're a thief!"

"I prefer the term 'discerning borrower.' We can return it . . . someday." She peers around the edge of the shelf and motions for me to follow.

She's right, we need the scroll, but I can imagine Nisai's dismay if he knew what we were desecrating in his name. "He'll be horrified," I mutter.

"Your Prince? He's into this kind of thing?"

I keep my voice as low as I can, even though there's no sign of the Chronicler or the acolytes among the shelves as we pass. "He'd live in a library if he had things his way."

"Surely the First Prince does what he wants."

"His life is the Empire's, not his own. They'd have him reviewing petitions and hosting receptions every waking hour if they could."

"But you at least know your way around a library, I'm guessing?"

"More or less."

"Right, then. Find us a way out of here."

I venture out into the side corridor, pausing at the junction with the main hall. The Chroniclers have scattered, scurrying across the floor like ants when their nest is disturbed.

"What's going on?" Rakel asks.

"Kaismap only knows. But something's got them spooked."

Figuring the best way out is the way we came, I begin to retrace our steps back to the main chamber. Our guide intercepts us along the way, her wrinkled cheeks pink and her robes scrunched in one hand so she doesn't trip on the hem.

"Our sentries report a group of soldiers entering the next branch of the canyon."

I tense. Rangers. They've tracked us.

"Quickly, you must go."

I don't have to be told twice.

We sprint for the entrance, our boots boomingly loud compared to the Chroniclers' slippers. We run headlong up the winding path, the still-healing wounds in my side protesting as I suck in larger and larger breaths. At the entrance, I throw an arm up to shield my eyes, momentarily blinded in the sunlight.

Rakel edges ahead of me, threading her way along the safe route through the rigged-up flagstones, toward the concealed entrance to this part of the gorge. Back in the main branch of the canyon, she sticks her fingers in her mouth and lets out a shrill whistle. The sound reverberates around the cliffs.

I groan. It would have been heard a mile away.

Then there are hoofbeats, and the black mare canters into sight. The three of us work our way along the base of the cliff until we find a path wide enough for the horse to climb out of the canyon. I admire the beast's courage as its hooves slide in the scree. At the top, I raise my arms over my head, catching my breath from the steep ascent.

Rakel climbs into the saddle and sniffs the air.

"What is it?" I ask.

"Sandstorm."

I follow her line of sight. Sure enough, the horizon is a blur of yellow-brown. A chill runs through me despite the heat of the midday sun. I've never seen a sandstorm, but I've heard enough tales of the abrading winds, of travelers blinded and flayed raw by the grit, of whole caravans buried, only to be uncovered a generation later by treasure hunters.

I cast about, realizing I've become completely turned around in this godsforsaken desert. "Which direction is that?"

Rakel grimaces. "South."

Oh, that's just priceless. My sense of direction may be off, but I've seen enough maps to comprehend that avoiding the storm will take us back toward Aphorai City. Into the path of even more of Iddo's scouting parties. Just when we might have the hint of a solution for Nisai.

I swallow hard and turn back to Rakel. "You know this land better than me. Got any ideas?"

She points toward the swirling wall of sand moving inexorably toward us. "That way."

"Have you lost your senses?"

"Maybe. But if you want those Rangers off our tail, that's your best bet."

I shake my head. "There's no way I'm going near that thing."

"Suit yourself." She nudges her horse with her heels. "May your gods keep you, Shield."

Then she's off, galloping headlong into the storm.

CHAPTER 23
RAKEL

He doesn't know I saw it.
But I did.

Back in the Library. That look on his face when I showed Sephine's vial to the Chronicler. The suspicion in his eyes. The way it all played out across his features until his hands were twitching, like he wanted to grab me and march us back to Aphorai City, or worse still, to the capital.

So eager to blame. So ready to think ill of my intentions.

So much like Barden.

He can keep his holier-than-holy view of the world. Let him run back to his fancy imperial friends and try to explain why he was even out here with me in the first place. I couldn't care a whiff.

"I work just fine on my own," I mutter.

Lil tosses her head.

"Yes, girl, I mean *we* work just fine together."

This isn't my first sandstorm. Doesn't mean my nerves don't fray as I ride straight into its path. The rumble grows louder and louder—thunder that doesn't pause for breath. Over that, the wind wails, like the ghosts of a hundred women screaming their frustration and fury.

At least my mood matches the weather.

A rocky outcrop lies ahead, where the dunes rise well clear of the canyon. Couldn't have asked for a better spot. I steer Lil toward the rock, giving her the reins. My hair begins to tug free of my braid and whip around my face. Overhead, the sun darkens, obscured by the raging clouds of dust and debris.

"Hold!" I call when we reach the rock. Lil's hooves slide through the sand and come to an abrupt stop. I dismount and undo her saddle straps, willing my fingers to work faster as the first grit of the storm bites.

"Down, girl," I say as reassuringly as I can. She folds her legs, lying pressed against the rock. I unfurl her saddlecloth and tent it over her back. She shifts her weight to help me tuck it under her bulk. It's not Lil's first sandstorm, either.

I'm preparing to crawl in beside her, when I see him. The Shield. Running across the dunes on a collision course with the storm.

Of all the putrid, fuming stenches under the stars, what is that boy *thinking*?

Guess he isn't. He grew up in the imperial capital, surrounded by green fields, without enough desert experience to even know not to eat akrol melon.

He hasn't spotted us. Part of me wants to let him keep going, the part of me that only wants to see him as a cog in the imperial machine.

But no matter what he thinks of me, I need him. It only took one glance at the scents-be-damned parchment in my satchel to realize I couldn't read it. Even if I did manage to put this antidote together, I don't know how to get it to the Prince without landing straight back in the dungeons.

And if I'm trapped in some dark hole under someone's palace, what then? If I never made it home, how long would Luz keep her side of the bargain? An image of Father comes to mind, his flesh rotting higher and higher, past the point anything can halt. Would our neighbors prepare his body to be sent to the sky like he'd wish? Or would they be too scared to go anywhere near a corpse consumed by Rot?

Sand lashes around the outcrop, hard enough to sting me from my thoughts, though not with enough force to scour the skin from my flesh.

Yet.

I *have* to get the Shield's attention.

There's no way I'll be able to shout loud enough to be heard over the storm bearing down on us—the only thing I'd gain is a gob full of grit.

I pull the last scraps of my old nightdress from my satchel. Wetting them from my waterskin, one gets tied around my forehead in case I need to swiftly cover my eyes, the other over my nose and mouth. I retrieve the yeb balm I'd used for a torch at the Library and push another strip of cloth deep into the jar of flammable paste.

This could go wrong. So wrong.

Crouched in the shelter of the outcrop, I use my flint to shoot sparks onto the cloth. The moment it catches alight, I toss it to the top of the outcrop and dive for cover.

I wait one, two, three breaths.

Nothing.

Stink on a stick. Did the wind blow out the flame?

Boom!

The explosion makes the storm a background hum. Lil rears. I lunge for her bridle. She snorts and paws the ground as shards of rock rain down on us. I catch the briefest scent of tangy smoke before the wind snatches it away.

If the Shield didn't notice that, he's beyond saving.

I peer around the side of the outcrop. Oh, he noticed. He sprints toward the promise of shelter, one arm up to shield his eyes.

Then we're both scrambling for cover.

Inside the makeshift tent, everything is black. Lil's head rests in my lap. I wrap one hand around her bridle while the other strokes her neck.

I'm all too aware of Ash pressed against my side, his scent a mix of sandalwood and the cedar I oiled his armor with back in Aphorai. Underneath, there's an annoyingly appealing hint of something akin to galbanum—earthy and green and musky in equal measure.

161

Thankfully the essential oils infusing his prayer band have faded to a murmur. I've never understood how anyone could stand wearing the scent of every god at once—they clash so badly it makes my stomach churn.

I can't see his face in the darkness, but his tense muscles tell me all I need to know. The last thing I can afford is his anxiousness agitating Lil.

"We'll be all right," I say, half to my horse, half to Ash. "It'll pass."

And it does. It just takes half the day.

When the wind leaves, it's as quick as an ungrateful guest. Lil rolls to her feet—eager to leave the stifling tent and straighten her neck. Her movement drags the saddlecloth down on Ash and me, and we're all flailing arms and clumsy feet as we try to fight our way free.

I muster what dignity I can, shaking out the cloth and throwing it over Lil's back. "Let's put some distance between us and them, eh?"

Ash nods grimly. "Let's."

We continue south, heading away from Aphorai and the main caravan routes. Not long before evening, I catch the scent of water. Sure enough, several dunes later I spot the green smudge of rock figs in the distance.

We make camp at the oasis. The pool at its center is smaller than the one at my village, and there isn't a dwelling in sight. Still, it's the closest thing I've seen to home in almost a moon, and I find myself equal parts heartsick and comforted as I feed Lil a handful of dried figs.

I chomp on one of the sweet fruits and regard Ash in the slanting rays of early evening. He's said barely a word since high sun.

I sigh. Better to lance this wound, otherwise it's just going to fester.

"I didn't do it," I say.

"Excuse me?"

"At the Library, all it took was a sniff of doubt about the vial of Scent Keeper elixir, and you were ready to condemn me."

"I didn't say—"

"No point in denying you thought it, that smoke's already gone to the sky. You need to make a choice. Either you believe me, or you don't. I had no part in what happened that night. I'll admit I had no warm feelings about . . . that woman, but I didn't want her dead. I don't want *anyone* dead. I don't want anyone even hurt. It's not who I am."

Ash leans back against the trunk of a palm, his face cast a deeper bronze by the sunset. "Back at the canyon, you said something about me being cosseted by palace life, of having no idea what it is to fear."

"And?"

He draws his knees to his chest and wraps his arms around his legs, seeming younger as he looks out over the oasis. "I didn't always live in the palace. There was a time, turns ago, when I didn't know where my next meal would come from, or if I'd survive to find out. Nisai saved me from that."

Huh. So this is as much loyalty as duty. Father always told me to remember the difference between the two—one is earned, the other is demanded.

"The Empire needs him. His father is dying. If Nisai dies, too, can you imagine the unrest that would follow? The provinces are already on the edge. You've seen it; Aphorai spares no love for the capital. But the thing is, nobody wins a war. Some people survive it, that's all. That's why I *am* afraid of something. Afraid of this"—he gestures around our camp—"whatever you call this thing we're doing. My fear is that this will be all for naught. That we won't find what we're looking for. That we'll be too late. That Nisai, at this very moment, is already lost to us."

His lips curl into a self-mocking expression, more snarl than smile. There's pain there. Raw, open pain. "You may not want to harm anyone, but I'm *trained* to kill. Back in Aphorai, I could have killed that lion. I should have killed it. If I'd fulfilled my duty, I wouldn't have been wounded; I'd have been by Nisai's side the night of the fire.

Whoever poisoned him wouldn't have been able to get near him. Then none of us—Nisai, you, me—would be in this mess.

"When you produced that vial, I did suspect you," he continues. Then he faces me, gaze locking to mine. "I was wrong. Whatever my apology is worth to you—I'm sorry."

My chest tightens with long-held grief. "I . . . I know what it's like to feel responsible for someone close to you to be . . . to be hurt."

Hurt? Hurt doesn't come close to the truth. My mother *died* from bringing me into this world. I can't do this. Not here, not now.

I clear my throat. "I'll tell you what else I know."

Ash raises his eyebrows, waiting.

"There's only one way out of this mess."

"And that is?"

"Through."

He nods in solemn agreement. "Through."

I hand him the scrunched scroll I'd stowed in my satchel. "Read me this formula again? It's written so flowery I can't tell sniffer from sitter."

CHAPTER 24
ASH

No wonder you couldn't read this," I tell Rakel. "It's Old Imperial." I smooth the parchment and hold it up to the fading light. It isn't the work of a single scribe. There are subtle differences in the hand, as if each line were written by someone new. I can decipher most of it, but I'm not as good at this as Nisai or Esarik.

I clear my throat and read aloud: *"When Riker's heart faced the eternal plight—"*

Rakel bursts into laughter.

"What?"

"Stop it already."

I raise a questioning eyebrow.

"Why are you putting on a Hagmiri accent?"

"I'm not."

"You are! Swallowing all your vowels like you left the mountains yesterday."

"That's how Old Imperial is spoken," I say tritely.

She has the decency to look abashed. "Oh."

"May I continue, supreme arbiter of all pronunciation?"

"You may," she sniffs.

I read:

> *When Riker's heart faced the eternal plight*
> *The sky was devoured and the Twins' lives sown*
> *When Azered's bones danced in the breath of blight*
> *Esiku's first children were turned to stone*
> *When the darkness bloomed across Kaismap's night . . .*

There's another line scrawled between the two stanzas. The ink is smudged in parts, as if whoever wrote it was rushed, or careless. But the surviving script is one I've never seen. That's if it even *is* script.

I stare down at the characters, my brow tightening. They're almost picture-like, at once foreign and strangely familiar. Perhaps they're just decoration? Some kind of illumination technique I've seen over Nisai's shoulder? Whatever they are, they're obviously not part of the main verse.

But the longer I scrutinize them, the more the designs seem to shift and swirl, as if they're smoke.

I blink once, twice.

The smoke returns to ancient ink on crumbling parchment.

Azered's breath, I must be tired.

It's then I realize I've gone more than a day without a dose. I retrieve the nondescript bottle from my pack and measure three drops onto my tongue. It's hideous enough in water, but straight up it tastes so vile I almost gag.

Thankfully, Rakel's not paying attention. She sits cross-legged, staring up into the rock figs, mumbling the first line of verse over and over. *"When the darkness bloomed in Kaismap's night. When the darkness bloomed."* Then she jerks to her feet.

"What is it?"

"The last thing Sephine said to me was 'the darkness will bloom again.' I figured she meant the dahkai plantation. That it could be saved."

"The dahkai?"

"The darkest bloom. It's what we call it in Aphorai."

"Because it only comes out on the Flower Moon—when both moons go dark at the same time?"

"Ah, mainly because it's black?"

I kick sand in the air. "Is everything going to lead us back to that godsforsaken city of yours?"

"It's not *my* city. And there's no point going back there. Maybe one or two of the bulbs survived, but the next Flower Moon is a generation away."

"Surely it grows somewhere else." But I already know the truth; I just don't want to believe it. Because that would mean the slimmest chance of saving Nisai went up in smoke before he even needed saving. "And if they are ingredients? How is that going to change the fact we've failed before we've begun?"

"Humor me."

I read out the section of the passage again.

"Bloomed," Rakel muses. "It's talking of something that's *already* happened. So if this is an ingredient list, it's not talking about the flower itself. Those must be harvested and processed immediately. They start rotting almost as soon as they've unfurled."

I double-check the scroll. "Past tense. That's correct."

"Right. Next line, then!"

"In case it had slipped your mind, the text suggests we need every single one of these things," I say, bitterness lacing my voice.

She rummages in her satchel and holds out a tiny blue bottle. "Good thing I had the presence of mind to bring this then, wasn't it?" She waggles her hand in front of me, clearly proud of herself.

I gape at her. "Is that . . . ?"

"Indeed. Dahkai essence."

"How did you get it?"

She shakes her head, expression wry. "It's a *long* story."

"We've got a long trip ahead of us."

"Then maybe I'll tell you. But first—is there anything else on the scroll?"

"There's a second stanza:

> *All must be pure and in sequence blown,*
> *If they are to serve both the dark and light,*
> *Only clouds will end what clouds have begun,*
> *The will of Asmudtag be ever done."*

"It sort of makes sense," she muses. "I've seen perfume formulas laid out line by line before. Ingredients, then method. 'Pure' is always a challenge, but if you're careful, a repeat distillation can usually do the trick. And then I guess 'clouds' means it needs to be evaporated? I don't know. I'll have to chew it over. In the meantime, though, we've at least got our list of ingredients, so let's focus on the next clue."

"The sky was devoured and the Twins' lives sown." Reading it aloud again triggers a memory—Nisai and Esarik debating points of history on the river barge. Thinking of their incessant intellectual

sparring makes something akin to grief swell in my chest. I shove it back down. "The Old Imperial name for the Hagmiri Mountains translates to something like 'the peaks that devour the sky.'"

Rakel's eyebrows shoot up. "Truly?"

"So a reliable source told me."

She grins. "Then I'd say that's as good a lead as any."

I shield my eyes, squinting as the sun descends behind the distant horizon. The Hagmiri Mountains. Any lead that takes us farther away from the Rangers is one I'm prepared to take, at least for now. "Agreed. We'll head for the mountains and search out this first ingredient. On the other side, there are villages and towns. Somewhere we'll be able to ask questions. Buy supplies. And a map."

"Sounds like a pla—" Her voice cuts off and she does a double take at me. "You left Aphorai without a *map*? Voluntarily?"

"I left in a hurry. I was coming after you. I wasn't intending on venturing far from Aphorai City, let alone leaving the province." The truth is, I didn't even think of it—I've seen enough maps in my time but never needed one to navigate for myself. I can almost hear Iddo's Squad Captain snickering. I turn away, a flush creeping up my neck—the heat of the shame a sharp reminder that it won't be long before I'll need to restock on Linod's Elixir. I add it to the mental list of things I'll need to find on the other side of the peaks.

Rakel shrugs. "Eh, maps are overrated when there's a fiery ball moving across the sky. If we keep our noses pointed south, we'll get where we're going." She gathers her things and mounts up. "But your Prince isn't getting any healthier while we stand around here."

It's a sobering reminder of the long road before us. And yet I find a tentative smile on my lips. Somehow, this girl has given me back one of the precious things I'd lost in the Aphorain fire.

Hope.

CHAPTER 25
RAKEL

The sky was devoured and the Twins' lives sown

There's good reason the Hagmiri Mountains used to be called "the peaks that devour the sky." We left the Aphorain desert three days ago to begin the climb into the foothills. Since, we've climbed and climbed and climbed—up ridge, down valley, up another ridge.

Then, fancy that, we climb some more.

My calves and thighs burn with effort whenever I give Lil a spell. Dunes and canyons keep you fit, but these slopes are something else altogether. I'd ask for a break, but I'd rather push through aching legs than the pain I'd face if the Rangers catch up with us. Even after a sandstorm, Ash says they would have our trail again now. Sure as stink on scat.

The slopes don't seem to bother Ash in the slightest—he keeps a steady pace, his breathing in time with his steps, face calm, impassive. Each time I change his dressings, I marvel at how quickly his wounds are healing. At this rate, his bandages will come off within days. Does it have something to do with whatever he keeps taking? Fancy medicine from the capital?

I skip a few steps to catch up to him. "What drug is it? Some kind of protective?"

"Excuse me?" he asks, almost too lightly.

"The way you heal. I've never seen anything like it. You're on something, aren't you?"

"Ugly habit."

I shrug. I'm not one to judge. "People do what they—"

"Ugly habit of *yours*—sticking your nose where it's not wanted." He strides ahead purposefully, then gives me a dismissive look over his shoulder. "Or needed."

I'm about to start after him when I hear Father's voice in my mind. *You get more with honeysuckle than bitter yolketh, Rakel.*

If only I had a zig for every time I've heard that. But thinking of Father, of the little time I have left to get back to him, reminds me of what's most important.

Ash can stew in his stinking mood until we find the cure, for all I care. One way or another, I'll figure out whatever it is he's taking. Because if it causes side effects or withdrawal symptoms, I want to be ready. Things are bad enough. Last thing I need is to be on the run with a Shield losing his mind.

We trek higher. The air cools and fills with moisture, so thick it seems you could close your hand around it. The vegetation begins to change, too. The resinous tang of conifer trees gives way to the honeyed pollen of dense kigtai forests. Barely any light penetrates the thick canopy, while springy moss grows underfoot.

Then there's the quiet.

It hangs over us, smothering the valleys. The higher we get, the more muted the world becomes. It's like nothing I've ever experienced or imagined. Even the scents seem muffled, the damp earth and decomposing leaves clogging each breath.

Eventually, we crest a ridge capped with exposed rock. Scrambling to the top reveals one of the most breathtaking views I've ever seen. A carpet of deep pink kigtai blooms unfurls across the landscape, and miles below the plains have receded to patches between the mist.

Above, snowy peaks meet the sky like the jagged teeth of their name. The temple says the twin deities, Zir and Tro, came from these heights. Which means somewhere, up there, is something to do with their birth. Or something they sowed. A tree? A flower? I don't know. But I'm going to find it.

Whooshing air buffets my face and I flinch. What in the sixth hell was *that*?

A huge butterfly, bigger than the largest desert vulture, swoops over me again. My heart tries to thump its way up my throat as the creature settles on the flowers nearby. The boughs dip under its weight. Twin circles of crimson decorate the bottom segments of its wings, as if they were red eyes staring out of the velvet black background.

Ash drops the scowl he's worn since I asked him about his medicine. His eyes go wide in boyish wonder, reminding me that he can't be much more than a turn or two older than me. "There's a tapestry in the imperial palace of one of these. I never thought they were real." He stretches his arms out to either side. "That thing's wings must be double my reach."

The giant butterfly flutters—if you can call its great wingbeats "flutters"—to the next lot of trees. It half perches, half hovers over the branches as it sucks nectar from the blooms through a long, thin proboscis.

I shudder. It may be beautiful, but there's something off-putting about the way it feeds.

"You know," I tell Ash, "there's this stall in the Aphorain market that sells exotic remedies from different parts of the Empire. The rarer, the pricier. There were these tiny silver butterfly chrysalises—dried with the creature mummified in their little cocoon. He claimed that when caterpillars seal themselves up, they turn to mush before clumping back together as a butterfly. The only parts that don't dissolve are the bits the butterflies grow from. Potent regenerative stuff, he claimed. Make a tincture from the cocoon, inhale the vapors, and you'll keep 'a youthful appearance.' I thought he was a charlatan, but the rich sorts used to snap up every shipment. Reckon they'd drink baby's blood if they thought it would cure wrinkles."

Ash huffs. "I wouldn't put it past half the nobles at the imperial court, either."

"I'm wondering—*The sky was devoured*—we're in the right place. *And the Twins' lives sown*. What if it's a play on words? Twin *lives*? A caterpillar and a butterfly? Both from the same parts. From the 'seeds'?"

Ash's expression turns thoughtful. "It's possible. You think your market vendor might have spoken the truth?"

"If his tiny specimens really had the restorative powers his customers swore by, then . . ." I gesture to the giant butterfly as it launches into the air, great wings bearing it toward the even higher slopes.

"Only one way to find out." He holds out his arm, like it's a bridge between our divide.

I take it, letting him steady me as I clamber down the rocks back to the forest floor.

When night falls, we camp under the trees. Ash builds a small fire. The canopy will dissipate the smoke, and the flames will be masked by the leaves. With no sign of pursuit since the desert, and given my light cloak does little to stave off the chill of the mountains, we're in agreement that it's an acceptable risk.

We settle on opposite sides of the fire, our thoughts our own. I twist my locket on its chain, still wondering why Sephine would have had it made for me all those turns ago, why Father wouldn't have told me its origins. If I'm ever going to learn the full story, I've got to get back to Aphorai and heal the Prince. Talk to Father. Maybe even track Luz down. One of my buyers or their associates must have a lead on her. I'd even stoop to seeking out Zakkurus one last time, if it meant knowing the truth.

But to have a chance at any of that, I need to solve another puzzle, with limited funds, half the Rangers in the Empire on my tail, and no idea whether the Prince will truly cling to life until some superstitious starwheel event.

I pull my cloak around me.

One scent at a time, I tell myself. *One scent at a time.*

* *
* *
*

Ash shakes me awake at dawn. The fire has been built back up and the savory aroma of roasting meat greets me. I sit up and look around. A small pile of russet fur lies crumpled nearby.

I grimace. "Squirrel?"

"Close," Ash replies. "Glider. Flying squirrel."

"Does everything up here fly?" I ask, scowling at the tree canopy.

He shrugs and hands me a sizzling skewer. "Alas, my wings are only ink."

"That was dangerously close to a joke."

"Hardly. A Shield is ever vigilant against the deadliest of perils."

I snicker.

Ash kicks dirt over the coals, a small smile quirking his lips.

I try not to think about where the meat came from as I pick it off the sticks Ash used to skewer it. I have to admit, once you get past all the fussy bones, it doesn't taste too bad.

By the time I've finished eating, Ash has packed our small amount of supplies back into Lil's saddlebags. I'm surprised she lets him anywhere near her, let alone stands patiently as he works. She doesn't even try to bite him.

We set out. About an hour's hike from camp, Ash calls my name from a dozen paces ahead.

"Stay here, girl," I murmur to Lil as I slip from her back.

179

I catch up to Ash, my breath fogging in the chill air.

He gestures ahead.

Is that a . . . chrysalis?

It's *huge*.

What I had at first glance assumed was a particularly thick tree is in fact a giant chrysalis hanging alongside a trunk. It's suspended from the sturdiest branch—half again as tall as Ash, and reaching almost to the ground, blending into the same russet-beige of the tree's bark. No wonder the flying squirrels were a similar hue. Everything up here is camouflaged.

"That's . . . a specimen," I manage.

"Isn't it just?"

I point to the giant chrysalis. "You think the Aphorain store holder was onto something? There's really some sort of 'seed of life' in those things?"

"We can't know for sure unless we open one."

"Wouldn't that hurt it?" I don't want to destroy an innocent creature on a whim. But I can't think of any other way.

Ash gives me a sympathetic look. "You'd rather I take the lead on this?"

I nod.

He crosses to the tree and reaches out, giving the giant butterfly casing a push. Something inside roils and twists, the skin of the chrysalis bulging and dimpling.

Ash jumps back with a yelp. "Perhaps not *that* one."

I can't help it. I burst into laughter.

He glowers at me and it only makes it worse. I brace my hands on my thighs, howling with mirth. "Watch out for the killer baby butterfly, mighty warrior!"

"Are you going to help, or are you just going to guffaw all day?"

I adjust my satchel strap and turn back to Lil. She seems happy enough cropping at the few blades of grass that have managed to poke up through the forest's mossy floor. I start after Ash.

We cross the next ridge and descend into a valley carved by a rushing river to find more chrysalises. The forest is so thick here there aren't even dapples, and it's hard to make anything out beyond the third or fourth tree in the gloom. Still, so many trunks receding into the distance appear too thick to only be that—almost every single one has a giant chrysalis hanging alongside.

There must be dozens of them. Maybe hundreds.

Ash stops in his tracks.

I step up behind him. "They're everywhere, aren't they?"

He nods. "Where do we even start?

I peer at the nearest tree. "If we're going to able to work out which bits are the 'seeds,' we'd need to pick the time between caterpillar and butterfly, don't you think?"

"Seems logical."

"My guess is that would be a dormant time. It shouldn't move."

"Agreed," Ash says, nodding a little too enthusiastically.

"So, we'll just go around poking them and see if they move like the first one we found. When one doesn't, you cut it open. Sound like a plan?" I hope it does, because I can't think of a better idea.

"Why do I have to be the one to cut it open?"

"The two swords strapped to your back might have something to do with it."

"Fair."

I take a deep breath, steadying myself. "This might take a while. You check that lot"—I point to the left slope of the valley—"and I'll take the other side."

"All right. But make sure you—"

"Stay in sight. Don't worry, I have no intention of taking any longer than needed."

He eyes me quizzically. "You were the one mocking me for being scared of a butterfly; what's changed?"

"I . . ." The truth is, I don't know. Maybe I'm just not used to the oppressive feeling I get here in the forest, so different to the dunes, the ravines, the open desert sky. Or maybe it was the way the first butter-fly we saw sucked the nectar from the flowers, its antennae twitching. Beautiful. Yet somehow unnerving.

"Shout if you find anything," Ash says. "And see that stretch of river edged in sand? Meet me down there if we get separated."

He lopes down the valley, leaving me alone in the gloom.

Guess I'd better get to work.

I move toward the first cocoon. I'm about to reach out and give it a nudge, when I think better of it and cast around the forest floor for a stick. I choose a forked branch, breaking off the unneeded twigs. When I prod the chrysalis, it undulates as the creature inside squirms.

Not this one, then.

I work my way along the trees, each bearing a dangling insect shroud that's big enough to fit me inside. Truth be told, it's cold enough that I'd almost like to crawl into one. Maybe it would be nice to hang from a tree in a snug cocoon and forget all this trouble.

With each chrysalis I test, they become less threatening, or maybe I grow bolder, wanting to know more about these strange creatures. I decide to try without the stick.

The cocoon's casing feels soft and warm, like the supplest leather. Its occupant wriggles against my palm, and I wonder if they're so creepy after all. You could almost imagine it's like stroking a pet.

Lil has drifted higher with me, and she looks up from where she's found another clearing of grass under a small patch of sun. She snorts and rakes the ground with a hoof.

"Calm down," I tell her. "I'm not trying to replace you with wings."

I move on to the next chrysalis.

When I poke it, nothing happens.

I try again. Still nothing.

Have I found one at the stage we need? Curiosity driving me on, I pull my knife from its sheath. Before cutting into the casing, I glance around. Lil watches me, ears laid back, teeth bared. What is she pick-ing up on that I'm not?

I sheathe my knife.

This can wait until Ash is here, too.

I scrape my boot through the leaf matter and moss, drawing a semicircle around the tree so I can find it next time. Then I retrace my steps, scuffing a mark every ten paces or so.

Back at the river, I cup my hands to my mouth. "I think I've found one!" I call to Ash, my voice uncannily loud in the damp quiet of the forest.

He comes jogging out from the tree cover. So much for staying within sight. With a few sure-footed leaps from stone to stone, he's across the river. "Let's see it, then."

I lead him back the way I came.

He folds his arms, sizing up the chrysalis. "What makes you so sure?"

"See for yourself."

He gives it a push. It swings a little, but that's it. He turns to me, expression excited, and draws one of the daggers at his wrist. "You found it, why don't you do the honors?" He holds out the blade, hilt first.

"How terribly thoughtful of you." This is not going to be pleasant.

The dagger is heavier than I expected. Adjusting my grip, I step over to the cocoon. I decide to start high—if what we need is liquid, I want to be ready to capture it.

I'm sorry, I tell it silently. *I wouldn't do this if I had another choice.*

Carefully, I pierce the chrysalis, making an incision downward.

Green ichor, so dark it's almost black, oozes from the cut. I thought it would smell terrible, but it doesn't. It's metallic, sure, but there are notes of something distinctive and sweet, almost like anise. Interesting.

I pause and look back to Ash. He gives me a nod. So far, so good.

The casing offers little resistance. I drag the blade lower, inch by inch, until the bottom of the cut is at eye level. No more ichor weeps from the wound. That's a relief. I expected there would be copious amounts.

I'm about to cut farther, when the whole cocoon shudders.

It starts stretching and morphing, bulging more violently than any of the others we've tested.

I jerk the dagger free and take a step back.

There's a horrible tearing sound. At first, I think it's the cut I've made splitting, but then I realize the sound is coming from behind me.

Another cocoon has a rend in it. Two antennae emerge from the gash, shorter and stubbier than a butterfly's, with barbed spikes running along their length. They're followed by an enormous head, wet and black, featureless but for a pincer-like mouth.

It gapes at me, displaying multiple rows of teeth. Then it lets out a bone-melting noise somewhere between a screech and a guttural snarl. Though it has no eyes that I can make out, it seems to lock its attention on me. Can it hear me? Smell me?

"They're waking one another!" Ash warns. "Get out of range. We don't know what they'll do!"

I retreat another step, only to find myself backing up against a third giant cocoon.

It begins to writhe.

A heartbeat later, its occupant bursts from its casing. Mandibles stretch wider than my face, and it's a sure bet that's where they're aimed. I heft Ash's dagger in my hand and stab at the side of the insect's head.

Jarring pain shoots up my arm.

I recoil with a cry of surprise, the blade scraping off without doing any damage. The thing isn't soft and gooey as I expected but covered in a hard casing, like it's wearing armor.

I realize I've dropped Ash's dagger. Stink on a reeking stick.

It's as if the creature senses I'm now defenseless. It looms closer and I edge farther toward the tree. Rough bark digs into my back.

With a hiss, the thing splatters ichor across my face. I squeeze my eyes shut and turn my head away.

Fetid breath huffs against my cheek.

I hope it's a quick death.

CHAPTER 26
ASH

The hissing monstrosity bares its fangs mere inches from Rakel's face.

I pull her back by the satchel strap and shove her behind me. My pulse quickens, hands and feet tingling as I bring my sword down on the snarling creature.

It shrieks.

This screech is different. Before it was rage. Now it's an unmistakable cry of pain as the creature shrinks back on itself.

I brace a foot against its carapace and wrench my sword free, the blade dripping with green-black ooze. Whatever these things are, they're thick-skinned. Tough, too. The wounded creature gathers itself to lunge again, and I barely avoid the snap of mandibles meant for my neck.

"Come on!" I grab Rakel's hand. "They're all fully formed. We must be too late in their season."

More and more larvae are waking around us, roiling in their cocoons, as if their first instinct, no matter what stage they're at, is to eliminate the invasion. Our invasion.

Rakel tries to pull away. "There's still one that's not moving. We *have* to get to it."

"More like we *have* to get away from here!" I pull her out of range of another hissing monstrosity.

But she's got that stubborn set to her jaw I'm beginning to recognize all too well. She yanks her knife from the belt at her waist. I know she tends it well, but that thing is for harvesting flowers. If she couldn't pierce the creature's armor with my dagger, she'll have no chance with her own blade.

She rounds on me. "If we don't get what we came for, we're not just risking our lives, but Nisai's, too!"

There's nothing that would let me forget that, but I also haven't forgotten that Rakel saved my life in the sandstorm. She could have left me there.

If we stay here, I'm not sure I can defend the both of us. But we both need this cure. And Rakel has shown time and time again she'll make her own choices, regardless of what I think.

I flick the ichor from my sword and square my shoulders.

Then I stride past her and into the fray.

More and more of the larvae nightmares have torn themselves free of their cocoons. They undulate across the forest floor toward us, hissing and spitting and gnashing their pincers. Periodically, one will let out one of those ear-bleeding screeches. Then the others rear up, slamming their front ends back against the ground in rhythmic thuds, as if they're communicating with the pattern of the beats.

I shudder in revulsion before bringing my sword down across the midsection of the closest beast. It glances along the thing's carapace before biting deep where two plates meet.

"If any get near you, go for the joints!" I yell. "They're weak points!"

At the edge of my vision, Rakel's horse rears and brings her hooves crashing down on the closest monstrosity. Rakel lunges, slapping her hand across the black mare's rump. "Go!" she shouts.

The horse turns tail and gallops toward the river.

Smart beast.

Pivoting, I avoid the clutches of the next creature, though not quick enough to escape a gash from barbed horns across my forearm. It's a flesh wound, but it burns like a heated blade. I mouth a silent prayer to Riker that these things aren't venomous.

I manage to slice my way through the next pair of giant larvae in our path.

It's replaced a second later by another.

And another.

My palms slick with sweat and I'm forced to alter my grip. I swing, only to have the blade snag in a carapace. I wrench it free, the shift in weight sending one foot sliding in the damp leaf mold. The closest creature hisses, spraying me with sticky liquid. Then I'm regaining balance, snatching a breath, edging closer and closer to the one unmoving cocoon.

Rakel follows in my wake. The forest floor is clogged with green-black blood, my boots slipping around lumps and chunks of insect. I'm breathing hard with the effort of the fight, sucking in air that reeks of death and bile and something overwhelmingly metallic.

When I finally reach the right tree, I cut the mute cocoon down. It falls to the ground and splits on impact, contents exploding like too-ripe fruit. Viscous liquid and half-formed butterfly parts spray in all directions.

I drag a hand over my face, wiping the bug guts from my eyes.

"You'll have to do the honors," I say, blinking through burning tears. "I have no idea what I'm looking for."

"You're *too* kind," she snipes, dropping to her haunches and plunging her hands into the goo.

"And you'll have to be quick about it."

It's no exaggeration. Farther up the slope, the creatures are still ripping free from their casings, another wave screeching and writhing their way toward us. There's still some distance for them to cover, but for all their seemingly ungainly bulk, they move fast.

Rakel swivels to face the oncoming black monstrosities, her eyes wide.

The first of the next wave reaches us, going for her rather than me, as if they've worked out she's the easier target. I lunge to her left, cutting another creature from mandible to midsection. The impact reverberates up my arm, muscles protesting.

I'm conditioned for close combat, but the training yard didn't prepare me for this.

How could *anyone* be prepared for this?

"Hurry! I'm not sure how long I can hold them off!"

Out of the corner of my eye I can see Rakel is elbow-deep in insect gore. The metallic stench of ichor is so strong now that between bouts with the creatures I'm swallowing hard to keep it together. I'm not surprised when Rakel doubles over to vomit.

Finally, she retrieves an odd-looking chunk out of the mess, wipes it off with her sleeve and holds it aloft. It's two barely joined discs of some sort of cartilage or chitin. Each is about the size of my palm but almost geometric in its perfect form, ridged in concentric circles like a section of sawn tree trunk.

I peer through the gloom. "Is that it? Please tell me that's it."

Her grin is almost feral as she holds up the discs. "Looks like twin seeds to me!"

"Then stay by me. There's only one way out of this."

She grips her prize in one hand, brandishing her knife in the other. "Through?"

I nod. "Through."

We run.

Racing headlong into the valley, our boots skid and slide down the slope. Each time one of us loses balance, the other steadies them.

By unspoken agreement we head for the river beach. It's clear of cocoons on either side, and the forest is free of them some ways beyond that. Either these things hate light, or water, or both, because they don't try to follow us beyond the tree line.

Seems Rakel's horse had already worked that out. She waits on the strand of river-smooth pebbles, eyes still rolling wildly.

"Oh, stench of stenches. I've really got to wash." Rakel's face falls from triumph at retrieving the ingredient to disgust at her gore-spackled tunic.

"You're thinking about grooming at a time like this?" I scan around us, up the slope where we fought off the larvae, and then to the other side of the valley, to where presumably hundreds more of the cocoons hang in the trees.

Rakel flips her horse's reins over her head. "They're everywhere, aren't they?"

I nod. "Seems the only place clear is the river itself." I set my shoulders. "If we stay close to the banks, we should be able to make it out of their territory."

"All right," she says, rubbing at an ichor-crusted arm. "But we're stopping as soon as we're clear. This doesn't just stink, it itches."

We walk in silence downriver, setting a good pace on the gently sloping banks. My eyes search the forest on either side but detect no movement. Rakel leads the mare and stares straight ahead except for when the rocks become too uneven to not watch her feet.

After we've put a safe distance between us and the insect horrors, I start unbuckling my ichor-sodden armor as I walk. Rakel's eyes go wide. Then they meet mine and dart quickly away, though not before I notice the color in her cheeks.

I remember her modesty at the desert canyon. She's not a soldier. She doesn't see a comrade engaging in a necessary routine, she sees a guy casually taking off his clothes.

She coughs. "Ah, what do you think about here for a camp? I can build a fire."

One look at the way her nose is wrinkled, at how she scratches at her exposed skin, tells me she needs this far more than I do. The ichor had stopped bothering me once it dried.

"I'll make the fire. You have some time to yourself." I gesture back to a low waterfall we just passed. "I'd bet it's the closest thing to a bathhouse out here."

She nods gratefully and begins to pick her way back up the rocks.

The one good thing about this forest is that the canopy's so thick there's quite a bit of almost-dry wood scattered over the ground. When I've a good blaze going, I head downstream so as not to disturb Rakel.

I leave my clothes and the pack safely up the bank and splash into the shallows. The water is the coldest I've ever experienced. Not wanting to dally, I scrub at myself with my hands. But it's not enough; the goo is too oily. It streaks and smears but stays irritatingly stuck.

"You'll need this."

I startle at the voice. Rakel stands on a rocky outcrop above the pool, her hair hanging in damp curls around her face. She wears a pristine tunic, much like that of the Chroniclers at the Library. When did she get the chance to ask them for a spare change of clothes? Then again, knowing her, maybe she didn't *ask*.

"Here." She tosses me a bar of soap. It's hard and translucent with a greenish cast, like an uncut gemstone.

"Thanks."

"And . . . I'm just going to leave this here." She holds up an identical tunic to her own, which she drapes over a dry rock. I give her a grateful smile, faintly amused at how she swings from caustic to considerate.

She nods and retreats toward the fire.

The soap is gritty with sand and smells pleasantly of mint. Scrubbing my scalp, I notice my hair is growing out. Given present circumstances, it's not the worst thing to have some of my most prominent tattoos obscured.

I attempt sluicing the bug guts off my armor. I'd never usually wash leather, but there's nothing to be done for it. At least the soap scours most of the carnage away.

As I work, thoughts of how close those monstrosities came to overwhelming us creep into my mind. Perhaps Iddo is right. I'm nothing more than a house cat, made soft by pampered palace life. Despite all those days in the training yard, the turns of running up and down the steep slopes of Ekasya until I thought my lungs would burst, I'm not suited for being out here, where I don't know what's around the next bend in the trail, what crouches behind each boulder.

The thoughts make my pulse quicken. Heat flushes my skin and an itching sensation begins, not everywhere but in too many places to pinpoint, like ants crawling through my flesh, pinching and nipping, eating their way free—

Get ahold of yourself.

I force myself to count my heartbeats.

One-two. Three-four. Five-six.

The itching subsides enough for me to think. I've got to get a dose, and soon.

I don't know what's to come, what shadows steal around us, but I do know one thing—there's no room for losing control.

*   *
*   *
*

Back at the fire, Rakel has made a makeshift drying rack out of fallen branches. I nod my thanks as I hang my sodden leather.

"I found these." She sits on her horse's saddlecloth and tosses an apricot to me. "Seems they grow wild here."

Separating it into halves, I happily chew the fruit, then take the pit and crush it against a rock with the hilt of one of my knives, revealing the kernel inside.

"Here." I gesture for her to give me the pit from her fruit. I split it and hand her back the prize.

"Never had them fresh," she muses, holding up the kernel in scrutiny. "Only ever seen them dried and salted. They're poisonous in large doses, you know."

"So I've heard," I mutter, stirring unwelcome thoughts of the night of the fire, of Esarik trying to eliminate which toxin Nisai had been felled with. Talk of poisons is still too close for comfort. But after witnessing Rakel hold her nerve today, I realize I've been so preoccupied with the quest, that I've been underestimating her.

It's a realization that piques my curiosity.

"How did you end up tied up in all this, anyway?"

She gives me a flat look. "You were there. You saw."

"I mean at the palace. You hadn't been there long, had you?"

"No, but it's a long story."

"Rather like how you came to be in possession of a vial of dahkai essence?" I gesture to our slowly drying clothes. "We've got some time to kill."

"Short version? I was trying to be something I'm not. And other people had . . . different ideas."

"Go on."

She sighs. "I wanted a perfumery apprenticeship. I could have settled for something more realistic for someone of my . . . heritage. But no, I wanted a top spot. One that would lead to becoming a master perfumer."

I smile, hoping it comes off as wry, not sarcastic. "You don't strike me as someone who would do that simply for the status."

"Ha!" She seems genuinely amused. "Pride did have something to do with it. But it was more, too. I wanted to make something of myself. Become independent. Find a place in the world from which I could make my own decisions." Her smile vanishes, and she pokes a stick into the fire. "My father was—is—ill. I wanted to be able to buy the best medicine, to find income more stable than what I'd been scraping together."

"I'm sorry."

"It's not your fault."

"That doesn't mean I'm not sorry for it. What ails him?"

"It doesn't matter. He's dying." She jabs at the coals, sending sparks flying.

Understanding dawns. "The Affliction?"

"Using a polite term doesn't change what it is. But yes. He's got the Rot. And yes, I realize there's no saving him. But I could have bought him time. If we could afford the things that can slow the progress of the ulcers, he'd gain turns. Half my lifetime again. Maybe more. It was worth the risk."

"The risk?"

"I made a bet with the wrong person. And I lost. And that's how I ended up serving Sephine."

"You became the Scent Keeper's apprentice because you lost a wager? Something doesn't quite add up here."

"I *wasn't* her apprentice." The last comes out almost as a hiss. "I was just a fool who couldn't smell the perfume from the notes. I was so intent on solving one problem I blundered into far bigger ones."

"Oh?"

She heaves a sigh and adds another branch to the fire. "I always thought my father so hard done by. He was a hero, you know? Military. Served the Eraz on the front line for longer than I'd been alive. I thought he'd received an honorable discharge to reward him for his service, with a full pension. But once he became ill, his pension was barely enough to cover the essentials—bandages, basic salves, the incense to mask the stench of the ulcers. How were we going to eat?

"So, I set about making money on the side. I learned the basics from the women in my village, and when I was old enough, I'd journey into the city and watch the traders at the night markets. With my nose, it wasn't hard to learn what worked and what didn't. What would sell."

Her voice swells with quiet pride. "And once I'd made a little money to buy ingredients, I started to experiment. Worked out better ways to produce things. It brought in enough, but it was always going to be tenuous. Who knew when the Eraz's regulators would find out? When the imperial tax collector and his thugs would come knocking? Or one of my buyers decided I knew too much about their operations and . . ." She makes a chopping motion in front of her nose at that last.

"But after my time with Sephine, I don't know what to believe."

She picks up a stick and starts pushing river pebbles around. "Was Father dishonorably discharged? He was ejected from the Eraz's army when they found out he had the Rot, but was that because he told them, or did he try to hide it? Could someone be that brave on the battlefield but so afraid of the consequences of his illness that he put his own soldiers at risk? Army camps keep people in close quarters. What if he had accidentally passed it on?"

"But you said there was money coming in, at least enough for his medicine?"

"A pension. I thought it was from his military service but maybe it was a caretaker's pension."

"Caretaker of what?"

"Me."

I raise an eyebrow at that.

She gives a tight little shrug. "Sephine claimed my father was lying, that she was paying to ensure I had enough. That I had a guardian until I was old enough not to need one. What reason did she have to lie about that? What was I to her? Why take the interest she took in me?"

She pokes at the fire. Sparks fly up from the glowing goals. "I still can't believe he would do that."

"Take the money?"

"No, that part I get. What I don't get is why, if it's true, he hid his condition. If he just owned up, things would have been different; surely he would have had an honorable discharge, and a pension. And even once he'd stunk everything up, why wouldn't he tell me? That's the bit that hurts. The lies. The deceit."

The pain in her expression moves me in a way I've not experienced for turns. I want to reach out to her, to comfort her. If only there wasn't much more than a campfire standing between us.

"I'll probably never know the whole of it. What secrets Sephine took with her to her pyre . . . if they even gave her one after what they think she did." She shakes her head and rises to her feet. "I'm going to refill the waterskins."

This is the chance to tell her, to admit my condition. Deep down, I know it's a turning point.

"He probably thought he was protecting you," I venture.

"Sorry?"

"Your father. I'd wager he was trying to protect you from the truth. People make mistakes. Perhaps he thought he could figure a way out of things, a way to make them right before you found out."

Her expression hardens. "Broken trust is the hardest wound to heal. And it always leaves a scar. *Always.*"

She gathers the skins and sets out across the stones to the water's edge.

I should follow her. Explain that I understand what it's like to be hiding something from the ones you care for because the truth can only hurt them. That you only intend to protect them.

But I saw the look in her eye as she spoke. Pain. Contempt. And a coldness that time will one day turn to indifference.

The fledgling trust between us is still so tenuous. I can't afford to put the mission at risk by telling her something that might make her see me in that same way.

CHAPTER 27
RAKEL

Esiku's first children were turned to stone

We agree to leave the Alet Range quick as milk sours in the sun. The trip down the other side will take us farther away from Aphorai and the last place we encountered Rangers. But while there's part of me that wants to take comfort from having found the first two ingredients for the Prince's cure, the other part wants to throw up my arms in frustration. Who knows if it's the right cure? Or even the right diagnosis? There are so many unknowns I could scream.

Where to next?

Our descent is mercifully quicker than the climb. That said, the ground is uneven and too corded with tree roots to risk riding Lil. My knees and shins start complaining. Soon each step jolts up my legs. Part of me relishes the pain. Next to the dungeons, I've never been so glad to be leaving a place behind.

Nightmares plague my sleep when we make camp—stinking ichor and black mandibles closing over my face until I burst awake, skin clammy in the night air. Then my eyes find Ash's silhouette in the moonslight, prowling between the trees on silent feet.

I try to take the first watch every time, because he never wakes me if I'm second.

He insists he's trained to need less sleep.

I'd be lying if I said I wasn't exhausted.

Worry is wearing me down. What other beasts does this strange land hold? Do the Rangers still hunt us? How does Father fare and did Luz speak the truth about the Order keeping him supplied, because if not . . .

And through it all: *Where to next?*

Shivering, I draw Lil's saddle blanket to my chin. Beyond the last embers of our pitiful fire, Ash guards a perimeter around me.

I fall into another fitful doze.

Ash is subdued as we descend into the river valley. I've learned he's usually quiet in the mornings, sitting tall and cross-legged at the edge of camp, greeting the dawn as prayer incense curls around him. But this is different. At first, I figure it's because he's on alert for more cocoons—even I'll admit I wasn't much help in that fight. When we've cleared the forest for cultivated land, quiet lanes crisscrossing terraces of kormak plantations, I begin to suspect it's more than that.

Up in the mountains, I let my mouth run away with me, exposed myself more than I wanted to. Does he think less of me, now he knows I'm the daughter of a disgraced provincial military hero?

I try to distract myself from brooding by concentrating on the remaining clues as we walk, repeating lines from the manuscript over in my head in time with my steps, trying to make sense of them.

When Riker's heart faced the eternal plight . . .

Esiku's first children were turned to stone . . .

When Azered's bones danced in the breath of blight . . .

Curse the ancients for being so cryptic.

Or just curse the Scent Keepers, ancient or otherwise. Because the way Sephine used to speak, this probably wouldn't even have been a riddle to her at all.

The sun is high overhead when Ash stops and points. A breeze blows from behind us, so that all I can smell is the humus-covered earth and the sun on the kormak—just as the drink, it's like pepper and orange blossom had a love child. I shield my eyes with one hand. Yes, there. Buildings.

"Let's take a break." Ash lowers his pack onto a fallen tree trunk, shrugs out of his cloak. He stretches, and scents be damned I can't look away as the muscles ripple under the tattoos running down his arms. Then his leather vest creaks. "Tro's stones, I cannot wait to get some oil for this."

I wrinkle my nose. I'm glad we had the sand soap, but there's only so much you can do with freezing mountain water. What I would give to be clean, to smell like myself again.

I squint toward the valley. "Do you think that town's big enough to have a public bathhouse?"

"Don't get too hopeful. Just because we haven't seen any Rangers since the sandstorm doesn't mean we can relax."

"We need supplies," I say flatly, planting my hands on my hips.

"If the gods smile upon us, it's a bathhouse for you, and first stop for me is something to eat. But I'd rather stay filthy and hungry than walk into a Ranger trap."

Imaginary sky friends or not, he's got a point.

We set off down the hill, the air and earth drying out, the plots of land getting smaller as we near the town. A herder and his flock of black and white goats block the lane and we stop to let them pass, newborn kids trotting along to keep up with their mothers—their warm, hircine scent an unexpected comfort after the dank forest and its horrors. Nearer to the town walls, we pass through a pomegranate orchard. Ash snatches two crimson fruits from the tree as we walk.

I raise my eyebrows. "Finally taking to some of my ways?"

He looks taken aback. "Hardly. Emperor's Rule. Anyone can take as much fruit from a roadside as they can carry in their bare hands."

"You wouldn't want to get caught doing that in Aphorai."

"Aphorai isn't exactly the pinnacle of civilization, is it?"

I roll my eyes.

"What a civilized response." He holds out a pomegranate. "Hungry?"

Before I have a chance to react, Lil swings her head around and snatches the fruit from Ash's outstretched hand. It crunches loudly as she chews.

"Hey!" I ruffle her mane.

She replies with a self-satisfied snort.

Ash throws his head back and laughs. It's the most uninhibited thing I've ever seen him do, and I smile despite myself. "Emperor's Rule," he manages between guffaws.

I reach toward another pomegranate tree. Maybe there are one or two good things to say for the Empire after all.

The town proper is much smaller than Aphorai City. Leading Lil through the gate, I'm mindful of what Father would say about its defenses. They're rudimentary at best—four wooden towers, ditches bristling with stakes. The air is thick with aromatic wood smoke— Hagmiri commoners burning in their hearths what only the rich could afford in Aphorai. Not that I envy them—flame is the last thing I'd want if my house was made of timber.

Strings of crystal beads hang in almost every doorway we pass, splaying tiny shafts of afternoon sunlight across the buildings.

I jut my chin toward the nearest of them. "What's with the door jewelry?"

Ash shrugs. "Wards. The Hagmiri ambassadors gift one to Nisai every time they come to court."

"Wards? Against what?"

"The armies of the Lost God. The Children of Doskai." A pinprick of light dances across his face and he flinches like he's embarrassed—a believer who has just blasphemed.

"Shadow warriors? That's cute."

Ash raises an eyebrow. "Is it?"

"You're not serious."

He keeps walking.

"You *are* serious. Nobody actually believes in any of those 'beyond the edge of memory' legends, do they?" I put on my best storyteller voice for the phrase that begins all the old tales.

I mean, warriors with the strength of ten men? Who couldn't be touched by blades?

Everyone bleeds, Father says. *You just need to know where to stab them.*

Ash hitches his pack. "Some do. Ever heard of the Brotherhood of the Blazing Sun? They're fringe—zealots who'd walk through fire if they thought it would resurrect the Lost God."

I whistle through my teeth. Even if you're not strictly religious, acknowledging Doskai isn't the done thing. Worshipping him? Outlawed. Taboo. And whatever superstitions people may have, wanting to invoke him is even more incomprehensible to me than placing faith in any of his siblings.

"Others," Ash continues, "find more accepted ways to hold on to the past. Tradition helps them feel less lost in the present. What do you think my tattoos are for?"

"So you look *fierce*?" I hold up my hands, curl my fingers into claws and make a noise somewhere between a meow and a roar.

He ignores that. "Partly, yes. But they're also a reminder. A symbol of what had to be conquered for the Empire to come into being."

I stop in the middle of the dirt road. "Do *you* believe in all that"—I twirl my fingers in the gesture for smoke—"Shadow Wars stuff?"

He squints toward the nearest doorway, where faceted beads glitter as they sway in the breeze. "I believe in the true gods. *Magic* belongs with our shadows. Behind us."

I'm about to tell him where he can stick his proverbs when a figure emerges from inside the house. A man about Father's age leans against the doorframe, arms crossed. The unveiled suspicion in his expression reminds me we're strangers here. Strangers who don't want to become familiar faces. I keep Lil between me and the houses and continue into town.

It doesn't take long to find the marketplace—a modest square with fruit and vegetable sellers displaying their wares on rough-hewn trestles. Artisan stores border them. There's a smith, an apothecary that doesn't look much more than an incense vendor, a potter with the smallest of kilns, and our destination—armorer.

Ash tightens his cloak and adjusts the linen head wrap I fashioned for him, pulling it down to make sure his scalp tattoos are covered. Then he enters the shop.

The armorer wears a stout belly, broad smile, and his own wares—he's dressed in bronze-studded leather from head to heel. He wipes his hands on his apron as he greets his new customer. Within moments, Ash and he are debating the contrasting qualities of various leather treatments.

"Best amber oil you'll find either side of Ekasya," the storekeeper says, proffering a strip of calfskin soaked in the stuff. "Pure Midloshian."

I haven't worked with amber before. Never really needed to. Barden always sourced his own, and I prefer cedar oil for my satchel, boots, and Lil's tack.

I drag the strip of leather across the counter and give it a sniff. "Midloshian?"

"From the Midlosh Sea. Off Los. The largest and best source in Aramtesh."

Ash nods and the armorer retreats to the store's annex to fill us a measure.

"Amber comes from the sea?" I murmur to Ash.

"The bottom of the sea," the armorer calls.

Got a pair of ears on him, that one.

He returns to the counter, sizing me up as if I'm simple. "Not any sea. Only where there used to be forests."

Forests? Under the sea?

Esiku's children grew only to drown.

I throw Ash a sidelong look. He glances back, realization clear in his eyes.

The armorer sticks his thumbs in the sleeve holes of his vest. "But the Losians guard their sources and methods as close as the Aphorains guard dahkai. Cagey lot, you northerners."

He looks pointedly at me. I tense. I should have known my accent would give me away. Should have let Ash do the talking.

Ash keeps his expression pleasant. "How much?"

"Decent lad like you? Let's call it a hundred even."

"Silver?" I snort. "Were you huffing dreamsmoke back there?"

The armorer keeps his eyes on Ash. "Thanks to your mouthy friend, the price has gone up. One twenty."

Ash clenches his jaw, the tendons in his neck going taut. He pulls me aside. "I'm short."

I look him up and down. "Above average, I'd say."

"I mean I can't cover it. Your mouth just cost me what I had left."

I scowl. "Surely you're not thinking of giving over that many zigs to this gouger?"

"What price do you put on your freedom?"

My scowl turns blacker, but I hand him the purse Luz gave me.

Ash pays for the amber and bids the armorer farewell. I follow him to the door, waving goodbye with the crudest hand gesture I know.

"What stink got up your nose?" Ash asks when we're walking away.

"You. Letting us get swindled worse than a widow at a soul-candle stall."

"We needed that ingredient."

"And we don't need to eat?"

"There's still enough in your purse to resupply for the next few days."

I could strangle that even-toned voice out of him.

Then he cocks his head to the side in that disarmingly boyish way of his. "It's not just the money, is it?"

Some of the anger seeps out of me. "When things seem to fall into place, at least for me, it usually means there's something else going on. Something lurking below the surface."

"What do you mean?"

"I mean, could the next ingredient really be amber? Something so common? What if we've got it wrong?"

"What if we've got any of it wrong? You said yourself we can't dwell on that. I know you've had to scrap and fight for a long time now. That doesn't mean something is less valid because it was easy. The world isn't constantly setting you a trap."

"You believe that?"

He glances sidelong at me, eyes giving away a barely hidden smile. "For a start, you're not that important."

I punch him not so lightly in the bicep.

He makes out as if I've dealt him a killing blow, doubling over with an exaggerated *oof* and a mock pained expression.

I shake my head but can't keep the smile from my lips.

When he straightens, his eyes turn serious. "Don't underestimate your own abilities."

I wave that away.

We continue browsing the stalls, Ash taking a moment to pick up the scrappiest of secondhand maps, chatting amicably with the seller about local crops and politics. I leave him to it, passing on replenishing my stores in the name of spending some of our last zigs on food. By the time I've noticed Ash has disappeared, he's exiting the apothecary.

He joins me, drawing near. "I can't be sure, but I think we're becoming a little too interesting."

I rummage in my satchel while I sneak a glance across the square. Sure enough, we're getting attention from other sellers, several of them murmuring to their neighbors.

I sigh. "Does this mean no bathhouse?"

"Is it worth the risk of finding out where the nearest Ranger might be?"

Of course it's worth the stinking risk, I want to tell him. All I can smell morning and night is the remnants of killer caterpillar sludge. But even though I *want* to wash away my nightmares, I *need* my nose attached to my face. Or my head attached to my neck.

"Let's go," I grumble.

That night, we make camp in a shallow basin some ways off the road, concealed by a copse of myrtles, their astringent tang the cleanest thing I've smelled for days.

Ash spreads his newly acquired map on the grass before us. "Aphorain dahkai. Losian amber. The butterflies of Hagmir. Each of the ingredients comes from a different province. If the pattern continues, that leaves Trel and Edurshai." He jabs a finger toward a small dot. "That town was Koltos. We're close to the Hagmir-Trel border."

"So Trel, or Edurshai?"

"Unless you've figured out any more of these ingredients and haven't told me, we're going to need help. We may not be able to consult Nisai, but we can do the next best thing. Word in the marketplace was that Lord Mur has called his son home to fulfill his duties as heir. There's to be a wedding."

I gape at him. "Hardly the time for a party, Ash."

"We're not going to the wedding; we're going to see the future bridegroom. He's a friend." He scans the valley as he rolls up the map. "At least, after what I've done, I hope he's still a friend."

$$* \quad *$$
$$* \quad *$$
$$*$$

The kormak terraces give way to rolling, crop-covered hills. Grape vines for Trelian wine. Row upon row of fragrant silver-blue lavender. Groves of oranges, the sun coaxing the fruit's zingy sweetness into the air. Each field is divided by lines of slim pines reaching toward the sky.

During those days of travel, I realize Ash and I have settled into a rhythm—hours where I'll ride and he'll lope along beside me, keeping pace with Lil's rolling trot. Other times he'll ride at my back, and at some point I realize it no longer feels like I have a stranger behind me. Then there's occasional spells where we'll all walk. At those times, like now, it seems companionable, like we're simply friends going for a stroll to enjoy the countryside.

Then I'll smell or hear or see something that reminds me of Father, reminds me time is evaporating for him just as it is for the Prince. I mustn't forget that anything pleasant about this smoke-brained quest is just a mirage.

And yet, as we crest each rise and take in the bounty of the next valley, my awe increases. Under other circumstances, I could imagine lingering here. And by the way Lil lifts her head as I lead her along the lane, her nostrils flaring at the new scents, I know I'm not the only one.

At a particularly pretty viewpoint, Ash flings his arms wide, as if he's gesturing to all the land before us. "The Garden of Aramtesh. Splendid, don't you think?"

"Wouldn't turn up my nose. But why don't more people live here?" We've hardly seen anyone since we made it out of Koltos.

His arms drop back to his sides. "The price of land. The Trelians have a saying: 'rich earth, heavy purse.' Most of the harvest will be transported elsewhere, so there's not much left to support a significant population."

I sniff. "Shipped to the capital, you mean."

He gives a conceding nod.

I'm almost sorry to have spoiled the mood. Almost.

It's close to sunset when we come to a gate in a stone wall that's been running beside the road for miles.

"Let me handle this?" Ash asks.

"First sniff's all yours."

The gate is old enough to be crusted in verdigris, but after Ash speaks with a gate guard in leather armor embossed with the Trel bull and a bunch of grapes, it swings open without a creak.

We're escorted up a wide path by two more guards. I nudge Ash.

"As far as they're concerned," he says in that husky attempt-at-a-whisper of his, "we're friends of the Mur heir making the most of the last days of our Kilda break from University."

"I doubt I look much like a student."

Ash arches an eyebrow. "And what does a student look like, exactly?"

I haven't thought of an answer by the time we reach a bridge over a still river. The water surrounds a huge stone building—squat and square with towers at each corner and a red clay tile roof. I wrinkle my nose. I can think of better defenses than stagnant slop. On the other side of the bridge, a courtyard of white pebbles is dotted with stone urns and statues of an elegant woman wearing a flowing cloak and cowl—the goddess Azered.

An equally beautiful youth sits reading on a bench against the side of the huge house, his long legs crossed at the ankles. The golden light of sunset gilds his hair. There's something familiar about him.

"My lord." One of the guards bows. "These two friends of yours?"

The young man sets his book aside and leaps to his feet, shielding his eyes against the slanting rays. "Ash? Stars above, is it really you?"

Ash steps forward and the two embrace.

Then the Trelian is looking at me. "Rakel!" He clears his throat and drops into a bow deeper and more graceful than the retreating guard's. "Please. Forgive me for being so familiar. I'm Esarik Mur. I was part of the delegation to Aphorai."

"Sorry. I didn't recognize you. It's been . . . some time." My words flirt with a lie. It's barely been a moon since I first saw Esarik back in Aphorai, and yet he looks markedly different—sallow and haunted. It makes my throat tighten. If someone young and healthy could go downhill so quickly, what state is Father in by now? I hope Esarik's mind isn't as tired as he looks—Ash seems convinced he's our best hope to decode the rest of the formula.

He eyes the scholar critically. "You've lost weight. It's not . . . Have you had word of Nisai?"

Esarik turns solemn. "He's alive. Iddo had him returned to the capital." He shakes his head. "I wanted to go along, impart whatever I knew to the attending physicians. But Father ordered me home. It appears he cares more about distancing himself from controversy than he does about Nisai recovering. *I* couldn't think of a worse time for him to announce my betrothal."

"Who's the lucky girl?" Ash asks, a strangely sour note in his voice.

"A river lord's daughter. The family has been noble for half as many generations as House Mur, but they're twice as wealthy. Astonishing revelation, no?" His last words are laced with bitterness. Guess there's no affection spared between the soon-to-be bride and groom.

"I'm sorry, Es. Truly."

"As am I." He looks away, out over the vine-covered hills. "As am I." Then he squares his shoulders. "What do you need, Ash? Money? Supplies? Father is due back from court soon, and if he finds you here upon his return, he'll—"

Ash holds up his hand. "By Azered's grace we'll be gone by the morrow. That's if we get started now."

"Started?"

Ash produces the formula manuscript. "What do you make of this?"

Esarik takes the parchment gently, even reverently. He studies it, eyes widening. "This is . . . This is . . ."

I shrug. "Old?"

"Pre-Empire," Esarik finishes. "For a start, there are no vowel diacritics. Then there's the width of the script strokes. And this is tulda vellum, highly durable." His eyes dart from side to side. How can anyone read that fast?

"It seems a formula. But . . . here . . . curious. These lines, they're in different hands. Each of the provinces use different classes of poisons. Perhaps many hands have come together to . . . oh. How terribly ironic."

"What is it, Es?" Ash prods.

"You remember, on that ghastly night, I talked about the ancient poison Ami and I debated? It was purported to be used by the small kings in their plots and schemes. From the surviving evidence it seems they were at war over everything—borders, trade, religion. And yet here we have a scroll suggesting they cooperated on one thing—poison craft." He looks up at each of us in turn. "Where did you find this?"

"You might not believe it," I begin.

He runs his hand through his gold-streaked hair. "When you study the past you come to believe a lot of things. Or go mad in the process."

"The Library of the Lost."

"It exists? Truly?" Our host's impossibly green eyes go wide and bright. "Please, join me inside."

Ash catches Esarik up on events to date, the pair speaking in low tones as we move through the Mur mansion. I hang back, awed by the riches we pass. Drapes infused with purrath blossom so that the scent gently releases in the sun. A contemplation niche laid out with jeweled boxes of solid perfume—someone having left the musk without its lid on as if it was of no consequence.

The scholar's study is no exception. Sunken lower than the hall, wine-red rugs stretch across marble floors as deep green as vine leaves. Candlewheels hang from the ceiling, their wax imbued with the sweetest of citrus oils. And everywhere—on shelves lining the room's perimeter, piled high on tables, and even in a jumbled stack in the corner, are scrolls and books.

I long to flop onto a bronze bench topped with silk cushions. But one glance at my travel-stained tunic decides me against it. I opt instead to perch on the cold marble steps. Ash leans against a wall. Above him, row upon row of paired swords, more ornate than his own, are mounted on the stone.

Esarik perches on the edge of another bench, a candleholder next to it piled high with endless nights of dripped wax. "Tell me. Have you discovered any indication of how long our Prince may endure?"

"Adirun, we think," Ash says. "Rakel's the one with the watertight memory."

"*When the lion wears the lost crown, he'll not live through the night,*" I recite. "That's what the Scent Keeper said. Something about the Lost God and the old calendar. Tozran's Coronation."

Our host furrows his brow, then crosses to a shelf of scrolls. He runs his fingers down their ends, stooping to pull one from the bottom of the stack. Not bothering to return to the table, he unrolls it on the floor. A myriad of lines crisscross the parchment, linking stars and different moon phases.

A starwheel chart.

"If my interpretation is accurate, and the Scent Keeper's words hold truth, the implication is that Nisai will indeed endure until the month of Adirun."

Huh. Guess Luz does know her starwheel.

"The night of the sixth, to be precise."

Ash and I exchange a look. Adirun sixth.

So definite.

So *close.*

Esarik rolls up the chart, the rasping of parchment unnaturally loud in the silent study. Shelving the scroll, he leans over a table spread with maps. "Down to the essence of the problem then, given time is not our ally. I daresay you're correct on your early assumptions. The darkest bloom is most certainly dahkai." He smiles at me. "And the seeds of life were very much in use in the early Empire, from the Monumental Age until the Great Bloom—multiple texts suggest there were far more adherents to their health benefits then than today."

Ash gestures to the poison formula scroll. "And the other ingredients?"

The scholar traces a finger across the Empire's province borders. *"Esiku's children grew only to drown,"* he muses, beginning to pace. "There used to be a sea in the Los province. Or, more accurately, Los was engulfed by the Midlosh Sea and then raised up again. It's all recorded in Akair II's *Cataclysms*—fables of when the younger gods first squabbled alongside the small kings. The Twins wanted to separate themselves from their older sister Esiku, but she didn't want to let them go. So Zir and Tro caused the rivers and ocean to engulf her most treasured forest—giant cedars that used to cover the land from the Cliffs of Lostras to northern Trel. By the time the waters receded centuries later, all that remained were remnants of tree resin as solid as stone. Or as solid as amber, to be precise. Your formula does indeed appear to stipulate amber from Esiku's forest."

"How do we even know that thing ever happened?" I ask.

"Cataclysm? We don't. But we are sure the land shifts over time— you've seen it in your own province, and in the Wastes of Los, fish skeletons have been found embedded in the rock. There's no debate there was once an inland sea there."

Ash raises an eyebrow at me. "Now will you admit that was silver well spent?"

"Only the smoke-brained pay that much for amber oil," I retort.

"Amber *oil*?" Esarik asks. "I'm not entirely sure it will be fit for purpose."

Ash stalks over to the table where the scroll is laid out. "You just said it was Losian amber."

"Indeed. But the second part of the passage is key. See?" Esarik points to the scroll and Ash reads:

> *All must be pure and in sequence blown,*
> *If they are to serve both the dark and light,*
> *Only clouds will end what clouds have begun—*

Esarik holds up a hand. "An understandable translation error. It's a quirk of Old Imperial. The second last line reads: *masaat asytaa amidak snalu masaat kiregtaa traalapaame.* We still use 'marsat' for cloud, but the other terms have no modern equivalent. If we were to be literal, *masaat asytaa* and *masaat kiregtaa* translate to 'wet cloud' and 'dry cloud,' more or less. But to a speaker from the first cycle of the Empire?"

"Steam?" I venture. "And . . ."

Esarik grips the table and bows his head. "Smoke. Smoke from the dahkai plantation going up in flames. The final ingredient in the sequence. If I'd known, I would have—"

"What could you have done, Es?" Ash asks gently. "What can even be done for plain old smoke inhalation? Wait? Hope?"

The scholar looks stricken. I know the feeling of figuring out something too late, like you can no longer trust your own wits, your own judgment. But dwelling on that isn't going to help Nisai.

"*Only steam will end what smoke has begun,*" I muse. "So . . . a steam distillate will cure a poison delivered by smoke!"

My excitement flees on the heels of another realization. Esarik's right about the amber. "But distilling the original amber from the carrier oil? It'd be like trying to unscramble an egg. Maybe with the right equipment, but we're talking serious setup. Master Perfumer level. Even if we could access that kind of apparatus, stench knows how many times it would need to be processed, and how many tries I'd need to get it right, the scent getting fainter and fainter each time. We could end up with nothing."

"How long would it take to find out?" Ash asks.

"Days? Weeks? I don't know. And amber isn't really . . . my thing." It was Barden's favorite. Not something I care to think about right now. "It'd be a surer bet if we found some in pure form. Probably safer for Nisai, too."

And much safer for us. There are very few places that would even have that equipment, and none of them where we could pass unnoticed.

Esarik glowers. "The Losians harvest every bit of the solid form. You might find some in Ekasya, for a small fortune. Be discerning— it's an antiquity, so fakes have flooded the market. Oh, and you'll need documents. The imperial regulators insist the system exists to protect purchasers from fraud, though one gets the impression it's more to ensure taxes are paid."

Ash twists away from the table, throwing his hands up in frustration. "As if I needed any more ways to bring the city watch down on our heads."

"Off you trot to Lostras, then," Esarik says, the bitterness of earlier back in his voice.

No wonder. Los's largest city is on the northern coast. The Empire's edge. It will take weeks just to get there.

I clench my fists in frustration.

Sephine used the last of her power to keep Nisai alive until Tozran's Coronation. We've already used up a moon. The last thing we can afford is a trip to Lostras.

CHAPTER 28
ASH

When Azered's bones danced in the breath of blight

The chagrin on Rakel's face mirrors my thoughts. We'll never get to Lostras in time, if indeed that's where we can find some of this legendary Esikun amber without instant arrest. I turn to the window and stare out over the moons-lit vineyard.

Something crashes behind me. Something heavy. Solid.

I spin to find Esarik standing over one of the swords previously mounted in the wall collection. He's lifting a heavy bronze bench and bringing one of its legs down on the hilt of the weapon.

Rakel stands with a mix of confusion and curiosity playing across her features.

The pommel stone—a clear golden-brown—shatters on impact. Esarik picks through the shards, holding one up to the light. "Shattered like glass. Anachronistic inclusions." He gives it a sniff. "Lack of coniferous aroma. It's a fake," he mutters disgustedly, taking down another sword, this one from the Mur coat-of-arms.

I take a step toward him. "What are you doing?"

"I was intending on saving you a trip. Alas, history is populated with as many rogues as the present. I can't provide the amber after all. However, perhaps there is a consolation prize." He grunts as he lifts the furniture again, nudging the sword with his boot so that it's positioned beneath the lounge leg.

"Esarik?"

Crash.

He crouches down and examines the warped metal. "Once more . . ."

This is a side to him I've never seen. Does a broken heart now command the usually mild scholar's behavior? It's always been bittersweet watching the affection between the scholar and Ami, the imperial library curator—not someone Lord Mur would ever let his son marry. Or has Nisai being poisoned cut him just as keenly as it has me?

He heaves the lounge up again.

Crash.

"Esarik!" I bark. "What are you doing?"

He pushes his hair from his eyes. "The Mur family has a long lineage. My ancestors were among the survivors of the Shadow Wars, and they exchanged gifts with their peers from the newly formed provinces at the Founding Accord's inception—symbols of unity after troubled centuries. Several swords in the Mur family collection were among these gifts. Including our own arms."

Rakel jumps to her feet, gaping at the warped hilt and broken blade. "You just destroyed your family's sword? Your *father's* sword? But he'll—"

"Experience the loss of something he loved. A pale approximation of how I feel."

"What about legacy?" Rakel blurts. "My father would be devastated if someone took to his sword like that."

"The stars know the legacy of my ancestors has been tainted. A sword on the wall can't change that."

In some ways we're so very different; in some ways our lives have played out along similar lines—at the whims of others. Esarik didn't choose to come to the palace, and then he didn't choose to stay. He didn't choose to study physiology. But he went along with all of that with characteristic affability. And now, even the life he had adjusted to, made the most of, has been taken away—banished back to his family's estate as soon as his father suspects there's more to gain from marrying him off to a rich local girl than keeping him in Nisai's circles.

When rain seeps into stone for turn upon turn, it can cause fractures where no eye can see, so that it's a shock when it finally crumbles. Perhaps Esarik's facade has been slipping longer than even I knew.

With a triumphant twist, he holds a pommel stone aloft. It shines clear as a diamond beneath the candlewheels. A flower has been sealed inside, frozen just at the point it began to unfurl its velvet black petals.

"I believe you can use this to save our friend."

Rakel's eyes widen. "Is that a—"

"Indeed. After the fire in Aphorai, this is possibly one of the only dahkai flowers left in the Empire. Sealed in glass at the point of blooming. While the essence you have acquired seems fit for the cure, I hazard to guess you'll need something solid to re-create the poison—your essence won't give off much smoke, even with its oils. This is useless for perfume now, a husk. But it should catch light serviceably."

"Re-create the poison?" I glance at Rakel. She's just as bemused as me.

The bitterness in Esarik's expression melts into wide-eyed earnestness. "Once you've made the cure, we must test it—we couldn't just dose our Prince with something for which we have no evidence of efficacy. And that means we'll first need to fabricate the poison. Once we've found the other ingredients, we'll find somewhere to retreat, where you can extract the flower from its casing, burn it as the final ingredient to dose me, then trial the cure."

"Poison you?" Rakel shakes her head. "I'm not poisoning *anyone*."

"Hold on a heartbeat," I say.

Esarik? Come with us? He's my friend, but he struggled with the pace of the trip to Aphorai, and that was with the luxury of an imperial delegation. And Rakel's impetuousness is more than a handful—the last thing I need is an erratic scholar falling apart at the seams.

"Es, the best way you can serve is if you get back to the capital as soon as you can. Nisai needs you. And if Rakel and I manage to somehow pull these ingredients together, we're going to need a friendly face at court."

He opens his mouth as if to speak, shuts it, opens it again. "But . . . I . . ."

"You know I'm right," I say as gently as I can.

Crestfallen, he hands Rakel the glass-encased flower. She stows it in her satchel.

Footsteps heavy, Esarik returns to the table and the formula. "You both need rest. I'll keep working on deciphering the final ingredients."

I cross my arms, about to protest. If we truly only have two moons to get an antidote to Nisai, I don't want to waste a moment. But then I look to Rakel, to her disheveled hair, the dark circles beneath her eyes, and I think better of it.

A servant shows us to our rooms, positioned on opposite sides of the main hall in the guest wing. Rakel opens the door to her chamber. The candlelit room beckons, a large copper bath positioned in the center. Steam rises from the tub. "I took the liberty of asking Esarik to have it prepared, I hope you don't mind. I just knew how much you wanted one and—"

"Mind? It's glorious," Rakel breathes.

Warmth spreads through my chest at the sight of her genuine pleasure. It's not an uncomfortable feeling, but it's strange to me nonetheless. "Good night, Rakel," I tell her, not sure what else to say.

She flashes a grateful smile. "Good night, Ash."

* * *

Dawn is yet to break when I awake to a knock at the door. Esarik slips into the room without waiting for a reply. I sit up, drawing my hand from beneath the pillow without the dagger I'd stowed there.

"Ash?" he whispers urgently. "Ash, get up. One of the cooks has just returned from the morning markets. She said there were several strangers in the village questioning folk."

"Tro's stones," I curse, swinging my legs out of bed and grabbing my trousers. "They must have tracked us from Koltos. I knew it was a foolish idea to linger there."

"This dangerous game has claimed us all." Esarik laments. He hands me a heavy purse and a folded parchment packet. "I've done what I can with the rest of the formula. You'll see I've marked the site of a cave system a couple of days' travel from here. Centuries ago, the locals referred to it as Azered's Grave. If I were seeking Azered's bones, that would be my wager."

He plunges on. "'Riker's heart' almost certainly refers to the traditions of the Edurshain people, who still revere the sagas and romances of the Great Bloom. But I haven't gleaned any specifics, and I don't comprehend a great deal about their venom work. You'll have to do your own research once you get there. I expect finding a camp will be your biggest challenge—the Edurshai Basin is constantly shifting."

"Shifting?"

"The rainy season in the Hagmiri Mountains floods Edurshai each turn. The land—*lands* to be technically correct—are predominantly peat islands. They float when the waters are high and settle in a different arrangement when the floods recede. So don't trust your map."

"Understood. And the other line? In the different script?" I ask.

Esarik grimaces. "Whatever it says, everything else indicates it's not part of the original formula. It's an afterthought. And the smudging suggests haste or little respect for the document. Possibly even defacement."

"It's graffiti?"

"Scribes are only human, they get bored, too. I've seen similar in other pre-Empire texts, few and far between as they are. I'm sorry, Ash, I wish I could do more. You can't imagine how much I wish for that. But please, for the love of the Prince, you must go. Now."

I gather my things and find Rakel, dressed but a little wild-eyed, in the hallway.

Esarik leads us to the servant's entrance. "I'll return to the capital as soon as I can, but knowing my father's predilections, this wedding extravagance will drag for a moon or more. If I arrive in good time before you, I'll make some inquiries into sourcing some amber. Discreet inquiries, naturally."

I clasp his arm. "Until then, stars keep you, my friend."

"And you."

The heavy oak door shuts behind us, leaving a pang of hollowness in its wake. I push it aside—going our separate ways to Esarik is the right thing—far more useful than having a friendly face around.

Rakel and I set out across the manicured gardens and climb the first stone wall between the manse and the fields. Beneath clear skies, the finches and blackbirds continue their song as we pass; anyone could be forgiven for thinking nothing is amiss. It's only when we're about to emerge from the last of the Mur family vineyards that I spot them. Three farmhands rounding a corner farther down the lane. Only farmhands don't wear swords.

"Down," I hiss. "Lil, too."

Rakel gives her horse a quiet command, and the beast folds her legs and sinks to the ground. I crouch next to them, sending a silent prayer to Esiku that we blend into the shade of the vines.

"Are they . . . ?" Rakel whispers.

I nod. I don't recognize any of them, but I'd recognize their ilk at twice the distance.

The three Rangers draw nearer, only their legs and boots visible beneath the leaves and bunches of grapes. But I can imagine the way their gaze will be roaming the vines, their ears alert for the barest out-of-place sound. I focus on controlling my breath, on keeping my heartbeat steady and even.

Rakel rests one hand on her horse's cheek, but the other is white-knuckled around the hilt of her knife. I'm reminded of when the three of us last huddled like this during the sandstorm, when she was the calm presence I needed, the one that kept me from trying to flee headlong into the arms of danger. I reach over and gently pry the blade from her fingers, covering her hand with my own, willing her not to spook.

The Rangers draw level with us, their hushed voices just out of earshot.

And then they're disappearing over the next rise.

Still, we wait there, in the vines, not daring to move for some time.

Finally, Rakel slips her hand from mine. "Are they gone?"

I nod.

For now, I want to add. But I keep my thoughts to myself.

*   *
  *   *
    *

On the second night after leaving the Mur Estate, we sit examining Esarik's notes alongside the ancient scroll. The evening air is mild, and with cheese and cold cuts from the Mur kitchens, supplemented with bunches of fat red grapes I'd cut from vines overhanging the road, there's no need for a fire.

I gesture to the map. "If the caves are beneath this ridge, we should reach their western entrance tomorrow, all being well."

Sure enough, during a golden Trelian sunrise, we cross the Ekasya river at a natural ford. Despite never having seen anything more than an oasis pool, Rakel's horse stoically bears us both across the rushing water, the current churning well above her knees.

As we near the map marker for the caves, the land turns rocky, the vineyards to olive orchards. Rakel dismounts, letting her horse crop at the grass tufting between the stones. We spread out to search for an entrance to the underground caverns.

"Here," Rakel soon calls.

I find her at the mouth of the cave, the entrance hidden behind a rocky outcrop.

She points to the ground. "The previous resident wasn't exactly a housekeeping champion." A trail of bones leads to the cave, bleached white in the sun so they blend into the chalky dust. They're far too large to be anything other than aurochs—the huge bovines used to plow the Trelian fields since the edge of memory.

"Could wolves have done this?" Rakel asks.

"Unlikely. A bear, possibly." I peer into the cave entrance. "It's blacker than shadow in there."

"Please don't tell me you're afraid of the dark."

"I'm just being cautious," I snap. "I doubt bone-crunching carnivores appreciate visitors."

"Whatever it was, it's long gone. I'd smell it if it were still here. This place is nothing like that. It's almost"—she sniffs the air—"clean. Minerals, moisture—that's about it."

She clinks around in her satchel before withdrawing a small jar. "Good thing Esarik's servants were generous with my supply requests."

I choose a torch-length bone from the pile and hold it out to Rakel.

"Oooh, city boy's learned a thing or two." She smirks, dripping contents from the jar onto one end of the bone. She sparks it, then blows gently to coax the flame to life.

I realize I'm staring at her lips and avert my gaze.

"When we get in there," I say, clearing my throat, "give me a moment for my eyes to adjust. I don't have your nose, and I'd rather be sure nothing sneaks up on us. Wouldn't want a repeat of the mountains, would we?"

Honestly, the blackness does unnerve me. The palace and the city of Ekasya below are never truly dark. There are torches along the main boulevard, lanterns lining the riverbanks.

Rakel shrugs. "The sooner we get in there the sooner we can adjust and see if we've come to the right place." She disappears into the cave.

Tro's stones. How does this girl keep managing to get me to follow her?

It's as if we're entering the jaws of a giant limestone beast. Fang-like rocks jut up from the floor. Their twins arrow down from the ceiling, drops of water hanging for impossibly long moments before plunging to the spike below. The last light coming from the entrance casts it all in shades of milky gray.

The entire cavern is silent, except for the occasional drip of water.

My eyes adjust just fine. But while I can see perfectly well, my palms have begun to sweat.

"Over there," Rakel says, torchlight flickering over her face. She points deeper into the cave. Incongruously, it seems less dark, even though it's farther from the surface. "That's got to be the way. Come on."

There's definitely some kind of light beyond this cavern. Perhaps a shaft leading to the surface. Rakel's probably right.

The walls of the cave narrow as we press on. Soon, it's not much more than a tunnel. The next thing, we're walking in single file. Then we're turning sideways to squeeze through the gap.

The close confines, the stone scraping against my skin, triggers a memory.

I'm small, younger than when I met Nisai. A trapdoor is closing at the top of a ladder, plunging me into darkness. I don't know when it will open again. It's damp down here. It's near the river and the water finds ways to seep through the rock. Something flutters against my cheek and I cringe away.

Voices argue above me. A man's shouted curses. A thud. A woman's shriek. My mother's.

Then silence.

Is she hurt? I want to call to her, but she told me not to.

Can you do something for me, my little hero?

I press my hands to the stone of the cave, my heart beating faster.

Can you be quiet? Quiet as a dockmouse? No matter what you hear?

It's so dark in here. As dark as the cellar—

But it's not dark. Not utterly, completely.

Light beckons.

I was following the light.

And Rakel's ahead, carrying it. We're here together. I'm not alone.

I take another step, the movement pressing my swords between the limestone wall and my chestpiece. They bring me back to the here and now. Steel and leather—protection. For me. For those I'm sworn to.

I push the memories away, into their own dark hole in the rock, and slam the trapdoor in my mind shut.

"Ash!" Rakel's voice echoes back to me.

One foot at a time, I edge forward.

It probably isn't much farther, but it feels like a mile before the cavern yawns wide again. Any lingering unease is stripped away at what lies before me. I balk, blinking in amazement.

I've never seen anything like it.

The floor of the cave gives way to a pool of water, its surface so unblemished it could put a polished gem to shame. But what's truly wondrous is the sapphire glow that emanates from beneath.

Rakel picks her way around the edge of the pool, her face lit, as if she's standing over blue fire. The color reminds me of the fireflies that dance at dusk through the Ekasyan summer. Except the light behaves like no fire I've ever seen. It's a steady illumination, like moonlight, not the flicker of flames.

Once my eyes adjust, I realize the light is coming from the plants growing on the bottom of the pool. They're shaped like small, leafless trees, with stubby growths instead of branches.

"What are they?" In the silence, my voice sounds uncannily loud.

"Bones, hopefully," Rakel says. "Living bone. They say it grows along some of the coasts in the color of rainbows, but I've only ever seen it sold in white powder. It's meant to help heal breaks and fractures." She pauses on the other side of the pool and produces a vial from her satchel. "This isn't the stuff you get in the markets. I'd bet on Esarik's theory. A place doesn't get called Azered's Grave for nothing."

"I'd wager you're right." And I would. I'd not have managed even half the things Rakel has figured out.

Kneeling at the water's edge, she reaches for the nearest plant. "Here goes nothing."

Through the ripples, she grasps the end of one of the branches.

"It's stronger than it looks." She frowns and shifts her weight, getting a better grip. "Easily as strong as bone. Maybe it's rock? Ow!" With a yelp, she draws back, shaking her hand as if something still clings to it. The vial splashes into the water and sinks into the bed of glowing bone plants.

"Rancid-reeking-Rot, that *stings*."

I'm about to move closer when something behind her catches my eye. The ripples caused by the dropped vial are doing something to the light.

It's changing.

"Ah, Rakel?"

She ignores me, too intent on examining her stung hand.

It's becoming more and more obvious. The light isn't changing; it's shimmering and pulsing.

Dancing, even.

And, one by one, the plants—whatever they're called—are going dark.

An inky cloud moves toward me as they shrivel and blacken, the die-off spreading like blood in water, like the tincture I take nightly and am running so low on, too ashamed to ask Esarik without the cover of Nisai's "migraines."

Rakel curses. "You're going to have to bottle it!" She's rummaging in her satchel again. "Don't disturb the water, and for your Prince's sake don't let any air in."

"What are you talking about?"

"*The breath of blight.* It's air! I let air in when I disturbed the water. And now it's dying. You'll need to get it from your side. I'll throw a vial. Catch!"

Instinct kicks in. I hear and feel the vessel hurtling toward me as much as I see it, and my muscles react. With a thwack, I've snatched the vial out of the air. Though it probably would have hit me in the chest if I'd done nothing. She's a good shot.

I struggle to uncork the stopper. Decay seeps nearer, relentless, unstoppable. It's like a game of shnik-shnik—the stone pieces falling into one another until none are left standing.

Then the vial is open and I'm dipping it slowly, slowly, ever so carefully below the surface.

"Make sure you submerge it at an angle!" Rakel calls across the water. "The bubbles will do you in otherwise!"

The advice comes just in time. One bubble surfaces and the tiny eddy stains the nearest glowing plant black. I tilt the vial so water rushes into the mouth, filling it to the brim before I lower it beneath the surface.

"It's submerged," I tell her. "Now what?"

"Guide the vial over a branch. Careful, now, you don't want to get stung more than you need to.

"Branch in the vial. No touching. Got it."

I try to position the vial over the next nearest branch. But the water is rippling now, glowing reflections wavering around the cavern walls. It's hard to pinpoint what's real beneath the surface and what's a trick of the light.

My hands threaten to shake, but I force myself to picture this as a battle, as facing down an armed opponent. One false move and their sword will open me from mouth to midsection.

It works.

The lip of the vial clears the delicate glowing branch.

"Great," Rakel calls. "You're doing great. Now, break off the stalk."

I move my other hand slowly, steadily, holding my breath.

The cascade of die-off still spreads, but I've got time. There's still time.

I pinch the stalk between my thumb and forefinger. It smarts and smushes against my skin and doesn't disconnect. Next thing, it's dying in my hand. Then the plant beneath it dies, and I'm left with one stung hand, the other holding a vial of blackened sludge.

I curse.

"No good?"

"It was fine until I tried to pick it."

"Wait there" comes her only answer. I hear more rummaging in her satchel before she speaks again. "I'm going to throw you some pincers. Use them to sever the stem—clean, in one pinch. But be careful of the tips. They're sharpened like razors."

"If I can manage to not cut myself on my swords, I think I'll be able to handle them."

"Ha-ha. Ready?"

"As I'll ever be."

This time, with both hands submerged in water that I'm at pains not to disturb, I can't lunge for the object hurtling toward me. The air moves over my shoulder and the plink of metal against rock sounds one, two, three times behind me. The tools have come to rest somewhere off to my left.

The plant beneath the jar is already black and decaying, the once-ethereal branch now sludge against the bedrock. I figure I'm not going to cause any further damage, so I lower the vial and let it rest on the bottom of the pool. Moving a finger with each heartbeat, I time the retraction of my hands from the water. Only the one plant seems to have died in the near vicinity, though the death from the other side of the pool is rolling ever closer.

I crawl along the rock ledge. My scrabbling fingers find sharp metal, and I withdraw them with a hiss, sticking my finger in my mouth and tasting copper.

"Ash? What's taking so long?"

"Lay off, would you?"

I reach out over the water again. Darkness rushes toward me, dread clawing up from the pit of my stomach in its wake.

I clench my jaw. Careful, so painfully careful, I submerge my hands again. One picks up the vial, the other poises Rakel's dagger-sharp pincers between thumb and forefinger.

The cloud of die-off has reached me now. The final plants are about to wink out, Nisai's only hope with them. I draw a breath, holding it in to hold myself together.

Somehow, I get one of the last blue branches into the vial. The pincers sever the stalk. I bring both to the surface, free the stopper from my teeth. The vessel is safely sealed.

I wait. One. Two. Three thumping heartbeats.

The chamber around me is completely black.

But inside the vial, cradled in my hands, the glow shines on.

"I have it!"

I have it.

Rakel's whoop of victory brightens the pitch-black cave. Then there's splashing and cursing as she makes her way toward me. The first thing that swims into view is her grin. She grabs my arm to steady herself, her hand warm on my skin where before there was the chill of the cave.

She draws close to peer at the precious vial in my hands, her smile softening to something resembling reverence as the last of Azered's bones defiantly continues to shine. The way the blue glow illuminates

her features makes her seem like she could be from the stars, as allur-
ing and distant as Azered herself.

"I thought for a second there it was over," she says. "That they
were all gone."

"They almost were," I admit.

She gives my arm a squeeze, then steps away, inhaling deeply. "Ah,
the sweet smell of success. Well, of damp cave more to the point, but
who's splitting hairs."

Her words set off a sensation I'd been trying to control since we
stepped foot into the cave. That smell. Of damp, underground places
walled in stone. Of being trapped, held prisoner.

With the adrenaline seeping away, the darkness comes crushing in.
My hands begin to shake.

I fumble.

The vial falls from my fingers.

CHAPTER 29
RAKEL

When Azered's bones danced in the breath of blight

Time stretches like tar.

One moment Ash is standing there with the glowing vial, awe
and wonder and victory playing across his usually stern features. The
next, he's looking troubled, stricken, almost panicked. He gasps for
breath. The vial and the precious ingredient it holds drop toward the
ground.

I lunge, twisting so that my shoulder hits the stone of the cave floor. A hiss of pain escapes my lips. But I get both my good and injured hand under my target.

Safe. The vial is safe.

"What's got into you?" I demand, scrabbling to my feet. "Ash? Ash, answer me."

The only reply is rapid, shallow breathing.

I know that sound. Remember it from when I was younger and it was loud in my own ears. Back when I hadn't learned to deal with the overwhelming rush of sweet and foul scents in the city. When the sense of myself and my own body separated, and I felt like I would drown in open air.

Something clicks into place. Now that the adrenaline, the urgency of what Ash calls "the mission" has abated, we're left in the dark. Before we entered the caves, it wasn't the traces of the long-gone bear he was hesitant about. It was this. The pitch-black.

"Ash?"

No reply.

"Ash!"

I hold the glowing vial out in front of me. It's a pitiful torch, but it's enough. Ash is crouched on his haunches, hugging his knees. He's murmuring so quietly I can barely make out the words. I lean closer.

"Don't-let-him-see-you, don't-let-them-see-you, don't-let-anyone-see."

"Ash, there's nobody here but us."

It's as if he doesn't register my presence. I crouch beside him and rest my uninjured hand on his shoulder, holding up the vial and its soft light between us. "Look at me. I'm here, you see? I don't know where you've gone, but I'm here." I give his shoulder a squeeze.

He blinks at me.

Good sign.

"We're going to get you outside. Try to focus on your breathing. It helps me when I'm overwhelmed. Deep breath in . . . count to five . . . and out." I breathe slow and deep, each inhale and exhale deliberate and audible.

Somehow, I manage to pry one of Ash's arms from around himself and get it over my shoulders, taking as much of his weight as I can. From the dim light of the vial, I guide us back the way we came. He's so much bigger than me, and though his feet are under him, sweat begins to sheen my brow, even in the cool of the cavern.

It's a struggle when the path narrows. We can't go through two abreast, so I turn us sideways and lead. The arm supporting Ash scrapes against the rock, and I bite back a curse. He's gasping for air now. I remember what that's like. I've got to move quickly, or he's going to faint.

As we near the entrance, the air brings promises of light and warmth and fields of fruit and herbs. Ash starts to straighten, his breathing still ragged, but slowly becoming more regular.

Outside the cave's mouth, I tilt my face to the sun, relief washing through me. "I thought for a second there it was all over. That they'd all die off before we could take any. But we did it."

Ash reaches out to steady himself against a boulder, and I ease out from under his arm. He's staring intently at the ground like he's deliberately avoiding my gaze. "They almost *did* all die. One stupid stumble and—"

"Stop," I say, squeezing his arm. "That isn't the important part."

He peers at me as if he's searching my face for any sign of judgment. He won't find any.

I open my satchel and nestle the glowing vial in a jar of dried saltwort so it's cushioned and hidden from excess sun, then replace the lid. Better to be safe than sorry.

I look to Ash. He's still wild about the eyes. Back when I was a child and used to get overwhelmed by scents, the best thing to do was to put as much distance as possible between me and the source of panic until I calmed. "Want to get out of here?"

He nods.

We set out, taking it slowly at first. The late-afternoon sun turns everything before us golden as we head southwest toward Edurshai Province. I decide to walk for the time being and lead Lil. It seems only right, given what we've just been through. And it seems only right to be on the same level when I start asking questions.

"Do you want to talk about what happened in there?"

"Would you mind if we didn't?"

I don't want to push. But I still know so little about him. I try something else. "You're not from Ekasya?"

"Does it matter? Unless we're successful I'll never be able to go back." He glances at me, sidelong. "What makes you think I'm not?"

"I heard the way you were cursing in there. That was as colorful as you'd hear in an Aphorain market."

He sighs. "I'm not from the imperial city. Not originally. When Nisai found me, I was province-less. I spent my childhood in the shadow of Ekasya Mountain."

I never would have guessed he's come from a harder background than I have. Even in Aphorai we've heard of the slums around the capital. "Then how did you end up in the palace?"

He considers that silently as we pick up the lane where it enters a field of lavender. Ash snaps a stem from the nearest plant and begins to pluck the leaves one by one. I used to find the scent calming, but the last time I smelled it so strongly was back in Aphorai when Zakkurus was about to turn my life upside down.

"I was about seven or eight turns old," Ash begins. "There was a royal entourage heading from the city to the river docks. Nisai hadn't yet been named heir, but he was already led by his curiosity. He strayed into my . . . 'Neighborhood' makes it sound more pleasant than it was. I'd fallen in with some older boys—older boys who were trying to find an out-of-sight place to light up some dreamsmoke."

I scowl. When I was a child, Father used to tell me terrifying tales about the drug and the monsters it makes of long-term users. As I grew up, I realized half of them are true.

"We ended up in an abandoned warehouse—that's when the others

229

noticed Nisai trailing us. They made him turn out his pockets, and when that didn't yield much, they started roughing him up. It was when they made him give up his shoes—they'd fetch a good price in the Scuttler's Market—that I stepped between them. Nisai was clearly rich, but he wasn't going to be able to give them what they wanted. The others backed off. Then ran. But it wasn't from my stand. They'd seen the Blazers come in behind us."

"Blazers?"

"Brotherhood of the Blazing Sun. Ever heard stories of Lost God worshippers snatching children off the streets?"

In some of those stories they disappear forever. In others, they appear moons later after their families meet rich ransom demands. They must have thought all their Flower Moons had come at once to stumble upon a prince.

Ash reads my grimace as acknowledgment. "The stories aren't unfounded. And there's plenty of theories about what they do to the poor wretches. All I knew back then was that anyone the Blazers took from where I lived never returned."

"You got away?"

He looks back to the cave mouth. "You learn a few things growing up in the shadow of Ekasya Mountain. Nisai was so grateful I got us out of the scrape, he petitioned his mother, Councillor Shari, and they took me back to the palace, where I began training to earn my keep. I've been by the Prince's side, in one way or another, ever since."

"What about your parents?"

"With me gone?" He shrugs. "One less mouth to feed."

There's pain there, but it's buried deep. It would be cruel to prod any further. Instead, I rummage in my things and pull out a bottle I'd been carrying since Luz returned my satchel to me in Aphorai. Its uses are many—migraines, aiding sleep, settling the nerves, and, importantly, helping to stave off the panic Ash lost himself back at the caves.

"Linod's Elixir," I say, giving it a shake.

Ash frowns at the bottle.

Many *would* frown. But I relied on the stuff when I was young and learning to deal with my sensitivity, albeit using a weak dilution. Fiercely addictive, its long-term users often develop resistance, requiring a higher and higher dose until the treatment becomes more dangerous than the problem.

But if I've learned anything about Ash, he's disciplined. He'd keep it in hand.

"Rakel, I don't know what to . . ." He averts his eyes again.

"We don't have to talk about this, either." I hold the bottle toward him. "It's what you've been dosing yourself with, isn't it? And judging by what happened in there, you've run out."

He reaches to take it, his fingers brushing mine. They're warm, but somehow send a shiver through me.

"This means . . . a lot," he says, finally raising his gaze to meet mine.

Our eyes lock. I'm acutely aware our hands are still touching, that I'm standing and staring and not so much as blinking. A flush creeps up my neck, but I can't move away. I don't *want* to move away.

Ash takes a step closer, his other hand wrapping around the bottle so my own is caught between his larger palms, his calloused skin rough against mine. "There's something I need to tell you," he says. "Something I wasn't entirely honest about."

I snatch my hand back. Whatever comes next, I've got a hunch I'm not going to like it. Nor will my stomach, judging by its churning.

He heaves a breath, gathering himself. "I need you to know that I wanted to tell you before, up in the mountains. I didn't want you to think I was . . . I didn't want you to think I would lie to you. But I wasn't yet sure."

"What makes you *sure* now?"

"Please, Rakel, what I'm about to say puts my life in your hands."

"I hardly doubt *your* life is in my—"

"Until Nisai is healed, our futures are inseparable." He opens his pack and holds out the Prince's journal. "And if you found the right sort of person to give this to, you'd have enough to denounce me."

231

I ignore the book—it's not like I have a clue how to interpret what I've seen in there—and start walking again, moving to the other side of Lil so my thoughts remain my own. "Spit it out, then."

"That day in the slums, when Nisai and I first met."

"Go on."

"We didn't escape the Blazers, as such."

The world grows quiet around me, making the buzz of bees flitting about the lavender seem loud.

"I killed them."

"Pff! How did a kid manage that?"

"I don't know."

I duck my head, frowning at him under the sweep of Lil's neck. "What do you mean you don't know?"

"I wasn't conscious."

"Hold up. Child—you blacked out, and in doing so killed two full-grown men?"

"I'm not certain how it went. But when I returned to myself, the Blazers were dead and I was covered in blood. And . . ."

"And? There's an "and"?"

"And-Nisai-said-there-were-shadows." He speaks the sentence so fast the words run together. "Something *happened* with them. They slowed the Blazers down. One of them started 'choking on darkness,' Nisai said. Yes. It sounds outlandish. Like I told you, I wasn't . . . *there*. I have to rely on Nisai's account. Even back then, he was fascinated enough by tales of gods and myths to believe it was some kind of magic. That *I* was magic."

"Ash, I know you're a believer, but . . ."

"A believer. Not a blasphemer. I've never told anyone any of this. Though I think Esarik may have guessed at some of it, given the way Nisai has been researching for any information that survived the Shadow Wars. Only, Esarik's much too circumspect to bring it up." He takes hold of Lil's bridle as if to steady himself. "I'm not lying."

Lil stops still without a whicker. I'm reminded I've never seen her allow anyone else to touch her without so much as a nip.

"I think my parents knew something of it, too," he continues. "I don't have a single memory of my father looking me in the eye. He used to mutter I was cursed, that he didn't want me beneath his roof."

"Cursed?"

"He was a devout man. He never missed an offering. Observed every portentous day in every turn of the starwheel and steeped my childhood in prayer. If I set a foot wrong, he would lock me in the cellar without food or water. Said I was tainted by shadow." His face twists at the last, as if he's tasted something foul.

"My mother pleaded for him to let me out. When that didn't work, she argued. Told me he was losing his mind. He wouldn't heed her words. They were both metalsmiths, and she was almost my father's match in strength." His eyes shine, but there's pride there, too.

"She wrested free, released me, and we fled. But what seemed emancipation soon became a trap. We begged in the streets, but there wasn't enough food. She fed me and went without. Soon she began to weaken, and when she contracted river fever, it was only a matter of time. My father was right all along. I *am* a curse."

"Your mother's death is on your father's head." I almost spit the words. Then I hear myself laugh, harsh and self-mocking. "I, on the other hand, killed my mother just coming into this world."

"She died in childbirth?"

"Not long after. But it was the injuries of birth that did it. My father almost never spoke of it. Like you said—I guess he wanted to protect me. And himself."

Ash grimaces. "I'm sorry."

"I'll always be sorry."

We continue walking, the plagued silence of earlier replaced with something cleaner, more breathable. Still, Ash's confession echoes in my mind. He really believes this. Believes he's somehow cursed.

But magic? Yes, I've seen incredible things I would never have imagined—giant butterflies and bones glowing with life. But *magic*? That's a leap of faith I can't make.

Eventually, the lane crests a hill. I let Lil graze while Ash and I scramble up a boulder for a better view. A patchwork of crops spreads out below, disappearing into the haze of a flat horizon.

This land is what people have made of it, but if they stopped tending it, nature would take it back. Sure as the land heaves under Aphorai. Not magic. Not gods. Nature.

"I don't believe in curses," I say. "In Aphorai, people kneel at the shrine to Zir and Tro all day, sniffing water lilies and melissa extract as if it's going to bring the river back. As if perfumed prayers are going to restore the Twins' favor. But I've seen enough springs to know that water flows where it will. A groundshake moved the river, not a pair of squabbling gods. Not a curse."

The breeze flutters my hair, and it takes my mind back to Aphorai again. This time standing at the top of the temple with Sephine. "The temple wants everyone to be a believer. When you believe, you pay the temple to make offerings on your behalf. In exchange, they're supposed to make sure the gods hear your prayers. But when my mother needed a miracle, did they make sure my father's prayers were heard? No. So either the priestesses are charlatans, the gods don't exist, or they're just plain cruel. You choose."

Ash stays silent beside me.

"And when Sephine could have healed my mother, did she? No. It was more important to send a message—no priestess must bear a child—than it was to save a life."

I look to Ash. "And those Blazers? You defended yourself and Nisai. People do what they need to do when their backs are against the wall. My father serves—did serve—in the Aphorain army; I've grown up on tales of unbelievable strength and bravery under duress. Feats so wondrous they may seem magic."

Ash gives me a sad smile. "I'm not sure it's the same."

"Have you done anything like that since? Blacked out? Hurt anyone?"

"Beyond the training field or in the line of duty? No, thank Riker. Sometimes I feel strange, but Linod's Elixir seems to . . . steady me. Even so, Nisai dedicates his spare time searching for an explanation for what happened that day, in case there's another way to . . . manage myself. I realized too late that part of his enthusiasm to get to Aphorai was to continue his research."

"Then I'd say you owe it to Nisai to spend your thoughts and energy on helping him. Make your actions in the here and now count the most."

I wonder at my own recent actions. Slaughtering rare butterfly pupae, however vicious. The dark fate of the wonders in the caves. So much destruction in the name of a single life.

I give myself an inward shake. That's a one-way thought trail. If I take too many steps down it, I know I won't return. All this would have been for naught, and it won't just be the Prince who will suffer for it.

I climb onto Lil's back. "Let's get on with it, eh?"

Ash tightens the strap of his pack and starts down the hill.

His steps are the lightest I've ever seen them.

CHAPTER 30
ASH

When Riker's heart faced the eternal plight

After the incident in the caves, I've increased my dose of Linod's Elixir—chagrined that my need seems to be growing faster than ever, yet thankful the higher dose takes effect quickly. Panic no longer simmers beneath the surface of every moment. I'm back in control. Where I need to be.

It's as much relief to my body as confessing to Rakel has eased my mind. I never imagined I'd be able to tell anyone else without them turning on me. Aside from Nisai, I've never felt inclined to trust anyone as easily as the way the understanding between us has unfurled. Perhaps because I've never met anyone who looks at the world as Rakel does.

We spend days crossing the fertile lands of Trel bound for Edurshai. The Basin comprises over a third of the Empire's landmass, but for the most part remains a mystery. The Edurshain people don't often travel outside their lands, and I can't imagine many outsiders would have reason to risk entering the Basin's ever-shifting landscape. It means that when Rakel peppers me with questions about the province at camp each night, I find myself woefully unequipped to answer.

"So the Edurshain like old stories of heroes and maidens and whatnot. Is there anything else we know about them that could help? Do they have an Eraz?" she asks over our well-concealed fire. "And what do they eat?"

"They're herders; they have milk and meat."

She shakes her head. "A person needs more than that to survive. If the Basin is as vast as you say, don't they grow crops?"

"I'm not an expert on the agrarian habits of every corner of the Empire."

"You seemed to know a lot about Trel. And even some about Hagmir. Why choose not to learn about Edurshai?" She pins me with her gaze. "Because they don't supply the capital with wine or kormak or precious-smelling dahkai, is that it?"

She's right, but she also seems on edge, each day's urgency wearing on her as much as on me. We blessedly haven't encountered any Rangers since the close call near Esarik's, but that's not the only force against us. With each passing night, time itself has become a pack of street dogs, snapping at our heels, just waiting for us to stumble down a blind alley while Nisai's life ebbs away.

"I guess I'd never thought about it before," I admit.

"Typical." Rakel sniffs.

I look to the stars. I can't help but think her newfound geographical curiosity is her way of avoiding the conversation returning to more personal topics.

I'm surprised when I realize that pains me.

*   *
*   *
*

Eventually, we crest the last of the Trelian hills to look out over the vastness of the Edurshai Basin. Heather grows shoulder-high, each branch covered with hundreds of tiny spiked leaves. A breeze sends the whole vista rippling from here to the far horizon.

The sight is double-edged. We're getting closer to the next ingredient, but first we need to battle through a veritable sea of thorns.

We decide to follow the myriad streams coursing between the heather-covered mounds, where lower-growing gorse and tiny blue wildflowers line the banks, making for easier going. Still, I soon end up with red lines crisscrossing my arms above my gauntlets, swallowing a curse when a thorn scratches my cheek deep enough to draw blood.

It's a strange feeling, walking on land that shrinks beneath our steps, cringing away from our feet only to spring back when we've left. Every so often, one of us sinks up to the ankle or knee, a sharp reminder we're far from solid ground. Beating back just enough brush to make camp each dusk and not being able to see more than a few arm spans in each direction unnerves me.

In contrast, Rakel seems calm. I suppose it's not all that different from the desert—open sky above but limited vantage points on the ground.

To me, it feels like we're ambush bait, and as the days pass, I begin to withdraw into myself, all energy spent on avoiding sinkholes, on trying to detect the presence of others—whether we're being followed by Rangers, or if we're on the trail of what we've come here for: the help of the Edurshain.

A distant noise, like vegetation snapping underfoot, snares my attention. Rakel's sensed something, too. She halts her horse so abruptly the mare tosses her head.

"What is it?" I ask, hands edging toward my swords.

From the saddle, she points out over the plain. "What are *they*?"

I'm forced to stand on my toes to follow her gesture.

Ahead, a swathe of heather parts before a herd of animals. They're four-legged, just like a camel or a donkey, and they're grazing, but that's where the similarities to any other beast in Aramtesh ends. Twice the size of Rakel's horse, their legs are long and graceful, short-haired coats pale and gleaming like liquid silver in the late afternoon light. Horns twist up from between the ears of the largest creatures.

Rakel drops her arm back to her side. "Are those . . . tulda? How big do they get?"

"*Big.*" I've never seen a live tulda before, but I've seen plenty of their spiral-horned heads on the walls of Ekasya's most ornate mansions. Trophies from the sport of noblemen. Though just like the lion hunt back in Aphorai, I see nothing noble about delivering any of the creatures before us the same fate.

"They're *beautiful*," Rakel breathes.

I burst into laughter.

She balls her fists at her hips. "What's so funny?"

"You should see your expression. A few days in the Basin and you're already as swoony as an Edurshain."

"I'm not," she huffs.

We draw nearer to find a girl of about twelve or thirteen turns wandering among the tulda, completely unconcerned at the prospect of being crushed beneath a giant hoof. She looks like she's made of moonlight, with pale skin, blond hair, and a white dress that flows to her ankles, the full sleeves billowing past her wrists. It hardly seems a practical ensemble for working livestock.

In one hand, the girl holds a herder's stave tipped with streamers of blue cloth. The other stretches up on occasion to pat a silver-pelted flank—the only substantial part she's tall enough to reach. Occasionally, one of the animals will bend down to press its nose to her shoulder in a way that resembles Rakel and her horse.

When she catches sight of us, the girl smiles and waves.

"Is it just me," I murmur, "or is she grinning at us like we're dear friends returning after a long journey?"

Rakel gives a one-shouldered shrug. "One of those things is almost true. Guess we're about to find out if we can make good on the second one."

"Greetings!" The girl beams at us. "I wonder if you could help me?"

"Someone doesn't waste any time," I mutter.

She rests the pole against her shoulder. "Please, this is my first venture with the herd by myself." Her sigh verges on the melodramatic. "Alas, they won't listen to my songs."

"Won't listen to your songs?" Rakel asks.

"I thought they would. Truly! I'd practiced around camp for moons. Mother was doubtful, but I insisted. Now the two youngest calves have gone missing. If dark comes and I'm not home . . ." The girl appears forlorn. "I'll not be trusted to lead them again. I'll be stuck at camp cooking for the rest of my turns. Or cleaning." She shudders at the last.

I spread my hands. "I'm sorry, but—"

"Of course we'd be happy to help you," Rakel finishes.

I shoot her a frown.

She beckons me over. "Esarik said we'd find the fifth ingredient with the Edurshain. You're no expert on this place, but even you know they keep to themselves, right?"

I incline my head.

"Then here's a chance to meet them on friendly terms."

"The Basin stretches over more land than any other province. We could be searching for this girl's tulda for days. And if we start and then don't complete the mission, what will we do then? Better to simply get directions to her camp and send one of her own people to help."

Rakel glances at the girl, who has retreated far enough along the trail for the rustling of the heather to cover our whispers, and politely turned her back. "Mission? We're helping a girl humble enough to ask for our aid."

I study her, my thoughts momentarily turning inward. "I think you and Nisai would get along well."

She seems taken aback. "Would we?"

"Indeed. I look forward to the day you meet."

"Did I just hear you"—she leans down from her horse, eyes squinting as if she's having trouble seeing—"being positive?"

"Does it suit me?" I turn to the side, one hand on hip, nose to the sky.

She snorts. "Too early to tell. Maybe I'll have a better idea by the time we find this girl's strays." She clucks her tongue and Lil walks forward. "I'm Rakel. This is Ash. We'll help you."

The girl beams at us. "I'm Mish. The calves were over here last time I saw them." She disappears into the heather, the blue streamers on her herder's pole flapping above.

Rakel's horse proves an asset in the search. She moves easily through the scrub, seemingly unbothered by the prickles, her hooves and broad chest cutting a new trail that gives Rakel a vantage neither Mish nor I can command.

"There!" Rakel calls. "A stream's up ahead. They, ah, seem to be playing in it?"

Mish giggles. "That will be them."

She leads the way, and we soon pick up the trail of flattened gorse left by the calves. Then she begins to sing. It's a wordless tune in a minor key, her voice high and pure. Soon, there's an answering call, somewhere between an aurochs's lowing and a goat's bleat. Two tulda calves, all legs and knock-knees, come cantering down the path toward us.

Rakel smiles at the trio, clearly satisfied. "I think you were wrong, Mish."

"Oh?"

"They do listen to you."

"That's kind of you to say, but . . ." She catches herself and straightens, holding her herder's pole upright as if she's a soldier on the parade ground. "You must accept my family's hospitality tonight."

Of the few travelers that do return from Edurshai, all speak of their festivities as if they were from the heroic sagas. They could last for days. "We couldn't impose—"

"We would be insulted if you didn't." She regards us with wide-eyed innocence, but there's a mischievous lilt in her voice.

Rakel laughs.

I resign myself not to argue the matter any further. I know when I'm outmatched.

We follow Mish into the fading light of dusk. Occasionally, she pauses, using her pole to test the ground ahead, leading us around what are presumably sink holes. She seems unbothered by the hazards of the landscape, chatting animatedly, asking questions of us. Though she nods sagely and subtly changes topic whenever the answers Rakel or I give seem strained. She'd be a natural at the imperial court.

The camp comes into sight just before sunset. We emerge into a clearing where a lower-growing type of heather is dotted with fat red berries and a stream meanders in an almost full loop. A herd of tulda, double the size of Mish's calves, line up to drink, some of them frolicking in the shallows, spraying water across silvered coats.

Not far from the banks, a score of round tents dots the clearing, their sloped roofs high enough for the likes of Iddo to stand upright inside. The exterior of the dwellings are decorated in green, as if they were merely another mound in the shifting landscape.

Mish invites Rakel to leave her horse grazing among the tulda, assuring her the land there is safe. Lil seems happy enough alongside the calves, so our guide leads us through the camp.

The evening bustles with activity. Women and men—clad in the same billowy-sleeved fashion that could have sprung from a historical epic—smile and wave at our approach. We pass pots being scrubbed, spices being ground, and a haunch, large enough that it could only be tulda, slow-roasting over a bed of coals.

My stomach rumbles audibly. Our guide claps her hand over her mouth with a giggle and ushers us toward the largest of the tents.

Rakel whistles through her teeth as we step inside. The interior is decorated in tapestries as intricate as those from the Ekasya palace. Scenes of strength and beauty, violence and romance play out across the walls, and above us, the domed ceiling depicts the constellations of the starwheel.

Such artistry is the last thing I was expecting in the depths of the Edurshain Basin. Rakel was right about my ignorance.

Mish points at a pair of floor cushions as other members of the camp begin to file in. Everyone sits in the round, so I'm challenged to identify any leaders.

"Elelsmish, won't you introduce your guests?" asks one of the women. Her accent is lilting and her tone strangely formal, like the troupes of theater players who visit the Ekasyan palace. The creases about her eyes suggests she's old enough to be Mish's mother, but the spray of freckles across her nose gives her a youthful visage.

The girl cringes at the use of her full name. I've done that more than once or twice.

"This is Rakel. And this is Ash." She lifts her chin. "They're on an important mission."

The woman nods. "I warmly anticipate discussing this matter of great import." Merriment shines in her eyes. "Once hunger has been vanquished."

The last members of the camp enter the tent, bearing platters. There's roasted meat, cheeses shaped like the Edurshain's domed tents, and a stew made from unfamiliar greens I discover are a fresh and herby accompaniment to the richness.

Rakel chews enthusiastically. "Best meal I've had in a moon," she mumbles between mouthfuls.

"Are you criticizing my cooking? Think you could come up with culinary masterpieces over a campfire in the middle of nowhere?"

She elbows me and grins, then pops another chunk of cheese into her mouth.

After dinner, the woman who questioned Mish rises from the circle. "I'm Ziltish, Elelsmish's guardian. Would you perhaps desire to see more of our home?"

Rakel and I both nod, and our host beckons to the tent's exit.

Outside, the twang of stringed instruments being tuned competes with a growing chorus of insects. The Edurshain woman smiles. "We will have songs this evening. Once the crickets seek their slumber. Perchance you will join us?"

I find myself warming to these people. "Very well."

Rakel pales, her smile wan.

"Not musically inclined?" I murmur.

"Let's just say I'd rather bathe in the rotten-egg reek of a Losian sulfur pool than sing in public."

"Noted."

The evening air is cool as we follow Ziltish between the stream and the camp.

When we reach the last tent, our guide turns to face us. "Your mission," she begins without preamble. "It wouldn't concern the ill fate that has befallen the First Prince, would it?"

My footsteps slow. I wonder if the Edurshain in the meal tent are the only ones here. If the situation deteriorates, I might have a chance. After all, I didn't see any weapons on any of them. Though hidden arms wouldn't be the first thing about this camp to surprise me.

"Please do not be perturbed. News reaches us from time to time, especially when it is of such magnitude. One has to admit the reward is a handsome sum."

Rakel bristles. "Reward?"

"For your capture and surrender into the custody of the Imperial Rangers."

I draw a breath.

"Worry not," Ziltish continues, "we've agreed your aid to our daughter warranted our respect."

My shoulders slump in relief.

"We?" Rakel asks.

She gestures around the camp. It seems most of the Edurshain have now gathered around the fire and the musicians.

Rakel frowns. "You didn't even discuss it."

"When you are close to others, it only takes a glimpse to know their mind." Ziltish pulls the tent's entrance flap aside. "Please, after you."

The interior is as close and warm as the Ekasya library after a summer heat wave. Between braziers of banked coals, waist-high baskets of dried and woven grass line the walls.

Ziltish opens one of the baskets and lowers her arm in past the elbow. "If your Prince was bitten in Aphorai, you've come to the right place." She straightens, a slender python now coiled around her wrist.

Rakel takes a hasty step back, hands up in surrender.

"Do not fear." Our host chuckles. "Old Kab was defanged turns ago. She helps train the new diviners."

"Diviners?"

"Members of the herd who inherited Dallor's divine blessing. When a tulda can survive a snake's venom, then their blood can help save the bitten."

Rakel lowers her hands. "No offense, and not that I'm a temple-goer, but I've never heard of a god called Dallor."

"That's because there isn't one," I say, striving to keep my voice level. Have we wandered into a camp of heretics?

The snake flicks its tongue against Ziltish's shoulder. "Dallor wasn't always divine. Before the edge of memory, the god Riker wandered in all his beautiful youth. He came to the Basin and heard a young woman singing beside a stream. He knew such a voice could only come from the purest heart. Disguising himself as a trader, he began to court her, court Dallor."

Rakel rolls her eyes.

I scowl at her.

Ziltish seems oblivious as she paces the room, her gaze softly focused. "But Dallor was already in love with an Edurshain woman, Trishaw. Riker promised she would regret rejecting his advances, and when she had learned her lesson, she would sing for his return. Turns later, Trishaw was bitten by a river snake. Desperate to save her love, Dallor sang for the god.

"He appeared in his mortal guise as a young man, swaggering because he had won the object of his obsession. But rather than fall into his arms, Dallor begged Riker to save Trishaw. Certain Dallor would refuse, Riker offered to turn her into a tulda, whose blood was able to resist venom, and could save Trishaw. Dallor agreed, willing to do anything for her love, even sacrificing her human life."

Old Kab slithers its way farther up Ziltish's arm and stretches its head out to nuzzle her cheek. "Thus Dallor became the first of the diviners. The most effective of the antivenoms we make still honors her name: Dallor's Sacrifice. And Riker was left to that fate most cruel: unrequited love."

Rakel's wearing that contrary expression I've come to know too well. I try to signal to her with my eyes, but it's no use. Here we go.

"But how did a tulda know how to heal a human? And how did she do it? Never heard anything like it."

Ziltish strokes the snake on her arm, seemingly oblivious. "I wouldn't have expected you to. It's as rare as the kind of love Dallor had for Trishaw. So rare that the Losian Eraz has bought all we've produced back until the Founding Accord."

"Why the Losian Eraz?" Rakel inquires.

"So many questions." Ziltish chuckles. "You could be Edurshain. Why do we sell to our brethren in the far north? Simply because Los is infested with every kind of asp, viper, and cobra known in the Empire."

Rakel sniffs. "I think you'll find Aphorai has its fair share."

I shift closer, elbowing her lightly in the ribs.

Her gaze meets mine in confirmation.

This has to be it. Dallor's Sacrifice. *When Riker's heart faced the eternal plight.*

"We have reason to believe this antivenom could be essential to the First Prince's recovery," I say carefully. "If we could just purchase a small amount from you, we'd be most grateful."

Ziltish shakes her head. "Our contract with Los covers all we produce. Every shipment is measured to the last drop. I'm afraid I couldn't help you with anything less than an order from the Emperor himself. Even that would . . . complicate things. Are you sure it's Dallor's Sacrifice you need? I can give you all manner of other antivenom."

Rakel nods vehemently. "We're sure."

Ziltish affects a melancholic expression that wouldn't be out of place in a courtly acting troupe. "I appreciate your earnestness. I truly wish I could help. Not turning you over to the Rangers is one thing. But risking my family's livelihood and the Losian Eraz's retribution? That's a whole other basket of serpents. One that we cannot afford to open."

CHAPTER 31
RAKEL

I'm fuming.

After her refusal, as flat as the stare of her pet python, Ziltish invites us to join the camp in their evening song. A night of merry music? As if nothing's amiss? These people are more brazen than a knockoff incense merchant.

I force myself to unclench my fists and follow Ash from the serpent tent.

Outside, cool evening air whispers against my skin—sweet relief after the stifling closeness. Ziltish goes on ahead, her steps light, as if she has no idea of the weight of what she has just done.

I look back to the tent, not bothering to repress a shudder.

"Don't care for snakes?" Ash asks as we wander back toward the center of camp, shoulder to shoulder so as not to be overheard.

"Can't say I'm overly fond of them. And that stink? Ugh. Dust and musk and dead mouse." I swallow down the mustiness coating my tongue.

"At least we didn't have Kip with us. Things could have gone even worse in there."

"Kip?"

"Losian Ranger in the delegation. On the road to Aphorai, she'd pin every single snake she found with a forked stick and slice off their heads with her dagger. Then she'd cook and eat them." He mimes chewing appreciatively.

"Right now, I wouldn't stand in her way if she wanted to burn down that whole slithering tent just to warm her hands."

"Nor would the other Rangers, I'd wager. Used to make them a bit wild about the eyes. I doubt any of them shed a tear when she was reassigned."

"Oh?" I try to keep my voice light.

"Iddo—the Commander—made her interim Shield to Nisai in my incapacity."

"Sounds like there could be worse choices."

Over at the fire, a harpist begins to play. I grimace at the two gaps in the seating on opposite sides of the circle. Seems we're meant to mingle. "Ready to join in the fun?"

"No." He sighs. "But it'll keep us as gracious guests while we figure out how to obtain some of this Dallor's Sacrifice."

"I could . . . *collect* some once everyone has turned in for the night." I waggle my eyebrows. The gesture succeeds in drawing a faintly amused smile from Ash.

"It may come to that." He squares his shoulders and leads us toward the fire.

As soon as we're seated, we're handed prettily engraved silver cups of what appears to be some sort of milk drink. I give it a sniff. Rich and sweetly fermented, with notes of sunny meadows. I take a sip. It's good.

The Edurshain are born entertainers. We listen to several ancient ballads—"Tamin's Five Trials" and "The Fall of Emarpal" among them. The harpist follows up with a solo of "Kesnai's Betrayal," the haunting melody as ethereal as purrath blossom.

My neighbor leans over to refill my cup and I smile my thanks. The drink may smell like goodness, but it's strong, too. My cheeks feel warmer than they should on a cool night, even with the blaze before us. Even with my frustration at being so close and yet so far from the next ingredient.

Ash meets my eyes across the fire, his expression unreadable. He raises his own cup to his lips. My face flushes even more, but I don't look away.

I take another gulp.

He tilts his cup and drains it, setting it down decisively. Then he stands, shrugs out of his cloak. His black hair has grown in a finger width, hiding the tattoos on his scalp. But in the firelight, the ink running down his neck and trailing along his arms only emphasizes the tendon and muscle. We've been in close quarters for so long, yet I've never run a hand over those planes and ridges. My fingers begin to tingle at the thought of—

I look down into my cup. How strong *is* this stuff?

Ash moves to speak with the Edurshain harpist, but I can't hear anything over the happy murmurs of the couple next to me.

What is he playing at?

The harpist nods enthusiastically. Ash straightens and takes one last glance at me over the other musicians. He tilts his face to the sky, as if orientating himself.

Then he begins to sing.

I almost choke on my drink.

His singing voice has the depth of his spoken one, warm as the sandalwood he wears and dark as smoke. But there's something else, too, a raw edge that hooks into me.

I realize I've gone completely still.

A quick glance around confirms I'm not alone. Every one of the Edurshain is leaning forward on their woven mats, giving Ash their rapt attention. The tulda beside the stream have stopped their grazing, horned heads lifted in silhouettes against the stars.

The song's words are in a dialect I don't wholly understand. Some words are familiar, some unknown. But after a few bars, the tune begins to tug at my memory.

I've never heard it sung with such anguish in the Aphorain streets. There, the chorus was a signal of dusk, a farewell to the day, when the servants of the less grand houses collected water from the plaza fountains.

It's a song of longing despite knowing you'll never be able to be with the person you love. Thoughts of Barden flit through my head, of how I continually brushed his affections aside. But the thought is fleeting. Because this is a song about falling for someone beyond your reach, about wrestling with duty and forsaking your heart.

Ash's notes soar, his features sorrowful in the light of the fire. And that's when it occurs to me who he is singing for. Who he's thinking of when his voice takes wing into the night.

Duty.

Love.

Nisai.

Ash is in love with Nisai.

He looks over to me. It's a look of complete vulnerability.

I flinch. *He knows that I know.*

Scrabbling for my satchel, I lurch to my feet, legs unsteady.

Everyone else is still intent on Ash. Small mercy. I take a couple of tentative paces backward, but Ash just watches me retreat, not skipping a note, his gaze searing into me.

I escape into the welcome embrace of the dark.

My feet take me along the stream, past the tulda, beyond the camp. It's not until the heather rises to shoulder height on either side of me, that I realize I can only barely hear the final notes of Ash's song. I slump down onto the bank, not caring that one of my boots splashes into the water.

Why didn't he just tell me? After all we've been through, does he not trust me? Why keep me in the dark?

Then I'm suddenly furious with myself. How could I have not seen this? He wouldn't be the first Shield to have fallen for their charge, if the sagas hold even a whiff of truth.

I take a deep breath and concentrate on singling out scents. The campfire, the tulda, and hoof-crushed heather leaves and berries, the faintest hint of the blue flowers. I lie back on the cool earth and trace the stars with my eyes. They're the same stars, if slightly differently placed to the Aphorain sky. I wonder if Father is gazing up at them right now, sitting outside our house with bergamot incense curling around him.

A pang of longing for home, the strongest since setting out on this smoke-brained quest, throbs in my chest. I close my eyes, letting myself imagine I'm small again, and Father is stronger than anything the world can throw at me. Strong enough to bear me on his shoulders through the streets. Strong enough to tell me the truth.

A tear slips down my cheek.

I wipe it away.

Father lied to me. And whoever is behind Luz and Zakkurus and this Order of Asmudtag business, to them I'm just a tiny piece on a vast game board.

Still, *Ash* didn't lie to me. He told me who he is, despite the risk. And now he's trying to tell me whom he loves.

Just as quick as my anger arrived, it's replaced with shame. Why wouldn't Ash love Nisai? If I had just looked beyond my own nose, I would have seen it.

Slowly, the burning in my cheeks begins to subside. Definitely enough party milk for me tonight.

I realize my absence will be getting noticeable. I heave myself to my feet and start back toward camp, cursing my squelching boot.

Ash finds me along the way.

Thumb hooked in my satchel strap, I try to appear nonchalant. "A singer, hey? You never mentioned that."

He plucks a stalk of heather and begins to tear off the spines one by one. "There are still a few things you don't know about me."

"Is Ash even your real name?"

"It's the one I was given." He doesn't look at me when he speaks. "Well, part of it."

"Then it's short for . . . ?"

"Ashradinoran."

I burst into laughter. I laugh so hard I clutch my hands to my stomach to ward off a cramp. "Sorry," I manage. "Mustn't have heard you right. I thought you said *Ashradinoran*. Legendary warrior of old. Giant of mythical strength and prowess. Wooer of fair maidens and goddesses alike."

"That's the one." He plucks another stalk. "And you should be thanking this mythical hero, not mocking him."

"Thanking you? For what?"

"Hold out your hand."

I hesitate.

"No snakes, promise."

I do as he asks, and he places a small vial in my palm.

"Is this . . . ?"

He nods. "Dallor's Sacrifice."

I stare at my palm, blinking. After this, the only ingredient left to find is Losian amber. This seemed an impossible quest. But is this the first whiff of the victory to come?

I throw my arms around him. "You did it!"

He embraces me in return. "*We* did it," he whispers, lips brushing my ear, sending a shiver through me. I'm suddenly aware of his hands against my back, strong but gentle. I haven't been held since I last saw Barden. Back then, I was captive to his desire for more than I could give, and to my need for reassurance in the only place I could find it.

This embrace means something else.

And I bet Ash is thinking of some*one* else. Thinking of the Prince.

I step back, the scent of sandalwood and galbanum quickly fading. But cedar still clings to me. I wish I hadn't started him using one of my favorite oils on his armor.

I hold up the vial. What could have made Ziltish and her lot change their mind? "How did you get this?"

He grins. "If I knew one thing about the Edurshain, it's that they're romantics. Seems my, ah, performance convinced them that our need outweighed their risk."

Our need. Our need to save Nisai. The only thing we both share.

I force a bright tone into my voice. "So it's onward tomorrow, then?"

He nods.

Not knowing what else to say, I stow the antivenom in my satchel. We head back to camp and are shown to our quarters for the night. Two bedrolls of beautifully embroidered blankets have been set up in the same tent, though a curtain of heavy felt, imbued with the balsam of vetiver to aid, er, *relaxation*, can be drawn between them.

We've been on the road long enough that privacy is a novelty. And after this evening's revelations, I'm glad I'll be able to have some space to myself.

I set down my satchel and reach to draw the divider. "Good night, Ash."

"Rakel, I . . ." He looks at me, at the floor, at me again.

"Yes?"

"Do you . . ."

"Do I what?"

He shakes his head. "Nothing. Good night. Call if you need anything."

With the curtain closed, I strip off and climb under my blanket.

I lie still, listening to Ash's nightly routine. His quiet footsteps circling the tent like he's staking out the perimeter of our camp. The telltale sounds of him checking and stowing each blade—one always under his blanket. The waft of Linod's Elixir as he takes his evening dose. The long, slow sigh he lets out when he first lies back.

Outside, the camp grows quiet, and a hush descends across the Basin, with only the occasional stir of breeze through heather. It seems like half the night before Ash's breathing falls into the evenness of sleep on the other side of the curtain.

It's even longer before mine does the same.

* *
* *
*

We leave the Edurshain camp at dawn.

Once we're clear of the Basin, we'll strike out toward the Great River Junction, where the major rivers of Aramtesh meet. There, we'll need to make a choice. Ekasya, where we'll risk immediate arrest but Esarik may have been able to source the final ingredient—true amber. Or Lostras—more likely to provide amber without incident, but so far away we might not make it back within the moon. Nisai's last moon, if we don't succeed.

I turn the options over as I ride. I've heard stories of Ekasya. If they bear truth, I'd be lost in a city that size. I wouldn't know where to start searching for the equipment I'll need to make and test the formula—and asking questions would only attract attention in the home city of the ailing Prince. And what if Esarik hasn't yet returned?

And Lostras? It may as well be *on* a moon.

Ash is surlier than normal. Walking ahead, he's barely said a word all morning, and when he does turn around, his expression is as sour as vinegar fumes. He shaved his head before dawn. Maybe he was trying to clear it. Truth be told, mine's a little foggy after last night's Edurshain hospitality. Still, I expected him to be happier now we're one step closer to healing Nisai.

The thought makes me curious, and I rummage in my satchel for the vial of antivenom. It's bloodred, and I expect it to smell of copper and whatever scent the venom holds. Instead, it smells of . . . berries?

A picture of the Edurshain camp springs back to mind. The lower heather surrounding the tents, laden with ripe red fruit. For all their love of heroic sagas, the Edurshain sure lack for a sense of honor. Have they sent us on our way with a vial of berry juice?

Ash halts, cocking his head to the side. "What stink got up your nose?"

"The *wrong* stink."

I'm about to explain when he lifts a hand so sharply the tendons go taut in his wrist, silencing me. He points to his ear and then out into the shrubland.

Lil gets the hint that something is amiss, her ears twitching. I slide from her back, landing on my toes to muffle the drop.

"What?" I mouth.

"Rangers," he returns silently, then motions for me to follow. We creep through the heather, leading Lil in single file, keeping both our heads low. Ash turns one way, then another, down different animal trails, moving as quickly as possible while keeping as quiet as possible.

A high whistle rings out. It's answered by a distant shout.

It takes all my restraint not to jump back up on Lil and ride headlong in the opposite direction. But even if I could outrun the Rangers, it'd only take one sinkhole in this never-ending bog to lame Lil.

I lose track of how long we go on like that, but my stomach soon begins to rumble in protest at not stopping for lunch. My head pounds from afternoon sun. We take narrower and narrower trails until we're pushing through the branches. Spiked leaves tug at my sleeves, claw at my calves and wrists until the skin is crisscrossed with red scratches. At least Lil's hide repels the worst of it.

Dusk falls. My whole body stings and itches, but Ash still won't let us ease up. We keep moving through the evening, the insects drowning out our whispered voices.

"They've built a campfire," I sputter as a whiff of distant smoke reaches me.

"Don't think it ignorance. Rangers don't make mistakes. They want us to know where they are. Or they want us to *think* we know."

"How did they find us?"

It isn't Ash who responds: "The camp elders, I'm ashamed to say."

Ash's swords are in his hands before the owner of the voice has materialized from the heather.

She's without her staff, and she's wearing a pack almost the size of her, but I can make out enough of her pale hair and features in the moonslight. I motion for Ash to lower the blades. "Mish!"

"You shouldn't be here," Ash rumbles.

"Please don't worry, it wasn't an arduous effort. I know this land. To me, your trail was obvious."

Ash sheathes his swords, muttering something between a curse and a prayer about being tracked by a thirteen-turn-old girl.

I size Mish up. "Why?"

She gives the closest impression of a shrug that her pack will allow. "After you left, I overheard the elders. I was vexed when I found they'd given you a heartbreak potion in place of what you needed. Dallor would be mortified, too, if she were still alive."

"The lovers of love stories sold us out," I huff. "So much for romance."

Ash rubs his hand over his scalp. "You would say that."

Mish rummages in the billowy sleeve of her dress. "It was I who invited you to camp, after you'd come to my aid, no less. I knew I needed to set things right. Here. True Dallor's Sacrifice."

I take the vial. "You came all this way for us? Mish, you're a hero."

"Well . . . In the same meeting, the elders agreed to revoke my herding privileges. Nobody is going to make me scrub pots at camp for another turn. I decided it was time to seek my fortune."

"Your fortune? Go home," Ash tells her. "It's dangerous out here. Too dangerous for a young—" He grunts in surprise, looking down at his arm. In his bicep, just below his prayer band, a dart protrudes from his skin.

"Don't worry, *that* one isn't dipped in deadly venom."

I snort. Seems Mish can handle herself.

"You should go. I'll lead them in a merry dance, but once they realize I don't have a horse, the gambit will be up. Farewell!"

And with that, she disappears back into the heather.

* *
 * *
 *

Ash sets a punishing pace.

He says we don't have a choice—Mish may have bought us time, but there's no way to cover our trail while we're still in the Basin, with our passage through the heather marking our route plain as day. Every ounce of my energy is spent on keeping going, so that I barely notice the sun rise and set, rise and set.

I'm about ready to drop when the river comes into sight late one night, a mile-wide ribbon of black silk dotted with silver stars. I was born too late to remember the river in Aphorai, so even through the exhaustion, I'm awed to see so much water flowing freely.

The Great River Junction is a town unto itself, lit up with torches and braziers. Ash and I thread our way through the outskirts and toward the river. At first the streets are lined with quiet houses and shuttered stores, but as we near the docks, they become rowdier, with taverns and dice houses and dreamsmoke dens. Beyond, the bobbing lights of barges beckon.

Down in the last streets before the river, we pause in the shadow of one of the traders' warehouses, their floors raised head-high on stone pillars. Guess it floods this close to the banks.

"Over there." Ash points to a dock flying the imperial phoenix, the thread of gold shining in the torchlight. "Those barges are bound for Ekasya."

I grimace. They're also the most heavily guarded.

Ash lets out a low curse.

"The boat guards?"

"No. Rangers."

He juts his chin. "Over there, see? Fellow leaning against those sacks of grain? And the woman over there? She's only posing—tax collectors don't bear arms; they get someone else to do the dirty work."

I bite the inside of my cheek as he picks out several more. If he's right, they've surrounded the entire dock area on this side of the river, blocking our way back into town. There's nowhere to run, and I have no idea which boat is going where. We could chance the water itself, but I've never swum anywhere as far, and nowhere with such a swift-moving current.

"Someone's coming. Quick." He pulls up the hood of his traveling cloak.

I reach up and tug my hair from its braid, letting it fall forward around my face.

Ash nods approval. "This way."

Next to Ash's silent grace, I feel clumsy trying to lead Lil and move quietly as we steal from warehouse to warehouse.

Then I trip.

I desperately cradle my satchel as I fall, but the clink of glass still rings out in the night. Pain burns where my hip and shoulder graze the ground, but I'm more intent on checking nothing's broken. Especially the living bone from Azered's caves. Breath held, I search through the compartments.

There it is. A soft blue glow.

I bow my head in relief.

It's only when I hear Ash's snarl that I realize I didn't trip. Someone tripped me. And now he and Ash face off.

"I thought I could smell something rank," the Ranger drawls as they slowly circle each other.

"Let us pass," Ash grates, the daggers he keeps at his wrists in each hand. Too close quarters for swords.

"Orders are orders. You can come easy like, or I can bring the sixth hell down on you. What's it to be?"

Ash doesn't speak, only keeps his eyes trained on the Ranger. Then he's moving, and the two men become a blur in the dark.

There's a grunt.

A muffled thud.

A slow, sickening wet crunch.

Ash lowers the man to the ground. He wipes his blades off on the Ranger's coat, casual as a baker toweling the flour from his hands. Daggers sheathed, he turns to me.

"Are you hurt?"

I shake my head, wide-eyed and numb. Father was a soldier, but I've never seen a man killed before.

"Good." Crouching, Ash takes the Ranger's purse, then rolls his body under the warehouse. "That won't keep him hidden long—they'll have a rotation report pattern. We've got to move."

We hurry along the riverbank. I walk stiffly on tense legs, trying not to think about what an arrow between the shoulder blades would feel like. Or a dagger blade under the ribs. Beside me, Lil's ears constantly swivel. I'm not the only one feeling threatened.

"Try to relax." Ash places a hand on my lower back, large and surprisingly comforting considering what he just did with it.

As we head away from the imperial dock, the vessels gradually decline in size and upkeep. The torches change to tallow candles, their smoke making my eyes water and the smell of rancid fat stinging my nose.

We pass a group of men gathered around what looks like a game of Five Cups in the dirt. Others have a girl about my age, blindfolded and sitting on one of their knees. They're waving a dreamsmoke pipe under her nose and she inhales deeply. Skin traders. If they're anything like the worst of that sort in Aphorai, they're keeping the girl so doped up she doesn't know what day it is.

Ash pulls me into his side, wrapping his arm around my shoulders. On reflex, I move to shrug his hand away, but then I notice the men's stares. They're so measuring, I can almost feel hands crawling all over me. I shudder.

"Please permit me," Ash murmurs into my hair. "Just for now."

He's right. And if I'm honest, I feel far safer tucked against him. I fall into step.

He steers us toward the second last boat. Its tented cabin is the shabbiest of all we've passed, but its hull shines in the moonlight. It's in good repair.

A man stands on the dock before the twin planks crossing to the barge. He's lean, with a scar giving his lip a permanent sneer. Smoke curls from a pipe in his fingers, but it's clove and tobacco, not dreamsmoke. His hands are steady.

"You the cap'n?" Ash's voice is gruff and heavily accented, like the day back at the caves.

The man nods.

"Room for a pair?"

"What's it worth to you?"

Ash jangles the Ranger's zig purse. "And the horse comes, too."

259

The captain gives a barely perceptible nod.

"How much extra for casting off now?" Ash tosses him the purse.

The captain's eyes drink in the silver glinting up at him. "That'll do."

"And quietly?"

"As a dockmouse."

The captain signals to his crew, all dressed in ragged clothing, but moving with an efficiency that speaks of experience. I won't be asking *any* questions about what these men are transporting.

We board the boat, and I risk a glance behind. No Rangers. Just the rough and tumble of the low end of the docks.

One of the crew casts off the mooring rope.

We're away. I breathe out audibly. Ash's eyes are intent as he watches upriver, arms crossed, each hand resting on the dagger sheathed at the other wrist. I try not to think about what those daggers recently did.

When the Junction has vanished around a bend in the river, I smack my palm on the barge rail. Even if we can find what we need outside Ekasya, we're going the wrong direction. Navigation isn't my strength, but you don't need to be top note in the perfume to realize that anything downriver takes us away from the capital and away from Lostras.

Away from Nisai.

I turn to Ash. He's conferring quietly with the captain. Then he returns, spreading his tattered map on the deck before him. "Esarik was right. Even if we can find some amber in time, the only way we'll know whether the cure will work is to test it. Yes?"

"Once we have all the ingredients, the poison seems fairly simple—expose the target to smoke in sequence. But to make steam for the cure? At the very least I'll need perfume-grade mortar and pestle, alcohol, possibly some acid, and a distillation apparatus."

"Then a barge bound for the east coast isn't the worst thing in the world, even though I would never have gone there by choice."

The coast? I raise an eyebrow. "See those two glowing things in the sky? They're called moons. In case you hadn't noticed, one of them keeps passing closer to a certain lion made of stars. This isn't the time to take the scenic route."

"Not another route, another destination. Somewhere we can find everything we need to determine whether returning to Ekasya is even an option."

"Oh?"

"Lapis Lautus."

CHAPTER 32
ASH

Lapis Lautus.

Nisai once told me the name means "grand jewel" in the language of the people from across the Normek Ocean—the vast waters that so few ever cross and live to return.

Grand Jewel. Ironic, given Lapis Lautus is a city constructed from the garbage other civilizations left behind, figuratively and literally. Built out into the sea centuries ago by raiders turned traders who wanted to avoid imperial sanction, it's said that for the right price, you can buy anything in Lautus.

You can buy any*one*.

The river carries us swiftly, and the captain obliges us to disembark before we enter the Trel Delta. We strike out cross-country and camp in thick riverland forest. After spending recent nights barely one step ahead of the Ranger patrol, and keeping vigilant on the barge, I do something rare and accept Rakel's offer to take first watch. For a few merciful hours, I sleep like the dead.

The next morning is thankfully uneventful, even pleasant, as we hike through the sun-dappled trees, birds trilling like they haven't a care in the world. I sorely envy them.

Before the sun has reached its zenith, Rakel halts, sniffing the air in that deerlike way that's become so familiar.

"What is it?" I ask.

"Something I've never smelled before. Like old fish, but not. Mud? Soggy plants rotting in the sun? Like . . ."

"Salt?"

She nods vehemently.

"The sea. I think we're near the sea."

Sure enough, the coast soon comes into view.

Rakel lets out a low whistle beside me. "That there is something to behold."

"You could say that."

It's not like the stories told in Ekasya—they speak of nothing but lawlessness and filth and squalor worse than the slums in the shade of the capital. Lautus rises from the end of a man-made promontory jutting over a mile out from the coast. There may have once been a natural island underneath, a beating heart to the sprawl, but it's long buried beneath the layers and layers that came afterward.

To say it's nothing more than a home to brigands and black markets, effluent and underworlds, would be to deny its beauty. It *is* a jewel. Out of reach of siege engines, its spires are elegant rather than squat, walls soar rather than hulk, and though they're each made from a different stone or wood or metal it all somehow hangs together—a beautiful mess.

Docks reminiscent of the spokes of the starwheel splay out from the city, ranging in richness and permanence. On one side of the causeway, stone marinas rise proudly above the water, crusted with turn upon turn of barnacles. On the other side, lashed-together wooden rafts make up the jetties with a floating market between them—sellers hawking their wares from skiffs they guide with a single long oar. The remainder are hidden from view by the city itself.

"Who built it?" Rakel asks, her voice tinged with awe.

"Smugglers. Pirates. Merchant princes from across the ocean. If it's not on the Emperor's lands, it doesn't pay the Emperor's taxes or abide by the Emperor's laws."

"Serious? Someone went to all the effort of building a city out of the sea just so that they could do things their own way?"

I shrug.

She snorts with laughter. "I think I'm going to like this place."

We take one of the lanes leading through the farmlets lining the coast, which I expect supply much of Lautus's fresh produce. I nod to Rakel's horse. "It's probably best we stable her. I've heard there are thieves in this city who can steal your undergarments while you're fully dressed."

"Speaking from experience?"

"As I've heard."

She chews thoughtfully on her lower lip, her eyes taking on that distant cast that I now recognize means her agile mind is formulating a plan. Then her gaze arrows back to me.

"Everyone may speak Imperial, even here, but there's only one truly universal language."

"Scentlore?"

"Hardly." She scoffs. "Zigs. Hand me your purse."

"Excuse me?"

"You want me to leave Lil with a stranger? Hand me your purse. I'm running low."

I take one look at her stroking her horse's neck, feet planted and jaw set. I decide not to argue. A wise soldier does everything they can to avoid an unwinnable battle. Instead, I make a mental note to thank Esarik for replenishing my coin.

Rakel steers us toward one of the smaller holdings, its fields and fences laid out in an orderly grid. We find the farmer, a broad woman with laughter lines and silver at her temples. Rakel presses several coins into her hand for feed, and I promise to make good on double that upon our return if the horse is in good condition.

Rakel's smile is a mix of gratitude and something else I can't quite place. Then she turns her attention to her horse.

"Be good."

The mare snorts derisively.

"I mean it, Lil. No biting, no kicking, no crushing this nice woman against the stable wall."

The only reply is flat ears and a black nose in the air.

"I'm glad we had this conversation." Then she flings her arms around the horse's neck. "I'll miss you," she whispers.

We set out. As we near the coastline, I swap my pack from my back to my front.

Rakel gives me a questioning look.

"What? I've been to the seedier side of town before, you know."

"I've never doubted *that*."

All the same, she tightens her satchel strap.

Guards station the entry to the causeway leading out across the water. I tense, half expecting them to recognize and apprehend us. Then I notice they're wearing both the insignia of the merchant princes and a glaze of boredom. True enough, they only seem interested in the gate fee.

"Twenty zigs," the largest of the lot says. It's a moment or two before I can process the demand. In the slums of Ekasya, people drop the last consonant when they speak, but the Lautian guard bites off entire syllables.

I balk at the amount. "Twenty? You just let that miller and his wagon through for a quarter of that."

"Miller had a pass. And didn't have an imperial bounty on his head."

Rakel stiffens beside me. I glance around. Two guards this side of the causeway, two on the other, and I'd wager at least half a dozen more stationed in the gatehouse. None of them as sleepy as they're making out to be.

"I'm afraid there's been some kind of mistake—"

"No mistake." The guard shrugs. "You don't last in Lautus if you don't use all your senses. Now, if I walked in your boots, I'd want to enter the city quiet as mice. And I'd want the protection of the merchant princes. The *last* thing I'd want is word reaching the Imperial Rangers as to my whereabouts."

"Twenty it is," I grumble, handing it over, sparing another thankful thought for Esarik's generosity.

Rakel watches the guards warily as we pass through the gates. Then we're on to the causeway, and her eyes widen at the aquamarine water either side.

"You've never seen the ocean."

"Oh, yes," she says loftily. "I used to go on a seaside jaunt every other moon."

"It's new to me, too." I raise my hands in surrender. "Sometimes I don't get you. One minute you're prickling at being thought provincial, the next your spines are out because I mistakenly assume you've seen more than you have."

She huffs a stray tendril of hair from eyes alight with indignation. "Then don't assume! Ask. Simple."

Movement in the water snatches her ire as quickly as it flared. She hangs over the side of the causeway, pointing. "What are they?"

"Dolphins." I wouldn't have known, either, if I hadn't seen them in Nisai's journal. A group of the smooth-skinned creatures frolic in the crystal waves, leaping in an intricate game only they understand. I'm astounded at how clean the merchant princes manage to keep the waters around the city. Don't crap where you wash, I suppose.

Ekasya could learn a thing or two from this place.

"And those fish!" Rakel leans so far over the water I have to resist the urge to grab on to the back of her tunic in case she falls.

An old man with a fishing pole sizes us up. "Don't think of poaching. You take from the merchant princes, they take from you."

I glance down at the hand that steadies his fishing pole. It's missing two fingers. "Thanks for the warning. I wonder if you could help me with something else," I say, flipping a copper to him.

Missing fingers or no, he catches it just fine.

"What's the best route to the market?"

"Which one?"

"I don't know, that's why I'm asking you."

"No, which market? Vegetables? Spice? Carpet and cloth? Beast and bird? Celestial instruments? Fruits of the sea? Jewels and antiquities?"

"Jewels and antiquities." Sounds just the place to find some black-market amber.

"Fancier than you look. Central District. Middle of town. Can't miss it."

Rakel adjusts her satchel. "And we're after some . . . remedies."

"Ah." He gives us a knowing look that more than slightly perturbs me. "Apothecary Lane. Fifth Sector, off the main avenue. Try Atrolos's place. He specializes in the good stuff."

Rakel beams. "I'm *definitely* going to like this place."

I flip him another coin. "For your discretion."

He chuckles. "Don't you worry, boy. Two fingers are enough. I'm not about to risk my tongue, too."

CHAPTER 33
RAKEL

We sniff out the Fifth Sector without too much trouble. It's in a neighborhood of three- and four-story town houses built from sparkling pink stone. A luxurious incense I've never smelled before burns in street braziers, so that the entire neighborhood seems to whisper of wealth and untold secrets.

Apothecary Lane begins at a narrow arch leading away from the main street and into the shade between buildings.

"I'm surprised they get any business down here," I muse.

Ash shrugs. "People don't want to be seen coming in and out of these places. Fires up gossip."

"Because they're ill? Or because they're looking to make someone ill?"

"Either. But it's probably the first as much as the second. What are they ill *with*? They'd get tonic from the market or elixir from the temple for anything routine. Here, they'd be seeking something else. Something that makes you stop pissing razor blades or deals with the warts you've found erupting on your . . ."

"On your what?"

He coughs politely.

"Oh!" I wrinkle my nose.

"More common than you might think."

I try to push the image of anything erupting on my netherbits out of my mind. Which only leads me to think of whether—

"And *no*, I've never needed to visit one of these places myself, thank you very much."

"I didn't say a word," I retort, assuming a prim expression.

"Your thoughts were shouting at me."

Heat prickles my cheeks and I make like I'm carefully picking my way over the uneven cobbles. By the time we find ourselves standing under a sign bearing a beaker held by metal tongs, set discreetly back beneath the eaves, I've regained my composure.

"Proprietor: Kreb Atrolos," Ash reads. He tucks one hand behind his back and dips into the most courtly of bows. "After you."

Sometimes I forget he lives in the imperial palace. *Lived*, I correct myself.

I pull at my sleeves, as if straightening them could make them less travel-stained, and push open the door.

Who knows what I expected to find, but it wasn't this.

The shop is large, but filled with so many shelves and stands, hooks, and racks that it feels like a lair in a jungle of remedies and relics. Jar upon jar of herbs and powders line the walls. Statuettes of naked people with the heads of beasts—serpent, lion, eagle—perch on a side table. Strange instruments are laid out in a silk-lined box that looks eerily like a sarcophagus. Animal skulls loom from the ceiling, and a human version sits plain as stink on the counter, its hollow eye sockets following anyone who comes through the door.

The only light comes from beeswax candles haphazardly arranged around the room. They throw unsettling shadows but are imbued with something even more decadently sweet than their honey base.

"Can I help you?" A man appears from the rear of the shop. Thin as a reed, pale as a corpse, his closely cropped beard is shot with white. He wears a short robe that buttons up to his neck with matching black trousers, and a line of winking gems studded up the edge of one ear.

"What's that scent?" I breathe.

"The candles. We have several sizes if they please you."

"I realize it's the stinkin' candles. But what's in them? Beeswax, a little cinnamon, and . . . ?"

"The lady has a refined nose, if not a refined demeanor. Is that an Aphorain accent I hear?"

Ash draws a breath behind me.

But this city isn't imperial, and the apothecary isn't going to call for the Rangers. I meet his curious stare. "It is."

"I made the journey myself once. Quite a trip. Tell me, do they still play that Death in Paradise game? A fine sport."

Not if I have any choice in the matter, I think, the memory of my last trip to Zakkurus's establishment still sharp. "I've played a round or two."

"But are you any good?"

"I'm still standing, aren't I?"

He steeples his fingers, and I can't help but feel I've passed some sort of test. "What you detect in the candles is vanilla. From the Forests of Rain on Gairak. I like my customers to feel calm and welcome."

"Gairak?"

"Of course, I wouldn't expect you to know the name. A tiny island in an archipelago flung off the Losian coast. Only pollinated by hummingbirds or a very particular bee native to the island. Incredibly expensive. But worth it, wouldn't you agree?"

"I can understand how others would think so." I turn up my nose, even though I find the vanilla nothing short of delicious. "A little too cloying for my liking."

"Then let me recommend an alternative. Or perhaps something for this fierce-looking fellow?" The apothecary glances at Ash, his nostrils flaring almost imperceptibly. "Ah, a woods man. Cedar, mainly? But really, I think you'd do much better adding some spice. Might make you seem less . . . one-note."

Ash replies by hefting his purse onto the counter. Suddenly I'm grateful for the miserliness he's stuck with up until this point.

The apothecary's eyes widen ever so briefly.

I clear my throat. Here goes nothing. "We've not long arrived in the city. I dabble in scentlore and would like to do so again."

His eyes go flat. "I'm not hiring."

"Oh, no, it's only a hobby." I wave a hand, flippant. "Strictly personal use. I just need to purchase a few things."

I relay the list of equipment I'll need, and we set to haggling. Ash makes an awkward show of refraining from inspecting the shelves and wall-mounted curios, as if he's terrified that picking up a relic might instantly convert him to some heathen religion.

Later, I find myself standing over a great chest filled with flasks and pipes, mortars and grinding stones, and carefully wrapped bottles of processing solutions. Atrolos drives a hard bargain, but he runs a well-stocked outfit.

He grunts as he tries, unsuccessfully, to move the chest across the floor. "This may be too heavy even for your manservant."

Manservant? I suppress a giggle.

Ash glowers. I can't tell if it's because his strength or his station has been insulted.

"I'm sure he'd be able to manage," I say. "But I'll be keeping his hands full with some other shopping first. It wouldn't be any trouble for you to hold this for a while, would it?"

He inclines his head, the purse on the counter catching his eye again. "There's nothing else I can help you with?"

I turn away and run a finger along one of the shelves. "There is something, now that you mention it, but I'm sure we'd have to seek it in the antiquities market. It's very rare. Highly regulated in the Empire. Not the kind of thing I'd expect you'd have in stock." I look slyly back over a shoulder, seeing if the challenge has had the desired effect.

He sniffs. "I might surprise you."

"And tell me, what kind of records do you keep for your rare items. Do purchases get reported to any . . . particular authority?"

"This is Lautus, my dear. Each to his own business."

I raise my eyebrows as if duly impressed. "I need Losian amber. Solid, not a liquid dilution."

The apothecary's eyes dart to the door, then to the soot-stained window on to the empty lane. "Even if I did have such a thing, it would command a princely sum. More princely than your manservant's purse."

I take the vial of dahkai from my satchel and place it on the counter before him.

"And this is?"

"Smell for yourself."

He carefully unseals the vial, just enough to let a vapor escape before shoving the stopper back in with a satisfied huff. "My ear heard true, then. That is a *genuine* Aphorain accent."

"Does it matter?"

"My dear, with half of this"—he gestures with the vial—"the only thing that matters to me is what's on your shopping list and . . ."

"And what?"

"And whether you're as good at Death in Paradise as you say you are. It's been an age since I last played a worthy opponent."

Stink on a stick. He can't be serious.

But he's off, rummaging in a jumble of metal cups.

I sigh. "So be it."

CHAPTER 34
ASH

Outside the apothecary's store, Rakel pats her satchel, now complete with the fifth and final ingredient, a translucent golden-brown gem the size of her thumbnail. I'm still processing the revelation that the three rounds of the so-called Death in Paradise game she just played to acquire it could have gone a very different way.

"Think you could give me some warning next time?"

"There won't be a next time if I can help it." She gives me an alley cat's grin. "Now, you know what shopping always makes me feel?"

"The warm glow of an acquisition? Victorious in the battle for a bargain?"

"Hungry. I could eat my way through a market."

"Food? Now?"

"Let's just say it would be a bad idea to take poison, even a slow-working one, on an empty stomach."

I jerk to a halt.

"How else did you think we were going to test the cure?" She skips ahead, then turns to face me, spreading her arms at the city around us. "Just say you knew you were going to die, what would you request for your last meal?"

"I don't know."

"Oh, come on. Everyone has a favorite food." Her eyes narrow and she starts walking slowly backward. "Don't tell me it's horse. I mean, maybe that would explain a few things but . . . Please don't tell me it's horse."

"It's *not* horse."

"Then what's the problem? Here, I'll go first. I love chicken char-grilled with lemon and topped with goat curd, and spiced barley salad comes a close second. Was that so hard?"

"Fine. Rose cake. I love rose cake. With pistachios. And carda-mom. Drenched in syrup."

She gives me an arch look. "Finished with a petal on top of each slice? All pretty like?"

"Exactly." I wait for her to mock me, or at least laugh. The gruff warrior loves his sweet and delicate baked goods. But all she does is lengthen her stride.

"Me first, then. You can choose dessert."

We set out toward the food market, picking up the pace as we draw near, the scent of flour and yeast billowing around us. "If we weren't an entire province away, I could almost imagine that's Ekasyan bread fresh out of the oven."

"Seems you could buy anything here. What's going to make capital-style bread an exception?"

I sniff. "It's a very particular bread."

When we arrive at the food market, I realize I was wrong. Completely wrong. Not only is there Ekasyan bread here, but no less than half a dozen baker's stalls are churning it out like the starwheel is about to stop turning. I purchase a couple of loaves—amazed at the ridiculously low asking price—and we keep moving, coming to a cluster of vendors selling savory pastries.

"These are some of my favorites," I tell Rakel when I've bought a half dozen alob dumplings. They're filled with white cheese and herbs. Steamed first, then fried in a heavy pan. Crispy and chewy and melty all at once. "Here. Dip them in this spicy sauce. I defy you *not* to like them."

She bites into the dumpling. Her eyes light up.

"Good?"

"Mmmhmph!"

"And these ones?" She points to a tray of plump pastry-encased triangles, baked to a golden sheen and sprinkled with sesame seeds.

"They're filled with various things. Mutton. Camel. Some will be horse."

She shudders.

"But I like the ones filled with spinach, onion, garlic, maybe a little squash. Here, these." I gesture to the seller and hand over a couple of copper coins. "Go on, take one."

She's halfway through chewing, when she wrinkles her nose.

"Don't like it?"

"The pastry is just fine. But *what* is that stench?"

I catch scent of it on the next drift of the breeze and smile wryly. Of course, she's never been anywhere near fishing docks, river or ocean. "My guess? Fishmarket."

"It's so . . ." She brings the neck of her robe up over her nose.

"Pungent?"

"That's one way to put it."

We skirt the edge of the fishmarket, past trestles heaped with goggle-eyed trub fish and silver-finned sheklaws, snake-like lossol eels and huge blacktails. Smaller specimens, sandzigs and hullsuckers, are piled high in barrels. There're even some things I haven't seen— strange creatures with more legs than I could count and eyes bulging at the ends of long antennae.

"What are those?" Rakel points to tray upon tray of pearlescent shells, disgust wrinkling her nose.

"Oysters."

"Ugh. Looks like someone hawked them up and spat them out. How could something so much like snot be so popular?"

"They say they're an aphrodisiac."

"Do they now?" She eyes me sidelong.

"Are you trying to make me blush?"

She winks. "Trying would imply it hadn't worked."

I shake my head but don't hide my smile.

We take our food down to the stone marina, upwind from where the fish sellers have begun to slop out their stalls for the night.

Rakel shucks her boots and perches on the edge of the pier, dangling her legs over the water. She gazes out toward the horizon, then gives a wistful little sigh. "Have you ever thought about what's on the other side of the sea?"

"If I'm honest?" I ask, settling beside her. "Not really. When you're in the capital, it's easy to forget how much world is out there. Nisai wanted to travel. But the Aphorai delegation was the first trip his mothers had permitted him to take since he'd been named heir. And I only go where he goes, present circumstances excepted."

She appears to mull that over, then asks: "Mothers? Plural?"

Her voice is strangely tight. Of course. Old wounds run deep.

"The Council of Five."

"Calling them all his mothers is a bit rich."

I lounge back on the pier, propping my weight on my elbows. "They didn't all bear him. But they all take personal interest. They named him heir, after all."

Rakel tears off a piece of dumpling pastry and throws it to a swooping gull. "Politics aside, wouldn't you like to know what's out there?"

"I don't need any more mysteries in my life," I say, tracing a finger along the pier where Rakel's shadow ends and the sun begins, the stone worn smooth by wind and water and uncountable footsteps. "There's too many I haven't yet solved."

She snorts. But a moment later she turns to catch my eye. The ocean breeze has tousled her hair, and I reach out and push a stray tendril behind her ear. Her eyes widen; then she ducks her chin and looks away.

Stupid, stupid, stupid, I curse myself.

"Well then," she says, her tone strangely high and light. "My belly is full. Time to hit it with something it's not going to like nearly so much."

I jerk upright. "What are you talking about?"

"The sooner we find somewhere I can fabricate the poison and cure, the sooner we can test it out"

"I haven't forgotten the plan," I say, stalling for time. "But I definitely missed anyone saying anything about *you* being the one to test this out." It's the gods' cruel joke that Rakel was caught up in all this. The last thing I want is for her to deliberately risk her life, though I doubt that would be enough to convince her.

She lifts her chin. "And why shouldn't I be?"

My chest constricts at the emotion in her eyes. There's the usual defiance, the stubbornness I once thought pride but now realize is a strength forged amid the kind of battles I haven't had to face in turns. But it's not the tenacity in her gaze that makes words catch in my throat. It's something searching. As if the question that hangs between us has nothing to do with poisons.

"We can't risk you," I venture. "If it works, you need to know how and why. If it doesn't, you need to watch that happen, too. There might be clues. Should the worst come to the worst . . . you're much more important than I am—you'll have a far better chance on your own to keep going and figure this out."

"And if it doesn't work?" It's barely more than a horrified whisper.

"I knew from the day needle and ink pierced my skin that another life came before my own." Another life. One. A Shield shouldn't have deep loyalties beyond the oath made to their charge, let alone voice them.

"But without you, how am I going to get anywhere near the capital, let alone the Prince?"

"I have faith you'll find a way." I sound calmer than I feel.

"I don't even know the way to Ekasya!" She's running out of excuses.

"You'll use the map. Just like I have been."

She presses the heels of her hands against her temples. "I don't want to lose you!"

The pain in her voice is a blade-sharp shock. How long has she felt this way?

No. I can't think about that. I will my muscles to relax and try to keep my thoughts in the moment, listening to the wavelets lapping against the great stone pylons, the birds squawking over the remnants of the day's trading. "Please, Rakel. Let me do this."

Her shoulders slump with a defeated sigh. "We should probably find a guesthouse."

"Stay a while longer? I'd like to see the sunset."

It could be my last.

Her expressions softens. "We'll stay as long as you want."

We sit side by side in silence as the horizon changes from blue to gold, through red, pink, purple, and indigo. Each time either of us stretches or shifts, the gap between us grows smaller, so that the deep velvet night finds us pressed together from shoulder to knee.

"Ash?" Rakel asks, her face turned up to the stars.

"Yes?"

"Do you love Nisai?"

"Of course."

"No, I mean, do you *love* him?"

Ah. So that's what this is about.

"In another life, perhaps Nisai and I would have had another relationship. In this life, Nisai serves the Empire. I serve to keep him safe. Nothing must ever get in the way of that, even each other. My loyalty to him is borne of love, and it always will be. But anything beyond the fraternal was set aside turns ago."

She's quiet for a moment, then swallows audibly. "Have you ever cared for anyone other than him? I mean . . . *really* cared?"

My heartbeat is suddenly loud in my ears. There are so many things I should say, that I'm duty-bound to say. But there's something else, something I've known for days, even a moon now, but kept confined behind the fortifications I'd long built around yearning or desire.

If I don't say it right this moment, I may never have another chance.

"Truthfully? Not until now."

When my hand finds hers, she wraps her fingers in mine.

CHAPTER 35
RAKEL

We're quiet on the walk to find a guesthouse. But with my hand in Ash's warm, callused palm, I feel like my churning emotions are being shouted to the world.

Yet nobody in the crowded streets pays us any heed, as if we're just another pair of lovers strolling on an evening grown cool from the ocean breeze. We blend in—from the anywhere accents to the myriad dress styles to the openly displayed affection between the people around us. And when we arrive at a guesthouse not too far from Apothecary Lane—I tell Ash it's to save him lugging the chest too far, but it's more in case I need any further supplies at emergency notice—nobody bats an eye.

Lautus seems as much for freedom as it is for free trade.

Our silver is running low after today's shopping, so we ask for the most modestly appointed room at the back of the building. The fewest number of people passing by, the better.

When we've closed the door behind us, I draw the drapes and set to work, boiling water in several pots over the hearth, setting up the most basic of distillation apparatuses, checking and double-checking the solutions from Atrolos's store.

Ash hangs his cloak at the door and strips off his boots to sit cross-legged on the bed, watching me work.

Though I'm itching to check his expression, I avoid meeting his gaze. The last thing I need is a nervous fumble.

"Are you sure you want to do this?" I ask.

He rises with his usual fluid grace and comes to stand before me. Resting his hands on my shoulders, he leans down to look me in the eye. "Yes. There's no other way."

"There might be. We could figure something out. It'd be an ugly thing to do, but we could try testing it on an animal first. Maybe two. Or maybe we could even pay someone to—"

He shakes his head. "Neither of us would be able to live with ourselves. And even if we could find some willing subject, it would risk exposing us, or take time that we don't have."

My shoulders slump under the weight of his words. He's right. We've not caught any new gossip from the capital since Edurshai. And this city cares naught for the imperial family, so I'd question the reliability of the word on these streets.

All I can do is try to make this as safe as possible for him. "You should probably leave the room, then," I tell him. "Save you breathing any of these things until they're ready."

He folds his arms. "And leave you with nobody around to help if something goes wrong? Not going to happen."

"Then open the window and stay by it. If you begin to feel anything strange, however mild, you have to tell me. This isn't the time for bravery. Agreed?"

He pulls a bench over to the window and sits. "Agreed."

I wrap the perfumer's scarf I'd picked up at the apothecary's over my nose and mouth and set to work, relying on turns of experience and experimentation, and a large dollop of instinct.

Producing steam is more complex than simple smoke. First, I'll need to transform half of the solid ingredients—amber, butterfly parts, living bones—grinding and separately dissolving each in processing solution, then distilling it into concentrated liquid. It's painstaking waiting for each ingredient to condense, balancing hot water and cold to keep the correct temperature in the different flasks and tubes.

Ash observes calmly, taking all this in like it's just something normal, mechanical. But this is going to be more alchemy than chemistry. Despite the simple-seeming instructions, I feel as equipped to formulate this ancient recipe as I would turning my boots to gold.

Admitting the truth of it sends a shudder through me. Ash could die. And it would be my fault. But if I don't try, more will be forfeit. Our lives. Father's. Nisai's. I swipe the back of my hand across the sweat beading on my forehead and focus on the task before me.

The last ingredient to be distilled is the cave bone-plant, still alive in the water from the pool we collected it from. Glowing specs swirl into the receiving flask, suspended like stars. Then they wink out, leaching all color from the liquid as they go.

The recipe calls for a sequence for both poison and cure, but curiosity drives me to mix a small portion of antidote distillate together. The solution swirls as if it's somehow alive, the combination smelling in turns familiar and foreign, each ingredient accenting the one before.

Hesitant, I remove my scarf and give the final result a sniff. The air that greets my nose makes me reel back in surprise.

"Rakel? What is it?"

I stare, incredulous. "Nothing."

"Clearly *something* has your attention."

I hold up the flask of formula. "Nothing. I mean, it looks like nothing. It *smells* like nothing. It's as if I had a bowl of rain, and even then, it would smell of sky and . . ."

"You think that's a sign we've got it right?"

"I can only hope so." I gulp. "Right, then. I guess this is it."

I douse the flames in the fireplace. The plain steam and woodsmoke seems such an innocent introduction for what's to come. I yank the mattress from the bed. On the floor, it's revealed to be more straw than feathers, golden tufts poking through as I drag it before the hearth.

Ash gives me a questioning look.

"The chimney will draw the smoke so it doesn't fill the room. But I don't know how you're going to react to the poison, or even to the antidote. If you begin to have a fit, I don't want to be preoccupied with making sure you don't fall off a piece of furniture and crack your head open." I position a bucket next to the mattress. "Nor do I want you choking on your own sick. The rest is in the hands of whoever came up with this Rot-be-damned formula in the first place."

He settles cross-legged on the mattress. "This really isn't going to be pretty, is it?"

"Probably not."

I set up a small brazier on the hearth and lay out measuring bowls in succession. A few drops of Edurshai antivenom. A sliver of Hagmiri butterfly. A section of glowing bone, still in just enough water to keep it alive. Losian amber ground to a powder. And Esarik's ancient dahkai flower, pried from its glass pommel, the petals now too dry to start decomposing.

Five provinces.

Five ingredients.

Five times I'll be going against everything I believe in and helping someone harm themselves. But this harm is the only way to help others. Nisai. Father.

And it's the only way Ash and I will ever find freedom.

"Sit over the brazier and tent your cloak over your head. *In sequence blown*, the formula stipulates. Light each ingredient with the candle and breathe the smoke. It might burn your sinuses. You'll probably be queasy. Light-headed. If you feel faint, just say." I point to the window. "I'll be right over here."

He nods, though his breath comes a little quicker. Seems that calm exterior is taking effort to maintain.

"Are you ready?"

He reaches out and takes my hand, his fingers enclosing mine. "Whatever happens, remember why we're doing this. Why I'm asking you to do this." He rubs his thumb over the back of my hand.

I don't meet his eyes.

"Rakel?" He brings his other hand to my chin, tipping my face up toward his. "I mean it. If this goes bad, it's not on you. I asked you to do this."

"But if I got the formula wrong, then—"

"What do your instincts tell you? Do you think you're wrong?"

"No." And yet every fiber of my being tells me to study the components further, to understand them better.

"I doubted you back at the Library," Ash whispers, "with the Scent Keeper's elixir. I promised I wouldn't doubt you again."

He nudges me gently toward the window.

Then his cloak is over his head and shoulders, he's tipping the anti-venom into the brazier and taking up the candle. His bulk blocks my view, but I hear the hiss and bubble as it catches light. Soon all the liquid will evaporate and what remains will char and smoke.

I press my scarf over my mouth and nose. We're trusting in a legend, in ancient scribes, and a translation on top of that. All of a sudden it seems more than folly. It seems downright stupid.

But it's too late for that kind of thinking—I catch the barest whiff of scorched blood before it's gone.

Ash has already inhaled the possibility of death.

He sits back, and I rush over, searching for early signs of poisoning. His pupils might be a little dilated, but no more so than the dim, candlelit room warrants.

"How are you feeling?"

"I wish I could get this stench out of my nose, but otherwise I'm fine. Next?"

I grimace.

He takes that as agreement. I return to the window and he lights the next ingredient. And the next.

He coughs, then shrugs off his cloak.

"Anything yet?"

"A little thirsty."

I pass him a cup of water. He gulps it down. "Easy now, you don't want to—"

He grabs the bucket and throws the water back up. When he's finished retching and spitting, he sits back, a little shakily this time.

"Do you want to take a break?"

But he's already measuring amber powder into the brazier.

When he next sits back and throws off his cloak, he's shaking. Dampness sheens his brow. "Ash . . . Tell me how you're feeling. Any other symptoms? Cold?"

"No . . . Hot. Too hot."

He loosens the laces of his leather vest and lifts it over his head. He's wan and sweat runs in rivulets down the contours of his chest, the ink of his tattoo shining like obsidian.

My heart skips. I knew this was a possibility, but knowing and witnessing are very different things. I glance to the antidote ingredients. All I want to do is give them to him, to make this be over.

"Keep talking to me," I say, fighting to keep the unease from my voice. "Can you tell me the sensations?"

"Like . . . River Fever, just after it breaks. Going to lie down for a little while."

"I can't let you sleep. It's too dangerous when we don't know what's going on with your body. Here, stand up, walk with me."

He's shaky on his feet so I duck under one arm. "Lean on me. This is no time for pride."

He smiles wanly. "No time for pride? I remember saying the same to you once." But he still lets me take some of his weight.

"One foot in front of the other. Go on. Now, focus your mind. Think of somewhere you wish you were."

"A place I'd rather be?"

I nod. "Tell me what it's like living in the capital, in the palace."

"I wouldn't know where to start."

"Smells? Do they have gardens like at the Aphorain Eraz's estate?"

We slowly circle the room. Ash insists his sense of smell is blunt, but then he speaks of the flowers in the palace gardens, how the bouquets change from moon to moon. He describes the terrifyingly exquisite perfumes of the Council of Five, and the everyday hint of toasting barley and overripe fruit from Ekasya's brewery when the wind blows just so. The scent of the palace library, of the cinnamon used to ward off parchment-eating insects, and how in springtime, Ami, one of the curators, brings posies of lilacs to work with her so that the early imperial history section smells like new beginnings.

"Lilacs soon became Esarik's favorite scent." Ash chuckles, then winces. "Now I bet they make him feel sad. Ami, too."

"And your favorite scent?" I prompt.

"Ekasyan bread. Ever since I arrived at the palace, Nisai and I would steal away down to the kitchens before dawn, before our lessons started, before duty got in the way. At that hour, it would be all rising dough and flour-dusted aprons and warmth. The cooks would make a fuss over us, and we'd always get a slice of the first hot loaf to come out of the ovens, piled high with fig preserve or soft cheese.

Before the palace, I'd never imagined any place could be safe. But nothing bad could ever happen in those kitchens."

"That's a nice memory."

He sighs. "Perhaps that's all it will ever be now."

We shuffle around like that, sharing and talking for what seems like hours. Finally, he moves back to the hearth. "Four down, one to go?"

"We should wait a little. Make sure you've got the strength for the last ingredient. And that I've got everything in place to administer the cure."

"But we don't have time to—"

"If we don't *make* time to get this right," I say, picking up the bucket, doing everything I can to not gag on the acid reek of bile, "we could be condemning Nisai to death. We've spent this long, we've got to hold our nerve. If there's one thing even I have patience with, it's an experiment."

He grimaces at the bucket. "I'm sorry."

"I've seen sick before, don't get in a lather over it."

"Bit late for that," he says, dabbing at his damp forehead with a cloth. He gives me a wan smile as I close the door behind me.

Though I'm not the one who has been taking lethal formula, dread sits cold and heavy in my stomach, like I've swallowed a rock. There's no going back once Ash breathes smoke from one of the dahkai flower petals. And even if the cure works, he's going to suffer a lot more between now and then.

When I return, Ash sits on the mattress, his demeanor calm, except for the slight wobble as he places the dried dahkai flower in the brazier. "Ready?"

With heavy steps I cross to the window and cover my nose.

Just like with the others, he's businesslike. And then it's done.

We stare at each other, waiting. In the hall, a couple giggles their way back to their room. Outside, the guesthouse's relatively quiet neighborhood has settled for the night.

Soon, Ash's eyelids begin to droop.

"No sleeping," I remind him. I'm about to prop myself under his arm, when he slumps over.

"Ash?" I give his shoulder a shake.

He doesn't stir.

Fear quickens as I gently roll him onto his side. He's still breathing, though it's shallow. I check his pulse. Slower than it should be.

I've got to hold my nerve. If I try the antidote too soon, before all the symptoms appear, we'll never know if the poison was the same as what felled Nisai. We'll be back at square one. It's the last thing Ash would want, especially after all he's suffered.

Yet every moment seems to stretch longer than the last. My fingers on his wrist begin to tremble as his pulse weakens. And still no sign of the key symptom—darkness spreading across the skin.

I check his eyes. Nothing.

I snatch up the first of the cure liquids. We'll have to find another way to test it.

My hands shake as I try to work the stopper free on the anti-venom distillation. I've got to get him breathing the antidote sequence. Now.

But the stopper is sealed so tightly my fingers can barely get purchase. Why in the sixth hell didn't I loosen it earlier?

Sweat slicks my palms. I wipe them on my robe and try again.

It's not working.

I glance to Ash. His chest is barely rising and falling.

I pull my knife from its sheath and wedge the blade into the hairline gap between the vial and the lid. Gritting my teeth, I try to put the same pressure on bracing and lifting. The knife slips, catching the end of my thumb where it holds the vial, slicing through the nail and into the flesh.

A hiss of pain escapes my lips, and I only manage to hold on to the vial through sheer will. I stick my bleeding thumb in my mouth, tears of frustration pricking my eyes.

Then I notice it.

At the center of Ash's chest. Darkness. Growing and twisting like a vine's first tentative tendrils.

I set my jaw and add the first liquid in the oil burner. The scent is horrid as it heats—simmering blood and something worse. I double over my scarf and tie it around my face, then struggle to lift Ash back into a sitting position, mimicking the tent he made with his cloak, this time so he's engulfed in steam.

In sequence, I add the ingredients, one after the other. It reeks worse with every addition, so that I have to run to the window and gulp fresh air for fear of passing out. Finally, I add the last liquid. A drop of pure dahkai essence.

All scent vanishes from the mix.

When enough steam has risen that beads of liquid run down Ash's face, I fling his cloak aside and lower him to the mattress. Then I watch. And wait.

The veins of darkness spread down his sternum.

Dread clenches my stomach. No. It's not supposed to be like this.

The poison is winning.

I can't lose him. Not now. But what can I do?

I could run, run as fast as I can back to Atrolos's store. If I knew what to ask for. If we even have enough zigs left. If Ash could survive that long.

I grab for my satchel, pulling out vial after packet after jar, searching for anything that might at least act as a temporary inhibitor, something to buy us time.

My fingers meet the tiny faceted vial Sephine dropped the night she died. The liquid inside is almost black, though holding it up to the candlelight reveals it's the darkest blue.

I've grown up despising the temple, hating Sephine for how she turned her back on my mother. But what if I've been shortsighted? What if I wrote off the powers Sephine revered because my grudge was more important, filling the spaces of things I'd lost, things I'd never had.

If Sephine could buy Nisai time, could I do the same for Ash?

What had the Chronicler said? Back at the Library of the Lost? If you survive "the first imbibing," you can use it to "channel the will of Asmudtag." Use it to heal.

Questions whirl. Will it kill me? How does this stuff even work? Once I've taken it, what am I supposed to do?

Now shadows seem to move under Ash's skin, as if they've broken off from his tattoos and are seeking a different home. Is that real? Or is my panic imagining the demons of impending death?

It doesn't matter. His life ebbs away before me. I have to do something. Even this. I wouldn't have got half as far alone on this quest, and I'll never make it into the Ekasyan palace without him. But it's not just that. I *want* him healed. I *want* the cure to beat this poison for him.

Because, with Ash, things are different. I've had people around me my entire life—you can never escape them in a village. But I've always kept myself apart. A volatile essence, too mismatched to mix with anything else. Yet getting closer to Ash has felt as natural and grounding as the scent of pure cedar.

It's worth the risk.

I work the stopper free from the Scent Keeper's vial. Before I hold it to my nose, I'm tempted to pray for the first time in my life . . .

Ash stirs under my other hand.

I rock back on my heels. Is it wishful thinking? Or has the black-vein halted its spread?

No, I'm right. It's receding.

I feel for his pulse. Each beat throbs stronger than the last.

It's working!

I lose count of how many times I watch his chest rise and fall into a settled rhythm. Slowly, tentatively, I lower and recap the vial.

After a while, Ash drifts in and out of a doze, mumbling in his sleep. Something about shadows and never being able to find an answer. I reach for Nisai's notebook from Ash's pack and thumb through the pages, wondering at the sketches, even if most of the text is lost to me. What answers did Nisai seek in Aphorai? Why did he want to believe so badly? And what did Sephine know of it, if anything?

"Rakel?" Ash blinks up at me.

I guiltily hide the notebook in the nearest place—my satchel.

His eyes are beginning to focus. "What happened? It's cold. Why's it so cold?"

He's shivering, his teeth chattering between his words. I crawl on to the mattress beside him, drawing the blanket over us. Carefully, I tuck myself under his shoulder, hand on his chest, hoping my body heat will seep through him.

His arm tightens around me.

I sigh in relief, finding his other hand under the blanket, lacing my fingers in his. Tears well behind my closed eyelids, one escaping to roll down my cheek. He's still here. He's still with me.

Our nightmares could soon be over. We have what we need to cure Nisai.

We just need to make it back to Ekasya. To somehow convince the imperial family to let the two fugitives they think played a part in the Prince's attempted assassination try to undo it. All in less than a moon from now.

It'll be a sniff.

CHAPTER 36
ASH

We spent two more nights at the inn. I wanted to leave earlier, but whenever I mentioned it, Rakel would fold her arms and tell me I could go on ahead if I truly thought I'd be useful to Nisai keeled over in a roadside ditch before even coming within sight of Ekasya. We must, she insisted, be sure the threat from the poison had passed.

I sat by the window in our room at the guesthouse, watching the sky as I worried at the braided leather of my prayer band and willed my strength to return. The Lost God's moon was almost full as it arced across the stars of the Tozran constellation. It sent a chill through me.

Next time it passes, it will be completely full.

The lion will be crowned.

Nisai will die.

When we finally leave Lapis Lautus, that knowledge makes the journey to Ekasya seem the longest stretch since leaving Aphorai. I turn to look at the skyline of the smugglers' city one last time, still amazed at how different the reality was to the tales I'd heard of cut-throats and chaos.

After retrieving Rakel's horse from the farmer, we risk taking another smuggler's barge upriver. We spend two days in the wake of the hypnotic rhythm of oars, two nights watching the moon. With Linod's Elixir proving less and less effective, my mood swings like a priestess's incense censer. Morbid to hopeful. Calm to agitation.

We make land before the River Junction and take lesser-traveled lanes, some not much more than a goat trail. I chafe at the delay—the imperial road is the swifter, more direct route. Continuing upriver would be better still. But we saw how that went last time, and by Kaismap's eyes I won't let us be apprehended before we make it back to the capital. There's only one person I'll be handing myself over to once we reach Ekasya. One person I trust to hear me out—if I can just get to her.

Nisai's mother.

Shari.

The terrain becomes flatter and drier as we travel on to the central river plains. Soon after, irrigation channels begin to web the land like veins. We're getting close to the capital.

We pass a group of people straggling by on foot. Judging by their plain-spun robes and the worn state of their sandals, they're pilgrims. The stench of putrefying flesh announces several are also Afflicted. I'd wager they're making a tour of every pre-Empire temple—or what remains of them—an ancient, meandering journey that takes more than a turn.

A small child riding on her mother's hip stares at me. Her lip trembles and she bursts into tears. I have no idea what to do, which way to look, so I look back to Rakel. She leans down from the saddle, pokes her tongue out, and crosses her eyes. The child's crying bubbles into laughter.

Farther up, an old man rests in the shade of a scrawny tree, leaning on a cane as knotted and gnarled as his wiry frame. His eyes fix on me as closely as the child's, though the knowingness in his gaze is far more unsettling.

He raises a pointed finger, a tremor shaking his hand. "You are of the shadows, boy."

The sun is warm, and with no sign of Rangers, I'd been chancing some time without my cloak. While the fanged jaw etched over my scalp is becoming concealed as my hair grows back in, the Aphorain lion of Nisai's forebears claws from my shoulders and down my arms, the ink marking me as Shield.

The old man states the obvious.

"No, no, no. Not *those* shadows." He grins as if he has just delivered the punch line of a joke.

I stiffen. There are fortune-tellers working the alleys of Ekasya who say they can read minds and see beyond the realm of men. Soldiers visit them before leaving for battle, seeking assurance that this will not be their last. I won't be played by their ilk. It's sacrilege, presuming to know the will of the gods. I would have expected more from a pilgrim.

"Explain yourself," I demand.

His only reply is a high, rattling cackle. Despite the heat, it sends a chill through me.

I walk on, quickening my stride.

When the pilgrims are behind us, Rakel slides from her horse. "What was that about?"

"He . . . said he saw shadows around me. How could he know?"

"Probably just meant your tattoos."

"No. They're believers. Intrigued by anything that hearkens back to the edge of memory. Same as the quartz hanging in the doorways back in Koltos. It was something more."

She sniffs the air. "More likely they were just overwhelmed by your magnificent cologne."

"I'm not wearing cologne."

"Then I guess it was just your natural aroma." Her nose wrinkles, but not before her lips twitch into the hint of a smile.

*   *
 *   *
   *

The next night, we make camp away from the road, in a copse of trees marking the boundaries between one landholding and the next.

"Just for a few hours," Rakel says. "We need at least some rest."

It's a balmy evening, the breeze a warm caress, both moons waxing bright above us. With no need for a fire, we've set our bedrolls up side by side and lie on our backs, staring at the sky. If only I could think the sight beautiful, rather than a marker of Nisai's ebbing life.

"Look," I say, trying to find a distraction. "We caught the jackal chasing Esmolkrai."

"We did what now?"

I stretch an arm up. "See that bright star? It's the eye of Esmolkrai, the serpent, who rises each night and sets like a snake going into hibernation. There're arguments between the university and the temple about whether it even is a star."

"What would it be otherwise?" Rakel moves closer, so that her hair tickles my shoulder. I inhale deeply. The scent of desert rose calms and stirs my blood in equal measure. How is that even possible?

"Another moon," I say, voice hitching in my throat. "Or a sun. Or even another world. Whatever it is, where I lived as a child, people say it's a good omen. An auspicious time. Anyone who lives in the slums needs all the luck they can get. And so do we. May as well try to think of the vial as half full."

Rakel lets out a low laugh. "Someone's swapped bitter yolketh for purrath blossom."

"Someone was a good influence." I reach out a hand, searching. Our fingers meet, entwine. Her palm is cool against mine.

It's then that I realize I'm sweating. Profusely.

She pulls her hand back and sits up, her silhouette turning toward me. "How are you feeling? Any lingering effects from the testing?"

"I can manage."

I should tell her. Explain that it's not the poison, that I felt restored from its effects following the first night of full sleep after the test in Lapis Lautus. I'm quick to heal, after all. What's stalking me now is very different. It runs in my veins. It's as familiar as the fine lines crisscrossing the backs of my hands.

I told her I'd not had an episode since I was a child, and that's true, but I've been close. I'm taking more and more Linod's Elixir and yet it's doing less and less to suppress those feelings. I'm losing control.

Parts of me that have long been dormant are stirring.

"We can't have you just 'managing.' You need to be at your best. And if there's something that's gone wrong with the cure, a slow side effect . . . We don't want to put Nisai in further danger."

The last thing I'd want to do is put myself between Nisai and a cure. Especially now, with just days on our side. But after what happens in Ekasya, I may never see her again, let alone together like this. Would it be so terrible to enjoy this last night of being the closest to happiness I've ever been?

Then her words come back to me, the ones from when we were in the mountains, waiting for our clothes to dry after the ordeal with the butterfly pupae. *Broken trust is the hardest wound to heal*, she said. *It always leaves a scar. Always.*

As I look up at her, outlined in stars, I realize in my blood, my bones, that I can't lose her. In her trust, I've found something I sacrificed to duty and never thought I'd deserve again. Something I'll never even have with Nisai.

Because I'm not Rakel's Shield. I don't have to guard against everything the world could throw at her.

I don't have to protect her from myself.

She is my freedom.

"It's not a side effect." My throat constricts, voice so thick it could be a stranger's. "I keep taking my Linod's dose and don't feel any steadier for it. Like I'm chasing an equilibrium that's no longer there."

Every muscle goes rigid, but I force myself to admit the shameful truth: "I need more."

My confession hangs for an eternity in the darkness between us. Each heartbeat aches deeper in my chest.

She gives a long, audible exhale.

"Rakel?"

"You're spiraling." Her tone is concerned but devoid of judgment. There's no admonishment, no scorn. "It happens to everyone who uses Linod's for a long time. You need to ease off. Deliberately. Methodically. And most importantly, slowly. It's won't be easy, but you have to start. Soon."

"Not yet. I must be in control when we get to the palace."

"Ash, if you increase your dose, or even keep up your current levels, it could kill you."

"How long?"

She lies back down, this time beside me, her head on my chest. "I can't say for sure. A moon? More? Less?"

I don't respond. What else is there to say? All I can do is hold her until her breathing evens into sleep.

Gazing up at the stars, I pray to each of the gods in turn that I'll be able to keep myself together long enough to fulfill my duty. To find freedom for all of us.

I reserve a final prayer of gratitude to merciful Azered, for at least one of the knots in my stomach has unwound, knowing I won't have to face tomorrow alone.

*   *
   *   *
      *

Somewhere in the night I find rest, because when I open my eyes the sky has turned predawn gray. There's a small fire nearby, dug into a pit to conceal it. Rakel must have been up for some time.

"Glad you got some sleep," she says, pressing a cup into my hands. "Inhale the steam, then drink it. All at once. It'll taste like a slurp from a tanner's vat, but it'll restore you. At least in part."

I do as she says. She's right. The tincture is vile. "What was in that?"

She gives me a wry smile. "You don't want to know."

"I wouldn't have asked if I didn't."

"Believe me, you *don't*." She grins.

I never thought I'd be so relieved to be mocked. "You're enjoying this, aren't you?"

Her smile widens.

"I thought you were all about healing people, not relishing their suffering."

"Eh, I get my thrills where I can." She moves off to ready Lil for the ride to the capital.

Funny thing is, once I've finished stowing my bedroll and splashed water on my face, I do feel a little better. I decide not to increase my Linod's dose for today and shoulder my pack.

"Ready?"

She nods.

Ekasya Mountain is the only major uprising out of the plain

between the Alet Range, the north Trelian coast, the Losian Wastes and the Edurshai Basin. The border of every province lies in view of the capital, and it is where the gods reside when they visit the mortal realm. If there is no time or space for your prayers to be lost on the wind, you must burn them on the great stepped pyramid of Ekasya.

From there, they will surely reach heaven.

Dawn overflows onto the plain. In a few hours, the mist hanging over the river will burn away. For now, it obscures the base of the mountain, so that the entire city seems to float above the earth, already a step closer to the sky than the rest of the Empire.

Rakel draws level with me, gapes up at the black granite skyline. "It's . . ."

"I know. I grew up in its shadow, and it still takes my breath away."

When I was a child, I used to think the mountain intimidating. Now that I'm a fugitive, about to march to the gate and hand myself over to the guards, the sight prickles my skin to gooseflesh.

So much has happened since I last laid eyes on this place. So much has changed, been lost. So much has been risked, is still at risk.

Rakel leans her head against my shoulder.

And, perhaps, something has been gained, too.

"The only way out?" she asks, taking my hand.

I give her fingers a gentle squeeze. "Through."

CHAPTER 37
RAKEL

I expected we'd run into trouble as soon as we arrived in the city.
    I wasn't wrong.

Guards seized us as soon as we passed between the huge gates. They confiscated everything but the clothes on our backs and my locket nestled safely out of view. Another led Lil away. She tossed her head, jerking the reins clear out of her captor's hand to look back at me.

"It's all right, girl," I called after her. But it wasn't all right—maybe it never will be—and my eyes stung as she vanished from sight.

At least Ash's presence was enough to convince the gate guards to bring us to the imperial complex.

If only we'd made it farther than a holding cell in the barracks.

Ash's whole bearing changes. Despite the aurochs leather cuffs we've both been clamped in, despite his twin swords being seized, he holds himself straighter than normal, shoulders back, chin lifted. "I demand an audience with the Council. Immediately. It's my right as Shield."

One of the guards stationed outside the door chuckles.

The other hefts one of Ash's swords, testing its weight for himself. "Last I heard you were no longer Shield. And you won't be going anywhere except on the orders of the Regent."

"Regent?" I murmur.

Ash doesn't answer, only paces the cell, his bound hands clenched at his back.

I slump to the floor. There's no time for this. We need get to the

Prince. Every breath takes us closer to the moment Sephine had said his life would falter.

And yet the day marches by, while we wait, powerless. We're brought meals—richer than I've had in my life—and given a few minutes free of our cuffs in which to eat.

I've no appetite, especially not with several guards watching our every move. But I eat, because I need Ash to eat. He's starting to look wild about the eyes, and there's a tremor in his hands each time they're unbound.

The next morning, we're manhandled out of the cell by four guards and led without explanation farther into the imperial complex. As we climb the great staircase toward the palace, the wind picks up, whipping my hair into my eyes.

I stumble and fall, somehow managing to roll onto my side to keep my face from smashing into the steps. Baked clay bricks are a mere inch from my eyes. Each one has an indented set of initials—the stamp of some long dead Emperor who wanted everyone to know he gave the orders to build this place.

Ash bends over me in concern, but his hands are as helplessly bound as my own. One of the guards grabs the chain between my wrist and yanks me up. I manage to get my feet under me before my shoulders pull from their sockets.

At the top of the staircase, a group of guards stands in formation. Their leader steps forward as we approach.

Recognition knifes through me.

His features seem harder, more set than when I last saw him, like here's the solid bronze statue when I'd only ever known the wax mold. The passing moons have changed him, but it's a scent I'd recognize anywhere, anytime. Amber, orange oil, thyme. Familiar sweat.

Barden.

His sash is imperial purple now, and there's a phoenix stamped in the leather of his kilt. The Kaidon phoenix. Somewhere in all this he's risen three ranks and been redeployed to the capital. I wonder who he snitched on to get to this position so quickly; who was the casualty of his ambition this time?

He comes even closer, and locks gazes with me. What's that in his dark eyes? Guilt? Regret?

Whatever it is, he can keep it to his stinking self.

"You found her," he says.

"Indeed," Ash replies.

I glance between them. "What in the sixth hell—"

One of the gate guards clears his throat. "Sir, they say they have a cure for the Prince. Regent says if it's true, admit them."

"Where is it, Rakel?" Barden's voice is level, detached, so different to the way he used to speak to me.

I muster my mildest expression. The last thing I need is for the cure to be confiscated, it's the only thing between me and the executioner's knife.

He sighs. "You can either tell me, or you can be searched."

However much I hate to admit it, he speaks the truth. "My locket," I tell him through clenched teeth. "On my locket chain." I try not to cringe at the thought of him putting his hand down my tunic to retrieve it. But he doesn't move.

"Let her go," he says to the guards holding me.

"Sir?"

"I said, let her go! Unbind her. Now. The Shield as well."

I don't meet his eyes.

He signals to his men. "Form up a rear guard."

The main imperial hall is as big as an entire wing of the Aphorain Eraz's estate and twice as loud as a marketplace. Crowds of courtiers fill the space, wearing a clash of colors and the most decadent scents, setting my stomach to churning. When the rich sorts begin to notice our presence, a hush falls like dusk. Soon after, a pathway clears.

The Prince is laid out on a platform before the throne, as if his bedroom has become a public spectacle. A tall Losian stands guard over him, a picture of alertness and lean strength. Kip, I assume.

Beside them, in a plain wooden chair—an oddly everyday item amid the riches of the great hall—sits Nisai's brother. It's a battle with my own instincts to keep moving one foot after another, getting closer to the man we've been trying to stay one step ahead of for the past three moons.

Commander Iddo's face is schooled to blankness, just like Ash's always used to be. What a thing it must be to be able to keep your emotions hidden from the world. But when I look to Ash now, hope is painted so raw and vulnerable across his features that it halts me in my tracks.

I can feel tension crackling in the room, smell the anticipation of the crowd. Like unbroken horses, they'll spook at the first movement or noise that snags on their unease.

"Commander." Ash executes a stiff bow.

"Ashradinoran. I thought you'd be wise enough not to show your face in the capital again."

"Commander, I"—he glances to me and clears his throat, clearly speaking for the entire room—"*we* believe we have a cure to what ails the First Prince."

"How can I believe a word you say? You're the first on the scene of a crime. You defy a direct order and desert with a suspect. You resist arrest. Kill a Ranger officer. How do I know you haven't simply returned to finish the job on my brother?"

Ash bristles, then reins himself in. "Because you know I had nothing to do with it in the first place. And that should the First Prince die, I would be required to fall on my sword." He takes an obvious survey of the room, to walls lined with palace guards, Barden among them. The guards are interspersed with a handful of men in black robes.

I spot a familiar face among them. Esarik. He made it back to the capital in time. What a relief. We're in desperate need of a friend.

"And," Ash continues, "you'd have more than enough witnesses to ensure that I did my duty."

Iddo stares at us for a long time, his brow furrowed. Somehow his considerable height seems even more imposing when he's sitting.

"Very well," he finally says.

"Commander, no!" The voice comes from the shortest of the black-robed men.

Ash bristles beside me.

"Forgive me, Commander," the man fawns. "But should we not study this so-called cure before allowing it to be administered to the Prince? The Guild advises empiricism over—"

Iddo raises a warning eyebrow.

The short man stutters to a halt.

But the first voice of dissent has opened the sluice gates.

"Tests," another black-robed man insists. "We need tests. Proof of concept at barest minimum."

My eyes dart around the room as more and more voices erupt. The Commander drums long fingers against the arm of his chair. Are they convincing him? I can't face another poisoning.

"A bodyguard and a provincial find a cure before the Guild of Physicians? Preposterous!"

"Surely suspected assassins shouldn't be permitted near our Prince?"

"Trial! Put them on trial!"

"Enough!" Iddo roars.

The throne room falls silent.

"You've been studying the First Prince and his condition for moons and come up with nothing. So much for your empiricism. Ashradinoran is well aware of the stakes here." He motions for us to come forward. "If you can heal my brother, do it."

My hand trembles as I approach the platform and Nisai's unmoving form. His face is pale, the skin webbed in so many veins of black it looks as if he's made of broken eggshell. I don't dare to move his robe aside, but it's clear the darkness has spread—down his neck, onto his chest. Tiny threads have crept right down his fingers and under the nails. He's covered in it.

But I must not let them see my doubt.

"I need an oil burner and a cloth!" My voice rings out across the throne room, sounding more confident than I feel.

Esarik must have been prepared. He approaches with the very things I need, along with my satchel. I resist the urge to hug the scholar for finding a way to retrieve it from the guards.

I turn my attention to Nisai. "Lift him to sitting?"

Ash moves to do as I ask, cradling the Prince as gently as if he were a newborn. I'm reminded of how deep their care runs for each other, how it goes beyond loyal servant and ruler. For the sake of that love, and for whatever it is I now feel for Ash, I hope I've got this right.

I *have* to be right. Otherwise more than the Prince will suffer.

Carefully, so carefully, I measure the first vial into the oil burner. I try to relax as the liquid takes a moment to heat. Once the steam starts to rise, I tent the cloth over Nisai's head and follow suit with the remaining four vials.

When it's done, Ash lowers the Prince.

Not daring to look at Iddo or the guards surrounding us, their spears at the ready, we wait.

And wait.

There's nothing happening. Nothing at all.

My stomach churns. Why isn't it working? Maybe the Prince doesn't have enough fight left in him. He's spent so long on the verge of death, maybe it's easier to keep sinking than it is to find his way back.

Or are we already too close to Tozran's Coronation?

Are we too late?

Ash and I lock gazes. All that running, all the risks we've taken to get to this moment, all for nothing. I swallow, throat painfully tight. I have no idea what to say, where to go from here.

Then the Prince's head rocks back, his face contorting into a rictus snarl. His limbs stiffen.

"He's seizing!" I unsheathe my knife.

"Not another move!" Iddo shouts.

Nisai's feet jerk and begin a rapid drumbeat on the bed.

I turn to Ash, pleading. "If I don't do something, he could choke to death."

"I trust you." With a grim nod, Ash turns to face the encroaching guard. People he once served alongside. People he once trained or was trained by. People he now draws his swords against.

I wedge the hilt of my knife in Nisai's mouth, careful to keep his tongue clear of his teeth. "Keep fighting. Find your way. Please." And then something I never thought I'd say of an Aramtesh ruler slips out. "The Empire needs you."

"Has it worked?" I hear one of the guards ask.

"Witchcraft," hisses one of the black-robed physicians.

"Stay back," Ash growls, his hands held just wide of his hips, as if he's simply relaxing between bouts on the training ground, not poised to strike.

My heart fills with admiration. Right now, we need calm. For the Prince's sake.

Iddo rises to his feet. "Stand down, house cat."

CHAPTER 38
ASH

I can't do that, Commander." My tone is formal. A soldier's words.

"Don't make this worse. Step away from the Prince."

I cast about, desperately seeking a friendly face. A voice of reason. My eyes find Esarik, urging him to speak. One of the black-robed physicians speaks something in his ear. The Trelian looks stricken but stays silent.

"It worked once," I say. "We tested it. It will work again. Just give her time."

"Time is not on anyone's side, least of all yours. Now stand down." There's something so calm about the Commander, even more than his usual aura of authority. Why does he not seem distraught? At least disappointed? Is it that he'd long given up hope for his little brother? Or did he expect all along that the cure wouldn't work?

"Iddo," I implore. "I understand. You're a pragmatist. I am, too. But the things I've seen over these past moons, the things Rakel has done . . . I believe she's Nisai's only hope. Please. I love him every bit as much as you do."

The Commander's calm shatters. "How *dare* you speak of love. The love of a traitor is no love at all." He draws himself up to his full height, head and shoulders above me and almost every other guard in the room. "This is your last warning."

"No." For the second time since arriving at the palace all those turns ago, I'm disobeying a direct order from a member of the imperial family. I thought I'd be in turmoil, but this time, I know my own heart.

The Commander appears incredulous. "No?"

I hold my ground. "You heard me."

Iddo signals one of the guards. Behind me, there's a commotion.

"Ash?" Rakel's voice quavers.

I risk a glance over my shoulder. They have her. One of the guards points his blade at her throat as he maneuvers her away from Nisai's still-trembling but comatose form.

And at that sight, how they hold the lives of the two people I care most for in this world in their hands, something shifts in me. Something that I've kept bound, caged, and cowed for half my life, trying to forget that it lurks inside me. That it's a part of me.

The edges of my vision darken.

The midday sun suddenly casts shadows where it shouldn't—in the light streaming from the balcony, where the gilt mosaics lining the walls should be glinting.

Deep inside, I feel something shift and stretch, uncurling from its crouch. With each beat of my heart it grows larger, stronger, filling me up as it feeds on my rage.

No. Keep control.

You are a boy, not a beast.

I'm less than ten turns old again. Standing in an alley with my back to the wall, side by side with a young prince. A boy just like me. A curious boy who has wandered into the wrong slum at the wrong time and will pay the price if the two Blazers closing in on us have their way.

A boy, not a beast.

I turn to see Rakel's eyes go wide. She begins struggling against the guard holding her with his knife blade to her throat, an inch from slicing her life away. A bead of blood trickles down her skin and falls onto the white linen of her robe.

A boy.

The beast sees the redness, too. Deep, mortal crimson. I fight it, try to hold it, keep it down, tighten my grip.

But today, the beast is stronger.

CHAPTER 39
RAKEL

My captor stinks of layer upon layer of sweat, salty new to sour old and everything in between. Part of me wonders what would happen if I stomped my boot down on his sandaled foot.

But there's another part. One that imagines what could happen with the knife at my throat if I did.

My neck stings where the blade nicked the skin. And there's a maddeningly slow trickle of wetness. The copper tang of blood fills my nostrils. Ash must see it, too, because his whole bearing is changing.

I can't be sure of what's shifted. Maybe it's the way he now holds himself—stiff, not poised. Maybe it's his expression that looks somehow pained and furious at the same time, like he's fighting some sort of internal battle.

Whatever it is, there's been a change. Something different in the light, the way it falls across the polished basalt floor. The way it meets the shadows. Almost . . . wavering.

And then I hear it. A sound so guttural and harsh it could have come from the sixth hell itself.

I was scared a moment ago, scared that my throat would be cut.

That fear seems suddenly small.

It's replaced with cold dread at the sight before me.

CHAPTER 40
ASH

It's been half a lifetime, but I'll never forget the feeling of the shadow unfurling. Back then it was a doubling, like I was in one place, while another, impossible version of me, a dark, angry, amorphous version, went for the Blazers.

This is nothing like that.

When it starts, the burning is almost bearable. Like I've spent too long in the sun on the first day of high spring. A prickling, just-too-hot sensation. It intensifies to a scald, and then the searing heat of what it must be like to be branded, what the Noseless Ones must feel when their wound is sealed by blistering hot metal.

Fire courses through me, rushing along the lines of ink that trace my torso, my arms, the backs of my legs, my scalp. But the worst, oh sweet mother Esiku, the worst of it is where the wings fold over my spine.

I'm being torn open in a hundred places at once, each line of my inked skin splitting like a ripe pomegranate.

Somewhere from inside the pain, white and scorching, I register the moment of imminent separation. I couldn't stop it now even if I wanted to. And now that the rage has built, that it courses through me thicker and more life-giving than air or blood, I *want* to let it go.

The beast leaps from my shoulders, raking great talons across my already-lacerated flesh as it takes flight.

I slump to the floor, bleeding and unable to do anything but watch, with a clinical sort of detachment, as a winged lion made of shadow lunges at the guards, claws extended. It slices limb from torso, rending hardened leather armor as if it is silk.

Some guards stand like statues, feet locked to the marble floor. Others cower and back away. The bravest prepare to fight. But their swords and spear points, even if they do connect, pass straight through.

The only prize each strike fetches is a howl of rage as the beast, part lion, part eagle, part me—

CHAPTER 41
RAKEL

The guard with his blade to my throat takes a step back, his grip tightening.

Then it goes slack.

Because he's running. Running as if his life depended on it.

The throne room erupts into chaos.

Above, a huge winged lion—ink black one moment, as translucent as smoke the next—swoops through the air, diving on the guards one by one, talons ripping and shredding with horrible wet tearing noises, spraying red in its wake.

Waves of stinking carnage swamp me—metallic blood and acid-sharp piss and panic-loosened bowls. I lurch over, hands on knees, and gag.

I glance to the Prince in front of me. He's still unconscious. Maybe he's a little more ashen, but his chest has begun to evenly rise and fall again. I dearly hope he's returning from danger.

But I'm not.

And I'm not the only one.

Below the platform, halfway across the room, Ash lies splayed facedown on the floor. Lacerations cover him from scalp to ankle, blood pooling on the floor around his prone body. I'm paralyzed by the sight before instincts kick in. I've got to find a way to stop the bleeding.

I start moving toward him, crouched low, hoping the shadow circling above doesn't decide to make me a target.

It wings nearer, then wheels away, diving on two guards standing back-to-back. Their shouted curses turn to the screams of dying men, until the roar of the beast cuts off their last voice.

"Rakel." The voice is familiar. It comes from what I had thought to be another dead body strewn over the floor. There. A shock of gold-streaked hair.

"Esarik?"

Deep wounds have been gouged in the lower half of his torso, bloodied loops visible in the worst of them. The stench tells an undeniable truth. There's nothing I can do for him.

"It's all right," he says through a gurgling cough. "I know I'm dying. But please. Do something for me?"

I hunker down next to him. "Of course."

"Tell Nisai . . . I'm sorry."

"What are you talking about?"

Tears of pain well in his eyes. "At first I refused. But they took Ami hostage. The fire . . . I thought smoke inhalation would be the worst . . ."

"Who did, Esarik? You're not making any sense."

"Please. If he wakes, he's in danger. The book? Where is the book?"

"Danger? From who?"

Esarik draws a ragged breath, moaning as it shifts his mangled torso. "I don't know what they'll do to Ami."

"They still have her?"

The shadow beast wheels overhead and lunges for another knot of soldiers with a sickening, wet crunch.

"No time. There's a letter. In my pocket. Take—"

He shudders and goes still, eyes staring undeniably into nothing.

Gingerly, I rifle through his robes. My fingers touch parchment.

Somebody grabs me by the arms. It's only when they begin shaking me that I realize they're shouting. With some effort I focus my eyes on the face before me.

Barden.

"There's a servants' staircase in the next room," he says. "Behind the curtain. Get to the bottom and follow your nose to the kitchens. Take the path to the small gate where they bring in the supplies and you'll be able to clear the walls. Find the residential sector. Go. Hurry."

"But Ash. He needs me."

Footsteps pound out in the hallway and more guards race into the room.

The pool of blood under Ash seeps farther across the marble.

"Look at him! It's too late. You won't get another chance. If the guards regain control, you may live to see the dawn, but they won't let you see many more. A trial will only be a formality."

"Barden, I—"

"For anything we ever were, Rakel, go. Please."

Though I want nothing more than to run to Ash's side, he'd want me to stay the course, to keep fighting to save Nisai. Not just for the Prince, or for Ash, or Father or even me. But for something bigger. Something more important.

The chances of any of us getting out of this are slim at best. The chance of me being able to do anything to help them after today are slimmer. But there'll be no chance whatsoever if I'm killed or taken prisoner here and now.

With one last look between Nisai and Ash, I make up my mind. Something inside me tears open, guilt flooding in. But it's the only way.

I gather myself and give Barden a nod.

Then I run.

A great tapestry hangs in the next chamber. I don't pause long enough to take in the scene. Sure enough, behind it is a narrow staircase, carved in stone and descending in a tight spiral. It's lit by a series of mirrors capturing the light from a high window and smells faintly of the last time it was scrubbed down with vinegar and lemon. I take the steps two and three at a time, one hand against the curved wall to steady myself.

I descend flight upon flight, the doors that appear along the way gradually getting smaller and plainer.

Finally, the heat of the kitchens whooshes up to greet me. It bears the smell of baking Ekasyan bread. Ash's favorite scent. The scent that he told me made him feel safe, warm, loved. Accepted for who he is.

It's the scent that finally breaks me.

But if there was ever a time for crying, this isn't it.

I swipe the tears from my cheeks and keep running.

CHAPTER 42
ASH

I'm not sure when I lost consciousness, but when I come to, the first thing I smell is death.

And I don't care.

Because everything is pain.

My skin is split in so many places that each breath hurts a hundred times over. There's another sensation, too, a more pleasant one. Like warm, soothing balm is being dripped across me in the bathhouse.

But it's not fragrant oil. It's blood.

The guards left standing are shouting at one another. In between, something growls and roars and there's the terrible crunch of human bone breaking.

Then it's quiet, quiet enough to hear nothing but the beat of huge shadowy wings. Quiet enough for me to hear my own life pumping slowly but inevitably onto the floor as my beast swoops and circles the air over me, searching for more prey.

Then there's another shadow over me, and it's much nearer, and it's human. It's that guard from the Aphorai palace. What was his name? I can't remember. Did I know?

"Rakel." My voice feels foreign in my throat, as if it's not my own. "Where is she?"

The guard's face blanches as he looks down at me. "Gone. Escaped in the chaos."

Relief washes over me, stronger than the pain, stronger than the shock.

"Please," I croak. "Please, just end it."

He looks to the ceiling high above us, my eyes following his gaze, sure that this will be the last thing they ever register. Then he draws his sword.

The pain threatens to crowd out my thoughts.

But there's still something beneath . . .

Her defiance in the face of the sandstorm. Her smile across so many campfires. Her voice guiding me from the caves and my own darkness. Our embrace at the Edurshai camp. Taking my hand as we sat on the Lautus causeway, legs dangling above the water. Warmth curled against me the night I shivered and sweated through the aftermath of testing the cure.

"Survive," I whisper.

My chest lowers with a ragged breath.

I let my eyes close.

CHAPTER 43
RAKEL

The main streets of the Ekasya imperial district splay down the mountain. From the peak, they seem like spokes of the starwheel and you're at the center.

When you're not at the top, things get a *lot* more confusing.

I try to keep to the backstreets and away from the main boulevards. Crisscrossing my way down the slopes soon leaves me lost in a maze of shaded laneways. Balconies thick with vines block the sky, the houses crowding together. Jasmine sweetens the air, masking the unpleasant scents of the city.

But jasmine alone can't mask the metallic stench of blood.

I come up against a dead end. How many of these blind alleys does this too-good-for-stink city have?

I cast around. Back up the alley, there's a pile of clay shards higher than me. Guess one of the buildings that backs on to here must be a potter. It's a good enough place as any to hold up for a breather.

I slip behind the heap of broken clay and strip off my tunic, replacing it with the Chronicler's linen robe I took from the Library of the Lost. That seems like turns, not moons ago. At least the change of clothes dilutes the blood stink.

In this city, even the alleys are sealed. I let myself sit on a sun-warmed paver—the few rays that make it past the hanging vines just enough to draw the chill from the black stone.

It's quiet. Quiet enough to hear my racing heart begin to slow, to hear my own breath in my ears. The sounds of the city are still there, but they seem distant, muffled by the vegetation. In Aphorai, it'd be the kind of hush you'd only find in the most secluded of gardens.

I fish in my pocket for Esarik's letter. The seal makes me hesitate, but any niceties flew on the breeze when Ash—

I don't even want to think about what Ash did back there. What Ash *is*.

The letter is written half in what looks like Old Imperial, given its similarity to the formula scroll. The other half is in a language I've never seen. I slam the heel of my hand on the pavers in frustration. The movement dislodges something from the packet. It bounces, tinkling, across the lane.

A golden-brown bead.

Losian amber.

Esarik had tried to atone until the end.

What else had he said? Something about a book? Could he have meant Nisai's journal?

I rummage in my satchel. I haven't looked at it since the night we tested the poison, and Ash never mentioned it. I'm not sure if that's because he didn't notice it missing, or if he noticed and decided not to ask.

Now, thumbing through the pages, almost none of it makes sense. There's at least three, maybe four different scripts, and I can only read the few snatches of imperial text.

Useless.

I bite back a scream of frustration. It's been four long moons since I last saw my village. Three of them spent on the road. We heard snippets of news about Nisai the whole way, but that's because he's a Prince. I've no word of Father. And when I last saw him, the Rot seemed to be winning, eating higher and higher into his flesh . . .

My eyes ache with unshed tears at the possibility this could all have been for nothing.

I shake my head. If Father is gone, I'd be better off disappearing somewhere. Maybe even back to Lapis Lautus. I reckon I could make a living in the city on the sea. I'd open my own apothecary. Keep busy. Find solace in small things. I'd close up shop in the evenings and go down to the marina and watch the dolphins play. Pick up some cheese dumplings on the way for supper, the ones with the spicy sauce just like Ash showed me.

In Lautus I wouldn't have to deal with whatever Ash and I have become. Or temples and palaces. Priestesses and princes. Poisonings and politics.

Journals in multiple languages.

Coded letters.

Shadow beasts—

Something wafts through my mind, like finally working out a complex perfume's subtlest note after you've been smelling it for days.

I snatch up the notebook and flip the pages, desperate to find the right place before I lose the thought. There. Symbols. Like the ones

313

scribbled on the formula scroll. And Nisai's translated some of them into Standard Imperial.

I pull out the manuscript to compare with the notebook. Only two match, but it's enough.

Shadow.

Beast.

I start pacing from one side of the alley to the other. *Think, just think.* There's something I'm missing here. Something just out of reach, like trying to turn your head fast enough to see your own ear.

Then it clicks into place. Those Blazers weren't after Nisai and the ransom he would bring when Ash and he were kids.

They were after *Ash*.

The Brotherhood of the Blazing Sun wanted a shadow warrior.

All the clues were there. The way Ash heals so quickly. The old pilgrim man talking about shadows. The illustrations in Nisai's diary . . . Why Nisai would even want to meet alone with Sephine in the first place. Ash getting edgy when he ran out of Linod's Elixir—I'd thought it was merely for his nerves and when he tried to explain, I'd reasoned everything away. Dismissed as impossible anything I'd not seen with my own eyes.

If only I'd smelled the forest for the pines and just *listened*.

I snap the book shut.

I'm only a few paces back down the alley when my nostrils flare. Huh? I could have sworn this was a dead end.

Amber. Sweet orange. And the barest hint of tanner's thyme.

A hand falls on my shoulder.

I slip its grip and spin around.

"Shhh. It's me. It's only me."

I stamp my foot. Hard. It comes down on Barden's toe.

He bites his lip and glares at me accusingly.

I retreat a step, my back finding the wall. "What in the sixth hell do you think you're—"

He holds up both hands, a show of peace. "I couldn't bear Aphorai after you'd gone. When Commander Iddo recruited extra guards to transport the Prince back to the capital, I seized the chance to go with them. I guess I proved myself, because I've been here ever since. Today, when the next lot of guards arrived, and we got the Prince out of the throne room, I slipped away."

"But how did you know which way I'd gone?"

"You're more predictable than you think, the way you move through a city, the things you avoid. I've always known how to follow you." He looks as if he's trying to smile, but it's more like the sad look he gave me the night Nisai was poisoned. "If only I'd made more use of that, maybe we could have avoided getting caught up in all this."

"What are you talking about?"

"What if I'd stepped in sooner that night?"

I fold my arms. "Which night?"

"When you risked more than you realized. When you went to Zakkurus. I should have stopped you from even going into that place, saved you from doing something that—"

"Have you learned *nothing*?" It's more exclamation than question. I throw up my arms. "You've always been trying to *save* me, like I'm a bunch of flowers to be cut and dried and kept safe in a vase forever. You did what *you* thought was best for me. What about what *I* wanted?"

"I realize that now. I do. But . . ."

"But what?"

"Just because I can't go back and change things doesn't mean I can't be of help to you now. Does it?"

I eye him skeptically. "If I let you help, it has to be my way. Sure you can do that?"

Now his real smile appears, broad and white-toothed in the shade of the overhanging jasmine. "What do you need?"

"I need to get back into the palace."

Barden huffs. "Have the stars stolen your wits?"

I hitch my satchel and push past him.

"Rakel, wait. I'm sorry. This will just take a bit to get used to. What do you need back there?"

"I have to find Ash."

"Your partner in crime sealed his fate back in the throne room. Did you have any idea what he was going to do? Did you know what he *was*?" He spits the last word, horror and contempt combined.

It's not his tone that makes me reel. It's the word. *Was.*

"Is he—" My voice catches. I try again. "Ash, is he dead?"

"If he isn't yet, he will be soon. Even if they don't execute him, that was a lot of blood. A lot of it his."

"But you didn't *see* him die."

"Rakel . . . He was in bad shape. That thing that came out of him, it . . ." He clears his throat, looking decidedly uncomfortable. "There was a lot of blood," he repeats.

"But you don't *know*."

Barden takes a step back, his brows drawn together. "Why are you so . . . Do you have f—"

"You said you wanted to help? I need to get to Ash. He's the key. I didn't realize it before. But now I do."

"I don't understand."

"It worked before, Bar. The cure. It *worked*. We *tested* it. So why didn't it work on Nisai?"

I pace back and forth across the alley. "It was never about an ingredient to counter each province's poisons. The provinces didn't even exist before the Founding Accord. It was an ingredient from each *god*. And the sixth ingredient was missing when I gave it to the Prince."

"Six gods? But the Twins are as one."

"Under the Empire, yes. But before that, there was the Lost God. Doskai."

"You're saying the Prince was poisoned by a *god*?"

I shake my head. "Not *by* a god, by a poison from the *time* of the gods. None of the palace physicians have any idea how to approach the cure, do they? They're not trained for it. None of them have seen it before. It hasn't been seen for lifetimes in the Empire, possibly since even before the Empire. Sephine was the oldest Scent Keeper in Aramtesh, and even with all her scentlore she *died* trying to save him, and Emperor Kaddash drove the Scent Keepers out of Ekasya, the only people who might have known how to help his son . . . The only people who know about . . . magic."

Barden exhales a low whistle.

"But that doesn't matter now. None of it matters. What matters is that I've worked out why the cure didn't work on Nisai. Why it worked on Ash. We were missing an ingredient. Ash is the key. He's not just a Shield, he's a *shadow warrior.* A child of Doskai."

Barden grimaces and glances toward the mouth of the alley. "If what you say is true, how are you going to get to him? He'll be in the dungeons by now, if he's not yet dead. You'll never be able to find him, let alone get close to him."

I fold my arms. "I thought you said you would do things my way from now on. Or was that talk of yours all smoke and no scent?"

"I won't be a part of you going back into the lion's den."

"The *world* is the lion's den for me now. If I escape the city, and that's a big 'if,' then Ash dies. The Prince dies. If the Rot hasn't taken him already, my father dies, soon enough. And stench only knows what kind of chaos will follow. I can't walk away knowing I might stop this before it's too late."

"Last word I had from our village, your father's still alive. My sister said he'd been visited regularly by a caravan trader bringing supplies."

Luz. Whoever the girl who sprang me from the Aphorain dungeons was, it seems she's true to her word. A part of me that has wound so tight over the past moons begins to slowly unravel in relief.

"When was this?"

Barden taps his fingers as if counting off days. "Mirtan's had her hands full with the new baby. Sometime in Borenai, I guess?"

Last moon. My nerves ratchet tight again. If there's anything I've learned recently, it's that a lot can change in a moon. And even when things seem bad, they can still get a lot worse.

I take a deep breath and square my shoulders. "This is bigger than us, Bar. We have to find a way to get to Ash. We *have* to."

*　　*
*　*
*

Hours later, I find myself taking one last look up at Shokan, the larger moon full but for a slivered edge, before descending back into one of my worst nightmares. Last time I faced a sewer, I was breaking out.

This time, I'm breaking in.

I don't want to separate the scents, don't want to know about the cured meat experiment that went wrong in the kitchens, don't want to know that half the staff had bad river fish for dinner last night and it's been troubling them all since.

Even Barden presses his arm to his face, his nose and mouth hidden in the crook of an elbow as he leads the way.

We didn't dare bring a torch, fearing it might be seen at a junction or through a grate in the floor of some cellar. So I'm listening to the changing tones in the flow of effluent, the slightest of breezes that tells me there's an opening up ahead as well as back the way we came, the feel of the stone wall under my hand as I pick my way along the narrow path.

If I didn't have a nose, I might be able to admire the genius of a waste system that fully contains every rotten thing the palace produces, carrying it away from the buildings and streets to a place where anyone who is anyone in this city doesn't have to get the barest whiff.

I suppose it has to come out somewhere. Presumably that somewhere is farther downriver. Oh. On the last night Ash and I camped before arriving at the city, I *bathed* downriver.

I push the thought away.

318

The only thing I have room for now is keeping one foot moving after the other on the slick stones and making it to Ash. Because if he's anywhere, Barden says, he'll be in one of the prison cells deep below the palace, like the one I was in before I fled Aphorai.

On a curve in the tunnel, my foot slips. A section of path breaks away, plopping into the sludge. My breath catches in my throat, bringing with it the very *taste* of sewer. It's a struggle to keep my stomach from rebelling.

"Stick to your left." Barden's hoarse whisper seems uncannily loud down here. "The edge is crumbling."

"You don't say," I retort.

I've lost track of how many turns we've taken, junctions we've crossed, grate-covered openings we've wiggled through when Barden calls a halt.

"If he's anywhere, he'll be on the lowest level. That's where they keep the most dangerous prisoners. There's a vent in the next passage."

"And you know this how?"

I imagine him shrugging in the darkness. "People say all sorts of things in front of servants. And I'm quick at making, ah, friends."

I roll my eyes. "How could I forget your friendly disposition?" If Barden was ever elevated to aristocracy he'd henceforth be known as Lord Flirt.

He ignores that. "Once we're through into the dungeons, I'll stay by our exit route and keep watch. You remember filching oranges from Old Man Kelruk when we were kids?"

"Uh-huh." The burst of citrus sweetness each time I dug my thumb into the fruit's skin will never leave me.

"You remember the plan if we got caught?"

"You'd puff up your chest and pretend to be the newest orchard boy who'd just caught me orange-handed?"

"Exactly. We'll play it the same. If anyone comes along and we've got no other choice, I'll make like I got there first and arrest you."

"You really think that kind of smoke will rise?"

"I'm pretty convincing when I want to be." I can hear the smirk in his voice.

"But what if they figure out you've helped me already? From the throne room?"

"They won't."

"How can you know for sure?"

"Nobody who witnessed you leaving the throne room lived to tell the tale."

"Oh." I grimace in the dark. *Except you.*

"And, Rakel?"

"What?"

"Be careful. Please."

After the time I spent locked up under Aphorai, I would have been happy not to see another dungeon for the rest of my life.

The Ekasyan version is worse. Cheap tallow torches smoking at regular intervals, stinking of rendered animal fat. Hot, fetid air. Guess the black stone retains the heat of the sun. It makes it seem like I'm descending into the belly of a beast.

Farther down the corridor from where I crouch, someone moans in pain. An all-too-familiar reek reaches my nose. I flinch, imagining Father's bandaged ulcers. I hadn't noticed a single infected beggar as I ran through the streets above. There wasn't time to think on it earlier. Now a shiver slinks up my spine, lifting the hair at the back of my neck. Barden's "the most dangerous prisoners" takes on a whole new meaning.

Anger simmers up from my core. Does anyone who gets the Rot in the capital get thrown down here?

I'm so preoccupied with my outrage, I almost walk straight past Ash's cell.

Unlike the other prisoners I've passed, he isn't just locked behind bars. He's shackled to the wall, arms wide, wrists pinned by manacles fixed into the stone.

Dark blood cakes his face. One eye has swollen completely closed. If it wasn't for his tattoos, I might not have even recognized him. The weak light of the torches flickers across his chest and I gasp. All his wounds from the throne room are healed, apart from where the scars from the Aphorain lion hunt have reopened.

I'm about to whisper through the bars to him, when I hear the hollow bang of a door. Heavy boot strikes start down the corridor toward me.

I slink back out of the light.

CHAPTER 44
ASH

The cell skitters with rodents.

A slow drip plinks on the stone, though I couldn't tell if it's in my cell or the next or the next. My wrists are bound in iron manacles bolted into the wall above me in unwilling surrender. I don't know how long ago I lost feeling in my arms, but my shoulders make up for it. The joints scream in agony.

If I could just keep my legs beneath me, it might be better.

But I'm tired.

So tired.

The wounds from my episode have healed. How long have I been down here? I chew my lower lip, half expecting to find beard, but there's no more than when we arrived in Ekasya.

I've always mended fast, but this is something *else*. The skin beneath my tattoo is smooth, except for the lines of scar tissue where the lion raked its claws down my torso in the Aphorain desert. Those wounds have split. Judging by the heat that pulses through the surrounding flesh, they're not in good shape.

Any other damage came courtesy of the guards who dragged me down here. Lacerations and bruises, a gash across my brow, one eye puffed closed.

If only they'd finished me off. The big Aphorain had his chance. Azered take him for not following through with it.

A change in the light seems a ghost at first. Then it becomes real— flickering through the bars. Have they scheduled my trial already and come to drag me to the headsman's block?

I lift my chin from where it lolls on my chest. Pain shoots down my neck with the movement. My good eye squints at the invading light, so used to the dark have I become. Fitting.

Then there's the telltale scrape of boots on stone. Ranger boots.

The cell door swings open, the moan of the hinges almost as loud as those from the other prisoners in the endless night.

The silhouette in the torchlight is much taller than the jailers. "Those are some nasty-looking gashes you've got yourself there, house cat. Cut yourself on your own claws?"

"Iddo." The name comes out thickened in the middle by my split lip, broken at the edges from parched thirst. "Have you come all the way down here to taunt me?"

"Nobody could frequent this place for mirth."

"Get on with it, then."

"You're hardly in a position to give orders."

"And you're now in a position to give even more of them. Regent? How well you've benefitted from your brother's downfall. Almost suspiciously so."

"You went rogue, house cat." He grates. "We needed information. Where do you think we would find the most information? From the perpetrator of the crime. You cost us that, and then you failed to get justice for my brother."

"All this time you've been seeking justice. *Your* justice. I was trying to *save* him."

"Saving? The massacre up there? I'd think you a traitor if you weren't too much of a fool." He takes a deep breath, visibly reining himself in. "I won't stand here and justify myself to you. My brother's welfare is no longer any of your concern. There's nothing you can do now except bring more shame upon him than you've already wreaked." He holds the torch out toward me, and I cringe back from the light. "You hear the truth in my words, don't you?"

Bring shame to Nisai? Yes. With a messy public execution during which I might lose my nerve. Because that's how any trial of mine will end. There's no escaping it. I can't be tolerated, not after serving the imperial family for as long as I have and yet putting them in danger day in, day out.

Iddo takes my silence as agreement, if not acceptance.

"I'll promise you this. You can go to the sky knowing my brother will be avenged. I'll make sure of it."

He holds something in his other hand. It takes me a moment to realize it's a sword. One of my own. He steps forward, leaning it against the wall beside me.

"He would have wanted me to afford you this dignity. I only desire to save you both the disgrace of a trial. Because my brother *knew*, didn't he? He never breathed a word to me, one of the people who needed to know the most. But he knew."

A flash of the horror in the throne room jolts me. Iddo's right. Whatever his future is, or his legacy, Nisai is better off without me. They're all better off without me. It'll be a relief if I die, if not at the hands of the guards, then here, by my own hand. Better. For everyone.

I stare hopelessly at Iddo before letting my head slump to my chest again. There's nothing to say.

Moving almost gently, he reaches up to where my manacles are bolted to the walls. A key scrapes. The locks release, and I crumple to the dank floor in a knot of chains and agony.

I catch my breath, then ask: "Will there be a chance to at least say goodbye?"

"Goodbye?"

"I know I can't see him in person. But a letter perhaps? For if he ever wakes? At least to . . . explain."

"A letter? No, Ashradinoran. You said your farewell when you slunk off into the Aphorain night. And after what your desert rat girlfriend did, I doubt my brother will read anything ever again. He's been shifted to the temple."

I flinch. The temple? An image appears behind my swollen eye—Nisai's body laid out on a pyre at the summit of the stepped pyramid.

Iddo watches me for a long moment. Then he nods to the sword. "I've done you this courtesy; my conscience is clear. Now it's time to fulfill your last duty as Shield." With a sigh, he turns and leaves the cell, shutting the door behind him. It clangs into place with morbid finality.

As his footsteps recede, I hear him muttering. I can't make out all the words, but one part does make it through. "It didn't have to be this way, house cat."

I contemplate the sword leaning in the corner.

If I don't use it, a trial is inevitable. If a miracle happens and Nisai wakes by then, would he speak out for me? Surely he'd see that would be a catastrophic move to make before his reign has even begun. They'd find out that he knew about me. That he knew all along and didn't denounce me, didn't leave me on the street that day all those turns ago. He'd condemn himself.

After this, it's undeniable. I'm a throwback to the Shadow Wars. Children of Doskai, Nisai said my kind were called back then, when the Lost God was still commonly worshipped; when the Lost God was yet to be lost. When soldiers' wraith forms made up the vanguards of armies, fighting battle after battle until daylight turned dark and the rivers bled with rage.

Just like the throne room bled.

Because of me. Because I wanted to escape the slums. Have a chance at a better life, one with meaning. Because I'd never had a friend before Nisai. And look how I repaid him.

Iddo's right. There's only one more thing I can do now to honor my duty. Protect the Prince. Even if it's from himself.

I take up the sword and wrap both hands around the hilt.

CHAPTER 45
RAKEL

"Ash," I whisper.

He doesn't answer; he's too intent on the sword the Commander left. I only caught hints of their conversation from the alcove I hid in nearby, but enough reached me to know what the weapon is for.

There's no way I'm going to let that happen.

I creep closer. "Ash!"

He doesn't get up from the floor but does tilt his head toward my voice. "Rakel?"

I point through the bars to the sword. "Tell me you're not going to use that."

He turns away. "It's the only way I can honor—"

"Honor? Honor can go broil in shit and sulfur. I can't believe he *got* to you. This is the last thing Nisai would want."

"Just like your father didn't want you to be a fugitive, presumably?" There's a dark edge of self-loathing in his voice.

"That's not fair, and you know it."

He heaves a sigh. The movement makes him cringe and press a hand to his side. "You're right. But so am I. Your father wouldn't have wanted this, but you cared about him so much that this is where we are. It's the same with Nisai. I must do what is best for him, even if it isn't want he'd want. You were there. You saw what that thing did. What *I* did."

"That wasn't you." My voice is steady, but my heart wavers in guilt-ridden beats. Did Ash know what he was doing? Did he have any control over that thing? Could he have stopped the air filling with screams and the stench of death? But then I remember him unmoving on the throne-room floor, blood pooling across the marble. "It wasn't *you*."

"Then who was it, Rakel? Everyone will be better off without me. Safer. That includes you."

I wave that away. "Nisai was researching how to help you, wasn't he?"

He hangs his head. "Nisai's been trying to find a solution for half our lifetime. If there was an answer, he would have found it by now. And even if he was onto something, his research is long gone, no thanks to me."

I pat my satchel. "It didn't get far."

"You have it?" He pushes himself to his feet, taking an unsteady step away from the sword.

I retrieve the notebook with a flourish.

He moves closer, squinting into the torchlight, hands wrapping in tight fists around the bars.

Good. There's a spark left in him. I need that. "You said it yourself. Our futures are inseparable. The Commander isn't going to let me go, even if I can help Nisai. I need you to stay alive, as a witness to everything that has happened. And I need something else, too."

"What?"

"Your blood."

"My *what*?"

I wave the book, trying not to let my voice rise with enthusiasm. "The cure? It wasn't based on the poison craft of each province. It was from the time of the gods: the Shadow Wars. It worked on you because you're Doskai's part in the poison—*and* the cure."

I hold the book up, flicking to the page I'd found. "See, look at Nisai's translation. That symbol is 'shadow.' That one is 'beast' and I'd bet my nose that third is the Lost God. Those very same symbols were in the smudged note on the scroll. It's *you*, Ash. The final ingredient is you."

He staggers back, snagging the sword with his heel. I cringe as it clatters to the stone floor, the noise echoing up the hall. We both catch our breath, waiting to hear if any footsteps follow the commotion.

When none come, I nod to the sword. "May as well make use of that thing." I retrieve an empty vial from my satchel and hold it out through the bars of the grate. "A thumb is probably best. Just a small cut."

Ash winces as he bends to retrieve the weapon. He holds it up to watch it gleam dully in the flickering light. "Are you sure?"

"I believe it, Ash." I marvel at the truth in my words. "I believe you're the key."

He clenches his jaw and nicks his thumb on the blade. Blood drips into the vial. When it's safely stowed in my satchel, I hold out my hand to the bars again.

"That's it?"

"One more thing." I fix him in a level gaze. "I'll have that sword."

"What for?"

What for? *So you don't stick yourself with it in a mess of self-loathing*, I want to say. But glibness isn't going to help either of us. "So that when Nisai wakes up he'll believe my story," I tell him.

He weighs my words for a long moment. Then he sheathes the blade and passes it, hilt first, through the bars. "Be careful who sees this."

I loop the sheath's straps into my satchel's, settling the sword on my back in a vague imitation of Ash's harness. Then I wrap my hands around his where they still grip the bars, my fingertips reaching the softer skin of his inner wrist. His pulse is steady and strong. As it should be. As I want it to be.

My throat tightens as he meets my eyes. There was always something dark at the edge of his gaze, but now it's haunted.

I lift a hand to his stubbled cheek. "Ash, I—"

"Come here," he says, voice husky. "Please."

I edge forward.

He loops an arm around my waist and easily pulls me to the bars. His uninjured eye roams my face, as if he's trying to remember every detail, while his hand trails a tingling path up my spine, higher and higher until he's cupping my neck in his calloused palm.

On the road, I'd sometimes imagined what this would be like. Back then, I thought of heat and hunger and escape. Now Ash's lips meet mine with aching softness.

Longing wells up inside me. For what was. What we might be if we only had the time, the chance.

The air around us is tainted by the lingering horror of the throne room and the bile of the sewers. But I keep searching until I find him underneath it all. Warm sandalwood. Cedar, green and earthy. A hint of galbanum-like muskiness I've come to identify as purely Ash.

I inhale deeply, drawing those three precious scents down into my chest, to where memory will keep them safe until my last breath.

With a stifled cry, I tear myself away and stumble back the way I came.

* *
* *
*

It's more early morning than late night when Barden and I make it out of the sewers and steal through the near-empty streets to take refuge in what must be the seediest guesthouse inside the imperial walls. Dawn is yet to kiss the sky, so the moon is stunningly bright, shining through what would be a window if it had glass or shutters.

When Barden bolts the door behind us, I report what I witnessed. Most of it, anyway.

"They've moved the Prince to the temple," I sum up, not taking my eyes from the silver orb creeping closer to the stars of the winged lion.

"I'm not surprised. It's the only way he'll be welcomed in heaven, to join the ranks of god-kings."

"I doubt Nisai would care about that."

"But the people do. And the Council will be keen for an immediate transition. The sooner it's done, the sooner the succession can take place. They won't want his death to leave room for political instability, to question their next choice. That'll open the door for a full conclave and—"

"No," I say.

"What do you mean, no?"

"I mean we're not going to let that happen. *I'm* not going to let that happen. I haven't weathered the storms of the past four moons just to tuck tail and run. Even if I could escape Ekasya, I'll be watching over my shoulder for the rest of my life, just waiting for one of the Commander's Rangers to appear."

"You have a plan, then?"

I give him my sweetest smile. "Go see if the innkeep's still awake, would you?"

*   *

* *

*

Barden stands over me, brandishing the razor blade he'd sweet-talked out of the innkeep.

Clumps of hair litter the floor. It takes more time than I would have expected, and I flinch when he nicks the skin just behind my ear.

When it's done, he rubs rosemary oil over my bare head. The scent sends a pang of almost grief through me, churning up memories of Father. Then my scalp begins to sting like wildfire.

I hiss in a breath.

"Shhh, it'll feel better in a minute. Just wait."

He's right.

I run my hand over my scalp, awed by its smoothness. "Part of me wishes I'd done that turns ago."

"You look . . ." He clears his throat. "It brings out your eyes."

It's an effort not to roll them at that.

"Right. Are you sure . . . ?"

I nod. "I need to do this alone. You'll only rouse suspicion." I reach out and squeeze his arm. "And thanks, Bar. I mean it."

He pulls me into a brief but fierce hug. "Stars keep you."

"And you."

He pokes me between the shoulder blades. "And keep your back straight. Priestesses don't slouch."

"Slouching is the last thing I intend to do."

"Oh?"

I gesture to where I'd leaned Ash's sword against the wall. "Help me with this, would you?"

*   *
* *
*

The stepped pyramid of the Ekasyan temple is far higher than its Aphorain counterpart, just like everything in the capital is bigger or grander or more finely decorated.

The Aphorain temple proudly bears the scars of centuries of

groundshakes, its sandstone floors worn smooth by thousands of feet. But this place is all angles and a high-sheen polish that captures my reflection like the building itself is watching me. The chill I feel looking up at it is almost enough to make the Aphorain temple seem welcoming.

Almost.

As I climb the ramp above the city, I keep my chin up and resist the urge to watch my feet. The thought of dislodging Ash's sword from where Barden helped me strap it across my back, concealed under the Chronicler's robe, is enough to keep me ramrod straight.

At the first platform, I slip off my sandals and cross the lawn of holy thyme. The scent of crushed leaves drifts up to me. At least that's the same as the Aphorain temple. Fingers crossed the inner layout is also similar.

I enter the dimly lit corridor under a portico flanked by carved likenesses of mythical firebirds, women with wings and claws. First door on the right should be the administrator's offices. And indeed they are. Here's to small victories.

I pause in the doorway, waiting to be noticed by the firebird sitting at a desk piled with scrolls and a pair of tiny scales. When she doesn't look up, I cough politely.

"Yes?"

"I'm from Lostras," I say, mustering my best Losian accent, all twangy vowels like my nose is blocked. "I'm reporting for second-level training."

She raises her eyebrows, the wrinkles on her forehead bunching. "We weren't expecting anyone today."

I curl the fingers of each hand and hook them together, trying my best to look pious. "It's true. I'm early. But, you see, I've been dreaming of here almost all my life. When I passed my initiate exams, I couldn't find a single reason I shouldn't hasten into service."

The priestess narrows her eyes.

Humble. Be humble.

"Please, I won't trouble you at all. I'll sweep cells, scrub dishes, change the floor rushes. Whatever could help."

Something in her demeanor softens. "There aren't any rooms in the initiate quarters. Most won't be moving on until ordinations next moon. Hence why we weren't expecting you. But if you'd be willing to take a cell in the—"

"All I want is to serve," I gush. "And to do so under this roof? It's all my prayers come true, it is."

I wonder if I'm trying to add scent to a perfume, but she seems to accept it, gesturing me to follow her down the hall. I try to mimic her silent footsteps so the only sound is our skirts sweeping along the stone. I count two left turns on our route, a right, another left, before we arrive at a wooden door that seems built for a child.

She pulls a ring of keys from her skirts. "There is a fountain that way, if you wish to wash. The water bubbles warm from inside the mountain. Breakfast is an hour before dawn, in the fifth sector. You'll find your way by ear. We're a talkative bunch in the mornings."

I fight off a grimace. Talk? Before breakfast? This *is* penance. "Please, what should I do in the meantime?"

The priestess looks askance. "Why, prepare yourself. One does not enter service lightly."

I thank her in the simpering tone I'd affected since my arrival and shut the door behind me. The cell is tiny. With a sigh, I shrug out of the straps securing Ash's sword to my back and flop down onto the pallet.

Instinct tells me to go now. Find the Prince before the moon rises. But sense tells me to bide my time and wait until most of the temple has found their beds.

There is no window as such, but there are slits in the stone. When daylight no longer streams through them, I rise and check the vials strapped to one thigh. I feel naked without my satchel, but there was no way I would have made it past the temple estate guards as a devout initiate if I'd tried to bring it with me.

The door to my cell opens with a Rot-awful creak. Gingerly, I edge it wide enough to slip through.

*   *
*   *
*

The only thing between the top of the temple and the stars is prayer smoke. Frankincense dominates, but there's an undercurrent of myrrh. Clearly those in charge are convinced the Prince has already begun his journey skyward.

When I lay eyes on him, I realize that's in part true. He's stretched out on his back on a bier, covered to the chin in heavy silks. Even in the low light of the temple braziers, I can see he's worse than yesterday. The web of black veins thicker and starker, in places knotting together.

Guilt seizes my throat.

He's worse because I got it wrong.

Because Ash tried to tell me the truth and I was too confident in my skepticism. Too arrogant.

Above me, the larger moon is entering the house of the winged lion. There's no time for burning bitter yolketh.

I press myself against a wall as two firebirds talk in hushed voices.

"You must honor the watch," the first says, her tone an order. "If we miss the moment, he'll wander the five hells forever."

The junior priestess bows, her senior counterpart already walking away. Leaving the Prince so poorly attended? Even the firebirds must truly believe he's lost.

I wait for her footsteps to recede and then count five counts of five before stepping into the light of the braziers.

"You shouldn't be up here, initiate."

"I'm sorry. I'm new. And I'm afraid I'm a little lost. I'm meant to see to the Abbess's ablutions."

She narrows her eyes. "It's quite late for that."

I scramble for an explanation. "She was in a meeting. With a member of the Council of Five."

"Oh, I see. You'll need to go back the way you—"

The moment she turns toward the stairwell, I step up behind her and press a cloth soaked in liquid torpi over her face. She struggles, and I fight down panic that I might not be able to hold on long enough. But once she's inhaled enough of the sedative, she slumps against me like a sack of barley. *Sorry about the headache.*

I manage to lower her gently to the floor, though not without an *oof* escaping my lips.

The sound of a blade being drawn rings out behind me.

"Turn. Slowly."

I do as I'm commanded. In the gloom, the figure before me stands as tall as Ash, especially when you factor in the battle braids, and her shoulders are nearly as wide.

Kip. Even if everyone else has given up, Nisai's interim Shield remains.

Her eyes pin me, making it clear I'm prey and she's predator. "You," she says, half accusation, half disbelief.

"Please, there's not much time," I beg, holding up my hands.

"Don't. Move."

I do as I'm told.

Behind her, another woman appears from the shadows. We're of a height, but the regal tilt to her chin makes her seem taller. Her perfume drifts toward me, so intricate and complex that for a breath I can't think of anything else.

Kip moves her bulk between the three of us. "Talk."

The woman wears a string of amethyst and rubies across her forehead, and imperial purple robes embroidered with winged lions. This must be Aphorai's representative on the Council of Five.

Nisai's mother.

Shari.

I direct my answer to her. "I didn't poison your son. I got it wrong in the throne room, and I cannot tell you how sorry I am for that. But now I know how to help him."

Kip grunts. "You might have fooled my predecessor, but you don't fool me."

"Ash? I didn't *fool* him. He knows I'm here now. He wanted me to come. Even from the dungeons, he's still desperate to save the Prince."

Her flat stare is unwavering. "I was in the throne room. Saw the blood. The Shield's dead, along with a score of palace guard."

"He's not." I gesture to my back. "Let me show you."

She gives a grudging nod, and I shrug out of the sword straps, carefully guiding the sheathed blade from under my robe. I slide it across the stone floor.

Recognition dawns on Kip's features.

"Now, may I?" I reach for the letter again, this time with no resistance.

Kip takes it from me, unfolds it, shakes it out, runs a finger around the seal, and finally gives it a sniff. Only then does she hand it to Shari.

I can barely breathe as she reads, hoping it was the right move, that Esarik spoke true and it's the confession I need to clear my name. When she's done, she raises her eyes to meet mine. I've never before felt so much as if my mind was being read like a scroll.

I jut my chin toward the bier. "He's dying. The physicians have given up. They would have fought against bringing him here otherwise—seems they have the ear of the, ah, Regent. There's nobody else who can help him. I promise you I mean no harm. Look." I retrieve the vials of antidote, unstopper the first, and let a drip fall on to my tongue. "See? It's not poison. Please. Let me try."

"Let her through."

Kip straightens, still staring at me down the blade of her sword. "Sorry, Councillor?"

"I said, let her see to my son."

Experimentally, I inch a foot toward the bier.

Kip doesn't move.

I take a step, hands out.

She gives a flick of her sword in a "go on" gesture.

I don't ask twice.

Nisai's body is emaciated, the contours of his bones obvious under the silk covers. How could he have wasted away further in such little time?

I kneel on the cushioned step running around the bier and gesture to the oil burner at Nisai's shoulder—presumably Shari's personal prayer kit. The Councillor nods permission, and I begin heating each of the essences in turn.

Steam curls around the Prince's face.

I try to interpret no reaction as a good result—given what happened last time. But worry still permeates my every thought like a stench that can't be washed clean. Kip leans against the wall, her flat stare unwavering on the bier.

I peer at Nisai. Did his eyelids flutter?

My fingers go to his wrist. His pulse is stronger. Undoubtedly.

"I think it's working," I say carefully.

Kip huffs and steps closer.

"His heart, it's beating stronger," I tell her, earnest. "And look, between the black veins, his color's improving."

Her eyes go wide. "Azered's stinkin' breath, I never thought . . ."

Then the nearest candles flicker. Several snuff out.

The black veins stretched across Nisai's skin begin to move, slowly at first, but then as if they're alive and squirming for a way out. I recoil, every part of me wanting to shrink away from the wrongness of what I'm seeing.

Dark vapor begins to seep from the Prince, as if it's growing from his very pores. I sniff the air. It's not smoke. The shadow, growing blacker and swirling thicker into the air above the bier smells of carcasses rotting under a blazing sun. Then it starts to take on form—twining in the shape of flower-covered vines one moment, massing together in a silhouette of some hideous, fang-jawed creature the next.

"What *is* that?" Kip holds her sword at the ready. "What have you done?"

I swallow. "I don't know."

Sephine's last words whisper in my mind.

The darkness will bloom again.

And at that moment I realize. She wasn't talking about the dahkai plantation going up in flames. She was talking about this. She was warning me.

Doskai.

The Lost God.

His essence is still *here*.

And unlike Ash, Nisai isn't a shadow warrior. The poison isn't already part of him. He's still in danger.

The shadow roils and darkens, as if it's getting stronger. When it's ready, will it turn on the Prince? Finish the job it started? Or will it come for me?

I glance at Shari, who looks like she'll lunge to her son's side any moment. Off to the side of the room, the young priestess groans as she comes to.

"Keep them back," I tell Kip, surprised at the authority in my voice.

There's still some liquid left in the vials of cure ingredients. Could direct contact have a stronger effect? Sprinkling it over my fingers, I fling precious drips toward the shadow.

It hisses and steams like water drops on a scalding pan. Then it contracts into something solid that seems to clamp down on Nisai.

I watch, horrified as the smoke-thing coils into a knot of serpents. The largest slithers toward Nisai's lips and parts them, seeping into his mouth. His body jerks as fingers of darkness spread down his throat, suffocating him.

"Esiku's tits . . ." Kip's voice trails off behind me.

"Maybe it can be severed! Try!"

Kip slashes at the air barely above Nisai's nose, but her sword passes through the dark mass. The thing seethes and Nisai seizes again, his torso bucking off the bier and slamming back down. There's a sickening crack as his skull hits the stone.

No, no, no. I will *not* have another death on my hands.

"Do something!" Kip says.

I could only slow its progress, Sephine said as she lay dying.

Used to channel the will of Asmudtag, the Chronicler explained.

My last chance.

I fumble for the vial of Scent Keeper elixir, bring it to my nose, and breathe in.

It's sickly sweet. An almost-repellent sweetness, thick through my sinuses, like fruit rotting in the sun, or the nectar the siblesh plant uses to lure insects into the maw of its flower. I don't know what I expected, but there's no burning. Maybe a little tingling.

I inhale again. Deeper.

This time it burns like concentrated smelling salts, like I've poured activated zesker essence up my nose. My eyes fill with water. I blink, once, twice, tears running down my cheeks.

Everything still looks the same.

Everything *feels* the same.

Except the darkness before me. Now I can sense its presence, the weight of it, the . . . rage.

It's as if the roiling mass of darkness has sensed something new, too. It continues forcing its way down Nisai's throat, though moves away to the other side of the bier.

As if it's wary of me.

Tentatively, I reach out. It evades my grasp.

I lunge across the bier. My hands sink into the shadow, nails digging into something solid, finding purchase. I begin to pull it away from Nisai.

It doesn't budge.

Deepest instinct, or maybe it's the elixir, tells me it's going to be a battle of wills. And whether or not the legendary Asmudtag chooses to make an appearance, I'm not going down without a fight.

You will not have him.

The dark mass writhes in my hands, snaking tendrils around my wrist, burning my flesh wherever it touches, searing into my veins.

I grit my teeth against the agony.

If the smoke-creature takes Nisai, in one way or another, it takes everything I care for.

Ash.

Father.

My village.

Peace.

I'd rather it take *me*.

Sweat pours down my brow, the tendons of my arms straining. I brace my feet against the bier as the darkness slithers farther up my arms. It takes on the form of vines one moment, thorns biting into my flesh. Vipers next, fangs sinking deep. Then it surrounds me, blocking out the light of the candles, the moon, the stars like I'm trapped in my own pitch-black cave.

"You won't have him!" The words rip from my throat.

But it's no use. The darkness grows, around me, around Nisai. I can hear myself crying, the sobs racking my body, and with each breath it's like I'm falling deeper into an ocean, the shadow the liquid that will drown me.

I sink to my knees.

I'm not strong enough.

"Kip! Help me," I manage, not daring to turn in case I lose my grip. "I can't do this alone." The last sounds barely more than a child's whimper.

"Move, soldier!" It's Shari's voice, snapping the command like an army officer.

Then Kip's close, her powerful arms wrapping around my waist, pulling me back from the bier.

It feels like I'm being torn in two.

Every instinct screams for me to let go, to flee, to make the pain end. But I lock my fingers into rictus claws, forcing them deeper into the shadow.

With the strength lent by my helper, I edge one knee backward. Then another.

The blackness under Nisai's skin begins to recede. First his fingernails fade from jet to pale amber. Then the tendrils retreat from his hands, up his wrists. I grit my teeth and keep pulling. As each inch of solid shadow comes free, it begins to waver, to fade, like it's changing back into the smoke it first seemed.

When the last of it loses contact with Nisai, I'm engulfed in charnel house reek. The smoke coats my skin, hot and rancid and stinging like vinegar in a thousand wounds, burrowing into my every pore.

Then it's gone.

Absorbed.

In me.

I collapse to the floor, groaning. Every muscle in my body feels heavy enough to sink into the stone, my joints aching like I'm in the throes of sand-stinger fever. I try turning my head, and the candles dotted around the room flare brighter than they were before. Too bright. Pain stabs at the back of my eyes. I gasp and scrunch them shut.

"Here." Someone helps me into a sitting position. Kip.

My arms are lead, but I manage to bring one up to shield my gaze with a shaking hand. The moon has passed over the winged lion. "The Prince. Is he?"

"I can't tell," she says. "Think you can stand?"

I nod, wishing I hadn't—pain flashes behind my eyes again.

Kip gets her arms under my shoulders and lifts me as easily as someone might lift a child. The room swims, the shadows in the corners rippling. I squint, not able to tell if it's the effect of the Scent Keeper's elixir, or if there are some remnants of what attacked Nisai left in the room. A deep breath does more to reassure me—the reek of dead animals bloating under the sun has completely dissipated, the stars once more obscured only by prayer incense.

I plant both hands on the bier, steadying myself.

Nisai is still too pale, and the skin below his eyes is bruised dark. He shifts, as if dreaming, then lets out a moan and stills again. I place my palm on his forehead. He's not deathly cold, but his skin's coolness is the kind that only comes with deep, unmoving slumber.

"Prince Nisai?"

His eyelids flicker, then open. His gaze is bewildered, but the whites of his eyes are white again, the irises a dark, warm brown. He attempts to speak, but only manages a weak cough.

I glance at the stone basin on the opposite wall, water burbling from a pipe like a natural spring, used for cleaning bodies in preparation for funerals. "Get him something to drink?" I ask Kip. She nods, marching to the basin and returning with a simple cup.

She gently lifts the Prince into a sitting position and helps him to a few sips.

"What . . . what happened?" His voice is scratchy with disuse.

Kip thumps a fist to her chest in salute. "You've been out for a very long time, my Prince. You were poisoned."

His eyes begin to regain focus. "Mother? Is that you?"

Shari takes her son's hand, her face a picture of relief. "I'm here."

"Smoke. I remember smoke. The dahkai crop. Then . . ." He looks to me. "I know you, don't I? You're Sephine's apprentice?"

Apprentice. Not the first time I've been mistaken for that.

Maybe it wasn't so much of a mistake.

"Sephine is dead."

He gives his head a disbelieving little shake, then winces. "Dead? But how? She was . . ."

"A Scent Keeper? Yes. She died trying to save you. She *did* save you."

He attempts to get his legs over the side of the bier, but they're weak and wasted, not much more than bone, and they only tangle in the heavy silk covers. "Where is my uncle? I must see him."

I grimace. He thinks he's back in Aphorai, thinks that time has stood still since the night before the Flower Moon. "Steady now. You're home. The capital. It's going to take some time yet before you'll be back on your feet." *If you'll ever be back on them*, I think, but don't want to disturb him with that news quite yet.

"Where is Ash? Did he recover from his wounds?"

I'm taken aback. How could he know? Was he somehow conscious during the throne room carnage? But then I realize. The lion. He means Ash's injury from the lion hunt.

"Those ones, yes. But I'm afraid Ash is in a much worse state now."

"Where is he?"

Tears well in my eyes, hot and inevitable like my grief and anger. I blink them back before they can band together and fall. "In the dungeons. He had . . . an episode. He—"

Nisai whispers, quiet enough for only me to hear. "You saw it? The shadow?"

I swallow, not trusting myself to speak.

And it turns out I don't have to, because movement in the doorway catches my eye.

Commander Iddo ducks under the lintel and strides toward us.

On instinct, I cast about, searching for a place to hide. It's only when Kip salutes him that I realize I've never seen the Commander without at least a pair of Rangers at his heels. Yet here he is, alone. A memory pops into my mind: After the perfume trials, when Sephine had me brought to the Aphorain temple, the firebirds turned back Father's old comrade Lozanak at the entrance. No soldiers on consecrated ground.

As stand-in Shield, Kip's an exception.

Guess Iddo also gets a princely free pass.

The Commander reaches the bier. "I wouldn't believe it if I wasn't seeing it with my own eyes. How are you feeling, Little Brother?"

"Iddo," Nisai breathes. "It's good to see you."

The Commander squeezes Nisai's shoulder, his expression and the gesture surprisingly gentle.

"Iddo, I want to see Ash."

The older Kaidon's hawklike features harden. "I'm afraid that's not possible."

"I'm aware he's been incarcerated. However, he is to be brought here. On my orders."

"You don't understand, Little Brother. Ashradinoran is dead."

No. I raise a trembling hand to cover my mouth.

"His wounds from the—" He clears his throat. "His wounds from the incident festered. They poisoned his blood."

I don't believe it.

When I last saw him, Ash's wounds from the shadow beast had healed, except for the split scars from the lion's claws. And even those healed quickly the first time around.

Incredulous, I look to Nisai. Pain is written across his features. He slowly raises a shaking hand, presses it against his temple. "I want his body brought here. He died in service, he will go to the sky."

"Died in service? Brother, I hardly think—"

Like a window cover rolling down, Nisai's face schools to unreadable. "I want his body brought here," he repeats.

"I can't do that."

Kip glances between the two brothers, warring emotions playing across her usually flat stare.

"Not through any of my own desire," Iddo continues. "But the body has already been disposed of. Physician Alak saw to that."

Nisai blinks. "Who?"

"Zostar Alak. He thought it safest that the Shield's remains be immediately incinerated at high heat, lest the contagion—"

"Contagion? You're talking as if Ash had the Affliction."

"He was afflicted with *something*. And after what I've witnessed, I'm becoming more convinced that something was behind your . . . illness."

"You let our father's physician make decisions over the fate of my closest friend? What about Father? What did he say of this?"

"Nothing. He's ignored any briefing or official duty since he signed over the Regency to me." Iddo pinches the bridge of his nose. "Ash was a Shield. A *servant*. Remember that, Little Brother."

"Leave us," Nisai orders, his expression cold.

Iddo stiffens. "Surely you're not—"

Shari rises to her feet, her voice lashing out like a whip. "The First Prince has made his desires plain, *Commander*." She wields the title like a weapon, leaving no doubt what she thinks of Iddo's regency.

"Little Brother?"

"Dismissed."

If Kip seemed nervous before, now she looks like she's about to vomit. But she steps pointedly between the bier and her former Commander.

She's made her choice.

Iddo takes one long, hard glare at her. Then he salutes the Prince, the Prince's mother, and the former Ranger, turns on his heel and strides from the room.

I sink to the floor beside the bier, the dread in my stomach replaced with a gaping, hollow emptiness.

Ash is dead.

CHAPTER 46
ASH

After Rakel left, the claw-shaped wounds down the side of my torso continued to throb. More than once, I've wondered if the heat was from my body's effort to heal the split-open scars, or if the wound was festering.

I hope it's the latter.

And I hope it travels fast.

I promised Rakel I'd not hasten my own demise. But if the gods keep her and Nisai safe, they can take me however they wish—a fever almost seems too merciful for the damage I've caused.

Slowly, in the dungeon's timeless dark, my side crusts over with scabs. Fast healing has always been something I've been grateful for. Now it feels like a betrayal, prolonging the agony of knowing I'll never again see the friend I dedicated my life to protect. Never see the girl who gave me hope above what I deserved, who I could have followed to every horizon.

What's more, the swelling in my face has reduced, the vision in my right eye is returning, and my mind is clearing with every passing hour. Still, when a figure appears outside my cell door, even a sharp mind can't comprehend why I'm being visited by a member of the Guild of Physicians.

And not just any physician.

The face that peers through the grate takes me back to Nisai's father's quarters, to before we left for Aphorai, before I'd met Rakel.

It seems like turns ago, but I can still hear the young page's announcement echoing in my mind: *Zostar Alak, by personal appointment to Emperor Kaddash IV!*

Old Black Robes himself. The man I once stood and watched puff himself up with self-importance as he fussed over the Emperor, bowing to Kaddash's whims, playing to his addictions.

What in Kaismap's all-seeing name does he want with me?

I stay where I'm sitting, propped against the warm stone. I'm not about to dignify his appearance by rising to greet him.

He eyes me up and down, gaze lingering on the wounds at my ribs. "Interesting. I had expected you to have completely healed."

I give him a flat stare. "If you want to gloat, I suggest you attend my trial."

He heaves a melodramatic sigh. "There won't be a trial. While our esteemed Regent may fixate on honor, I have a much more holistic view. We couldn't have emotions running high. When powerful people get emotional—well—it just opens all sorts of conundrums for the perversion of justice. That would be entirely unsatisfactory. No, my wondrous little shadow. To anyone aboveground . . ." He looks up, as if he can see through the low-ceiling of the catacombs. "Which really is a long way up, isn't it?"

I don't reply.

"Where was I? Oh yes, to anyone up there, you're already dead."

"Nobody will believe that without a body," I scoff. "The Commander—"

"After your failure to complete your final duty to the Kaidon dynasty, the *Regent* was suitably disposed toward delivering you into my custody. And as for a body—it was quite simple to rough up Ebos enough for him to be sufficiently unrecognizable before his incineration. A street artist with a bit of parchment ink did the trick for the tattoos. Nothing complex, really."

Ebos? But he was one of the best out of the household guard. Steady. Disciplined. Loyal to Nisai.

Perhaps that was his downfall.

Bolts of anger course through me. I roll to my feet. "Why Ebos?"

"Why *not* him?"

"No. Why not *me*?" I demand.

"Because you're too important to the cause."

"The cause?"

"There's so many things we don't comprehend about your kind. Things that could be key to saving the Empire."

"Saving it from what?"

He tugs on the hairs growing from a mole at his temple. "From your Prince."

Is this some kind of trick? Some last twist of the knife, as if the guilt and pain weren't already enough?

"The Council has the temple on lockdown, so I'm yet to see it with my own eyes. But the smoke going to the sky suggests he may be cured."

Nisai lives. He's awake.

My heart surges. Rakel. She did it. Despite me, despite everything.

Black Robes sniffs. "Your young female companion is full of surprises. One has to respect such talent in youth, however grudging. I was quite gifted myself. And I do respect skill. Value it. Highly. I'm sure she'll see reason and join me. With a little persuasion."

I surge forward.

Though the heavy bars of the cell stand between us, Black Robes takes a step back.

"Don't you touch her."

"You won't achieve anything by getting yourself in a lather. I've had Linod's Elixir carefully added to your water for some time now."

I pause at that. There's nothing stirring inside me. No prickling across my skin. Black Robes speaks the truth. I'm equal parts relieved and chagrined.

"The First Prince's recovery really is unfortunate. He should never have been named heir. For one, it was premature—the Council tripped there, what could we truly expect from a group of women? For two, he is blatantly ill-suited to ruling. Indecisive. Naive. Weak. And worst of all, he is tolerant of the whims of the provinces."

"Of course he's weakened. He was poisoned!"

"Oh, no, it's been heading this way for far longer than that," Zostar continues. "This"—he waves a hand—"this rotting from the inside out, as if the Empire itself has succumbed to the Affliction. I know it. You know it. The Empire's enemies know it. There are wolves at the gates. And if we're not ready, if we don't prepare, if we're soft, they'll take us all alive. And your young prince lacks the—how should we put it—the temperament to do what needs to be done. Someone needed to step in."

"*You* poisoned Nisai?"

"Alas, I was not the one to commit the final act. However I do claim credit for the idea, along with the exposure to the initial ingredients. It's what led me to suspect what you were—my incense never seemed to weaken you as it did the Prince and his jelly-spined father."

Bereft of any other weapon, I spit at him, a viscous gob that splatters across his cheek.

He produces a white silk kerchief from inside his black robe and dabs at his face. "I'm sparing your life. Would it be too much to expect some gratitude? Some basic manners?"

"Gratitude? I'd be happy to drag you through the five hells by your stones. Does that suit?"

"I was afraid you'd view it that way." He lets the kerchief float to the muck-covered floor. "Pity. This could have been far less unpleasant than it's going to be."

"This?"

"We're going to need to run a few experiments." He sniffs, rodent-like nose twitching. "You're not the ideal specimen by any means, but we so rarely find one of your kind that we have to make the most of each discovery. And the last one died before we could really learn anything new."

The last one? He knew of others like me?

"My people will see to you presently. Oh, and when the time comes? Feel at liberty to scream. You won't be disturbing the neighbors."

His footsteps recede into the dark.

I slump against a wall, mind reeling. Nisai is alive. Rakel is with him. Neither of them know the face of their enemy.

But I do.

There's no choice now. I need to find a way out of here.

I must survive.

CHAPTER 47
RAKEL

The evening breeze carries notes of jasmine and spiced incense to the highest platform of the Ekasya temple. Behind that drifts the toasting barley of the breweries, just as Ash described on the long night we tested the cure.

Farther beyond, so far down the mountain it's barely discernible, the decay of garbage and the damp funk of exposed river mud permeates the slums. The backdrop to Ash's childhood.

The temple balcony runs around each of the stepped pyramid's five sides. I cross to Azered's edge, leaning out over a balustrade woven with wreaths of cypress—the tree of mourning. Snapping off a sprig, I bring it to my nose, so that all I can smell is resinous sap, all I can feel is the salt of silent tears drying on my cheeks.

Somewhere beyond the horizon, the best part of a moon's travel from Ekasya, there is a place I used to think of as home.

I wonder what's left for me there.

I wonder what's left for me anywhere.

The Commander spoke of fears that Ash was a contaminant. Am I now one, too? Is Nisai? Does any of the darkness still lurk inside him? And what have I become? Sephine died taking as much of the poison into herself as she could. What will it do to me?

A thud-scuff interrupts my thoughts.

Nisai joins me on the balcony. His steps are slow and careful, but after several days' rest he's able to walk with the aid of two crutches. Who knows how long it will take for his atrophied legs to bear weight again. If they ever will.

Kip stations herself by the door, arms folded. I catch the scent of leather armor, coconut hair oil, and nothing else, as if she's scrubbed with grit soap. I can only imagine what it would be like to grow up with slurs about the sulfur stench of the Losian Wastes. Unpleasant smells are easier to wash away than cruel words.

The Prince nods in greeting. "I was hoping I'd find you here."

I shrug. "Where else would I be?"

"My pardon is valid outside the palace. You may go wherever you wish."

"So could you, technically." He looks older, as if the starwheel has turned half a dozen times since he stepped into the Aphorain palace hall.

I'm not surprised he's aged. I can't imagine how it would feel to know that someone wanted you dead so badly that they found a seemingly incurable poison, dredging up magic outlawed so long ago it should have been well beyond the edge of memory. Not only that, but they had enough power to blackmail one of his closest friends to deliver that poison.

Shari handed Esarik's letter to Nisai not long after he revived. No wonder I couldn't make anything of the script, the first section was in Old Imperial, the second in a language they made up when they were younger to pass notes in their palace tutorials—if the message were intercepted, its contents wouldn't be compromised.

The letter admitted full guilt, though explained his blackmailers had told him to set the fire in the dahkai plantation to discredit the Scent Keeper. It was only when Ash and I visited had he deduced that the smoke he had released was to be the final ingredient, the trigger, in a series of poisonous substances the Prince had already been exposed to.

It was more than politics.

It was assassination.

He begged Nisai's forgiveness, telling him how he'd married Ami, the curator, in secret because his father would never let him shirk family duty for an aristocratic match. When she was taken hostage, he felt he had nobody to turn to.

He had me. Nisai's voice was full of sorrow as he closed the letter. *I could have helped him. We could have found a way.*

But the letter revealed nothing to Nisai about who had taken Ami, who had put Esarik up to the poisoning, who still seeks the Prince's death.

And that only makes me think of Father, who lives with the knowledge that something is trying to take his life every day.

"I have to leave the capital," I tell Nisai. "Soon."

He inclines his head.

I return the nod, as if it's some kind of unofficial salute. To him? To a mission accomplished? Or to the memory of his closest companion, who spent the last day of his life underneath this mountain. Grief ignites to rage as I picture Ash's unmoving body being dragged from the dungeons and shoved into an incinerator, his remains charred to dust without the honor of a fragrant wood pyre or the incense to honor his beliefs.

Nisai sighs and pinches the bridge of his nose.

It's a reminder he shares my pain. I'm not completely alone.

The image burns away.

"Are you unwell?" I ask.

"Only in my thoughts. I'm not sure who I can trust anymore. Other than my mother. Kip. And you."

I raise an eyebrow. "What makes you think you can trust me?"

"You risked everything to save me."

"I didn't have much choice."

"Ash trusted you."

I have nothing to say to that.

Nisai clasps his hands in front of him, managing to look thoughtful and composed despite the situation. One day he'll make a formidable statesman. An *Emperor*, I correct myself.

"We always have a choice. Even if it is between seemingly impossible options." He shields his eyes from the setting sun, squinting out toward the west, over the riverlands to the smudge of dust haze on the far horizon. "I've had word from my mother. Until we discover who is at the bottom of the assassination attempt, she thinks it's best I make myself scarce. I'll be coming with you."

"What? To Aph—"

"Keep your voice down."

"Oh. Sorry. But do you think that's wise? After the last trip . . ."

"If there's one thing my mother—Shari—is, it's shrewd. You don't get to her position on the Council being anything but. She knows my great-uncle, the Aphorain Eraz, has all the reason in the world to want to keep my head on my shoulders and my nose sharp. And it's the last place almost anyone else would expect me to be. After the previous trip, as you say."

Then he squints slightly in appraisal. "I'm going to be in need of people with expertise in a particular set of areas. Scentlore, not least among them. Do you happen to know any suitable candidates?"

"I might know someone. But that depends."

"Depends on what?"

"On how much you're paying. Seems like it's dangerous work being anywhere in your vicinity."

He gives me a wry, lopsided smile. "I think appropriate compensation could be arranged. Starting with this. The temple administrator was reluctant to part with it, but lucky for me she wouldn't deny the First Prince." He reaches into the ample sleeve of his robe and hands me a tiny bottle made of pure quartz crystal. Carved with a pattern I've seen before but can't quite place, it's the most beautiful workmanship I've come across.

Nisai nods. "Go on. Open it."

I work out the stopper.

Dahkai.

"Some of the last in any market of Aramtesh, I'd expect. It can't give you or your father back what you've lost these past moons, and for that I'm sorry. But it should be more than enough to buy the best available treatment."

He hands me a small scroll sealed with imperial purple wax stamped with a winged lion. It's a note of imperial provenance, legally assigning me owner in the eyes of the regulators.

"Thank you." Those two words sound so completely inadequate. I may have played a key role in saving his life, but there was nothing that forced him to pardon me, and what's more, to trust me. Let alone turn over such a rich reward.

But I don't know how to put my immense gratitude into words. I reseal the bottle and dip into an awkward half bow. "Thank you, my Prince."

*   *
*   *
*

We leave that night.

Once the temple priestesses saw the Prince, they calmed down about my impersonating a Losian initiate and drugging one of their own. The administrator I'd fooled scowled, but suggested the best way to get Nisai and me out of the imperial complex and then the capital would be as pilgrims.

Kip insists on remaining in the Prince's service, muttering something about the Rangers not being able to find a turd in a shitstorm, so why should she bother with them. I smile sadly at that, wishing Ash could have been here to hear it, knowing the turds she's referring to were a pair of fugitives—us.

We're to join a flotilla of barges headed downriver, full of devout sorts who seek to pray at the five major temples of the Empire's provinces. I'm skeptical as to whether we'll be able to blend in.

An imperial heir recovering from an assassination attempt.

A Losian Ranger turned bodyguard.

An Aphorain village girl turned Prince saver.

But when we arrive at the docks, I realize devotion doesn't discriminate. All ages and provinces are represented in the passengers. Some of them reek of weeks of unwash. Others must scrub with pumice stones until their skin is raw and they're as scentless as a human can be. A few stick out with undeniably aristocratic perfumes that shout louder than anything a plain-spun smock can hide.

Once we're aboard, I turn back a last time, to where the palace and temple crest Ekasya Mountain. Braziers glow in the night, the whole city lit up so bright that I can't see all the stars, the mix of smoke and incense and tallow and beeswax lost in the multitudes of scent. But the winged lion constellation shines through it all, flying toward the desert, toward home. Gazing up at it, I find myself saying my first ever prayer under my breath.

"Asmudtag, if you're out there, if there's something after this life, please, guide Ash home, too."

* *
* *
*

The journey is long and uneventful.

Another time I might have enjoyed the novelty of the river barge, but that only lasts a few days.

Then it's step by penitent step overland to Aphorai.

Nisai and Kip recount how when they last passed this way, the delegation was attacked by a group of brigands. I guess a band of gray-robed pilgrims isn't worth the effort, because we see nobody except the odd merchant caravan.

Sometimes we trudge in silence, sometimes the pilgrims sing. I hate it when they do. It makes the grief at Ash's loss well up inside me, blurring my vision. Lately things have looked watery enough. Like the edges of distant objects have become soft, less distinct.

I shake my head. No doubt I'm getting a bit of sun brain out here.

Which is probably why I don't recognize the lone rider until he's almost upon us.

"Rakel!" he calls, sliding down from his camel while still awkwardly holding the reins of a horse. The mare is blacker than the night sky, her ears laid back and teeth bared as she repeatedly attempts to nip the hand holding her bridle.

My throat constricts with emotion—gratitude and relief and amazement. "How did you find us?"

Barden taps his nose cunningly. "I knew the Prince had been saved once the smoke went up from the temple. And I knew if you'd succeeded, you'd be heading home as soon as you could. So I asked around at the docks, getting an idea of which barges left recently. Figured there was a good a chance as any you'd be stowed away among the pilgrims. Then I bribed the guards at the palace barracks stables, dropped the rest of my wages on a camel and passage on a merchant barge, and struck out after you. I always know how to follow you."

I fling myself half at Barden, half at Lil, so one arm ends up hugging mane, the other, man.

Man?

I step back and look up at my oldest friend, realizing we know very little of what each other has gone through these past moons. Part of me aches at the thought of what we've lost. I'm not sure I'll ever be able to reconcile the Barden who betrayed me, no matter his reasons, with the Barden who stands before me. But his journey must have come with its own demands, its own threats, and I can only guess at them.

Good thing the road to our village is long.

*   *
    *   *
      *

I smell home before I see it.

Cooking fires.

Desert roses whose perfume will dissipate when the sun rises.

The first water for miles.

We crest the last dune and look down on the oasis I'd begun to believe I'd never see again. The village is just beginning to stir in the predawn light.

Father stands outside our house, crutch under his arm for balance, watching the eastern horizon. Whether he waits for the coming dawn, or somehow for us, I don't know.

And right now, I don't care.

I slide down from Lil's saddle and break into a run, skidding down the dune, kicking up sand as I go.

All the questions, all the grudges, all the accusations vanish as he wraps his arms around me—mint soap, old leather armor, rosemary beard oil.

But something's missing. There's no bergamot to mask the stench of rotting flesh.

I barely even catch a hint of rotting flesh.

I step back to see Kip and Nisai making their way toward us,

Barden carrying one of the Prince's crutches and supporting him with the other arm as they descend the dune.

Nisai. First Prince of Aramtesh. Here in my village.

"Father, you might want to sit down." How do I even begin to explain I've brought the heir of the Empire home with me?

"I'm fine, really," he says, one arm still around my shoulders, his chin pressed to my hair. "Now that you're home."

"This may be hard to believe." I swallow, suddenly feeling inadequate to the task before me. "May I present First Prince Nisai?"

Father doesn't seem the least bit surprised, stooping into a bow that is surprisingly graceful considering the bandages around what's left of his leg.

I frown. "Father, I'm not joking."

"I realize that. I had advance word."

"Advance word?"

A figure emerges from the doorway behind him. The loose robe and long sleeves say traveler. The leather vest and kilt strapped over it, scaled with bronze discs, say something more. A knife for hire. Is this the caravan guard Barden mentioned?

I peer closer. Dark hair cropped to chin length. Paler skin than any caravan guard has the right to possess. And deep, deep blue eyes.

The traveler watches me with an amused smirk, then turns to Nisai. "My Prince. I must say, it's such a pleasure to finally make your acquaintance. Luz Zakkurus, at your service."

Luz Zakkurus.

Luz. The beautiful servant girl who broke me out of the Aphorain dungeons.

Zakkurus. The youngest Aphorain chief perfumer in history, who rigged the perfume trials against me and sold my indenture contract to Sephine. In a way, the person who started this whole thing off.

My nostrils flare.

Violets.

Both Zakkurus and Luz smelled of the most exquisitely delicate violet water. My eyes may have been deceived, but my nose told me they were one and the same long before now.

I plant my hands on my hips. "What in the sixth hell is going on here?"

But I don't get an answer. Instead Luz, or Zakkurus, no *both*, steps closer, taking my chin in hand, turning it to either side, staring into one eye and then the next. "You survived the first imbibing, then."

"What are you talking about?"

Sweet clove breath. Long, elegant fingers cool against my skin. "You took Sephine's elixir. You haven't noticed anything different? Any cloudiness to your vision?"

My jaw drops. I'd told nobody about the headaches, about the feeling that distant objects had lost their sharpness. I thought it merely lingering exhaustion since healing Nisai, that it would pass. "How did you know?"

"Asmudtag is all. Light *and* dark. Do calm down, petal. And come inside. You, too, my Prince. We wouldn't want the neighbors getting fragrant ideas. There's much to discuss. And, as ever, time is of the essence."

The last is said over a mailed shoulder: "Oh, and your mother asked me to pass on a message."

My *mother*?

"Welcome to the Order of Asmudtag."

ACKNOWLEDGMENTS

Wahey . . . do I smell a cliffhanger?

If that's not the most pleasing of aromas to you, feel free to curse every stench under the starwheel. I'll wait. But when you're done, rest assured that Rakel, Ash, and many of their friends (and frenemies, and enemies) will return. I hope you will, too.

In the meantime, please know that I'm so incredibly grateful to you, dear reader. Without you—and the amazing booksellers, librarians, and reviewers who may have led you here—I would not have had the opportunity to spend as much time in Aramtesh. Your support is worth more to me than dahkai.

Every book is like a complex perfume—with so many ingredients contributing to the bouquet. This one is no different. On that note, thanks go to:

My agent, Josh Adams, the most awesome ally and advocate—I couldn't have dreamed of a better champion for me and my books. Thank you for believing! I'm also incredibly grateful for Caroline Walsh's wonderful support and guidance in the UK. Josh, Tracey, Cathy, Caroline and Christabel—I thank my lucky scents you're all in my corner!

Editors extraordinaire Linas Alsenas and Mallory Kass—what can I say? From our first conversation, I knew Rakel and Ash were in safe hands. Thank you for giving this left-of-center book a home, for your engagement and patience in what's been a truly rewarding and collaborative editorial process, and for challenging me to dig deeper to make *Shadowscent* the best possible version of itself.

The wider team at Scholastic UK, with special notes to: Lauren Fortune, Pete Matthews, Lorraine Keating, Emma Jobling, Antonia Pelari, and Tina Miller. Liam Drane—thank you for the shiniest cover, incorporating so many intricacies of the story and world. And Chie Nakano and Tanya Harris-Brown—I'm so grateful for your tireless work to send Ash and Rakel adventuring in other languages!

Shadowscent takes place in a secondary fantasy world. While it is impossible to escape all influences from our own world, Aramtesh is not an analog of any one location, culture, or historical era, and was instead built from the ground up to have its own internal logic. For this, I relied on so many smart and generous people. Linguist Dr. Lauren Gawne created Old Aramteskan, a new language specifically for a society in which daily life revolves around scent. Experts shared knowledge on everything from chemistry to moon-orbit calculations to lion behavior to neurotoxins. Sensitivity readers (both known and anonymous to me) gave time and energy to examine Aramtesh's intersections of representation. That said, any shortcomings remain my own.

My mentors, critique partners, early readers, and sounding boards—Amie Kaufman (you never gave up on your Baltimore Keith!), Laura Lam, Pam Macintyre, Kat Kennedy, Sophie Meeks, Serena Lawless, Katherine Firth, Mark Philps, Chris Stabback, Jasmine Stairs, Liz Barr, Kirsty Williams, Nicole and Shane Rosenberg, Claire Gawne, Amber Lough, Eliza Tiernan, and Mel Valente. You're indelible. I couldn't have done this without you.

SCBWI British Isles (with special shout-outs to The Saras and the Undiscovered Voices team, and to Southeast Scotland local network organizers past and present), Book Bound UK (especially Karen Ball who encouraged me to keep going with this after reading the, ahem, rough first chapter), and Scottish Book Trust for my New Writers Award and all the assistance and opportunities since.

My support networks: House of Progress and the Aus retreat gang, Clan #becpub, Ladies of Literary License, Clarion Narwolves, Plot Bunnies, and the We've Got This crew.

Friends: In addition to those already thanked above, my gratitude to Brendan, Jack, Andrew, Martyn, and Andreas for the homes-away-from-home at such important junctures—I am eternally appreciative. Alison—now there's a thesis and a book inspired by Mavis.

Family: Guess all those effing oil burners paid off with this one, Mum. My godmother, Alexandra, for all those imagination-fueling research trips across the world. Phil and David: You can't choose your in-laws, but if you could, I'd choose you. Dida and Manu: Home smells like eucalyptus and mountain mist, cracked sunflower seeds and swimming pool chlorine in a warm car.

And Roscoe? Thank you is not enough. I love you.

ABOUT THE AUTHOR

P. M. Freestone hails from Melbourne, Australia, and now resides in Edinburgh, Scotland, with her partner, their Romanian rescue dog, and a collection of NASA-approved house plants. She is a Clarion Writers' Workshop (University of California) graduate and a Scottish Book Trust New Writers Award winner, and holds degrees in archaeology, religious history, and a PhD in the sociology of infectious diseases. She's only ever met one cheese she didn't like.